Jason Franks writes comics, prose and source code. His first novel, BLOODY WATERS, was short-listed for the 2012 Aurealis Award for Best Horror Novel, and his second, FAERIE APOCALYPSE, was a Ditmar Award finalist in 2019.

Franks is the writer of the THE SIXSMITHS graphic novels (a Ledger Awards finalist) and the comic series LEFT HAND PATH (also shot-listed for an Aurealis Award), as well as numerous short stories in prose and comics. A collection of his mainstream short stories was collected in UNGENRED by Black House Comics.

Jason has published work in most genres, but he is most comfortable at in the darker reaches of speculative fiction, although his writing is often humorous. His protagonists are likely to be villains or anti-heroes and the Devil is a recurring figure in his work.

Franks has lived in South Africa, the USA and Japan. He currently resides in Melbourne, Australia.

T0165064

Jason Franks Titles By
IFWG Publishing International

Faerie Apocalypse
X-Dimensional Assassin Zai Through the Unfolded Earth

X-Dimensional Assassin Zai Through the Unfolded Earth

by
Jason Franks

X-Dimensional Assassin Zai Through the Unfolded Earth

All Rights Reserved

ISBN-13: 978-1-922856-03-6

Copyright ©2022 Jason Franks

V.1.0

Printed in Palatino Linotype and Berlin Sans FB

IFWG Publishing International
Gold Coast

www.ifwgpublishing.com

For Professor Joe and Sensei Fred

Acknowledgements

It takes a village to raise a child, and the same is true of a novel. A great many people put in a lot of work helping me to realize *X-Dimensional Assassin Zai*.

Firstly, thank you to my wife Yuriko and my conversation teacher Akira Saito, for helping me to keep the language and cultural aspects of the book authentic. Any errors are the fault of the village idiot (me) and not the villagers.

I must also thank the early readers who helped me to find the proper shape of the story and the principal character here: flinty-eyed Jason Nahrung, who showed me what was wrong with it; lion-hearted Marta Salek, who convinced me it was worth finishing; and sparkle-handed Jason Fischer, who showed me what it was missing. Cheers to Steven Mangold, Justin Jordan, and my dearly missed great aunt Celia Franca for early feedback and encouragement. Ta to Michelle Goldsmith for her notes late in the process.

A hearty big thank you to Edwin Rydberg, for publishing chapter 6 ("The Wild Hunt") in the *Assassin's Canon* anthology all the way back in 2009, before this was a complete novel—just in time to prove I didn't steal these particular ideas from Iain Banks. And finally, *arigatō gozaimasu* to Gerry, Maria, Stephen, Daniele and the IFWG team for making this book an artefact of actual reality—the one with the usual number of folds.

#1: The Arisen City

When the immigration officer looks up at me, I smile and try to look more like my passport photo.

The lenses of his spectacles turn an opaque blue, then fade back to transparency. He turns the passport over; looks at the chrysanthemum embossed on the red cover. Let him look. Everything about the document is genuine except for the name.

The immigration officer goes through my passport page by page, examining the stamps and visas from all the places I have been. There are a lot of them.

My attention starts to wander. Fifty hours in transit has not improved my powers of concentration. I wonder if the damage to my digestive system by seven consecutive airline meals will be permanent. I am tired and queasy, and I want a shower more than anything in the world.

"Mr Zai."

"Eh?"

The immigration officer's glasses are now yellow. "Mr Zai, I see that you have just arrived from the United of States, Mr Zai."

"That was just a stopover. I departed from Tokyo."

English is not the officer's first language. It's not mine, either. "So you are a not-American, you?"

I shake my head. "Japanese." As it says on my passport.

"What other destinations have you visited on your way to Karachidor?"

"I flew here directly."

"You stopped in America."

"I stopped in Heathrow, Dorval and Logan." I know that's a ridiculous itinerary, so I add, "I came the long way."

"The Way is always long," says the immigration officer, nodding. "Mr Zai, you do a lot of travelling. What is your usual occupation,

1

Mr Zai?" I can't work out whether bracketing each question with my name is some form of polite address, or whether it signifies aggression.

"I sell handcrafted coffins." It's a line I use often and it's close enough to the truth.

"Are you here on business?" The immigration officer's glasses are red now.

"No. I am on a holiday." I do not know if there's a visa requirement for business travel and I don't know if the paperwork provided by my agent, Federico, contains such a visa.

"Mr Zai, what sights are you most looking forward to the seeing of, here in Karachidor, Mr Zai?"

"I suppose I'll go to the History Museum." I had never even heard of Karachidor before Federico gave me the tickets and I have no idea what there is to see here, but a history museum sounds like a safe bet. I try to look a little bored. "Really, I am more interested in the shopping."

The immigration officer inspects my arrival card for the third time. "No things to declare?"

I shake my head.

The immigration officer's glasses turn green. He stamps my passport with an ink that sizzles on the page, and hands me back the folded document. He does not welcome me to the country of Karachidor or to Mesra City.

I make a little bow. When I straighten up, the immigration officer is already looking to the next traveller. His glasses have turned orange.

My luggage hasn't made it to Karachidor with me. It takes me about twenty to describe the item (black, with wheels and an extendable handle) to the airline's representative, who speaks considerably less English than the immigration officer. I leave him with a bag-tag and what I think is the address of my hotel. The documents Federico gave me are written in the local language and I can't even recognize the alphabet it uses.

I am unfazed. Lost luggage is not a new experience for me.

Since I am unable to read any of the signs, I follow the crowd towards the exit. The locals look Mediterranean-Caucasian, but with startling, colourless eyes. They speak in an even-sounding language full of looping vowels and low consonants. Karachidaean fashion is very Western—suits and skirts and jeans and t-shirts—but there is something unfamiliar about the cut and weave of the garments.

Usually, if I was traveling somewhere new, I would be better prepared, but on this occasion, I was in too much of a rush. Federico called and asked me to meet him at the airport, where he provided me with a ticket, a handful of currency, and a hotel voucher. There was barely time for me to memorize the slim file with details about my contact, much less receive a proper briefing. Federico assured me this was an easy job as I hustled off to board my flight, but now that I'm here I feel like a fool. Where is this place?

I tried to google 'Karachidor' from an internet kiosk in Heathrow, but the search engine found no matches and offered no suggestions. My itinerary offers no additional clues. Japan to Europe to Canada to the US to Karachidor? Either the earth has just grown larger, or Federico's travel agent is incompetent.

When I get home, I will ask him to use a different booking service.

The ground transportation area outside the terminal building smells of carbon monoxide and jet fuel. My eyes are gritty and watering from fatigue, but I blink them clear and try to find a way out of here.

I can't see a taxi rank. There are no vehicles at all with commercial markings; just a steady stream of quiet, mollusc-shaped motor vehicles, which drift up to the kerb to collect the arriving passengers. After ten minutes of looking for a taxi or a shuttle service I give up and I go back inside.

I ride an escalator down to the subway. There are no turnstiles on the concourse, and nobody seems to require a ticket, so I just follow the crowd on to the platform. I am the only foreigner waiting for the train, but none of the other commuters pay me any undue attention. Few people ever do.

A train draws up within a couple of minutes. I don't know where it's going, but since there are no other platforms and I assume that it will take me somewhere central.

The train is clean and eerily quiet. After the initial lurch, it accelerates away smoothly. A few minutes later, we emerge into the open air. Judging by the way the scenery rushes past the window, we're moving at *shinkansen* speeds: maybe 300 kilometres per hour. Grass. Trees. Hills. There seems to be an unusual amount of blue amongst the green. Perhaps there's a tint in the window glass.

A Tokyo native, I am no stranger to trains, and it is here that I realize what it is about the Karachidaeans that makes them seem so self-possessed: none of them are staring at their phones. Nobody is reading a book, or listening to music, or playing games on a tiny screen. They look alert and present in the moment, as if they are prepared for some imminent disaster. I wonder if Karachidor suffers terrorist attacks, but I quickly dismiss the idea. I have seen very little overt security in my short time here: no guards; no metal detectors; no CCTV cameras.

I left my own phone in a locker at Narita airport. I never take it with me when I travel on business. A mobile phone is a tracking device that records your every movement, even when it's turned off. Besides—it feels good to disconnect. What is the point of travel if you can't get away from your usual life?

Mesra City appears on the horizon. The train descends into a tunnel.

Most of the other passengers get off at the first stop. Since I don't really know where I'm going, I do the same. I follow the crowd up to the street and emerge into the CBD of Mesra City.

Most modern cities are more alike than not, but Mesra City is just a little more modern than any other city I've seen. A little more high-tech. A little cleaner. I feel a twinge of jealousy on behalf of my hometown.

I ascribe the cleanliness to the complete lack of vehicle traffic. There are no cars, buses, trams, or motorcycles in the downtown area. No bicycles or skateboards or Segways or scooters. The streets are uncrowned. There are neither kerbs nor sidewalks.

There are not many foreigners here. I spot a few clutches of Caucasian or Asian businessmen, and a single group of Africans. I see a woman wearing a feathered wig and a man with pale blue skin. Everybody wears sunglasses, although the sun is not particularly bright.

I'm tired, hungry, and sweaty. I have no idea where I am, and I can't communicate with anyone. I don't know where I'm going, or how I'm going to get there. The anxiety puts a spring into my step. It's a long time since I've been anywhere this strange or unfamiliar.

A bird perched on a street sign flaps away, leaving a stray feather and a streak of faeces. I cannot tell if it is a pigeon or a seagull.

The afternoon is fading to dusk, and I still don't know where to find my hotel. Out of the corner of my eye I spot an illuminated sign, lit up in dozens of languages. I see English. I see Japanese!

I elbow my way through the crowd until I get to the sign, which says, simply, 'books'. A wide flight of stairs leads me down to a small underground mall and the open doors of a foreign language bookstore.

As I enter, I feel a peculiar sensation on my skin, like I've passed through a spider's web. A pang of nostalgia: some feeling half-remembered from childhood, like the taste of a candy that is no longer available, and which I had forgotten existed. My ears pop.

I shrug my shoulders and shake it off. Jetlag.

Inside the bookstore the wares are not just limited to print. There are all kinds of media on display: optical disks, cassette tapes, hard drives, flash memory sticks, microfilm. There are texts cut into bark, scratched onto stone, etched onto steel. There are potted plants that have grown into runic forms. At the very back I glimpse tanks of clear fluid that contain organic shapes. Knotted-up limbs, scrawled over with tattoos. Eyes that roll to meet my gaze. Living tomes. Some kind of art installation, I suppose. Spooked, I hurry back to the front of the store, where the ink-on-paper books reside.

It takes me a while to find the half a shelf of Japanese language books, on the bottom row beneath what appears to be the self-help section. I decide to purchase a Japanese-to-Karachidaean dictionary and a second-hand translation of an Elmore Leonard novel.

I put down the books on the counter and the bored looking sales clerk just stands there watching me through half-lidded eyes. I smile an imbecilic tourist smile and say "Two books please!" I repeat this in Japanese, just in case.

The clerk looks down at the books, and so do I. The dictionary and a slim volume called *Doors and Ways*, by Raethe Marghison, which I have some somehow mistaken for the Elmore Leonard. I bow and hold up my hands. "Ah, so sorry." I return the book to the self-help section and come back to the counter with the novel.

The clerk grudgingly rings up my purchases. I flip through my wad of Karachidaean currency, but I can't match any of the numerals to those displayed on the till. I offer the sales clerk my American Express card. She rolls her eyes and shakes her head.

I offer my Visa card instead. The clerk takes it with a sigh and swipes it through a dusty reader terminal.

The symbols on the cash register change. Paper spools. The clerk tears off a slip and I sign it. She puts the books into a plastic bag with my copy of the receipt and I walk out of the shop. Buying books always makes me smile.

I sit down on a bench outside the bookstore for a few minutes, learning some phrases out of the dictionary. "Please", "thank you", "I don't speak Karachidaean". The local number system is, thankfully, base 10, but I still wish they used Hindu Arabic numerals like every other civilized country. At least they use the metric system.

I try to use my new language skills to purchase a pastry from on a street vendor, but he either cannot or will not understand what I am saying. In the end I just point to what I want, and he gives it to me. In return, I give him what I believe to be the appropriate denomination in local currency. The vendor returns most of the bills to me, shaking his head with exasperation.

The pastry tastes unexpectedly sour. What I had taken to be a sugar glaze turns out to be crystallized vinegar. Once I recover from the surprise it's delicious. I wander out into the swell of pedestrians again, munching on the pastry and feeling implausibly happy.

I head west. Many people are now wearing hoods, although the skies are clear, and humidity is low. Crowds of young people wearing skinny jeans and zippered shirts. More blue skin. Suits in grey, black, brown, red. A three-legged man with gelatine-like skin, dressed in a tartan kilt. I wonder if I'm delirious from jetlag.

I wonder if he can play the bagpipes.

The excitement has washed out of me, and a tide of weariness has risen in its place.

It's dark now, and I really do need to find my hotel, but even with the aid of the dictionary I cannot decipher the voucher Federico provided me.

I wave down a woman in a jumpsuit that looks like it was hand-knitted out of plastic twine. "I am for look," I tell her in Karachidaean. I offer her my hotel voucher.

She looks at the document, frowning, and says something I don't understand. I nod vigorously. "English," says the woman, with a snort. I am proud of my English skills and feel strangely insulted.

The woman grabs my elbow and leads me one block east and then another block north. She points at a building diagonally across the road and makes shooing gestures at me. The building does look like a hotel, although I can't recognize the name from the text on my voucher.

I thank the woman in English, bow to her, and then thank her in Japanese. She just turns and walks away.

The hotel lobby has faux-marble surfaces everywhere you are expected to touch; textured fibreglass mouldings everywhere you are not. The desk clerk says something to me that I don't understand while I fish out my now-tattered hotel voucher.

"Ah, Mr Zai am you, Zai." The clerk speaks with British accent that's as polished as her grammar is terrible.

"Yes."

"You room number and 2304 room." She hands me a keycard. "I do hope you will enjoy your stay with we, you."

"My baggage didn't make it all the way to Mesra City with me. Have you heard anything from the airline?"

"Us have not, us." The clerk smiles without sympathy.

I thank her, grab a fistful of tourist pamphlets from the rack beside the desk, and head for the elevator. I still don't know the name of the hotel.

I've been sleeping for a couple of hours when somebody knocks on my door. I open it to find a bellboy standing there with my luggage. I don't know whether or not to tip him and he gives me no indication either way, so I bow and thank him, and he goes away. My stomach has settled and now I am hungry.

After a mediocre dinner in the hotel's Americana themed restaurant, I head for the bar looking for a nightcap. The barman speaks English, so I ask him to recommend me something local. He pours me a shot of liquor that he identifies as *shnkwer*. It's harsh and clean and, once the kick wears off, it feels like a very gentle dentist has cleaned my teeth.

I order another.

I wake up feeling neither hung over nor jetlagged, and I attribute my unexpected good health to the double shot of *shnkwer*.

After all of the rushing to get here, it's a Saturday, and I have two free days before I can meet my contact. I pretend that it's reconnaissance, but I am quite excited to explore this new and mysterious city.

I eat a leisurely breakfast while poring over my stack of tourist brochures. I can't make much sense of them, even with the aid of the dictionary, so I pick out some destinations based on the pictures and show them to the concierge. He picks a brochure out of the fan in my hands like a magician drawing a card and offers it back to me: a ruined fortress on a hillside. The concierge tells me that the bus will be stopping at this very hotel in about ten minutes. He swipes my Visa card and directs me the lounge where three other hotel guests are waiting for the tour bus.

The interior of the oversized mollusc-mobile is not as exotic as its exterior: velour and foam rubber and plastic and sweat. The guide stands in the aisle, legs akimbo, and addresses in the looping Karachidaean language with all the drama of a stage actor. Occasionally, he also provides a terse summary in English, pitching his voice so loudly the PA buzzes.

Mesra was the first city founded in Karachidor, he says. Its name means 'the Arisen City' in the language of 'the ancients'. Calling it 'Mesra City' is redundant, like saying 'New York City City'.

The guide tells us that the highway we are travelling is two hundred years old. (I take photos of the highway.) The harbour has, obviously, been serving as such for two thousand. (I take photos of the harbour.) This forest is old growth, this orchard is new. (I take photos of the trees.) The native falcons have become endangered by the introduction of some kind of predatory megabat from Australia. (The bus is moving too quickly for me to change the lens in time to get a photo of the birds.)

The tour guide delivers a spray of unrelated of facts, which I punctuate with shutter-snaps. Every time he says 'obvious' or 'typical' I feel like I have missed some crucial piece of information; some in-joke. I wonder if my lack of comprehension is due to a problem with the guide's English or with my own.

We stop to inspect some ruins. Slabs of tumble-down masonry on an ancient hilltop, cracked open by weeds, worn down by wind and rain. Metallic ribs protrude from the stonework as if it was concrete. The guide says that the stones were not cut by masons, they were grown onto the metal framework by 'lithomancers' in the 'traditional manner'.

Apparently, it's been nine centuries since the structure fell. I am surprised when the guide explains that it was an apartment complex, not a fortress. I take three dozen photos.

We descend towards a small village for a lunch break and to do some shopping. In the souvenir shop I purchase a box of something I believe to be homemade fudge and an Authentic Lithomantic Artefact that resembles a stone lollipop on a steel stick.

After dinner I head back to the hotel bar for a nightcap. Tonight, I'm not alone in the bar: there is a young lady seated two stools away from me drinking merlot. She's a little thickset, with short dark hair and grey eyes.

When I order a shot of *shnkwer*, she looks up at me and says, "What is that, anyway?"

I look at the barkeeper and say, "Please make that two shots."

She's pleased to hear somebody speak to her in English, so we strike up a conversation.

The young lady tells me she's from Manchester. We have a not-very-interesting discussion about our jobs. Mostly about hers—I tell her I'm a salesman. Then we go upstairs to my room for some perfunctory sex.

The girl from Manchester does not ask if I am single, so I don't tell her that I am in an open relationship, or that I will report all details of the night's activities to my girlfriend Michiko when I get back to Tokyo.

Next morning, I brace the concierge again. He explains how to use the subway to get to the harbour, where the Ancient History Museum is located. It's an easy commute with only one change of trains, but I am proud of myself when I arrive at my destination: a disappointingly small, bunker-like building.

The bunker is mostly taken up by a reception area. The man at the desk hands me an English language guide booklet and waves me through: apparently there is no admission fee. A small sign with an arrow points me towards a downwards ramp and suddenly I understand. Most of the complex is underground.

The ramp spirals downwards through the strata of Karachidaean history. The display cases are with artefacts and artwork, maps and scale models. Nothing is animatronic or interactive; everything has been hand-made. I work my way though it in silence, absorbing Mesra City's history as best I can. All of the information displays are presented in Karachidaean, so I have to rely on the guide booklet's brief and badly written synopses. I'd find it funny if the text was in Japanese, but bad English makes my head hurt.

According to the booklet, the Karachidaean people washed ashore on this island as refugees roughly 2800 years ago. Most of the vessels in which they arrived—the diorama shows an odd mix of longboats, canoes and sailing ships—landed in the Mesra harbour, from where the population spread across the Karachidor.

Eventually, I come to a detailed map of the island. If I've interpreted the scale correctly, Karachidor is roughly a quarter of the size of India. I have yet to see a map showing the island in the context of the rest of the world, but I wonder how I could possibly have failed to notice a landmass this size lying between the Americas and Africa.

The new residents of Karachidor established cities and eventually built a new trading fleet. The island has extensive mineral wealth, and they quickly became rich. When the Romans took the Iberian Peninsula, the Karachidaeans became concerned that they would be swept up into the Empire and decided to conceal the location of their new homeland. Though they had no military, they had 'ways' of keeping their shipping lanes free of foreign vessels. Karachidor's policy of secrecy and seclusion has continued into the present day.

The Karachidaean economy is almost exclusively based on this secretive trading. Despite its high-tech landscape, very little manufacturing or engineering occurs on Karachidor. The Karachidaeans broker deals between countries and corporations; they ship goods; they provide 'management services.' They do not have the internet here. My father would approve.

The final room in the museum is covered with a faceted glass dome. Its panels light up in sequence to show a pictorial history of Karachidor spiralling down and around from the highest point of the ceiling.

I squint at the booklet, then up at the roof again. It shows the Karachidaeans' original home: another context-free island that the guide booklet identifies as the island nation of *Tlilnh Tsish*.

I roll that over on my tongue. Tlilnh Tsish: I'm not sure of the phonetics but it's not easy for a Japanese native speaker to pronounce. *Tlilnh Tsish, Tlilnh Tsish*. With Japanese phonemes the closest I can get is *chi-rin tsu-ishu*.

I walk the circumference of the dome and watch the light show four times through, hoping to see a map that shows Karachidor in context, or the location of fallen *Tlilnh Tsish*, but there is nothing. I read and reread the relevant parts of the booklet, hoping to discover some clue I have overlooked in the tortured English, and in the end that is where I find it. The book does not actually say that *Tlilnh Tsish* fell; it says that it *descended*. Perhaps they mean to say that it 'sank'.

Tlilnh Tsish.

I think I am currently standing on an unknown continent, which has been colonized by refugees from Atlantis.

█ head back to the hotel in a daze. Early to bed this evening. No drinking or bedroom sports. Tomorrow is Monday, and that means it's
time to go to work.

█ get up early the next morning and find breakfast in a café near the
central station. While I eat, I study a tourist map of the CBD. When
the waitress clears away my plate, I open my dictionary and ask her for
directions. She speaks a few words I don't understand and indicates a
route on the map.

It's about fifteen minutes' walk to the office tower where my contact
works.

Rows of windows slant downwards diagonally across the face of
the building: a triangular prism that widens as it rises. At the higher
levels, it is connected to adjacent buildings by a web of passageways.
There's no way I am going inside.

I hate office buildings. I hate office jobs and office culture. Suits
and briefcases and all-night drinking parties with the boss. Fawning
and bowing to corporate psychopaths. Ever since I was a little boy,
I knew I could never be a *sarariman* like my father. After college, I
joined the yakuza, but that was also suits and drinking and bowing to
psychopaths—with guns. When we started shaking down corporate
board meetings to affect their share price I knew it was time to get out.

I joined the army to escape the yakuza. No suits or drinking, but
there was still plenty of bowing and guns. I did like getting to work
outdoors, though. That is how I decided to go freelance.

Justin Jordan does not emerge from the prism until 1730 hours. He's
a big, shaggy American with light skin, light eyes. Beard, no moustache.
Nice-guy smile. He's wearing a polo shirt, long basketball shorts, and
sports shoes, and he's carrying a sports bag as well as a briefcase. I
follow him down the road until he disappears into a building that I
think is a gym. I wait in a coffee shop across the street.

At 1835, Jordan reappears, freshly showered and dressed in khaki
slacks and a fresh polo. He looks like he spends a lot of time lifting
weights, but he doesn't do enough cardio. Lot of muscle, but no
definition.

I watch Jordan go into a small bar. I linger outside for a while,
looking in shop windows, plotting a route to the nearest subway. Then
I follow him inside.

Jordan is sitting at a table, eating a steak. There's some green vegetable on the side that I can't identify, and apparently neither can he.

He's clearly not going to eat it. I belly up to the bar and order a beer. It comes in a bottle I don't recognize, but it's weak and dirty-tasting and might be American. It won't impair anything besides my tastebuds.

A Karachidaean woman joins Justin Jordan at his table. They know each other well. She orders a glass of wine while he finishes his steak. When he asks for the cheque, I slip out the door.

Justin Jordan and the woman enter the tube station together. I believe she is the second wife that has caused all of his impending trouble. Bigamy is a difficult crime to prosecute when your other wife lives in a place that doesn't exist.

I find a place to watch them from the opposite platform; in the shadows beneath a malfunctioning lamp; out of sight of the overhead security camera. It's less crowded on this side, but not deserted. I sit quietly and nobody pays me undue attention.

The Jordans' train arrives at 1950. Justin pushes to the front of the crowd, wanting to be the first to get through the doors. I think he wants to make sure his wife gets a seat—he has some country manners about him. In Japan, we do not hold doors. It amuses me every time I see a Westerner displaying such etiquette.

I board the next train and go back to my hotel. I have memorized the evening timetable traveling in both directions.

Tuesday evening, Justin Jordan emerges from his building at 1800 hours. Today he's dressed in business-casual: he's going to skip the gym, today, but not the pub. I follow him there. For the second night in a row, he does not notice me. I would be surprised if he had.

Justin Jordan orders some kind of poultry dish, which he eats slowly. He's drinking Bushmills tonight; straight, with ice. Later, he does a shot of bourbon. The woman that Jordan's American wife is so angry about does not put in an appearance.

I pay for the beer I've been nursing all night and head out. Justin Jordan, still finishing up his meal, does not even glance in my direction.

I'm on Justin Jordan's platform, standing in the crowd, when he steps off the escalator. He's panting a little—he's had to rush to make the 1950. When the glow of the train's headlamps becomes visible, the crowd presses close to the yellow safety line. Jordan goes with it, but today he's not inclined to push to the front.

The train itself comes into sight. I jockey for a better position; nudge a shaven-headed man in the ribs. He grunts and moves sideways, shouldering a middle-aged businesswoman aside. She makes an offended sound and steps to regain her balance, jostling Justin Jordan with her handbag. Jordan, irritated, takes another step forward, making a space at the front.

I slip in behind him. The slowing train is close; I can hear the hiss of displaced air as it glides up to the platform. People jostle around me. I stumble, reach out. My hands connect with the small of Justin Jordan's back and he tumbles down on the tracks in front of the decelerating train. Only a handful of people have time to express their shock before the engine strikes him.

A hush descends. The sound of Justin Jordan's bones being slowly pulverized is clearly audible above the ball-bearing glide of the train on its tracks. He does not scream; perhaps he broke his neck in the fall.

The braking vehicle rolls over Justin Jordan with no visible change to its momentum. Its gore-splattered nose drifts serenely out of my view. By the time the screaming begins I'm already on the escalator, halfway back to street level.

I walk about two kilometres to the next tube station and catch a train back towards my hotel, on the other side of the city. Outbound trains on this line have been delayed by a fatality on the tracks, but my train, headed the other way, arrives three minutes behind schedule.

Mesra City's transport system isn't as good as Tokyo's, but it's better than most I've seen.

At the hotel I take a shower and then head downstairs for dinner and a nightcap of *shnkwer*. I'm feeling relaxed and satisfied. A fun trip, a job well-done. I couldn't ask for more. I'm asleep almost as soon as my ear touches the pillow.

There's a knock on my door at 0100 in the morning.

I wonder idly if I've been caught. Have the authorities found me? Did I miss a CCTV camera? It's possible, of course, but the exercise yields only the slightest frisson of fear. In my experience, police do not knock politely if they come looking for you in the middle of the night.

I open the door. It's the girl from Manchester, clad only in a bedsheet. I step aside to allow her into the room.

When I awaken the next morning, I'm alone again. I feel refreshed and rested; invigorated by all the new sights and experiences. I pack up my luggage and head down to the restaurant for a big breakfast. I have fifty hours of travel ahead of me and if I eat well before I get on the plane, I might be able to skip a couple of bowel-destroying airline meals.

In the airport gift shop, I find a stand of sunglasses with opaque lenses that cycle through a series of tints and colours, exactly like the ones the immigration officer was wearing when I arrived. I can't read the tags, but I think they're on sale. Last season's stock. I'd buy a pair, but I can't find one that suits my face.

Sitting in the departure lounge I feel a little sad. Such a short stay; so much I didn't manage to see. I'll have to come back. I hope it will be soon.

Much as I'm looking forward to sleeping in my own bed, I'm already excited about the prospect of returning to the Arisen City.

#2: The Space Whip

Despite my best efforts, I am not much better prepared for my second trip to Karachidor than I was for my first.

When I returned home last time, I went to a cybercafé to look for information, but none of my searches returned so much as a stub Wikipedia page. None of my favourite travel websites recognized the airport code for Mesra International. When Federico came to me with another ridiculous itinerary, I tried to enter it as a multi-destination trip, but the browser crashed every time before I could specify the final stop.

Federico has no better an idea of where Karachidor is than I do. His client makes all the travel arrangements and it's as much a part of his job to be uncurious as it is to arrange for strangers to be murdered.

Karachidor is not connected to the internet. It does not, cannot, *should* not exist in what I think of as the real world. It's like I've unfolded a pocket map of the planet and found an extra page.

Fifty-something hours later I'm back in Mesra City. I collect my baggage and head down to the subway. This time I am staying in a hotel with a name written in a script that I actually read. It's called the Epsidor.

In my travels, I have stayed in every kind of accommodation, from youth hostels to timeshare resorts to hotels so exclusive they do not even warrant a star rating. I've slept in tents and hedges and ditches and luxury palaces and seaside villas. But I have never stayed any place like the Epsidor.

From a distance, the building looks like a two-dimensional image projected onto a particularly thick mist. It grows more solid as I approach it, but only if I look at it directly. In my peripheral vision the structure fuzzes and blurs as my perspective changes.

Once I pass through the main gates, the Epsidor resolves into three dimensions. Or four, or five: the hotel seems to rotate as I turn my head. It's like standing inside an MC Escher drawing.

The reception clerk speaks perfect Japanese. A bellboy who is just as fluent shows me to my suite. True luxury!

I steep myself in my private Jacuzzi for thirty minutes. Then I head down the stairs for a meal in the revolving restaurant on the top floor. The view from the window shows Mesra City's iridescent skyline. The rotation is slow enough to mitigate most of the hotel's parallax distortions—the effect is similar to being pleasantly tipsy.

The waiter provides me with a menu in my own language, but most of the dishes made from ingredients I've never heard of. In the end I order a glass of *shnkwer,* and a main meal called *szhtrltek hetjn szhtr.* The meat is a bit like lamb or goat, served with a starchy legume that tastes a bit like potato. The dish is jewelled with tiny blue and red capsules. The wine-based sauce changes its flavour according to the colour and quantity of the capsules in each mouthful. Dessert is a frozen confection with a molten core that's too sweet for my palate.

I am uncertain if this is traditional Karachidaean cooking or some sort of haute cuisine experiment, but it is certainly tasty. The bill goes onto my room tab, to be paid for by my mysterious clients. There were no prices listed on the menu, so I'm certain it was expensive.

The following morning I'm too nervous to try anything exotic for breakfast. I have a bowl of miso soup and a cup of weak coffee and then I head into town for my first meeting with my clients. I'm dressed in my usual traveling clothes: jeans, a Hawaiian shirt (blue, with pale green lilies), and hiking boots. I wouldn't dress like this at home, but when I'm abroad it's practically a uniform. Don't look at me, I'm just a tourist. I have yet to find a stronger variety of camouflage.

I did bring a suit with me, but I have decided not to wear it. I'm an assassin, not a banker.

The meeting point is in a park on the northern fringe of Mesra City's CBD. I arrive early so that I can reconnoitre the place, but spend most of the time looking for a public toilet where I can take a nervous piss before the meeting.

It is a beautiful park. Swards of lush, bluish grass. Beds of unfamiliar flowers, divided by hedges and rockeries. A pond filled with eels and koi. Copses of strange trees provide shade and hide all but the tallest of city buildings from view. An exotic floral scent on the breeze.

I find a large display map near the toilet block. Some graffiti artist has drawn a large X on it and written the word *gazebo* underneath it in katakana. What is a *gazebo*?

I head for the X, following the path into a stand of trees at the base of a hillock. As I step into the shade, I feel sensation like passing through a membrane that makes me recall the foreign language bookstore I visited last time I was in Mesra. Once again, there is some deeper familiarity...

Japan. A forest. A temple. Leaf litter and the smell of the sea...

And then it's gone. I cannot place the memory.

After the first turn in the path the grade levels out. It's darker here, and the trees are closer, although the sky is still bright and blue above me. The only sound is the foliage rustling in the sudden breeze. I can no longer smell the strange perfume. The path turns and then opens into a small glade, which contains an open-walled pavilion. Is this a gazebo?

There are four people under the awning. Two of them are sitting at a small glass table: a Karachidaean woman, wearing jeans and a tunic; and a Caucasian man, wearing a tailored suit and a tan that's verging on sunburn. The other two, both Karachidaeans, are standing on either side of the gazebo. They're not visibly armed and neither of them is physically imposing, but they have the alert-but-disinterested demeanour of professional bodyguards. Good ones.

"Ah, Mr Zai," says the sunburnt man. He speaks with an upper-class English accent. He's wearing a diamond stud in one ear and a Rolex on his wrist.

I bow from the waist.

"Please join us."

I take off my shades and sit down in the empty seat. "Ladies and gentlemen." I speak English, since that's the language in which I have been greeted. "How do you do?"

"Zai, we very well do, we thank you, Zai," says the Karachidaean woman.

The Englishman smiles at the woman's clumsy English in a way that makes me wish I could hear him trying to speak Japanese. "I am Jonathon, and this is my partner—"

"I am Vashya, I am."

The Englishman frowns at Vashya's interruption, but she ignores him. I doubt these are their real names. Zai certainly isn't mine.

"Now we all know each other. That's wonderful," says Jonathon. "I trust your accommodations are satisfactory?"

"Yes, thank you."

"The Epsidor is a darling place," he says. "What do you think of our *gah-zeh-boh*?"

Now Vashya gives him an irritated look.

"What is a *gazebo*?" The best way to defuse mockery is to fail to recognize it. Let him think I'm stupid.

"Gazebo. Never mind." Gar-zee-bow. Now I understand. "Shall we proceed with the business at hand?"

"Yes, please." Jonathon wants me to dislike him. It's working.

"Zai-san, our organization is looking for a new operative, and we have been impressed with how you completed your most recent mission."

"Thank you." How closely have they been watching me? I try not to let it worry me. If they have an operative who is capable of tailing me without me noticing, what do they need me for?

"We will, however, need to know a little more about you if we are to begin a formal arrangement, so we're going to ask some questions."

I do not respond, since he did not ask a question, but I'm not happy that this is turning into a job interview. I have no ties to any particular syndicate or political regime. I'm a freelancer and I'm a professional. If they're looking for the personal touch, they should talk to my hairdresser.

"If there's anything you don't want to answer, meeting's over," says Jonathon. "We all go home, no hard feelings."

"I understand." Corpses bear no resentment.

"Can you confirm the following facts for me please? You are the operative known as Zai Zen. First recorded activity under this name was on behalf of the Ishida organization of Tokyo-Shinjuku in 1998."

"Just 'Zai'." I am embarrassed: I dropped the 'Zen' from my nom de guerre within my first week as a freelancer. It felt pretentious. I'm also displeased that they know about jobs that I performed as an amateur. My work for the Ishida yakuza was a long time ago.

"Wakarimasu," says Jonathon. He pronounces the word as if it comes with a side of pappadums. "You have been represented exclusively by the Rio De Janeiro-based agent 'Federico' since 2002?"

"Yes."

"Military experience?"

"Yes."

"In the Jeitai? The Japan Self-Defense Force?"

I nod once, firmly.

"Special forces?"

"Catering."

"Active duty?" asks Vashya.

I shake my head. Japan has only sent troops abroad a few times since the forties, and then only on peacekeeping missions. Even if I had been deployed, I wouldn't admit to it. That would make it much easier for them to narrow down my civilian identity.

Jonathon does not look very satisfied. "Family. You're Japanese. Samurai blood?"

"Peasant class."

"Ninja training?" Jonathon asks. "*Shinobi*?"

"No." It's difficult to suppress my smile.

"Special weapon skills? Katanas? Nunchukas?"

I fail to suppress my frown of annoyance that he has pluralized the Japanese words. "No."

"Fighting style?"

"I do not fight." I look Jonathon right in the eye, and then Vashya. "My job is to kill people, not to…engage them in fisticuffs." I hope that I have pronounced that correctly.

"So…what are your special skills?"

I frown and purse my lips. "I am pretty good at camping?"

Now it's Jonathon's turn to look annoyed, but Vashya nods approvingly. "Zai, what is your motivation?"

"My motivation? For killing people?"

"Zai, yes."

"Money."

"Zai, there many ways are to make living, Zai."

"I'm good at this job. It's interesting. I enjoy the travel."

Jonathon looks at her and she nods. He looks back at me.

"Mr Zai," he says. "Our agency, Unfolded Enterprises, would like to represent your services to the international and extranational community."

I give a bow-nod.

"If you agree to work for us exclusively, you will be paid a half a million pounds sterling signing bonus, and the same for every successful mission that you undertake on our behalf."

Now he's speaking my language. "What about Federico?"

"Federico has been paid his usual stipend for setting up this meeting, and he has already negotiated a substantial finder's fee."

I'm a little annoyed that Federico did not share any of this with me before I left Tokyo, but he knows I would have refused to come if he had. I value my independence. I like freelancing. But is a *lot* of money, and the travel opportunities are very tempting. Also, there's the distinct possibility that they will kill me where I stand if I refuse.

"Hai. I agree to your terms." I hope I will not regret this.

"That's very good news," says Jonathon, "Because we have a mission that needs your immediate attention."

"Of course."

"Our man will meet you at your hotel with further instructions." says Jonathon. "They will involve murdering somebody. I hope you don't mind."

"Hai." And then, deadpan: "But, excuse me. I still don't understand *gazebo*."

I head into downtown from the park and take a train to the central station, two stops away. I want to find the foreign language bookshop while I have some free time in Mesra City.

I have been studying Karachidaean from the dictionary I purchased last time, and I now have a vocabulary of about 30 words—although I have no idea how to correctly order them into a sentence. I want to find a grammar book and perhaps a travel guide, in a language that I can understand.

I don't know the address of the store, but I have been interested in maps and navigation since I was a child, and I believe myself to have an unshakeable sense of direction. I do not get lost; not ever.

Except for this time. Apparently, the shop isn't anywhere near where I thought it was.

Perhaps it's closed down. I'm fairly confident that I recognize the block where I found it, but there's no sign of the underground mall. Perhaps they covered over the stairway leading down to it. Perhaps they demolished the entire building while I was away.

Whatever the case, the bookstore is nowhere to be found. I return to the hotel empty-handed and hungry.

A skinny Karachidaean man dressed all in black is waiting for me in the lobby of the Epsidor. When he spots me, he breaks into a grin and rushes over. My new employers' fixer. "Mr Zai!" he says. "Welcome to Mesra City!"

This is the first time anybody has bothered to welcome me to Mesra City and something about it rubs me the wrong way. "What's your name?"

"Zai, you can please call me 'Rambo' please," he says. "As do my friends."

I doubt he has many of those, and I doubt they call him any such thing. I have an instant dislike for Rambo-san, although I am grudgingly impressed by his English.

"*Hajime mashite*, Rambo-san." I speak Japanese out of some mild form of spite.

Rambo-san breaks into a massive and delighted grin. "Come on, buddy Zai. I'll give you a showing of my turf, home boy."

"I don't know," I say, shaking my head and revising my estimate of his fluency. I've already had enough sightseeing for the day, and I dislike guided tours.

"I will show you all the sights, Mr Zai." There's a pleading tone in his voice now. "All the places the tourist books don't say."

I would happily trade Rambo-san's company for a tourist book. "I'm feeling quite tired. For now, please just give me the briefing?" I'm glad we're speaking English. If we were speaking Japanese, I would find it much more difficult to refuse him.

Rambo-san's disappointment is obvious and crushing.

"Next time, I would be very happy to go on your tour." I regret saying the words as soon as I have uttered them.

Rambo-san leads me to a small garden which is either on-top-of or behind the hotel, depending on how you approach it. Lush, soft grass with an unusual texture, with potted palm trees and banks of succulents growing out of red mulch. There's a sharp, woody odour in the garden, as much like mint as eucalyptus.

We have the place to ourselves. Rambo-san pulls out a paper file and shows me the mission.

"Steven Mangold and Nathan Wiedemer." I read my contacts' names from the paper. There are photos of the two of them together and separately. "Who are they?"

"In technicality, you would call them scab-labour," says Rambo-san.

"Dock workers?"

Rambo-san nods. "Shipyards," he says. "Before the union they quit, these duo were superstar machineristers."

"And now?"

"Now they are consultants."

"For who?"

"Shady Operators," says Rambo-san, relishing the expression.

"And the union wants them dead? Or the shady operators?"

Rambo-san shrugs. "Does it matter, Mr Zai?"

"Not to me."

Rambo-san gives me an envelope full of travel documents. "Tomorrow, you are travelling to Station Bravo Tango. There, I shall arrange for you some weapons. What choices are yours, Mr Zai?" His eyes glisten as he says it, and his forehead gleams with perspiration.

"I won't be needing any weapons, but thank you for offering, Rambo-san."

"AK-47, Sig Sauer, TEC-9. I can get you anything!" he bleats. "Ghurka knife. Machete. Cyanide. Grenades of the hand."

I hold up one hand. "That won't be necessary, thank you."

"But..." Rambo-san's eyes narrow. "I see," he says. "You have your own weapons. I must warn you, customs are very strict, my old Holmes."

I shake my head. "Don't worry about it. I have everything I need."

Rambo-san blinks about six times. Then he stares down at my hands, as if they have turned into scorpions. "You are deadly indeed, Mr Zai."

All I can do is bow.

At the Port Authority, I show my ticket to a succession of officials, who patiently direct me to the ferry terminal and then to a waiting area. A scrolling sign above the gate says SPACE WHIP in English and Karachidaean.

Before long, a hydrofoil slides into its berth and the crew usher me and about forty other foreigners across a floating gangway and onto the vessel. None of the other passengers are Karachidaean. Once we are all aboard, the hydrofoil backs into the dark waters of the Mesra City harbour and turns for the channel exit. When we pass through the headlands, it accelerates and we're soon cutting through the open ocean at about 80 knots.

A sea platform that resembles an oil rig with a NASA launch-pad grafted onto its superstructure comes into sight. A thick cable woven from a material that is both fibrous and crystalline rises from it directly into the sky without the benefit of any scaffolding, like Jack's beanstalk to the land of giants. I cannot guess how high it reaches but I can't see the end of it. The cable itself is difficult to see, despite its girth, which I estimate to be fifteen meters in diameter.

The hydrofoil slews around, throwing me back into my seat. We decelerate sharply and drift in to dock beneath the platform.

Dragging my luggage, I debark with the other passengers. Armed guards watch us closely as we cross a long hallway to a series of immigration desks. The passport control officer doesn't even speak to me; she just stamps the document and waves me through. I follow everybody through an ordinary security checkpoint with an x-ray machine and then into another departure lounge.

I don't even have time to sit down before a crew member steps up to the podium and speaks into a squelchy microphone. The 'climber module' is here.

We file into a polygonal chamber filled with rows of chairs. There are no windows. I find my assigned seat and strap myself into the safety harness. I must look a little confused because the woman to my left—a buxom Indian lady with henna tattoos on her hands and a dot on her forehead—smiles at me sympathetically. "Is this your first time on the Space Whip?"

"Yes."

"It is like a rollercoaster," she says. "Only it does not return you to the place from where you started."

I smile.

"I hope you didn't have a big lunch," she says.

There's no safety demonstration. An attendant checks that we are all buckled in, then vanishes into another room. The cabin begins to shake and engines roar to life. Rockets blast the climber module straight up the cable. I lean back into my seat and clench my jaw. My cheeks flap around my teeth from the g-forces. Some rollercoaster.

After about twenty minutes the roaring dies away and we begin to decelerate. Now our ascent seems incremental, as if we are being hauled up a rope, hand-over-hand.

I ask the lady sitting next to me, "Is this a kind of space elevator?"

"Not quite," she says. She assesses me for a moment; an engineer trying to determine how technical an explanation can I can handle. "Do you understand how a gravity slingshot works?"

"Yes?"

"This is similar. A slingshot allows you to use the gravity of a nearby astronomical body to change your direction and acceleration as you pass it by. The Space Whip uses the gravity differential between the realities on either side of a space fold to similar effect."

I have to translate that into Japanese and think about it before I can formulate a reply. "Why is it called a whip?"

"You'll see." She sits back and smiles.

A rocket blast kicks the passenger module sideways. My stomach lurches as the cabin starts to spin. Acceleration pushes me back into the chair and suddenly it does feel like I'm on a rollercoaster; accelerating down a curve that never ends. Over the roar of the rockets, I can hear the module whipping along the flexing cable.

We arc out, decelerating into a gentler trajectory. An additional burst from the thrusters slows us further. There's a small jolt as we dock with the orbital station.

I wonder if it will be worse going back down.

We debark from the climber module through a series of airlock doors and emerge into a hall, where our baggage has been laid out for us. There's full gravity, somehow, but I'm unsteady on my feet as I find my suitcase and wheel it towards the exit. A sign overhead says 'Welcome to Station Bravo Tango' in English.

I follow the crowd to a transport hub and find a quiet place to inspect the map of the Maglev Transit network, which looks more like a nervous system than a railway. It shows plan and profile views, with stern, bow, port, and starboard clearly marked. Most of the stations lie close to the hull and it looks like the tubes are strung across on the exterior of Bravo Tango. The 'You Are Here' arrow puts me at the Space Whip Terminus, somewhere near the bow.

I join a line of other passengers waiting to ride the MT. It feels like I'm queuing up for a second turn on an amusement park ride. Finally, I get to the front and a door opens, granting me admission into a one-man capsule.

I secure my baggage in the stowage space provided and strap myself onto the plinth with some trepidation. When I am secure, the door closes and a screen folds out in front of me, showing a section of the transport network. I select the Hotel District station and press GO.

The capsule rotates alarmingly. The enclosing chamber vents with a sharp hiss and the capsule starts to move.

It's over in minutes. The capsule rotates to a stop and the doors open. Pulsing with adrenaline, I step out into a wide thoroughfare beneath a glassed-in roof, through which I can see nothing but the vacuum of space. The stars above burn more brilliantly than I have ever seen them. I smile as I steady myself against a post. Assassin Zai in Outer Space.

I put on my sunglasses to shield my eyes against the starshine and saunter shakily down the street, looking for the Hyatt.

I'm surprised at the size of my hotel room. I'd expected a cabin, like on a cruise ship, but it's the same suite you'd find at the Hyatt anywhere else in the world: roomy and a little fancy, right on the cheapest edge of luxury.

I'm too wired to sleep. I shower, button on a clean shirt (this one has stylized cuckoo birds running along the hem), and then venture out for a walk. Perhaps a coffee will calm me enough for sleep.

The wide streets of the hotel district are lined, perhaps unsurprisingly, with hotels, restaurants and gift shops.

I choose a café with a faux-Tudor facade because a sign in the window advertises Finest European Coffee, but the barista who serves me has an American accent, so I order a cup of tea. I am the only customer at this hour—whatever hour it is. The dark skies and fluorescent lights yield no clues as to the local time. I take my hot beverage and find a seat beside the electric fire. I sit back and look up at the sky and think about how I came to be sitting at a coffee shop that thinks it's a ski lodge while on board a secret space station.

"Pretty, isn't it?" says the barista, who has followed me to the sofa. She has long, straight brown hair and a fringe that practically covers her eyes.

"You can't even see the glass," I observe.

"It's not glass. It's...I don't even know what it is. Some material."

"Space glass?"

"Sure. Space glass." She indicates the couch beside me. "Can I sit here?"

"Please."

It's quiet for a moment. I'm too tired to think up any small-talk. There isn't much weather to discuss in space.

"Nobody ever asks for tea," says the barista.

I can't bring myself to explain to her, so I just say, "It's my culture."

The barista nods. "We don't get many Japanese up here."

"I thought I'd see more Karachidaeans."

"No," she says. "They don't travel. 'Security reasons.' They don't want anybody coming along and drowning their shit again."

"They are very good at hiding themselves."

"That they are."

"But, I admit, I don't understand how they have hidden *this* place."

The barista laughs. "They haven't," she says. "Karachidor is behind the fold, but that doesn't extend beyond the atmosphere." Behind the fold. I like that.

"How come no one knows about it, in that case?"

The barista shrugs. "Because governments don't want them to," she says. "That's why they let the Karachidaeans do all the accounting."

The barista and I take the MT out to a stop near an unfinished area of Bravo Tango. It has atmosphere and a controlled climate, she tells me, but it has not yet been added to the gravity grid.

We cross a narrow walkway, and the barista leads me to membranous aperture that I think is a temporary airlock. There is some wavering gravity, but it flickers out or shifts direction fractionally as we proceed. "Spill-over from nearby gravity nodes." I find her casual use of this jargon very attractive.

We proceed, crouching, down a low-ceilinged corridor to yet another airlock, which opens into a small plastic blister on the side of the station. I follow her through, swinging inside using an overhead handhold and into complete weightlessness.

The barista touches a panel by the entrance and the walls fade until they are transparent. Outside, the space station does not present much of a horizon and the sky fills a bigger arc of my vision than it ever has before. The Earth hangs huge and blue above me; spattered with brown and green and streaked with white.

Bravo Tango's geosynchronous twirl rotates the planet out of my view, so I turn to look at the barista.

"Can't see the moon; it's on the other side of the world," she says, "but I'll make it up to you somehow." She pulls her sweater over her head.

Sex in zero gravity takes some adjustment. It's difficult to hold a position for long; we have to constantly seek out new surfaces against which to brace ourselves. The barista and I literally have to bounce each other off the walls. My only regret is that I won't be able to tell Michiko about it when I get back to Tokyo.

Michiko and I share our exploits with each other. We chuckle together about other, temporary lovers' foibles; we show each other new things we have learned…but I can't share this with her. I can't bring her here. I can't tell her I was in space, or why I was sent here. I can't tell her about Karachidor, or Mesra City, or the Space Whip, or Station Bravo Tango. I can't tell her the truth about my job.

Perhaps one day that will change. Perhaps one day I will change. But I doubt it.

In the morning, still weary from travel and poor sleep, I head for the observation lounge: a gallery with a view of the docks behind approximately 100 square meters of the non-specular *space glass*.

Three big interstellar vessels hang in the sky a few kilometres out, fixed in place by force fields and thrusters and brute mathematics. Smaller vehicles shuttle between these ships and the loading bays. I take about five hundred megabytes worth of photos before my hands get tired. I lower the camera and just stand observing the ships coming and going.

A huge vessel that's far too large to have been manufactured in a gravity-bound environment shakes free of its tethers. It turns with impossible grace and glides away into the night. A burning swan: bound for places far stranger than I have ever seen.

For now.

I move to a balcony that affords a view of the loading bays, which are tiered like rice paddies. Forklifts and robot arms dolly up and down retractable piers, ferrying cartons and palettes. The piers are all oriented differently and have their own gravity fields. From my vantage, many of the vehicles are travelling upside down, or traversing vertical surfaces.

The shipyards where my contacts, Mangold and Wiedemer, ply their trade are on the far side of the docks, mostly obscured by the curvature of the hull. I will have to get closer if I am to observe them.

Station Bravo Tango makes no attempt to enforce day and night cycles. My body clock is so confused that I don't know whether I've missed a meal or not—but suddenly I'm starving.

In a chain restaurant near my hotel, I order myself a blue-plate special that's high in fat, salt and sugar. Then I go for a walk to the ski-lodge coffee-shop and order an espresso, which proves just as terrible as I feared: greasy and burned. My barista friend isn't on duty today.

I've only just had lunch, but I am suddenly convinced that it's evening, so I return to the Hyatt for a nightcap. I feel oddly small and lonely here, and the familiarity of a hotel bar is comforting. I've been to a lot of places, but this is certainly the furthest from home I've ever travelled. Off the map and into the stars.

I try three different beers, but they're all soapy American brews. I give up and order a glass of bourbon. They don't serve *shnkwer* here. The barman—a Regular Joe type with blue skin and white hair—tells me that the Karachidaeans refuse to export their elixir.

After a couple of drinks, curiosity overwhelms my manners. "May I ask where you are from?"

"Menlat Nir." He speaks English with an American drawl. "Ragev Tsul stratum."

"I don't know where that is."

"It's about three hundred klicks due east of Karachidor, and seven thousand meters above," says the barman. "This time of year, anyway."

I nod continuously while I try to make sense of what he just said. "It moves?"

"Every season. Sometimes more often, depending."

"Depending on what?"

"Oh, you know. Ocean currents. Business. Politics. Whatever."

"Do you miss it?"

"Well, the economy sucks, but the beer is good."

I nod and nurse my drink. I'm out of intelligent questions.

"Where you from?" asks the barman.

"Tokyo."

"Never heard of it," says the barman.

"It's wild."

"I'll bet."

Another pause.

I don't know exactly how to say this, so I dig for some kind of English idiom to lead with. "So, hey." I think that works. "So, hey. I want to meet some aliens."

He frowns.

I search my English vocabulary again. "Extra-terrestrials?" I am slightly drunk, and I say the difficult phrase slowly. It comes out with a thick Japanese accent, but I think the barman understands. "Is there a...a Mickey House, or some place?"

"What's a Mickey House?"

"A conversation lounge? Or a pub where aliens hang out?"

The barman shakes his head. "ETs mostly stay on their own ships. It's more comfortable for them." When he sees the look of disappointment on my face he adds: "I guess there's the Sector House. Kind of conference centre where they go if they have business to conduct or, like, disputes that need to be resolved. Neutral ground."

"Disputes?"

"Nothing heavy. No duels or politics, but...you know. Wheeling and dealing. Dickering."

"Can you tell me where to find this Sector House?"

The woman at the registration desk makes me sign in before she'll let me go into the Sector House, but she doesn't ask my business or check my ID.

The building is a maze of corridors; each one leading to an open lounge area and a cluster of glassed-in conference rooms. There are strange barriers that prevent me from entering certain areas: a wall of scent here; a squared off block of steam there; a passageway where some kind of friction field makes it feel like a sadistic masseuse is gently rubbing gravel against my skin.

The beings I see wandering these halls are difficult to comprehend, much less describe. None of them are humanoid, or even bipedal. Some of the aliens are glassy. Some are made of tiny liquid filaments. One of them is so opaque that its carapace reflects light perfectly: just flat colour, without shadows or highlights. Another being spreads gradually into dimensions that lie beyond my capacity to perceive. There are several creatures that I think are distributed organisms: disconnected pieces that sometimes operate independently and sometimes together. I am too intimidated to take any photographs.

I make no attempt to communicate with the ETs here. I wouldn't know what to say.

On my way back towards the MT station I see a more familiar creature pass me: a jellyfish-man in a tartan kilt, like the one I spotted on my prior trip to Mesra City. Perhaps it's the same one. How many could there be?

The Scottish Jelly Man freaked me out the first time I saw him, but now he just looks ridiculous. He looks fake, like a man in a rubber suit playing a monster in an episode of *Ultraman*.

I always did like the monsters better.

I change my Aloha shirt for a plain grey polo and take the MT to the shipyards, where my tourist persona would be out of place.

This area is much more downmarket than the hotel district. Diamond plate flooring and grungy, prefabricated stores. Not a souvenir stand in sight. The main thoroughfare is narrow and bends to accommodate the bulkheads and bulges of the station's integral structure. The ceiling is high but uneven, striated with pipes and cabling. Most of the businesses here are workshops or warehouses.

I eat a sandwich in a workman's café and buy an awful cup of filter coffee from a convenience store. Eventually I spot my two contacts, walking towards me on the other side of the street.

Steven Mangold is a big man with the hunched posture that you sometimes see on the very tall. Nathan Wiedemer's younger and slenderer and a couple of inches shorter, but he's hardly short. Both of them are wearing jeans and flannel shirts under high visibility vests. They are carrying old-fashioned lunch pails.

I shadow Mangold and Wiedemer until they stop in front of one of the larger workshops. The windowless metal façade bulges outward unevenly, as if it's absorbed a massive explosion from the inside. Mangold swipes an access badge over a reader and the door opens. Both of them walk through together, swinging their lunch pails. I can't hear their conversation but they both seem to be enjoying it.

I see no evidence of camera surveillance. On my way back to the MT station I purchase a high visibility vest from one of the shops that sells workman's clothing and tools. I take note of the time, which is displayed on a wall clock behind the counter. I will return tomorrow.

Twenty-three and a half hours later I return to Mangold and Wiedemer's workplace wearing my new orange vest and a pair of scuffed hiking shoes that can pass for work boots. I'm carrying half a dozen cardboard tubes that look as if they contain old fashioned blueprints, but which are in fact empty.

Thus encumbered, I make my way back to the hangar and begin clumsily trying search my pockets, as though looking for an access badge while juggling my burdens. Timing, as always, is the difficult part—but it's also the part I am good at.

Wiedemer rushes up behind me and swipes his badge. "Here you go, man."

"Thank you."

I waddle through the open door. Wiedemer follows, and Mangold is not far behind.

"You need a hand with any of that?" says Mangold, sympathetic.

"I can manage, but thank you." Neither of them seems suspicious. As union pariahs they're used to keeping their heads down.

"Don't mention it," says Wiedemer. They slope off to the right, already deep in some interrupted conversation about Iggy Pop and David Bowie. I go left.

There are partitioned offices around the perimeter of the workshop, but most of the activity seems to be taking place on the open main floor, where about two dozen mechanics are hard at work maintaining construction vehicles and other heavy machinery. Mangold and Wiedemer are headed towards the far side of the building, where three sets of bay doors are set into the rippled and buttressed wall. Yellow stencilled text informs me that this is, in fact, part of the hull of the station.

I dump my paper tubes in a recycling basket and then I walk around trying to look purposeful for a few minutes. None of the mechanics pay me any mind and the office workers stay in their offices.

Mangold and Wiedemer have disappeared into a prefabricated hut near the bay doors. There are no windows, so I loiter in the shadows behind a hump of machinery covered with a tarpaulin. Before long they emerge, clad in bulky space suits. I can tell it's them from the way they interact, even though the helmets conceal their faces. They enter a small airlock beside the bay doors and disappear from my sight.

The hut contains more space suits, hanging on racks; lockers; a table with two chairs; a refrigerator; and a supervisor's console that I believe would be manned, if my contacts were not scab labour.

Their lunch pails are in the fridge. I could poison them, but that will look like obvious foul play. Also, I didn't bring any poison.

There's a fifth of whiskey beside the console and two used glasses: these two cowboys are enjoying being unsupervised. I'm certain that whatever accident befalls them will be blamed on drunkenness. That's convenient.

The console shows different views of a space-going vessel under construction. The ship is a small one; about 250 meters long and shaped like a sausage link. Rocket engines ring its body at both ends. The hull is covered in scaffolding, draped with cables and spotted with telescope arrays. Alloy ribs stand free where the skin has not yet been fitted. This is no burning swan; it's one of ours. I feel proud of its homeliness.

One end of the sausage-boat hangs suspended from a gantry. Two small vehicles, each with a mounted pair of articulated arms, manoeuvre about on the apron beside it. They are completing the hull, attaching plates with fibrous metallic ligaments. Helmet cameras confirm that their operators are Mangold and Wiedemer.

Wiedemer's vehicles raise a sheet of material over a thick metal slab and brings some kind of arc torch to bear upon it, while Mangold beats it into shape with a battery of jackhammers. I pull on a pair of cotton gloves and raise my hands to the keyboard.

A login dialog prevents me from getting any further. The system has been locked by its prior user, CONST\NWiedemer. I don't want to try to guess his password—if I get it wrong, I might set off an alarm. Even if not, the most probable outcome is that I'll lock myself out of the system.

I rifle through the loose documents scattered around the console, hoping that the supervisor has been kind enough to write down the passwords on a sticky note. I don't find any sticky notes, but I do find a small tablet computer in a grubby neoprene case.

I press the button on the side of the tablet and the screen comes to life. A picture of a puppy playing in a sunlit meadow, overlaid with the grid of a pattern lock. When I squint at the screen I can see a line of finger-grease that runs through about six of the dots.

I remove my right glove and trace the pattern anticlockwise. The grid disappears and now program icons appear on top of the puppy meadow wallpaper. I flick through Wiedemer's email, his social media pages, his open web browsers, and finally his virtual notebook. He has a tab in there labelled PASSWORDS. I swipe it open.

Right there beneath INTERNET BANKING and HOME WIFI he has WORK LOGIN.

I put my gloves back on and try the password on the administrator's console. It gets me in right away. I nose around the desktop until I find a wireframe view of the construction site, with the gantry, the sausage-ship, and the two maintenance vehicles and the bay doors. By right-clicking randomly on the modelled surface I stumble onto a context menu that offers me a choice of arcane-sounding options. I choose GRAVITY GRID and then a LEVELS dialog appears. It's currently positioned at 1G. I drag it down to zero and click APPLY.

On the screen, I observe Mangold's vehicle begin to rise, swaying away from the apron after its hammer-arm. He flails, but there's nothing he can do without a secure base. The swinging arm with the anvil suddenly drops towards the apron as it wobbles into a cell with gravity and the body of the vehicle rotates after it.

The anvil smashes down onto Wiedemer's vehicle, crushing the cab and becoming snared in its windmilling arms. I turn the gravity up to 2Gs. Mangold's vehicle comes spinning down with enough force to crack the apron.

I restore the grid to 1G and clean my fingerprints off the screen of the tablet with a spritz of glass cleaner and my cotton gloves.

This is the first time I've dropped an anvil on someone.

The return journey on the Space Whip is surprisingly sedate. The sea platform draws the cable taut, and the climber module descends from Bravo Tango mechanically; hand-under-hand. It's not a very smooth ride, but at least it has none of the wild acceleration of the trip out to Bravo Tango. I fall into a doze and do not properly awaken until we're almost back at sea level. I am disappointed to have missed out on the view.

When I get back to the Epsidor there's a message waiting for me. I have a meeting tomorrow.

It's a rainy day in Mesra City, and I don't have an umbrella.

In Tokyo, you can buy an umbrella in every kiosk or convenience store, but I can't find one for sale anywhere in Mesra City. Perhaps they are out of fashion. Some of the locals are wearing waterproof hoods, but generally speaking, the Karachidaeans don't seem to mind getting wet.

It's bright and sunny in the glade containing the gazebo. The ground isn't even damp. I have an intuition that this glade is not a part of the usual geography of Karachidor, any more than Karachidor is part of the usual geography of my own world. I also have the feeling that the good weather has been orchestrated so that the Englishman can wear his sunglasses without embarrassment. I wish I had brought my own.

"Have a seat, Mr Zai," says Jonathon. The bodyguards don't even look at me.

Vashya indicates the empty chair. Dripping, I sit down carefully. "Zai, you've done very well, Zai."

I bow.

"Both contacts are dead," says Jonathon. "Some kind of systems malfunction, apparently. No evidence of wrongdoing. Both men had alcohol in their systems and the fault is likely their own."

I bow again. Jonathon purses his lips and looks at me through half-closed eyes. "Didn't think you had it in you," he says. "How did you manage it?"

"Stealth," I reply, because it sounds better than 'recklessness and luck.'

"You *are* a ninja," says Jonathon, grinning.

Vashya does not smile.

"Welcome, Mr Zai, to your new position as an official X-Dimensional

Assassin for Unfolded Enterprises, Limited," says Jonathon. I shake his hand, and then Vashya's.

XDA Zai. I like the sound of that.

#3: Doors and Ways

No map of the earth is accurate. The planet is roughly spherical; if you flatten it into two dimensions it's going to be distorted. Depending on how you project it, the shapes of the continents will be altered, as well as their relationships to one another.

Think of all of those different projections. The rectangular Mercator projection, with Antarctica smeared across the bottom. The Robinson, and the Winkel-Tripel, with curved lateral edges that give the passing illusion that the map is a sphere. The Dymaxion, which looks like a kindergarten craft project. The Authagraph, which you can fold into an accurate globe.

When I consider Karachidor, I think of the Homolosine projection.

The Homolosine looks like a peeled orange skin. The top of the map is round, with a cleavage separating North America from Europe and Asia. The underside has four lobes, one each containing South America, Africa, Australia, and open ocean. Imagine if you had such a map. Imagine that you knew it well; that you had travelled all across it so many times that it felt like a floor plan of your home. Imagine that one day you unfolded the map to find a fifth lobe, right between South America and Africa, containing a landmass you have never seen before.

That's Karachidor: a place that's only on the map if you unfold it correctly.

I'm on the last leg of my flight to Mesra City, and I'm trying to determine exactly where the transition from the Conventional Earth occurs. Where exactly is the fold?

I sit hunched over my entertainment unit, watching the icon for the plane as it moves along the flight map. The work is monotonous, but I have nothing better to do. I've already watched all the movies and I'm too uncomfortable to sleep. My eyes hurt too much for me to focus on my book.

Every sixty seconds, the map is replaced by an information screen showing air speed, altitude, position, time at destination, and other data. We're about two hours out from Mesra City when I feel a peculiar sensation. It's as though my skin has expanded fractionally, and the bones and muscles and organs that fill it have then swollen to match. Like I've grown just a tiny bit larger. When the flight map returns, it shows Karachidor's landmass, but without the context of the rest of the world. The icon of the plane shows that we are approaching from the north east.

The information screen no longer indicates latitude and longitude.

Rambo-san is waiting for me at the airport. Today he's wearing sweat pants and a hoodie made of some fabric that's cabled to resemble chainmail. He grins and waves like a fan at a rock concert.

"Mr Zai! Mr Zai!"

"Hello, Rambo-san."

He gives me a long, serious look, and then says, "I am feeling very privileged that you would call me that, buddy-man."

Before I can reply, he grabs my luggage out of my hand and starts to wheel it away. I blink twice, take a deep breath, and then follow him out to a strange local car, which he's left idling in the drop-off area. I'm shocked that he has managed to do this without drawing the ire of airport security, but he does not seem concerned.

Rambo gets behind the wheel and turns out into the traffic. "I am very sorry, Mr Zai," he says, "but there will not be time for the tour I promised you on this today. The boat to Sugdike goes only two times per week."

I lean back into the passenger seat and close my eyes. "That's too bad, Rambo-san."

The mollusc-mobile is quite comfortable, and the ride is smooth. There's a faintly floral smell in the car: the aroma of Rambo's beverage, which sits in a cup-holder where I would expect to find a gearbox and handbrake in a normal car. I cannot see a dashboard but, if I jockey around, I can catch a glimpse of a head-up display that's only properly visible if you are in the driver's seat.

Without taking his eyes off the road, Rambo-san hands me a paper dossier. "Your contact is named Gregory Vondruska."

The dossier contains photographs, maps, corporate correspondence. Apparently, Vondruska is a clerk at the Sugdike Institute. "What is a Sugdike?"

"Sugdike is special holiday resorting place."

"How special?"

It takes Rambo-san a while to formulate how to express it in English. "Some people, they did copy a Medium Evil village and that is made Sugdike."

It takes me a while to figure out what that means. "It's like a medieval Club Med? Why would anybody build such a thing?"

Rambo-san keeps his eyes on the road. "Touristism?"

"And this Institute where Vondruska works?"

"Research place," says Rambo-san.

"What kind of research?"

"Who cares?" he says. "It's for the tax advantage only."

"What did Vondruska do?"

"Vondruska has been selling the research secrets," says Rambo-san.

I need to kill a man for selling research undertaken for the sole purpose of earning tax breaks for a resort hotel. That sounds about right.

ambo-san drops me off at the Port Authority with a handful of tickets, which I use to gain admission to a river barge. I find a seat on the lower deck near a window.

By the time the barge puts out I'm drowsing queasily. I try to look at the Mesra City scenery, but that makes it worse. Dirty sunlight glitters off the ultramodern skyline, right in my eyes. I turn away, too lazy to put on my sunglasses.

I take my book out of my bag, but I don't even bother to open it. About five minutes later I notice that it's not the translated Elmore Leonard novel that I thought I was reading. *Doors and Ways,* by Raethe Marghison. I recognize the title, vaguely. I must have picked it up out of the seat pocket on the plane. I replace the book in my travel bag and try to locate the Elmore Leonard, but it's not there. I sigh and settle into my seat and close my eyes.

The vessel bumps to a stop and machinery rumbles. We're in a lock. The water drains; the boat shifts down, moves, then stops again. The process repeats. The final jolt is accompanied by the spider's web caress that I now understand indicates passage through some kind of dimensional membrane. I open my eyes.

The river is a lot wider now. Trees line the shore on both sides and the sky is cloudier than the one above Mesra City. When I look back towards the lock, I can see no sign of the city or its sprawl.

The barge makes a turn onto a canal. We are approaching a small town. Prefabricated buildings designed to look rustic line the shore, but there's an ordinary suburban precinct behind them. Most of the traffic consists of shiny white golf carts and utility vans, with the occasional sedan car.

The barge docks at a riverside quay and the crew herds all the passengers into a long, thatch-roofed hut. The floors are poured concrete, but the thatching looks real. The hut contains a single room furnished with rude wooden furniture. LCD screens fold down from the rafters and a smooth, a female voice with a British accent pipes into the room from hidden speakers:

"Welcome to Sugdike, the Village on the Edge of Yesterday—"

This is not a resort, it's a theme park.

Sugdike, the British woman tells me, is a genuine medieval village, filled with genuine medieval people—not actors. The townspeople have been taught to speak a relatively modern form of English for our convenience. They are used to the presence of tourists and will be very happy to assist guests with anything they require.

The screen flashes images of the various attractions of the village: blacksmithing, shopping for handicrafts, falconry, shopping, hunting, 'tavern culture', and shopping. All major currencies can be changed for local money at any of the businesses or outlets in the hotel district. For the sake of authenticity, merchants in the village cannot accept credit card payments.

I file out of the hall with the other new arrivals. We board a small wagon train of golf carts, which delivers us out to our various accommodations with an utter lack of dignity.

I check into the Hyatt and go straight up to my room and throw up in the bathroom sink. Then I sit down and squirt the contents of my bowels into the toilet.

It's mid-morning the following day when I emerge from my room. I pick at what's left of the breakfast buffet for half an hour, but my appetite hasn't yet returned. I spread a brochure-map on the table beside my half-finished plate.

It looks like the most direct route from the hotel district into Sugdike proper is the Woodland Path, although it passes through the Bright Glade, the Limpid Pond, and the Woodcutter's Clearing. The brochure cautions me that this is a mildly strenuous walk and offers several other routes into the medieval town which are golf cart accessible.

I push my plate away. I have a feeling that Sugdike's attractions will be best experienced on an empty stomach.

The Woodland Path is wide enough for four people to walk abreast. The sun slants down through the old growth forest. Songbirds sing and crows croak. The breeze smells like pine needles and damp leaves and tree bark and spring.

I tell myself that when I get back home, I'll try to get out of the city more. Perhaps I'll fly up to Hokkaido and go camping. Take Michiko and commune with nature. But I know I won't. I'll stay in the city until the ski season, and then my communing with nature will be confined to cursing the Nagano slopes every time I fall off my snowboard.

I'm actually feeling a little homesick by the time I come to the Bright Glade. It's a wide, naturally clear area amongst the trees, filled with light and chirping critters. I put on my sunglasses.

A massive oak tree presides over the glade. A hollow log lies carefully arranged in its shadow, and seated on the log is a bearded young man. Something about this place makes my skin prickle. I shake my head, but the feeling remains.

The bearded man smiles and stands up. He's wearing a tunic, pants, boots and a wide leather belt. According to the brochure-map, this area is off limits to the villagers, so he's probably a cast member for the theme park.

The bearded man looks past me, as if waiting for more people to show up. When no tour group materializes, he tries not to look disappointed. "Hello, traveller," he says. "It'd my pleasure to be your guide during your first visit to the village of Sugdike."

"I have a map." I show him the map with a gesture that's designed to shoo him away as well as to demonstrate my truthfulness.

"So, you do."

"Since I have a map, I don't think I need a guide."

"Are you good with maps, then?"

"Very."

"Well," says the guide, "I get paid to show visitors around. If I sit on my arse all day, I only get half wages." When he says that, I am unmoved. He then adds, "You wouldn't even have to tip me."

I'm not in the mood for this, but I do have to make at least a token effort to see the attractions. I hope there aren't any rides. And I'm already feeling guilty for my rudeness. "What's your name?"

"I'm Emmet," he says. He has an Irish accent, I think. I would have expected English or American with a name like Emmet.

"Zai." I suppose that my chosen is not commonplace to my culture, either.

We shake hands.

I snap a couple of quick photos of the Bright Glade. Emmet offers to snap a few with me in them, but I refuse him. I have cleared the memory card since my trip to Station Bravo Tango, but I don't like anybody touching my camera.

Emmet leads me back to the Woodland Path and we head in to Sugdike proper.

"You're Japanese, then?" says Emmet, after a few minutes of walking.

"Yes."

"You speak English very well."

"I have a degree."

"So do I. English Literature." Emmet smiles and shrugs. "That's why I'm a guide at a fucking theme park."

The Limpid Pond is nothing more than that: a still pool of water. Willows bend over it. We stand on the wooden viewing platform for almost a minute before I've had enough.

"Hardly seems worth the trouble, doesn't it?" says Emmet. "I think they only built this platform because the pond's not big enough to warrant a bridge."

There's no woodcutter in the Woodcutter's Clearing; he's already quit for the day. I feel irrationally jealous.

Once we're out of the trees, the Woodland Path becomes a dirt road, which terminates at the village common.

The village is composed of a few hundred well-maintained thatch buildings, clustered below a small and unimpressive stone castle. I had expected the streets to stink of human effluent, but it seems they have some anachronistic form of sanitation here. Sugdike smells like cropped hay and wood-smoke, with only the faintest traces of horse shit for colour. I wonder if Europe was this cheery in feudal times, because I am certain that Japan was not.

This is where most of the business—tourist business, anyway—is conducted. Emmet shows me the miller, the cooper, and the seamstress, the tavern. I see a few other gawping tourists—some of them in costume, some of them not. The 'locals' are all Caucasians who speak a modern dialect of English, but sprinkled liberally with 'ayes' and 'nays', 'thees' and 'thous'.

"Isn't there supposed to be a blacksmith?"

"Formerly our most popular attraction," says Emmet, pleased that I've finally asked a question. "The forge proved to be a bit of a fire hazard, though, so he's been relocated outside of the city limits."

"How far outside?"

"You could walk," he says. "But most people take a wagon or a horse." I have never cared for horse riding. Emmet notes my frown and so continues: "Or you take a golf cart from the hotel district."

I blink slowly. "Perhaps another day."

"Would you like to visit the castle? You won't be able to see the Duke until tomorrow, but the view from the battlements is quite good, and there's a changing of the guard at twilight."

"Is there a fireworks display?"

Emmet. "You'd have to go to the Enchanted Kingdom for that," he says. "There's no gunpowder in this era. We wouldn't want any anachronism, now, would we?"

"Is there a pub?"

"We already looked in on the tavern."

"A pub where local people go. Not tourists."

"There is indeed such a place."

The streets narrow as Emmet leads me away from the common. The sanitation that surprised me earlier becomes less evident as we get away from the tourist areas. Sugdike is bigger than I thought it was.

We pass a four-storey stone building with a sloping shale roof. It has no visible windows in the upper levels. The lower levels are concealed behind a seven-foot wall topped with a coil of razor-wire. "The prison?"

"The Sugdike Institute." The way Emmet says it, it sounds like place where they assess insurance policies. This is where Gregory Vondruska works. I don't want to look too interested, but from a first cursory inspection it does not look like a promising location to make contact. Probably, I will have to make a house call.

There's no sign to identify the pub, but the door is open and there is a hearth lit inside. It's a single, dirt-floored room containing two long communal tables. We seat ourselves on the raw wooden benches in a quiet corner. Emmet looks a little uncomfortable, but he smiles when the publican approaches. "What'll you have?"

"Two ales," says Emmet.

"Can I have what he's having?" I say, pointing to a drunk sitting further up the table. The drunk shoots me a surly glance and goes back to his trencher of stew. Gravy is literally dripping from his nose.

"Two ales and one food," says the barkeeper, turning away.

Shortly the barman brings us our drinks and my meal. I eat it slowly, because there's no cutlery. I think it's beef, stewed to the point where the meat is indistinguishable from the gravy. There's not a hint of seasoning, not even salt or pepper. It's very hot.

"Perhaps you can clear something up for me." I speak carefully, because I've burned my mouth on the stew. "Where is this place, Sugdike, located? Geographically, I mean."

Emmet thinks about it. "I don't know how to answer that question," he replies. "Nowhere, I suppose. This is a different universe to the one we are from."

"A parallel world?"

"Not exactly," says Emmet. "Just a different one, which contains an earth-compatible planet. Only one small island on one small planet in this entire reality has been settled for the Sugdike project."

"They have an entire universe and they used it to build a theme park?"

Emmet shakes his head. "Universes are plentiful," he says. "If you know where to look for them."

"That isn't what I asked."

Emmet sighs. "They didn't build this place," he says. "They copied it." He can see that I don't understand, so he continues. "They cloned the village from a real one and put it here."

"How can you clone a place?" I ask.

"As I understand it, it's a bit like making a mold of the existing article and then casting a new one from a compatible slice of space-time. When they created the place, it was an exact duplicate of the original town. Then they modified it until it was…this."

"Real estate must be really expensive in Karachidor."

"It's more of a quarantine thing," says Emmet. "Because of the research. In case something goes nuclear."

"If the people who run this place are able to clone a village out of time and make it a tourist attraction, I cannot imagine what kind of research they might do here in secret."

"Oh, it's not really a secret," says Emmet. "It's just that most people think it's too ridiculous to say aloud."

"Really?"

"You know that the big walled-in building we saw?"

"The Institute?"

"Its full name is the Sugdike Institute of Sorcery."

I take a moment to process that. "They have...wizards...in there?"

"More like test subjects, or inmates," says Emmet. "But yes, I believe so."

"Really?"

"You don't believe in wizards?"

I think about it for a moment. I think I do believe in magic. It's difficult to explain the unfolded world any other way. But Wizard School feels like s step too far into fantasy. "No. I don't believe in wizards."

"With good reason," says Emmet. "They're all dead and gone, aren't they? Your Merlins and Morganes and all them. Vanished into myth and folklore."

"Are they the ones who hide Karachidor?"

"Yes, originally," says Emmet. "Our thaumaturgical engineers have extended that work in the meantime, but I don't think any of them could have managed something on that scale again."

"*What* kind of engineers?"

"Thaumaturgical engineers," said Emmet. "They can do a kind of magic, but it takes permits and project plans and a lot of time and money. You want something that actually works, it needs to be properly designed, constructed, and installed."

I nod my head as if I understand what he's telling me. "So why put this Institute...here? In a theme park?" Rambo-san's explanation about tax breaks can't be the whole story.

"Well, like I said, we don't have any proper wizards these days. The Institute aims to make some new ones."

"In a theme park."

"The idea here is to see if these people, with this medieval mindset, can be more like the old school magicians." I can't tell if he's joking or not.

"Can I meet one?"

"A wizard? Sure." Emmet gestures to the drunk with his nose in his stew. "There's one right there."

"He doesn't look like a wizard to me."

"You've obviously not met a lot of wizards, then, have you?" says Emmet. "That over there is a classic specimen." Before I can stop him, he waves to the drunk. "Excuse me. Excuse me, sir."

The drunk looks up at blearily from his trencher of stew.

"Sir, would you happen to be a wizard?"

The drunk raises his chin and squares his shoulders, although he's still swaying in his chair. "I take my learning at the Institute, aye."

"Do you have any advice for the uninitiated?" Emmet gestures at me with one thumb.

The drunk rubs his mouth, removing some of the gravy from his chops. He looks at his hand, sniffs, and licks it. "Aye," he says, slowly. "Aye, I do, then."

The drunk slides down the bench unsteadily until he's sitting close enough to Emmet to make him visibly uncomfortable. He leans closer and takes a long, deep whiff. Emmet leans away as politely as he can.

"You," says the drunk. "You have no art, but you know the Ways. You have the stink of the Hill Folk upon ye."

"That's just my cologne," says Emmet.

"Laugh ye not," says the drunk. "The fey ones are not to be trifled with."

"I've always preferred plain old custard," Emmet replies. I'm not sure what this means but before I can ask, the drunk turns to me.

"You have some talents," he says. "Ripe, too. If you haven't awakened to them yet, you will soon enough."

Suddenly I'm just as uncomfortable as Emmet. I don't know what the wizard is going to say next, but whatever it is, I'd prefer he didn't.

The wizard sniffs the air again. "Topomancy," he says. "And some chronomancy. Aye."

I have no idea what he just accused me of, but it sounds like nonsense. I'm relieved he hasn't spilled any of my secrets.

"Topiary?" says Emmet. "Trimming hedges, and such?"

"Time and place, boy," says the drunk, still addressing me. "In the right time, and the right place, you will come to learn about time and place."

"Let's get out of here," said Emmet. "This man is drunk."

"You told me he was a wizard." I don't know why I'm defending the old lush now. Perhaps because he said I was special.

The drunk raises a hand angrily, pauses, closes his eyes, and throws up a mouthful of vomit on his jerkin. He lowers his hand.

Emmet is right. It's time to go. It's past my bedtime and the jetlag is brutal.

I am in the Bright Glade, looking up into the spread of the guardian oak tree. The sun is behind it and its rays dazzle me through the canopy. I know that I am dreaming.

The sound of a man vomiting draws my attention. The wizard from the tavern is sitting on Emmet's log with his head between his knees and his fingers laced behind his head.

I take a step towards him. "Are you alright?"

"I'm fucking drunk," the wizard replies, to his boots. He says 'fucking' like a foreign word. I expect that he picked it up from some other tourist.

"Did you come looking for me?"

The wizard unlaces his fingers, looks up at me, and wipes his mouth. "Of course not," he says. "This is *your* dream, not mine." I am conscious that we are speaking English.

The wizard spits a mouthful of bile on the ground.

"What happens now, dream-wizard-san? Will you take me on a magical journey?"

"It's your fucking dream," says the wizard. "If you want to go somewhere you can make your own fucking Door. Find your own damned Way."

I awaken before the sun is up. The dream conversation is still vivid in my mind, although I am sure there's more of it that I can't remember. I'm still unclear as to whether or not it really was a dream or an actual psychic experience.

It's Monday and I need to get to work, but I just can't bring myself to meet with Gregory Vondruska just yet. I have come to believe that something more important is at stake. More important to me, that is. I am certain it's not more important to Vondruska.

The Bright Glade is not very bright in the weak dawn light, and I have the place to myself. I am relieved the wizard isn't here, although I know that, since he's a villager, he is supposed to be unable to leave the town. There's no sign of Emmet. Maybe a big tour group came through. I am pleased by the solitude.

The Bright Glade still feels odd. It's not the spider-web feeling that comes when I pass through a veil between worlds, but it's akin to it. It triggers the same newly awakened faculty. It's a sensation like touch, if touch was directionless and did not require direct contact.

I explore until I find a place where this feeling is strongest. It's very subtle; a pressure behind my calves; a tension in my feet and hands. I reach out experimentally, flexing my fingers. There is something there, but it's like trying to open a polythene produce bag from a roll in a supermarket. I can feel the seam, but I cannot muster enough friction in my fingertips to open it.

Frustrated and more than a little guilty for all the time I've been wasting, I head back to the hotel. Enough of this witches-and-wizards nonsense; I have a job to do. I eat some grease for breakfast, with two coffees and a fistful of painkillers, and then set out in cargo pants and my blackest pair of Doc Martens. Time to earn my salary.

At the Radisson, two hotels down from the Hyatt, I commandeer a golf cart and go for a drive into the residential zone, where the non-medieval people live. It's very suburban: bungalows and low-rise apartments, convenience stores, supermarkets.

Gregory Vondruska's home is a two-storey place that only stands out from the other properties on the block because it has a triple garage. Low fence at the front, high fence at the back. There's probably a swimming pool in the yard. I park the cart around the corner from the house and find a quiet spot in the leafy park across the road, from where I can watch the house with some concealment from prying eyes. It's still early and there's not much traffic yet.

There are two cars parked in the driveway: a Toyota Echo and a big vehicle that looks like the lovechild of a Jeep Cherokee and a Plymouth Fury. I wonder why the Vondruskas need three cars? The hotel district is small enough that you can get anywhere you need on a golf cart. Are there roads out into the countryside? Is there a highway you can drive back to Karachidor? Or to other, more exotic places? Perhaps I should have asked Emmet, after all.

Around 0830 am Vondruska emerges from the house. He's a short guy with quick, intelligent eyes, quirky eyebrows, and hair close cropped around his pate. He struggles into the Echo and drives away. I guess the Jeep Fury is Mom's Taxi.

I pull the book out of my knapsack and settle in for a dull morning of surveillance. *Doors and Ways*, by Raethe Marghison. Okay, then.

The previous owner of *Doors and Ways* has marked some of the pages. Something is familiar about the annotations, although there is no writing—just some passages circled or underlined. I look at the table of contents. The book contains about a dozen essays, written by authors whose names I vaguely recognize but whose work I cannot recall. Sita Dulip, Temudjin Oh, Bill Roth. I flip to the front of the book and start reading.

Editor Raethe Marghison's introduction tells me that any journey, physical or mental, will yield an improved knowledge of one's own self. Self-knowledge can open the Doors to new Travels; set one upon the Ways to destinations undreamt-of.

I stifle a yawn. Reading prose in English always makes me sleepy.

Marghison goes on to inform me that there are many ways to open Doors, to travel the Ways: ritual, meditation, study; science, magic; subtle action, brute force; indulgence, deprivation; circumlocution, silence.

Double-barreled yawn.

I fan the pages of the book and open it again to the most heavily marked chapter, 'Traveling'. This chapter is also written by Marghison, in the same florid style. Lots of semi-colons and pompous clichés and very little actual explanation. Over the course of about fifteen pages, I learn that a Door is an opening that leads from one place directly to the next, even if they are not geographically adjacent. A Way is a non-linear trajectory that connects two places with a shorter actual distance than the direct route.

Ways require less effort/power/attention to maintain and are generally used for routes that are heavily trafficked. Doors are usually closely guarded secrets.

This is like listening to Jim Morrison reciting the Lord of the Rings. I feel bored but mildly paranoid.

Most Doors and Ways are duplex, but some only open in one direction.

The origin and destination do not have to exist in the same dimensional or chronological bracket.

Some few Travelers, Marghison writes, are able to open Doors or cut Ways of their own.

Topomancy and chronomancy. It takes some hard thought to forge the connection back to the drunken wizard's conversation. That's the problem with English: in addition to its ridiculous grammar, it is full of these words that draw meaning from its precursor languages.

I put the book down and look again at Vondruska's house. How can the magical textbook that contains some, or all, of the answers that I so desperately seek, be so boring?

It's late afternoon by the time I head into Sugdike. Alone, I wander about aimlessly taking uninteresting and carelessly framed photographs on my phone.

I watch an old woman chasing chickens. I watch children milking cows and tending to vegetable gardens. I watch a hostler shoveling manure out of a stable. I would rather be asleep in my hotel room.

I spot my friend the wizard coming out of the Institute. I hesitate for a moment, smile, give a tiny bow. "Hello."

He looks at me without recognition.

"Do I know ye?" His diction is a lot crisper when he's sober, although he is little red-eyed and looks hung-over. The wizard has changed his tunic for one that is stained but vomit-free.

"We met in the pub last night."

The wizard's cheeks redden. "I am sorry, sir," he says. "I have no recollection of the evening. I apologize for anything untoward I may have done." It sounds like an apology that he has issued many times.

"Please do not worry. You did nothing to embarrass yourself."

The wizard nods in gratitude and hurries along. I wonder again if my dream was anything more than a message from my own subconscious. Probably not.

Back in the town square, a falconer gives a demonstration for a small crowd of tourists. None of them seem much more interested than I am.

I make the hike out to the smithy, which is located in a shallow cave out in the hills, about thirty minutes' walk from the town centre. By the time I get there the smith is already done for the day. Everything he's made today, barring a pile of horseshoes, will be for sale in the village gift shop tomorrow.

I spot Emmet down in the common, taking a tip from a tourist couple in period costume. They struggle into a horse-drawn carriage and clatter off towards the hotel district.

The sun has just about set and it's Emmet's time to knock off as well. "Fancy a drink?" he says.

"At the wizard pub?"

"A real pub. By which I mean one that serves Guinness."

"They serve Guinness in Sugdike?"

"No," he says. "Come on, I'll take you where the park employees go."

Emmet secures a golf cart and drives us through the hotel district and out the back to the residential zone where park employees live. Gregory Vondruska's house is not far from here. Emmet parks out front of a strip mall and leads the way into a sports bar.

In the pub the TV is on, tuned to a Karachidaean news channel with English subtitles. It's not crowded. A few tables, a bar counter, laminated plastic menus with photos of the food on offer. Buffalo wings and hamburgers. We order a couple of pints of Guinness and find a booth in the corner.

Something is troubling Emmet, but I don't ask. I am a murderer, not a therapist. We just sit there and drink quietly and listen to the neighbouring conversations. A pair of young men compare the assets of various Sugdike characters who are in fact actors in the employ of the park: the milkmaid, the bar wench, the hostler's daughter. A woman complains that it's been her lifelong dream to work in a medieval theme park but, now that she's here, the tourists are ruining it for her. A couple wearing matching designer spectacles lament awful décor in the lobby of their building.

After a few drinks, Emmet looks me in the eye and says, "You know I'm more than just a theme park guide, right?"

"No?"

"I'm not just a guide, I'm a Guide." I think I can hear the capital letter, but it might just be drunken slurring.

"I'm sorry?"

"I'm a *Guide*." Emmet moves his head sideways every time he says the word. "A Guide who can show you the places that aren't in the tourist brochures."

"I see." After four pints of Guinness, I'm not thinking very fast, either.

"I'm a Guide..." he hesitates. "I'm a Guide who can take you off the *map*."

Drunk or not, after the dream and the book and my own jetlagged musings this alarms me, and I try to deflect it. "Are you talking about drugs?"

"No, I am not."

"Eh, *wakarimasen*." I pretend that my grasp of the English language is weakening. "*Off the map* is a...how can I say in English...a euphemism?"

Emmet opens his mouth, closes it, looks me up and down...makes a decision. "Ah, don't worry about it," he says. "Forget I said anything."

"Are you talking about a bordello?" I say the last word slowly.

"Ah," he lies. "Ah, yes. I am."

"I have a girlfriend."

"Understood," says Emmet. He seems relieved.

I start talking about Michiko. How I miss her, and how wonderful she is. I make up a fake name and occupation for her, of course. I drone on until Emmet gets bored, which thankfully doesn't take very long. He declares that it's late, so we settle up the tab. Emmet directs me back towards the Hyatt and I stagger off alone.

Emmet clearly has knowledge. He's a Guide. He knows about Doors and Ways. He knows about Travelling. He suspects something is unusual about me, but I can't ask him the questions I need answered. I am here to kill someone—I need to be an ordinary tourist whom nobody will remember.

I will have to find my own answers.

Back in my hotel room, I break open *Doors and Ways* and read a little more of Marghison's chapter.

There are many attributes by which Doors can be classified: free-standing, inset, or hidden; transparent, opaque, luminous, obscure; permanent or ephemeral; limited-in-volume or unlimited. Some Doors are concealed in reflective surfaces, like mirrors or still water; others in shadows or flames or puddles of blood. Some look like actual doors.

Maybe I'll die in my sleep, and then I won't need to read any more. If I see that wizard again, maybe I will ask him to read to me.

I need to meet with Vondruska tomorrow, if I am going to take the midweek barge back to Mesra City. I don't think my sanity will survive another three days here.

I'm back in Sugdike by 0930 and have to wait half an hour until the gift shop opens.

When the proprietor finally unlocks the door, I rush through. I make a small bow to the sales assistant and slip past before she can offer to assist me. I have no idea what it is that I am looking for with such unseemly eagerness.

At the back, there is a room full of ironwork. As promised, some of it is the work of the blacksmith, but there are cheaper items for sale, too. These are assembled in a workshop in the business district from kits manufactured in China.

I pick a Roman gladius: it's heavier than expected. The metal is soft; it won't hold an edge for long. I look at some other swords: a falchion, a two-handed sword, a scimitar, a cutlass, a rapier. Emmet's line about anachronism comes back to me and I shake my head. But I'm not looking for a weapon. I was never one for fighting, even in my gangster years.

I chest up to a suit of plate armour, but I'm afraid to touch it. It looks heavy and complicated, and I don't know how securely it's attached to the stand. There are individual pieces laid out on a small trestle table nearby for fat-fingered tourists like me to handle: greaves and breastplates and helmets and gauntlets.

I put on a helmet gingerly. It smells like blood. Even before I snap the visor down, my field of vision is uncomfortably restricted, and I'm sure it's not improving my hairstyle. I take it off and pick up a gauntlet.

The gauntlet is a nice piece of work; scalloped steel carefully articulated over a soft leather glove. I put it on and fasten the straps. It's heavy, but it feels good. I spread my fingers, turn my hand over, make a fist. It's one of the Chinese pieces but I'm so pleased with it that I don't actually care how authentic it is.

I have just enough currency on me to pay for it in cash. The clerk puts the gauntlet in a wooden, velvet-lined box and I leave the store with a much lighter wallet. This gauntlet...this is what I need.

I'm even proud of the box.

The Bright Glade is empty, and once again I find myself lingering there. Telling myself that I'm crazy, I walk a curving path around the perimeter of the clearing, looking for the soft place. Ah. There it is.

I waggle my fingers through the air as if playing the harp, and feel the membrane parting and closing around my digits. I need more friction.

I open the new box and spend a moment just looking at the gauntlet, lying there on the velvet lining like a dead crustacean on a bed of red ice. I put it on, and wave my hand around. It does not inhibit my ability to feel the crease in reality.

I make a sweeping gesture with the gauntlet and this time I feel the membrane part between my fingers. The rent immediately begins to close, but I clear it with a backhand stroke and draw it wider.

I have opened a Door.

On the other side of the Door is a forest, but it's a different forest to the one outside Sugdike. The light is different, the trees are different. The ground is sloped, and I am facing downhill. It's a different forest, and there is something wrong with it.

I can hear snatches of strangely orchestrated birdsong. The green of the flora seems unnatural, as though the colouring has nothing to do with photosynthesis. There are no odours: I don't smell forest; I don't smell clean air; I don't smell grass or soil. I don't smell anything at all.

I can't see a horizon for the density of the trees, but something strange about the perspective makes me feel like I am not standing on a planetary surface; I'm standing on a world that is flat, like a game-board. Or a page in a book.

I head downhill, moving carefully because I don't know where I am, and also because I am feeling a bit light-headed. At the tree-line I finally get a view down to the valley below.

A river runs through the lowest part of it, winding its way down out of the hills. There's a strange citadel standing upon a crest on the far side of the valley. It wavers and shifts before my eyes, as though some of its towers are photographic ghosts left by a double-exposure. I turn my head and observe similar citadels atop three nearby hills. When I turn my head back, I'm certain that the original citadel has relocated to a different hilltop.

A horn sounds in the distance and a procession of riders on horseback winds down from one of the citadels. Colourful banners stream from the riders' lances. The plumes on their helmets and the manes of their horses are equally colourful. I unlimber my camera, but it won't switch on. Disappointed, I watch the procession ford the river and continue on downstream with my naked eyes. The birds are now tweeting their symphony in march time.

I tell myself that I am hallucinating as I make my way back up the hill to the Door, but I know I am not. I have blundered into some kind of fairyland.

Heading to the hotel, I cross paths with Emmet, heading towards his pickup spot in the Bright Glade. He gives me an odd look, but he doesn't take off the headphones or speak as I pass him. I nod back. It's not until I get back to the hotel that I realize I am still wearing the gauntlet.

I put it back in its box. Then I take a shower and change into a clean shirt: purple, with red and white carnations on the hem. It's time go and ruin Gregory Vondruska's evening.

Vondruska's modest little car is parked in the driveway, but the Jeep Fury is gone. Perhaps the kids are at soccer practice. Perfect.

I let myself in the front gate. There are lace curtains on the windows, so I can't see inside the house. I cross the garden and push through the inside gate to the back yard. I was wrong about there being a swimming pool: instead, there is a swing set and a jungle gym and a sandpit full of spades and toy construction vehicles.

I contemplate the house for a moment. The second-floor windows are nice and high up. As I pull on a pair of cotton gloves, I find my thoughts wandering from defenestration to sightseeing. I really don't feel like tramping around this suburban hell when Fairyland is so close at hand.

I exhale a long, slow breath to purge the distraction. Focus. This is serious business.

The back door doesn't keep me out for very long: the deadbolt is off and the door handle lock yields to a loyalty card for a Tokyo department store that I never bothered to register.

It's completely silent in the house. Did Vondruska go to soccer practice along with his wife and kids? Is he out for a walk? I poke around in the kitchen and the living room, the dining room, the study, the bathroom, but I know he's not there. I look up the stairs, shake my head. The house is empty; I have a sense for these things. I sigh through a moment of frustration. I really do not want to come back here again. Focus. Be thorough.

I return to the kitchen and open the door to the laundry, which is the only room I haven't yet checked. There's another door past the dryer unit, which leads to the garage. As I approach the door, I can faintly hear an engine revving.

I open the door into the garage carefully. Halogen floodlights in the ceiling make the room startlingly bright. Sound-proofed walls. Benches covered with tools and engine parts, belts and filters and cans of car fluids and oils. Now I understand why the cars are always parked in the driveway: Vondruska uses the garage as a motor workshop.

And there he is, dressed in stained jeans and an old t-shirt, peering into the open bonnet of a silver 1968 Corvette Stingray. I'm not a car nerd; the only reason I can identify the vehicle so precisely is that there are posters of it all over the walls. The car howls like a gelded lion while Vondruska tinkers with the engine. Clouds of exhaust blue the air.

I walk up behind him quietly, although there's really no need for stealth—there are no shadows under the bright lights and there's no way he can hear me over the engine.

When Vondruska does notice me in his peripheral vision it's too late. I slap away the rod that's holding up the bonnet and slam the hood down on his head. Back in the 1960s they made car chassis out of steel.

Cautiously, I raise the bonnet again. I've caved-in Vondruska's skull.

The heat of the engine block beneath his face is slowly starting to cook his flesh. I don't bother to check for a pulse: even if he's still alive, he won't be for much longer.

I give Vondruska a small bow from the doorway and make my exit. Fairyland awaits.

By night, the woods outside the fairy citadel are moonlit and full of shadows, although I can't discern an actual moon overhead. The unflickering stars are bright enough to serve in its place.

The symphonic birdsong is gone, replaced by furtive noises and animal cries—some of which sound alarmingly like speech—as the nocturnal critters go about their business. There's enough creaking and rustling overhead that I wonder if the trees are also holding a conversation.

From the edge of the forest, the citadel seems closer than before. There's only one of citadel, now, lit in coruscating purples and blues. Perhaps it's a St Elmo's fire. I am literally looking at fairy lights.

There is some sort of a festival underway in middle of the valley. I leave the dubious safety of the trees and approach the cluster of stalls and tents. A band is playing stringed instruments on a stage across from an open marquee.

The folk taking their merriment here are a diverse lot. Some look almost human, but with pointed ears or compound eyes or spindly, many-joined limbs. Others have animal attributes, or appear to be composed of plant matter or more exotic materials. I see a man with a hand made of glass and a woman whose face appears to have been thrown on a potter's wheel.

The one thing common to all of these folk is that they are rapt in the throes of merriment; drinking and dancing and capering about; beating drums or eating or fornicating. None of them evince even the tiniest amount of self-consciousness or restraint. It feels a bit like an open-air music festival, but there's nobody selling band merchandise.

I do not try to speak to any of the revellers, and I know better than to partake of any food or drink. I just walk around, taking in the sights and sounds.

I am surprised by how good it feels to just witness everything without having to fuss over a camera.

In the morning I pack the gauntlet in with my checked baggage. I'd love to hang about and explore the fairyland some more, but it's going to get hot around here once the police begin to investigate Gregory Vondruska's death. Will I ever come back here? To this theme park I was so keen to escape just 24 hours ago? I shake my head and tug out the handle on my carry-on.

I ride a golf cart to the quay and board the vessel back to Mesra City. This time, when the barge makes its transition back to Mesra city it's obvious to me, although this Door has a different feel to the one in the Bright Glade. This portal feels somehow elasticated; the one I made felt more like a tear. Here, the membrane between worlds here is more rubbery than viscous.

In Mesra City, a bus takes me from the port back to the airport, and soon I'm on my way back to the real world, where the shortest distance between any two points is a straight line, and the quickest way to travel is the itinerary that does not stop in Heathrow.

Once the plane reaches cruising altitude, I reach into the seat pocket for my book—and then realize that my copy of Doors and Ways is in in my carry-on in the overhead locker. The pocket yields the translated Elmore Leonard novel that I lost on the way here. It even has my bookmark in it.

I pull out my boarding pass from my last flight to Mesra City and compare it to tab for this current flight. I am sitting in the same seat.

After the things I have just experienced, this coincidence hardly seems remarkable. I arrange an airline pillow behind my back and settle in with the novel. It's still going to be many, many hours until I get home.

#4: The Aerostatic Archipelago

My fourth trip to Mesra City is just as uncomfortable as the prior trips, but this time I welcome the misery of long-haul travel. Anything to distract me from my troubles at home is a blessing.

This trip is an escape, but I know that, if I survive, when I get back I'm going to have to deal with the awful truth.

She left me.

Once I have passed through Mesra City customs I collect my baggage and take the subway to the Epsidor hotel. This is routine now. I can get around Mesra City without actually having to speak to anyone. Without thinking about where I am going or what I am doing.

Perhaps it is my mood, but I am coming to dislike this place. The Karachidaean people are not particularly welcoming hosts. I would prefer some brash American behaviour right now to the local traits of being secretive and sly. This place is also efficient and well-organized in much the same way that my own country is. I feel oddly threatened here.

I really need some rest.

Thanks to the Doors and Ways manual, I now understand that the gazebo where I meet with my employers lies on the other side of a Way in place far from Mesra City's botanical gardens. I do not know whether or not they know that I have the ability to locate and to open Doors. Did they select me for this work because they knew of my potential talents? If so, surely they would have tried to help me develop them. Or perhaps they wanted to see if I developed them on my own. My employers have not exactly been forthcoming about anything, other than who they want me to kill.

Just as likely, they are completely ignorant of my abilities. I can think of no advantage to my telling them, so I resolve not to say anything unless they ask me directly.

Jonathon and Vashya greet me coolly as I approach. Their body-guards do not even acknowledge my presence. "Sit down, Mr Zai," says the Englishman.

I do as he asks.

Vashya hands me a thin folder full of photographs and addresses. "This your contact is," she says. "Razjhel Nabora."

The file contains photographs of a young lady with pale blue skin and red hair and an ambitious gleam in her eye.

"She wants to sell science to you people, does she," says Vashya. "United States of America to, Britain of the Great, Australia Land Down Under, China Republic of Peoples."

"Clean-burning engines and renewable fuels," says Jonathon. "Nabora intends to save the environment and the world economy, and of course she is interested in making rather a lot of money for herself, in so doing. As you can imagine, there are quite a number of people who want to stop her."

By the time he's finished speaking, I have memorized all the relevant details in Nabora's file. "I understand."

"Very good, then," says the Jonathan.

"Zai, you are going to Menlat Nir, Zai," says Vashya.

"It can be a bit of a difficult place to navigate," says Jonathon. "Our associate will meet you there and give you an orientation."

"Rambo-san?" I hope that I have managed to keep the annoyance out of my voice.

"Ram-bosan?" says Vashya, confused.

"That's the name he gave you, is it?" says Jonathon. "Rambo?"

I nod.

"Cultural appropriation, that is." Jonathon snorts and then grins. "I'd be offended, if I was an American."

In the morning, I return to Mesra City International Airport, where I board a transfer bus to a building that looks more like a sports arena than a flight terminal. The roof of the stadium is open, and I can see something bubbling just below its lip, like a soufflé rising from inside a baking dish.

Inside the stadium, the guards are members of the blue-skinned Menlat

Niri people. I have seen a few of these people in and around Mersa City, but Conventional Earth foreigners like me are more common.

I line up with the others to show my passport and my ticket for the sky city of Menlat Nir. I've been anxious to visit this place since I first heard about it, but today I am having a hard time mustering my usual enthusiasm as I trudge through the hallways of yet another airport.

After the security screening, the guards usher me through into a basket-shaped gate lounge. I flop into an empty seat and vegetate for forty-five minutes before a stewardess comes by with a clipboard, checking to see where everybody is sitting. She frowns and addresses me in a halting Karachidaean. "Sir, you must sit in your own seat, sir," she says. I think. My Karachidaean is even worse than hers. I stare at her, puzzled and annoyed.

I suppress a sigh and bow and say "I'm sorry," in Japanese, English, and then Karachidaean, my sincerity draining noticeably with each successive language. There are plenty of free seats all around, and I can't bring myself to believe that the gate lounge has allocated seating.

She says something about load balancing as she leads me to a different seat. She pats me on the shoulder and smiles as I settle in.

There's an announcement in Karachidaean and another language I don't recognize. I can't understand it, but it does draw me out of my reverie for long enough to notice that the room is in motion; rising with a gentle wobble. It's not the gate lounge; it's the cabin of our aircraft. An airship. The soufflé I saw earlier was the half-inflated balloon.

There's another announcement, after which some passengers start to move around the cabin. I go to the window and look out. We're over sea now. The shadow below us is massive and oval. I've been up in a hot air balloon, but I've never flown in a zeppelin before. This is much more comfortable.

I curse under my breath, grit my teeth, and try to turn off my brain again. I am able to stem the tide of memories from that balloon ride with Michiko, but the wedge in my gullet remains. Michiko.

The airship reaches cruising height at about one kilometre in altitude. I hear some new motors kick on and with a small lurch the dirigible starts to turn, and then to accelerate.

I drowse my way through another six hours. Eventually there's another announcement and people start to drift back to their seats.

Menlat Nir comes into view through the starboard window: an archipelago of bulbous shapes blown out of some lustrous material. The balloons at the lower strata are bigger and more distinctly ovoid than those in the higher ones. Most of the buildings hang below the envelopes like wasps' nests, but some of the smaller habitations grow up the sides of the inflatable surfaces, and others are strung between them. The whole city sways and bobs in the buffeting winds.

Most of the vehicle traffic consists of smaller airships, which swarm around the city like fat, slow-moving insects, but there's also a funicular system connecting the larger structures. I wonder if Menlat Nir has any kind of defence force. It would only take a single fighter jet to destroy the entire city.

The zeppelin bumps gently into a berth at the airport cluster and shivers through a mooring procedure. I follow the other passengers out through the airlock and down a swaying aerobridge. Although it's fully enclosed, the bridge is strung loosely, and the floor makes a steep curve down and then back up. Foreigners like me hold tightly onto the rail, but the Menlat Niri passengers and crew saunter up and down as if they were crossing level ground.

I tell the immigration guard that I am on holiday. She stamps my passport without even looking at it and waves me through.

I am just pulling my suitcase off the conveyor belt in the main terminal when I hear my name called.

"Zai! Mr Zai!"

"Hello, Rambo-san." I don't turn to look at him as I return his greeting.

"I'm so sorry I am late, Mr Zai! I had very much difficulty finding parking here and I did not see you get off from of the air-o-plane."

I incline my head and conceal my irritation.

"Come, Mr Zai," he says. "It is low oxygen out of here."

Rambo-san leads me to a small kiosk that sells batteries, chocolate bars, inflatable neck-pillows, and respirators. Rambo-san picks one out for me. It fits snugly over my nose and mouth without adjustment. After a few seconds, I'm barely aware that it's attached to my face. I can hear the carbon dioxide purged when I exhale, but it takes no additional effort to breathe through it.

Rambo-san finds a pair of matching goggles and pays for the whole kit with a Visa card. As we head for the doors, he puts on his own respirator and goggles. We have the same model, only mine is black and his is olive drab, matching the army fatigues he is wearing. He has put some effort into the costume, but I notice that he hasn't laced his boots correctly.

"Come on, Mr Zai," he says. "Let me show you my ride."

Rambo-san's ride is an Apache AH-64, stripped of its armaments. It's painted in the same olive drab as his pants. Some passers-by glare at it distastefully, but most pretend not to see it.

Embarrassed from my hair to my toes, I climb into the helicopter behind Rambo-san. He climbs into the pilot's chair and hands me a helmet with built in headphones and a mic. I am surprised an Unfolded Enterprises' gopher can pilot a helicopter, but I suppose they wouldn't have hired him without *some* useful skills.

Rambo-san pulls the control stick, and the chopper starts to ascend. I would like nothing more than to open a door and feed him up into the rotors.

Rambo-san explains the sights to me in his pidgin-American as the chopper passes them by. Menlat Nir is an archipelago of massive lighter-than-air ships. When it's travelling, the city-state extends into a convoy, but when it is stationary it reforms into a circular configuration with a massive turbine at its centre. Atmospheric tides drive the turbine to generate electricity for most of the city, along with solar panels on the dirigible surfaces.

When he's run out of things to show me, Rambo-san says, "I am feeling very thirsty, Mr Zai, and the beer in Menlat Nir is very good."

"I have heard that." The words have escaped before I can stop myself.

"Would you like to visit my most favourite bar, Mr Zai?"

"I am very tired, Rambo-san."

"It's right near here," he says. "And it's full of all the hot bitches."

"I have a girlfriend, Rambo-san." The lie hurts less than the prospect of going to the pub with him.

"Aw, you don't have to worry," he says. "What is happen in Menlat Nir is to staying in Menlat Nir."

"Thank you, but the only place I want to stay is my hotel."

I can't see much of Rambo-san's face behind his respirator, but his head wobbles slightly, and I believe that he's suddenly close to tears.

"Maybe tomorrow." I hate myself for saying it.

"I'll take you up to that," says Rambo-san. He tilts the stick and the chopper banks away from the city.

The Palisades Hotel is a tiered structure, widest through its middle floors, which hangs from three spherical balloons. Gas jets at its widest point are used to counteract the swing of the main gondola-building for the comfort of foreign guests. The hotel sign is printed in English beneath the open-faced Menlat Niri characters, and I wonder if 'Palisades' is a direct translation. I am not actually certain what a palisade is, beyond being a popular name for a hotel.

Rambo-san lands the chopper on a helipad that's uncomfortably close to the corrugated surface of the balloon. I climb down from the chopper and walk away with a little more haste than is strictly polite, holding my respirator tight against my face.

A porter takes my bags and I descend to the reception area, hugging myself to keep my clothes from flapping in the wind. An airlock door closes behind me and the wind ceases. I take off the mask.

There's a line to check in. Out of habit, I grab some tourist brochures while I wait, but the misery of my domestic situation comes upon me again and I can't even be bothered looking through them.

The clerk speaks good English, but I don't hear a thing he says to me. I just show my passport and sign the forms and take the key.

In my room, I drop my bags near the door, kick off my shoes, and climb straight into bed.

Oblivion comes like a mercy stroke.

I wake up at 9am local time, but spend all of the morning wallowing in bed, trying to figure out what I did wrong and whether or not I should attempt to win Michiko back. I could handle the situation if she had left me for somebody else, but she didn't. She left me because of my own shortcomings, and I do not know how to rectify them. I don't know if that would be enough to convince her come back to me.

In the early afternoon, I refuse to let the cleaners into the room. The stack of tourist brochures sits beside my bed, unread.

The phone rings at about five, but I don't answer it.

Two hours later there's a knock at my door. "Mr Zai, it is I, Rambo."

And so, it's an unwanted obligation that finally gets me out of bed. I told him I would go to the pub with him, and I have to follow through.

Rambo-san waits for me in the lobby while I shower and get dressed. I choose a silk shirt with flames and lotus petals on it, which I hope will embarrass Rambo-san into sparing me a long evening.

I suppose I should be grateful that he managed to get me out of bed.

onight, Rambo is wearing a sharp suit with his army boots, which are still incorrectly laced. He clearly has bigger ambitions for the evening than I do. We take the cable car to Zaspir Taul, the party district, because he doesn't want to drink and fly.

Rambo-san asks how my reconnaissance is going. I dissuade him with vague assurances and ask him about himself, which provokes him to ramble about guns and American military history until we reach our destination. He doesn't stop talking until it's time to put on the respirator.

We emerge from the funicular station into an open courtyard which is ringed with clubs and restaurants. Barrier walls keep the wind out, so it's relatively calm and quiet here. The gas envelopes above us are draped with lights, which strobe and spot the courtyard with multi-coloured bursts of illumination. At first, I think the floor is obsidian, but I soon realize that it's actually glass. The open ocean gleams black nearly four kilometres below.

Throngs of Menlat Niri citizens descend from tethered dirigible craft on rope ladders. Apparently, the cable car is only used by tourists and drunks.

Rambo-san forges a path through the milling crowds of laughing, chattering young people. It makes me angry to think they should be out here having a good time, in my presence.

Eventually, we arrive at a pub. I can't read the sign, but it has the feel of a local chain. "Food here is first," he says. "And also is beer."

I haven't eaten all day and suddenly I am ravenous. We find a couple of stools at the bar, and Rambo-san orders for both of us. I wonder if his Menlat Niri is as bad as his English?

The beers are too sweet for my taste, but very crisp and also strong. Dinner arrives promptly: a crusty pocket with a starchy, meaty filling. It's more like a crumble than a pie. The portions are large, but not very satisfying. When I'm done with it, I order some vodka. I feel like something heavy and punishing.

"It is time to find the hotness honeys," says Rambo-san, getting impatient.

"I am not on the market." I am pleased with my use of colloquial English.

Rambo-san shrugs. "You are then my wingman, buddy."

We split the tab and head for a nearby club called the Lord of Breath. A neon sign over the door shows a pink Death's Head. Neon blue mist curls from its hinged jaw. The music sounds like earth-side club tunes reinterpreted by Enya on a meth bender. Rambo-san winks at the bouncers, pays the cover, tips the girl at the register, and struts on through the doors. I follow with less enthusiasm.

The Lord of Breath is filled with artificial smoke, which billows in psychedelic, sculpted patterns under the strobing lights. I buy a round of vodkas at the bar. Rambo-san slams his gamely, but refuses a second. I order another one anyway and then follow him out into the club.

We patrol the perimeter of the main dance floor, but Rambo-san does not see any hotness honeys that he fancies. He points upwards, and directs me to climb to the second level using rungs set into support pillars. The Menlat Niri glide up and down without effort, but I see only one tourist try to ascend: a drunk, shirtless European. Halfway up the ladder he stops to wave his cap and falls off.

On the second level, there is a smoke-blowing competition in progress. Menlat Niri participants inhale from cigarettes, cigars, pipes, hookahs, bongs or spliffs. They exhale spirals, helixes, stick figures, smiley faces, yin-yangs. The winning entry is a long-necked shape that's either a giraffe or a cock-and-balls.

I lean over the railing and look down at the dance-floor. The clubbers are waving and gyrating, as they do in clubs everywhere, but there is a lot more leaping than usual — the Menlat Niri. There are enough tourists boogying away with a complete lack of coordination and rhythm that I am embarrassed to be one of them. Not that you would ever catch me on the dance floor. If I'm too old to be a punk, I'm too old to be a clubber.

"This place sucks," said Rambo-san.

I nod once. "I'm ready to go."

"Let's try the Drums of Heaven. The bitches are there more honey." I nod again, although I intend to beg off as soon as we get outside and go back to the hotel.

As we start to climb back down to the dance floor, I notice a Menlat Niri woman of about my age watching us. She's wearing black cargo pants, a black tank top, and a black, flat-topped cap. She smiles when I meet her gaze. I nod to her and turn to follow Rambo-san down the ladder.

I look up again when I step down off the last rung. The girl in black smiles down at me from the balcony and then vaults over the railing. It's a five-meter drop but she lands gracefully. I stand there, stunned, while she pads over to me.

"Do you speak English?" Her accent is peculiar; sibilant with hard vowels.

"English, yes."

Rambo-san is halfway to the exit when he notices I'm not following. Suddenly, I have an escape route. Rambo-san frowns, shakes off his disappointment, and gives me a leering double thumbs up. I wave to him with my left hand, since the girl in black is now holding my right.

She looks at me frankly and says, "My name is Zia."

"I am called Zai."

Zia laughs. I can't help but smile. "Shall we go for a walk?"

I give a short bow and say "Hai."

Zia and I wander, arm in arm, amidst the hedgerows and benches, fountains and sculptures. There are no birds or insects. The creaking of tether ropes and the murmur of low conversation swells around us. The glass floor is black as oblivion.

"Where are you from?" says Zia.

"Japan. You are a local?"

"Yes," she says. Obviously. "It is getting cold. Would you like to go for a drink?"

"I'm hungry."

"Even better," she says. "I know a Japanezi restaurant that is open late. It is nearby."

The 'Japanezi' place is a little sushi bar in an alleyway behind a complex of smokehouses. The chef is a Menlat Niri who is as skilled as any I've seen. It's a shame he doesn't have better ingredients to work with, but given the geography of Menlat Nir, I'm surprised there is any sushi grade fish at all. The sake is an excellent modern vintage, served chilled. It has never been a favourite drink of mine, but tonight I consume more of it than I should.

When I've paid for the meal, Zia says: "Take me to your hotel."

When I awaken the next morning, I am surprised to find Zia still asleep beside me. I sit up on the edge of the bed and rub my eyes. Hangover. I wonder what's in the minibar.

Behind me, Zia stirs and sits up. "Hello," she says.

"Hello." I can't look at her.

She moves closer, comes to sit behind me. I don't say anything.

"Are you cheating on someone, Zai?"

"Not really." Zia sits quietly until I turn around. "It's complicated. It *was* complicated."

"Why did she leave you?"

"I don't know."

"What happened?"

"I bought her a car."

"She didn't like it?"

"No."

"And then she left?"

"Yes."

"Did she say why?"

"She wants a man with a real job, not some fool who spends more time on the road than at home."

"You travel lot."

"It's my work. It was never a problem before."

"Before what?"

I turn away again. "I don't know. Before I had this success. Before I bought that car."

She leans her shoulder and head against my back. "I'm sorry. It isn't my business."

"Zia, at the nightclub…" I'm not sure how to finish my question, but she knows what I'm asking.

"Why did I choose you?"

"Yes."

"Because you look like such a nerd, in your tourist shirt," she says. "But there's something bad about you, also."

"How do you mean, bad?" I do not manage to conceal the wariness in my voice.

"I do not mean that you a criminal, or anything." She bites her lip. "I mean…dangerous. Wild. Like we could run off together and have adventures, and nobody would ever find us."

I can feel my cheeks redden. "I'm just a salesman."

"I'm just a chemical engineer with too many strange fantasies," she replies. "How long are you staying in Menlat Nir?"

"A few more days."

"And then you're going home to your girlfriend."

"Ex-girlfriend."

"She doesn't want a car," she says. "She wants more from you."

"She should just tell me what she wants."

"Yes, she should." Zia pulls me down onto the bed and says "Come here. You already know what *I* want."

After breakfast, Zia shakes my hand, kisses me goodbye, and tells me to look her up next time I'm in town—but she doesn't leave me a phone number. That's okay. She's made me feel a bit better about my situation. I haven't worked it out yet, but I now feel like I can find a way through to solve my problems—or to put them behind me.

Now I'm ready to go to work.

I take a taxi to the business district and get off at a docking node near the offices of Kejlat Nurn Industries, where my contact Razjhel Nabora is employed.

The network of suspension tubes that connects the buildings in this cluster sways and shivers as I explore it. I hang on to the guard rails while Menlat Niri workers float blithely past me in both directions.

The signposts at each intersection are all in Menlat Niri script, but big corporations have English on their logos. I find my way to the KNI office complex by following their advertising.

The KNI office complex grows over a series of conjoined balloons like a rough metallic fungus. I stand there looking at it for a good few minutes, because I don't have any ideas about how I am going to execute this job. It's very difficult to get around in this city. It's going to be hard to follow somebody unobserved and it's harder still to surveil a place without attracting notice. Getting away is going to be equally difficult.

I could just walk right into the office complex, find Nabora, and kill her. I could use my bare hands. I'm not much of a fighter, but she's a civilian, and most females are probably smaller than me. Anyway, who cares about escape? This mission is the only purpose I have remaining to me. I wonder if they have the death penalty here.

Or I could go for something spectacular. Like the Hindenburg, only bigger. I could climb one of the balloons. Find some way to set a fire. Try to take out the entire office complex. Although I know that, these days, dirigibles are filled with Helium or some other inert gas, so that probably won't work at all.

A recollection of Zia interrupts my death-and-glory fantasies. I find it heartening that this stranger believes I can repair things with Michiko. Perhaps she's right. Zia seems wiser in these matters than I am. Or perhaps she was just looking for a nice way to say goodbye.

I could really use a coffee.

I spend the rest of the morning in a Starbucks that's walking distance from the Kejlat Nurn Industries dirigible cluster. I have consumed an Americano, a Frappuccino and three different cakes from the display cabinet and still have no idea how to make this happen. Perhaps I need Rambo-san's assistance. The thought makes me want to climb out the window and try skydiving without a parachute. I hope he doesn't come back to the hotel again.

On the way out of Starbucks, I stop to tip my tray into the rubbish box. I feel greasy and a little bloated, but I am feeling a little better now. Are these mood swings permanent? Or was I just craving caffeine?

As I turn towards the door, a woman shoulders past me on her way in. At six foot she is nearly three inches taller than I am, but that's not the thing that surprises me. I am surprised because I recognize this woman. From a photograph.

Razjhel Nabora.

consider about shadowing Nabora back to the office, but the walkways are too exposed and even my usual tourist persona will be obvious, floundering around clumsily in a business district. Even if I get her somewhere private, I know I can't sneak up on her out here and I don't fancy trying to wrestle a bigger, more agile opponent over the rails. There's no way I can credibly accomplish this mission out there in the open.

But that's okay. I know where she lives.

retrieve my big camera from my suitcase at the Palisades and ask the concierge to order me a taxi dirigible to the nearest camera store, which, to my delight, turns out to be a Bic Camera.

Inside the store, all the signage is in Menlat Niri. The packages have translations in the local language stickered on them, but there's still plenty of Japanese if you look for it. Is this how Americans feel when they find a McDonalds in my country?

There's a murmur among the shop staff. I pretend not to notice as I browse an aisle full of macro lenses. Eventually, the murmurs subside and skinny clerk with his shirt tucked in too hard approaches me.

"*Nihonjin desu-ka?*" He speaks Japanese with the strangest inflection I have ever heard.

This guy is so crazy about photography that he has learned to speak Japanese in order to converse directly with the camera company sales reps. I am pleased to be able to hold a fluent conversation in my own language and I'm always ready to discuss the topic of photography. I have never allowed my enthusiasm for the medium to be diminished by my lack of talent.

I take out my camera and show it to the attendant: an old-fashioned pre-digital SLR. He is impressed when I explain that I develop all the negatives myself.

In the end, I spend one hour and nearly five thousand American dollars on some new optics. The attendant throws in some other supplies for me: film, a bag, some processing chemicals, and a fat little digital camera that he thinks would make a nice gift for a child. On the way to the register, I pick up a five-dollar digital alarm clock. The attendant doesn't even bother to scan it.

The bottom floor of Bic Camera hosts a drugstore, where I purchase a potassium chloride salt substitute, an instant cold pack, a bag of cotton wool balls, and a small flask of vodka. I pay in cash.

stay up half the night in my room making preparations. I have done this before, but my skill with explosives is more 'teen vandal' than 'demolitions expert'.

I use the cold pack, the salt substitute, and sugar from the hotel room's tea set to make potassium nitrate. While I wait for the saltpetre to form, I pull apart the alarm clock and remove the mains transformer. I attach the battery from the digital camera to make a crude spark generator.

I add the saltpetre crystals to a measure of sulphuric acid from the photo developing kit, to make nitric acid. I add more sulphuric acid and then soak it up with the cotton wool. Finally, I wash the cotton with fresh water and set it out to dry.

When I am done, my fingertips are a little scorched and my nasal membranes are stinging. I go to bed feeling pleased with myself for not to have blown up the room or set off any smoke alarms.

In the morning, I carefully pack the dried guncotton into the vodka flask before I head downstairs for a greasy buffet breakfast. It's going to be a busy day.

ask the taxi pilot to drop me at the shopping area in the district where Nabora lives. I'm expecting a strip mall or a department store, but what I find is a lattice of small, high-end boutiques suspended between a cluster of balloons. It looks like a model of some complex molecule.

The shops are connected with a loosely strung rope ladders and precarious suspension bridges. The locals swing and spin over the structure with arachnid grace despite the encumbrance of all their shopping. It's clearly not a place that's been built with tourists in mind.

On the taxi platform, I tighten my respiration mask and strap myself onto the network with a safety harness, a tether cable, and about sixteen karabiner clips. Then I try to figure out the best way to climb down from here into the residential district.

There aren't many people in the swaying pedestrian tubes. At least they are covered and I'm out of the wind. Here the street signs are written in English, which I take to be a mark of class here in Menlat Nir, as it was in Japan. Before long I emerge in an expensive neighbourhood where the homes look as if they have been blown out of glass. Nabora's house has four levels, each of which is composed of a number of conjoined globes: four on the top level, three on the second, then two, then one. Top-heaviness is a desirable architectural feature for a dwelling that hangs in the air.

The walkway leads to a door set into double globe, second from the bottom of the stack. The front door won't open, and I can't find the lock in its curving surface. The seals are airtight. I need to find another way inside.

There is a set of rungs, practically invisible on the mirrored surface, winding up the side of the entrance globe. I can see no other option, so I pull on a pair of leather gloves and adjust my respirator and goggles. Then I wind the nylon strap from my camera case around my right wrist.

The first part of the ascent, climbing the underside of the curving surface, is the most difficult. I secure my right wrist to each new rung by looping the camera strap through it. I do not know how long it will hold my weight if I slip, but hopefully it will buy me enough time to find another handhold.

The wind gusts around me as I pull myself up, hand over hand. My scalp is freezing under my tousled hair. One of my feet slips off a rung and for a moment I'm hanging, the wind swinging my legs away from the globe. I issue a grunt that sounds a little bit like a scream and try to draw my knees up, turning my hips in an effort to get my feet headed back towards the ladder. They skid off twice before I manage to hook one foot back onto the ladder.

I stay in that position for a while, breathing hard. My shoulders ache. My forearms burn. I can't feel my fingers.

Once I'm on the upper surface of the sphere, with gravity holding me in place, rather than my fraying muscles, I stop for a rest. The globe vibrates a little beneath me and I can feel the whole structure swaying. Hot sweat dries cold on my skin.

I don't rest for long. When the adrenaline wears off, I will be shaky and weak, and I'm still in a precarious position.

There's an access hatch on top of the globe. I use the tip of my Spyderco knife to dig out the seals around the bolts until I hear gas discharge. After that it's quite easy to pry it open. Through the aperture I can see layers of insulation, plumbing and electrical cabling. I drop into the crawlspace and pull the hatch closed behind me.

I find the trapdoor by touch and lower myself into the apartment.

I am in the sitting room. There are curving couches arranged around the perimeter and a circular coffee table at its centre. A bare coat rack next to the door. I am startled to discover that the exterior walls are one-way glass. Anybody inside the house would have had a clear view of me climbing the walls.

I ascend the spiral staircase to the floor above, which is made up of three conjoined globes: the kitchen, dining room and laundry. Another staircase leads to the top level, which is composed of a bathroom and three-bedroom spheres. The master bedroom is the only one that looks as though it has recently been used.

I return to the sitting room and then descend into the basement. As expected, it contains the utilities: hot water system, fuse box, heating unit. Excellent.

I set up the spark generator so that it will ignite the guncotton when the front door opens off. There's not enough of it to cause a huge explosion, but I don't need one. I just need enough spark to set off the propellant.

I return to the basement and open the taps for the gas fixtures. Then, using a hacksaw from inside the utility closet, I cut through the pipes connecting them to the hot water system, the heating, and the stove. By the time Nabora gets home the lower levels of the house should be full of flammable gases.

My pride in my own ingenuity doesn't last long. Now that I have set my trap, I cannot exit through the front door. I'm going to have to climb out the way I came in.

I spent the rest of the day watching the news on the TV in my hotel room. There is a cable channel which broadcasts with English subtitles but even so, almost none of the stories make any sense to me.

Finally, a report with a slightly hysterical pitch catches my attention. I hear the English word 'terrorist' several times. Footage that looks like it was taken by drone cameras shows the outside Nabora's home. The structure looks mostly intact, but the glass is blackened and cracked. The drones show a bodybag being loaded into an ambulance chopper, so I figure that this mission has been a success.

I need a drink.

I'm still eating breakfast when Rambo-san comes to collect me the following morning. I have to shush him repeatedly—I don't want to discuss business in the dining room. He sits fidgeting while I work through my meal.

The eggs are cold, but the toast is nice and grainy and dripping with butter. I resolve to start eating a proper breakfast every day when I get home, as part of my campaign to be a better man.

In the chopper, Rambo-san tells me that Nabora was halfway inside the apartment when the explosion blew the door closed. She died from a head injury incurred from the impact with the door.

I don't tell him that this was my error. If I had realized that the door opened inward (all doors do, in this dirigible city) I would have set the device in the kitchen.

Back in Mesra City, it's a beautiful day, and there are thousands of Karachidaeans outdoors enjoying the sun. I am not leaving until tomorrow morning, and I have the rest of the time to my leisure, so I decide to go to the beach.

White quartz sand squeaks beneath my every footstep. I take off my shoes and socks and walk the length of the foreshore with my feet in the surf. I didn't bring a bathing suit, but that's okay. I'm not much of a one for swimming.

There is an open-air market on the esplanade, where the salt breeze takes on the added aromas of cut grass and spun sugar. I buy some t-shirts with Karachidaean slogans printed on them. For lunch I buy a mustardy hotdog and a glazed doughnut from a stand blazoned with the American flag.

When the sun goes down and the vendors pack up their stalls, I walk back towards the station, carrying my souvenirs and my shoes, but I find my way blocked by some kind of parade. Drums boom and rattle in march-time. Ragged voices sing something sweet and sad. Dancers in loincloths caper through the crowds, on fire. I sniff the air expecting the odours of smoke, of gasoline and grilling meat, but there's no odour. Whatever is burning on them gives off only blue light without any heat.

A stranger gives me a pouch of pink baubles. They look like sweets, so I put one in my mouth. I test with my teeth, and it cracks open; crumbling into a waxy substance. Somebody nearby laughs at me—this isn't food. I hope it's not poisonous.

Embarrassed, I spit out the crumbs, and in so doing am further surprised to discover that my breath is blue and luminous. The crowd cheers, a circle forms around me. I smile, exhale some more blue fire. I take a bow. The applause rises and so does my embarrassment. I rush away as fast as my bruised dignity will permit.

The blue fire stays with me on the train. I try to breathe through my nose all the way back to the Epsidor, but even so, I can see tiny flames every time I exhale.

In my room I clean my teeth and rinse my mouth a dozen times, but I can't get the powdery taste out of my mouth. My sinuses and nasal passages feel strange, but it's not uncomfortable. I don't think I have poisoned myself.

I turn off the lights and climb into bed. Lying on my back, I watch the tendrils of blue fire uncurl in time with my respiration.

The universe has opened to me—and the universes beyond. It is now my purpose—my *duty*—to venture where others cannot or may not; to see the things others do not or will not believe. There are worse ways to earn a living.

And now I know exactly what to do when I get back to Tokyo.

Soon as I get off the plane, I'm going to call up Michiko and take her shopping for a ring.

#5: The Empire of Shaedows

The flight to Mesra City is as debilitating as usual. This is my fifth time making the trip and under normal circumstances I'd be irritable, right now it's going to take a lot more than mere travel fatigue to diminish my good cheer.

She said "Yes!"

In the morning, I take the train to the park for my usual briefing. I'm wearing hiking boots, polarised sunglasses, cargo pants and a greyish aloha shirt with purple flowers. The weather is cool today, so I am wearing a light canvas jacket over it.

I play it cool all the way to the boundaries of the park, but once I am off the street, I find that I am unable to restrain myself from executing a Snoopy dance on the grass. She said yes!

I take a deep breath and calm myself, exhale the foolishness. Then, I march directly to the grove where my handlers for Unfolded Enterprises hide their privacy pocket. Even so, I cannot help but noticing how bracing the air is; how floral and delicate and sweet.

Jonathon and Vashya are waiting, flanked by the pair of expressionless bodyguards that I recognize from prior briefings. They might as well be furniture, now.

"Zai-san!" the Englishman calls out to me, rising from his chair, a huge, fake grin on his face. Vashya stays in her seat. She does not feign any kind of emotion.

I bow as I approach. "*Ohayou gozaimasu.*" I feel like a character actor making a guest appearance on a single-camera drama, having unwittingly interrupted some moment of tension.

"Zai, have a seat please, Zai," says Vashya.

I sit.

Vashya and Jonathon lock eyes for a few moments longer, then look back at me. I just wait silently. Whatever is going on between them, it's clearly above my pay grade—but I suspect that I am the medium through which their dispute will be resolved. Am I going to have to choose sides? Will I have to kill one of them? Is there anything in the world worse than office politics?

The Englishman breaks the silence. "Let's talk about today's mission, shall we?"

"Hai."

"We have no dossier for you this time, Mr Zai," he says. "We can't send our man ahead of you because we don't even know how we're going to get you across the border. The truth is, for this mission we have very little intel whatsoever."

I am not worried about illegally crossing a border, and in fact I feel vaguely insulted. "Tell me what you know. I will find the contact and kill him."

"There's a bit of a story," says Jonathon, with a smile I do not like. "You might like to get comfortable."

"I am comfortable." This is as deep a lie as I have ever committed.

"Alright then. There is a place you may have heard of, if you know anything about Western mythology, called Fairyland."

"A Midsummer Night's Dream." Does he think I grew up without a television set? "Alice in Wonderland. The Magic Faraway Tree."

"Yes, exactly. Exactly," says Jonathon.

"The Wizard of Oz. Peter Pan in Never-Never Land."

"Alright, I take your point," he says, but I haven't even made my point yet. Does he really think that only Western cultures dream of magical worlds?

"Anyway, by now it shouldn't surprise you to learn that it's a real place."

It does not surprise me because I've already been there. I nod.

"About ten years ago, the Way from Karachidor to the Faerie Land was abruptly sealed and all commerce with the Realms ceased," said the Englishman.

"I see."

"Ordinarily, that would not be a concern for the likes of us, but now somebody has found a new Way in…"

"And they're using it to trade black market goods?"

Jonathon looks at me through narrowed eyes. I was a yakuza gangster, once. I understand how these things work.

"What are they trading? Drugs?"

"Well, it isn't knock-off Rolexes," says Jonathon.

"Weapons," says Vashya. "Some person selling weapons to Karachidor and America, is person. Bad weapons."

I raise an eyebrow, because they are waiting for a reaction.

"In the past, most of the arms exported from the Faerie Realms were duds," says Jonathon. "They lost all magical properties when they were shipped to our world. That is not the case with these new weapons."

"What kind of weapons?"

"Nasty stuff. Hand-to-hand. Swords, maces, axes, pikes. They're made of a substance called 'shadowsteel'. Supposed to be unbreakable. Never loses its edge. Looks bad ass."

"They sound pretty cool."

"They are," says Jonathon. "They're brilliant—except for the side-effects."

"Side effects?"

"Psychosis, in almost all cases. Often, physical mutations. Sometimes weirder effects, like draining the wielder's shadow. There's a theme, if you want to look at it that way."

"Zai, they becomes a monster, Zai."

I shake my head. There's no mission here. "This sounds like a job for Karachidor customs."

"Oh, they have tried to shut it down," says Jonathon, "But it's proven rather more difficult than they expected. Some of the local plods followed the smugglers back into the Realms, and never returned. Now the different law enforcement agencies are tangled in red tape, trying to determine who is responsible, who has authority, and what needs to be done...really, they'd all rather the problem just went away."

"Zai, that is where you come in, Zai," says Vashya.

"We need you to find a way into the Faerie Realms," says Jonathon, "and then eliminate the...*faerie person*...responsible for the weapons trade. All we know is his name: Ghesnuk Rethe."

"We found a Guide who is reputed to know his way around the place," says Jonathon. "He will find a way to get you into the Land and to survive once you've made the crossing."

"I can manage by myself." There's a more vehemence in my voice than I had intended.

"No, you cannot," Jonathon replies. "Something bad is going on in the Faerie Realms and we feel..." he looks at Vashya, who nods grudgingly. "We feel that it is necessary that we provide you with a Guide in order to maximize your odds of success."

"Something bad?"

"We don't know," says Jonathon, uncomfortably. "When the Ways were sealed, we lost all of our assets over there."

"Politics? Civil war? Plague?" I have been to Liberia, Sierra Leone, North Korea, Gaza, Ukraine. I have a difficult time believing that Fairyland might be more dangerous.

"I have heard it described as 'post-apocalyptic'," says Jonathon.

"I don't need a guide."

"It's not up for debate," says Jonathon. "He doesn't know your mission parameters, but he will help you find what you are looking for."

And then I finally understand. "Is this Guide named Emmet?"

Yet again, my employers exchange a complicated series of facial expressions with each other. "You were right about this one," says Jonathon.

Vashya does not dignify that with a response.

Emmet has shaved off his beard, but he is still recognizable. I am more surprised to see that he's wearing jeans and a t-shirt, and not the costume he wore in Sugdike. We exchange pleasantries and I do my best to conceal my resentment at his presence.

A guide. Do they think I am some kind of an amateur?

"So. Fairyland," says Emmet, once I've placed an order for two pints of *shnkwer*. We're at a booth in the pub where I stalked Justin Jordan. More than two years have passed but the place hasn't changed. I have chosen this bar because I am certain there's no surveillance here.

"The Faerie Land. It's a funny old place."

"So I have heard. But what does that mean? A place is a place."

"Not this one." He takes a drink, bites his lip. "The Land consists of many different Realms and Nations, but there's not really a...*geography*. There are no maps."

"No maps?"

"Every path just leads to where it goes but the distances between places aren't necessarily consistent with the length of the path. Physics and the like only operate in the most superficial of ways. It's all...false. Irrational."

"Is it real?"

"It's magical," says Emmet. "We've had this discussion before. If you don't believe in magic, I suppose the answer is no, it's not real— it's *surreal*."

I take a long drink of *shnkwer*. "I may have changed my mind about magic."

"That's marvellous," says Emmet, deadpan.

"Please explain how the Faerie Land is surreal." I try to pronounce it the way Emmet does.

"Well," he says, "it's unreal, in the way that dreams are. Everyday causality makes sense only within a very narrow context, which is based on storybook tropes, not logic or science." He frowns. "Although it can be surprisingly hard to tell the difference sometimes."

"For example?"

"For example, gravity is reasonably consistent, because if characters went flying off into space for no reason it would be bad storytelling."

"What else can I expect?"

"Well, prepare yourself for an awful lot of coincidences."

"Like you being my Guide?"

"Exactly like that."

"We're not even in the Faerie Land yet."

"Travelling the Realms is always a magical journey, and these journeys have to start off in some place that is real."

"There's a working Door to the Realms in Sugdike, is there not?"

Emmet is not surprised that I know about it. "There is," he says, "but it doesn't go to the true Faerie Land."

"There's more than one?"

"The Sugdike's portal leads to a...splinter," Emmet replies. "I told you the village was deep-cloned out of time, right?

"Yes."

"Well, that's the difference between a deep clone and a shallow copy. Ontological references connected to the cloned object are also cloned."

I stare at him blankly.

"Sugdike has its own fairyland," Emmet explains. "A replica, just as Sugdike is a replica. Disconnected from the original. A fragment, just as Sugdike township is just a fragment."

"Can we go to the real one?"

"Well, the Door I used to use has been sealed for a while now, but...I think it will open for us this time."

"Why is that?"

"Story logic," says Emmet. "Taking tourists for a look-around is not much of a story, but, if I am not mistaken, you and I are going on an actual quest."

Emmet and I have adjacent seats on the flight back to Heathrow. He tries to make small-talk, but the plane is not private enough to allow us to talk business and, without being rude, I do my best to shut down any personal conversation. I prefer to travel alone.

It's a relief when we separate in order to pass through customs—Emmet has an EU passport and I do not—and then meet up again in the Aer Lingus terminal.

The flight to Dublin is crowded but punctual. Emmet rents a car in the airport—he is used to being the guide. I am not used to following tamely along, but this is his turf.

It takes hours to drive from Dublin to Tramore. Emmet opts for the scenic route, along the coastal road as far as Wexford, where we stop for lunch. Then we get on the N25 and another hour later we are here.

Tramore is a resort town built up on the side of a hill facing the waterfront. Apparently, it's a good place to go surfing—if you're a polar bear. Visible in the distance is the Great Newton Head promontory, which is surmounted by three white towers. An iron sculpture of a sailor, pointing out to sea, stands atop the middle one. Emmet tells me that the sailor is known as the Metal Man. I've never been to this part of Ireland, and I'd like to look around, but there's work to do.

In town, we stop for coffee and then we head to a wilderness store to buy supplies for our trip: tents, hunting knives, rope, sleeping bags. We buy some canned food at the supermarket. "There's accommodation to be found in the Realms," Emmet tells me. "Inns and taverns and so forth. But usually there's plenty of sleeping outdoors." The way he says 'the Realms' makes him suddenly sound very professional and experienced. Perhaps he will be useful after all.

We're staying overnight in a B&B. Emmet seems to know the owners very well. They are all involved in the Unfolded Earth Guiding business. When they ask Emmet jokingly if he's going to take me into the Realms of the Land, Emmet's reply is a sombre one. "I'm going to try."

There's a moment of quiet, but they soon resume carousing. The whole scene makes me very uncomfortable. I don't want to hang about with people who might remember me. Worse, they know where I am going. This is why I didn't want a guide.

As soon as I can politely do so, I retreat to my room, claiming truthfully that I need to get my gear in order. First, I pack the kit I'm going to take into the Realms with me. Then I put a fresh set of clothes into the airport roll-along, along with a passport, credit cards, and cash.

Finally, I strip the identifying tags and badges from my main luggage.

Emmet and his family are still celebrating in the front room when I slip out the back door.

First, I deposit all my excess clothes in a charity bin at a nearby supermarket. I cut the lid off my old suitcase with the survival knife and ditch it in a dumpster behind the loading dock. Then I head up into the hills, dragging my carry-on. I also have with me an entrenching tool—a small, folding shovel—that I purchased at the wilderness store with Emmet.

The night is brisk, and the air is wet. I find a secluded, woody area, well off the road. Shining my flashlight around, I walk until I can no longer see the traffic or the lights. I take the entrenching tool and use it to dig a meter-deep hole.

I wrap my luggage in a plastic garbage bag, tape it closed, and put it in the hole. Then I cover it with dirt and replace the sod.

I dust off my hands and head back towards town. Getting away after this mission is going to need special care.

In the morning, Emmet and I strap on our packs and leave the B&B on foot. I am not sure what's heavier—my kit or the fry-up breakfast I consumed before leaving the B&B. Emmet wisely opted for cereal and toast. "Inter-dimensional travel unsettles my stomach," he tells me.

"Are we going to the standing stones?" I read some tourist brochures over breakfast; they seem a likely site of the local Door.

"We're not."

"The megalithic tombs?" I pronounce 'megalithic' carefully and get it mostly right.

"Nope."

We hike for about forty-five minutes until we reach a shabby-looking church: a box made from poured concrete with a slate roof and exactly one stained glass window. It's not old enough to be a tourist attraction, and there is nobody there on a weekday morning. "The old building burned down thirty years ago," says Emmet. "Local government was too cheap to restore it, so they put up this instead. Churchyard is still original, though."

He unlocks the gate padlock and leads me around to the back of the building. Aside from the graffiti and the litter, there isn't much to see. A couple of stunted trees and a dozen or so crumbling gravestones behind a small carpark.

"There's a Door to the Faerie Realms here?" If there is, my topographical senses cannot locate it.

"There is. Or at least, there was."

"I expected something more…pagan."

"They fey folk aren't pagans," says Emmet.

"I still don't understand why they'd put a Door into a churchyard."

"The Door was here long before there ever was a church."

Standing amongst the tombstones, I make an active effort to explore the place with my topographical senses. There *is* a seam, but it's been sealed and smoothed over. But the texture doesn't quite match the surrounding reality, and there is some roughness around the edges. "How do you open it?"

Emmet steps up to the edge of the rockery and clears his throat a few times. After a moment I realize he's speaking in Gaelic.

Minutes pass. Emmet keeps talking. I suppose this is some kind of magic spell.

"Oh, come on, you fucking thing." He stamps in frustration. "Open up, you fucker!"

Nothing happens.

Emmet looks at me sheepishly. "This one's still sealed," he says. "But there are other gates…" He doesn't sound optimistic. He clearly thought this one would open.

"Let me try something." I unsling my pack, open it, and pull out the steel gauntlet. Emmet gives me a strange look as I put it on.

I step up to the seam, shut my eyes, and extend my hand. The Door is patched tightly but I think I can unpick it.

It's hard and frustrating work. I growl, make a fist, punch the seal. It doesn't break, but the pressure of my blow weakens the adhesive and one of the edges rucks away.

I seize between metal fingertips and—

There. I have it.

"Take my pack and get ready," I say. "I don't know how long I can hold the Door open."

"You're an Opener?"

I shrug.

"I knew it."

"Do you want to go or not?"

"We'll talk about this later, Mr Zai." Emmet secures his own pack and then picks up mine with both hands. "Alright. Do your stuff."

I shut my eyes again, grab, and tear. It takes physical effort. I plant my feet, put my hips into it, and grunt. The Door opens raggedly and

Emmet jumps through the breach like a heavily burdened jackrabbit. I have to turn and step through backwards in order to keep the Door wedged open as I follow.

The Door slams shut behind me with a bang that is in no way metaphorical.

We are in a forest.

The trees are black, but they are not burned; they are just dead. The soil is dry and bare and also black. The sky above is bright and blue. There is no wind, and the temperature is quite comfortable. The silence is eerie.

Emmet looks right and left. He takes a couple of tentative steps, then turns back to me. "Oh, fuck," he says. "We're in the black forest."

"Is that bad?"

"It doesn't get much worse."

I look around but see nothing obviously threatening. "Are there... monsters?"

"No," says Emmet. "Just trees and dirt and death."

I look around sceptically. "I don't see any death."

"The trees," says Emmet. "The soil. If you touch them, you will die."

"Oh."

"We need to get out of here."

"You're the guide."

"I don't know where we are."

"You said we're in the black forest?"

"Aye, but I've never been in here before," he says. "That's why I'm still alive. The Door never used to open into here."

"Where did it used to open?"

"A different forest," says Emmet.

"A normal forest?"

"Normal for the Realms."

"Oh? With walking trees and talking animals and everything?"

Emmet does not appreciate my levity. This pleases me in some petty way. "We need to get out of here, Zai."

I look around, but there are none of the usual forest tell-tales to indicate direction. The sky is uniformly bright and there are no shadows, so I can't work out where the sun lies.

I close my eyes and extend my topographical senses. This place has the same flat feeling as the Sugdike fairyland, but there is a rumpled quality to it, like a sheet of paper that's been crumpled up and then smoothed out. I guess an apocalypse will do that.

Here in the Realms, my topographical perception is more detailed than ever, and my range is greater. It gives me a sense of the physical terrain as well as the weft of its inter-dimensional substrate.

I open my eyes. "This way."

"How do you know?"

"You said you wanted to get out of here."

Remembering Emmet's warning about the trees being deadly to the touch we proceed carefully.

Black trees, dead soil, bright sky. The scenery does not change.

We keep walking. The scenery continues to not change. It is hard to judge the time because the light does not change either.

"Do you hear that?"

Emmet pauses to listen. A muted roar; a distant rushing.

"I think we are near the sea."

Emmet stops dead in his tracks.

"Emmet?"

Emmet shakes his head. "There're no sea in the Faerie Realms; just Land and Sky."

"It sounds like the sea to me."

Half an hour later we emerge from the trees. Emmet and I scramble up over a sandy crest, which is patchy with black grass. We stand up there looking out at the rising tide of an ink-black sea.

"Well, fuck," says Emmet.

An odour on the breeze makes me gag; bitter and nutty. "The water's poisonous."

"But it's not like the trees," says Emmet. "There are things living in it."

I look, watching the waves shatter against the shores. There are shapes moving out in the foaming waters: finned, spiny, bony shapes. Teeth and tentacles and beaks and claws. It is fascinating and awful and I would love to take some photos, if I had a camera that would work in this place…but right now we have a different problem to deal with.

"Emmet." I speak quietly. "There's something following us."

Emmet turns around slowly.

A black-skinned, humanoid creature steps out of the black forest.

"Oh, shit," says Emmet.

The black thing is the size of a small adult or a large child. It's not black, like an African; it's black, as if it was carved from a lump of coal. Its eyes are black. Its hair is black. It's wearing garments of soot-blacked leather, bound up with straps and black lacquered buckles.

The black thing capers towards us. Emmet and I back away.

"What is it?"

"I don't fucking know," says Emmet, "but I it looks fucking dangerous to me."

"What should we do?"

"Run or parley," he says. He thinks about it for almost two seconds. "I suggest running."

We turn and run, stumbling down the crest and along the rocky beach. The sand chews at my boots, the stones wobble and slip beneath my feet. We have to get off the beach before one of us falls and breaks a leg, but there is nowhere else to go: we have the deadly forest on the left, the poisoned sea on the right, and the black thing behind us.

The black thing maintains its distance easily, jumping and skipping behind us. I can go faster, but it would be risky given the poor footing—and I don't want to get too far ahead of Emmet, who is already struggling to keep up.

The black thing is now close enough that I can see it grinning. Its teeth are as black as venous blood.

Emmet tries to make up some distance with a lunge that becomes an awkward stumble. I grab his jacket and yank to keep him from falling and almost lose my own balance. Somehow, I manage to stay upright and we forge on.

The black thing is so close that I can feel heat radiating from its skin.

The sea is close, and the ground is slippery from the salt spray. Stumbling and sliding, I scramble up a spur of volcanic rock, which is so sharp it draws blood from my hands. Emmet clambers up after me on all fours.

When I look over my shoulder, I can see the whites of the black thing's eyes. They, like its teeth, are a ruddy black colour. The black thing crouches below us, but it makes no further attempt to come after us. It cocks its head and says: "I'll catch up with you gentlemen later. Do enjoy your stay in the Shaedowlands."

The black thing turns and scampers away.

"Well, that was peculiar, wasn't it?" says Emmet, once he has caught his breath.

We take a moment to get our bearings. Ahead of us, the rocky ground ripples up in a series of jagged ridges before it terminates at a sheer cliff wall, hundreds of meters high. Surmounting the cliffs is a tower. Corrugated and veined and twisted, it looks as much like the trunk of a tree as it does a giant, diseased phallus.

"Looks like we found the Dark Tower," says Emmet.

"Have you seen it before?"

"No," he says. "I used to be clever enough to avoid this kind of thing. Your man on the beach had the right idea."

Emmet is right. The black thing stopped just before it came in sight of the tower.

"What are the Shaedowlands?" I make no attempt to pronounce the word the way the black thing said it.

"Best guess: it's what the Realms are called now," replies Emmet. "Or at least, some of them." He gestures around at all of the scenery: the black trees, the black sea, the black rocks, the black tower. "You might have noticed a bit of a theme going on."

A column of riders comes around the tower and starts down a treacherously narrow pathway that leads circuitously to us.

"Should we run away again?"

"How? Do you want to risk a swim in the poison sea, or would you prefer high tea with our new friend in the black forest?"

"There's only one of him."

"I'll take my chances with the riders," says Emmet morosely.

The riders are pale and thin-faced. They have dark hair and round, acutely-angled eyes and pointed ears. About half of them are female. They are wearing chainmail under plain black tunics and they are armed with lances with vicious, curved blades.

Four of the riders draw up while the rest canter around behind us, cutting off our escape. Their leader dismounts and approaches us on foot. She is very tall, with cockroach-black eyeballs and streaks of grey in her black hair. Up close, I can see that she has a crest on her tunic: the dark tower. Black on black.

The leader sizes us up. "Mortals." She looks disappointed.

"Aye, we are that," says Emmet.

"Are you seeking an audience with the Emperor?"

"The who?" says Emmet.

"The Emperor of the Shaedowlands."

"No," says Emmet, trying to ad-lib his way out of the situation. "We are far beneath the notice of such as he."

"He sees you, mortal—especially when you stand in sight of the tower."

"I mean no disrespect," says Emmet. "We are disoriented. These Realms have changed much since last I was here."

The leader inclines her head. "That they have."

"If we have trespassed in any way—"

The leader shakes her head tersely and he shuts his mouth. "No," she says. "The Emperor believes that his own kind should be allowed to come and go as they please. It was not he who barred the Doors."

"His own kind?" Emmet flashes me a warning look.

"He is a mortal, like you," says the leader. "Or at least, he was, before he was made Emperor."

"There was a...thing...that followed us out of the black forest," I tell the leader. "It chased us down the beach, but it ran off when we came in sight of the tower."

"What kind of a thing?"

"A black thing?"

The leader raises a hand and snaps her fingers. Her second-in-command walks his horse closer. "These mortals were pursued by a black thing."

"The Black and Crimson King grows bold," the second replies.

"Aye," says the leader. To her second, she says: "It has surely returned to the forest, but we must secure the beach. Go. I will report to the Empress."

The second climbs back onto his horse and mounts up. At his command, half of the company wheel their horses and gallop down the beach, in the direction the black thing went.

"You may continue about your quest," the leader tells us. "Stay away from the Darkling in the Woods, and hope that he will stay away from you."

The leader has one foot in its stirrup when Emmet speaks up: "We're looking for the merchant Ghesnuk Rethe."

"Of course, you are," says the leader. "You will find him at the Black River delta."

"Where is that?" says Emmet.

"In the place where the Tinker-folk once had their machine kingdom," replies the rider, swinging a leg over the saddle. "Where the ore-lands and the mountains meet the forests and the sea."

The remaining riders head back up the path to the tower.

I turn to Emmet. "Do you know what's going on?"

He shakes his head. "Emperors and Empresses...the King of Bloody Shite-stains...it's all new to me."

I think about that for a moment. Politics. "Alright. Let's go to the Black River delta."

"Sure, sure," grumbles Emmet. "I bet that's a scenic fuckin' place."

We follow the beach until the cliff wall splinters and slumps into hills. As we move away from the beach, the terrain becomes less bare, although it is a long way from the lush meadowlands I saw in the Sugdike faerie land. The landscape is black or brown or grey from horizon to horizon, and the low, cloudy skies that hang above it are stained bruise-purple or pus-yellow.

I sigh and we continue to trudge through the hills. This is why I quit the army. Too much marching around with nothing else to do.

When I say this aloud, for the fifth time, Emmet replies, "The journey will take how long it's meant to take."

"Are meant to wander here forever?"

"No. We'll end up where we need to go, have no fear on that account. Storybook logic is clear on that."

"Do these stories have happy endings?"

"Depends," says Emmet. "The usual thing is that it turns out that what you were seeking was with you all along, but you needed the journey to discover it."

"I don't think this is one of those."

"Well, there are other kinds of endings. Ones that go on and on and on," says Emmet, glumly. "Spanning continents and generations. Sequels and spinoffs."

We keep walking.

Emmet and I come to a river, clear and rapid. We follow it upstream until the light starts to fail, and the temperature starts to drop. Emmet stops at a shelf protected by a slab of fallen rock. "Let's make camp here. This will keep the wind off, at least."

Starting the fire is more difficult than I had expected. Emmet seems entertained by my efforts. "Matches won't work here. Or lighters." He produces a flint and steel from his pack. "If we're lucky, this will do it."

"And if it fails?"

"We can try rubbing two sticks together. Or pray for a lightning strike."

The flint works. We puncture some cans of food and cook them over the miraculous fire. After the meal, I boil some water and make coffee.

"Thought you'd be a tea drinker," says Emmet.

"I drink coffee also. Especially when I need to stay awake."

"There's not much in the way of nightlife around here, in case you hadn't noticed."

I shake my head. "We need to keep a watch tonight. I'm pretty sure the black thing's been following us."

"Are you shitting me?" says Emmet. "I thought those riders chased it off."

"It's keeping its distance, but it's still out there."

"Great."

We sit watching the fire and drink our coffee.

"You know," says Emmet, "I've met other Travellers before, but never an Opener of Doors."

I am reluctant to discuss the matter, although I'm sure Emmet can help me understand it better. These abilities are my deepest secret.

"Come on," says Emmet. "I've seen you open a locked Door. You can trust me, I promise."

"It's true. What else do you want me to say?"

"Tell me about the glove. Is it magical?"

"No. It just helps me to...grip...things better."

"A fetish, then."

"If you say so."

"Can you create new Doors?"

I drink the last of my coffee. The grounds are gritty on my tongue. I try to scrape them off with my teeth. "I wouldn't know how."

"Might be a useful ability to have," says Emmet.

"It might."

"Want to try and see?"

Emmet badgers me for another ten minutes before I take out the gauntlet and strap it on. I flex my gloved fingers, shut my eyes, and swirl my hand around. There are no nearby seams or nodes that I can perceive. I flex my fingers and try to gather up some of the unknown substance that forms a barrier between the worlds. To my surprise I find a fistful of the stuff. It stretches between my fingers, resists...then breaks free of my grip and snaps back into shape.

"Anything?"

"I don't know what I'm doing."

"Perhaps if you, like, *visualize* another place? The house where you grew up, or something?"

My parents still live in it and I'd rather not visit them right now. I try to set my goal a little closer at hand.

I try to visualize inside the tent, where I have left my iPod lying on my pack. The device doesn't work here in the Shaedowlands, but it's small and it's close by. I use both hands, pull a hole open...but when I let go with one hand and try to reach through it snaps shut. I snatch my hand back, worried that the closing portal will sever it.

Emmet is leaning close, squinting in case it will help him see what I'm doing. "What happened?"

"Didn't work."

"Try again?"

I draw in a long breath and make another hole. I gather the edges with the gauntlet, close my eyes and reach through with my ungloved hand...

...and my fingers close on empty air.

I open my eyes, turn over my hand, and open my fist, just to make sure. It's empty. "Are you satisfied?" I feel a little disappointed. I start to remove the glove.

Emmet blinks a couple of times, takes a deep breath. "I think you did make a small portal," he says. "But it didn't lead anywhere. It was just...it was like your hand went out of sync with your arm."

"Okay." I flex my naked fingers. "So I can make doors that don't go anywhere."

Emmet is still curious, though. "But, hmm, yes. There was definitely a latency," he says. "A good three seconds between your hand going in one side of the portal and coming out the other."

I close the gauntlet up in its box with a snap. The exertion, followed by failure, has left me tired and frustrated and I do not want to talk about this anymore.

Emmet scratches his chin. "You remember that wizard we met in Sugdike?"

"I thought he was a drunk?"

"Wizards usually are, in my experience," says Emmet. "Remember what he said?"

"I remember he vomited on himself and then we left."

"Topomancy and chronomancy," says Emmet. "Those are your talents. That's the chronomancy we just saw."

"I can open a Door three seconds into the past? That's very useful."

"3 seconds into the future," says Emmet. "But that was just your first time, wasn't it? And you weren't even trying to open a time Door. Want to try again?"

I shake my head. "I have a headache."

"What's wrong with you, man? You might have the ability to travel through time, and you don't want to try it out?"

"Time travel gives me a headache." Or maybe it's just this conversation.

Emmet gives an exasperated sigh and reaches for his bedroll. "First watch is yours. Perhaps that headache will help you stay awake."

The moon above looks like a piece of silver that's been hammered into a flat disk. Its wan light does little to drive back the shadows at the edge of the firelight. I know the fire is more likely to draw monsters than to scare them away, but it comforts me to have it going. I wish I had some marshmallows.

Emmet is snoring loudly when the black thing comes. I somehow feel embarrassed on his behalf despite my own rising levels of terror. The black thing crouches just beyond the circle cast by the flames, watching me with its black, black eyes; grinning at me with bloody black teeth.

"Hello." I do not know if I'm speaking so quietly because I don't want to waken Emmet, or because I am trying to remain calm.

"Hello, Opener." Still crouching, the black thing moves into the circle. The light of the flames serve only to darken its appearance.

"Can I help you with anything?"

"No," says the black thing. "I just wanted another look at you."

"And now?"

"Now I have encountered you twice," it says. "By storybook rules, that will almost certainly become thrice."

"And what will happen then?"

"We will see," says the black thing. "Though I am sure it will be dark." It bows and backs out of the circle. "Sleep well," it says. By the time it finishes speaking it has disappeared.

I let Emmet sleep for another three hours and then we trade shifts. I do not mention the black thing's visit, since it has imparted no useful information.

I awaken at sunrise to find Emmet asleep at his post. Somehow, the fire is still burning. I tell him that he's lucky he didn't fall in, but he just shrugs.

"Zai, I've been thinking..."

"Yes?"

"If you can open a Door through time, what would happen if you went through it?"

"Are you asking if I am a time traveller?"

"I don't think you're weird enough to be Doctor Who," he says,

"But I've been wrong before."

"Who?"

"You've never watched Doctor Who?"

"Is it a TV show?"

"Never mind," says Emmet, stoking the fire with a stick. "You see the coffee pot?"

I pass it to him.

"Anyway," he says. "Time travel. We know it's possible to…"

"Time travel is shit."

Emmet stares at me as if I have sprouted a third arm from my forehead.

I rub my eyes. "I have seen all the movies. I know the stories. You travel in time. Meet famous dead people. There's a paradox that is the problem and also the solution. You save the world, or ruin it. It never makes sense. Time travel is shit."

"But…you just did it."

"Going forwards in time doesn't count. That's just…" I struggle to find the word. "Relativity."

"If you're at the speed of light, it's relativity," said Emmet. "Sitting with your arse on a log making your hand go into the future? That's time travel."

"It's shit."

"You're not thinking of the possibilities," says Emmet. "We already know you can go forwards. That's just relativity, like you said. But if you could make a Door into the past…"

"The past is for the dead," I say. "Why would I even want to go there?"

Emmet tips some coffee into the pot. "Never mind why. Let's say you had a pressing need. If you went through the Door, and you changed events, the future *you* might not ever go through that Door. So where did the first *you* come from?"

"Wait, now there are two of me?"

"Maybe?" Emmet pours some water from a canteen into the coffee pot. "Probably there's some quantum thing." He puts the coffee pot into the fire and tries to push it to the hotter part with a stick.

"You mean, like…the cat that's alive and dead at the same time?"

"That's the one." Emmet prods the coffee pot a little too hard and spills its contents into fire. "Ah, shit!"

That's what I have been trying to tell him. Time travel is shit.

We tramp through the hills for two more days, following the river. We stay up late and rise early. I do not bother to set watch again. The black thing has had plenty of opportunity to kill us already, if it really wanted to. I cannot tell if it's still following us, but I have seen no sight of it since its visit.

On the third day a crescent-shaped mountain range appears in the east....or at least, in the direction from which the sun rose this morning. I am fifty percent certain that was north the day before. Emmet says that that sun's passage through the sky can vary from Realm to Realm, and so can the sun itself. Some Realms have their own suns. Some Realms trade suns between them.

It takes us days to skirt the mountains. When I ask Emmet if there isn't some shortcut through, he says, "Of course, there are passes and tunnels, but they're infested with monsters and psychopaths. It's ambushes a-go-go, and I forgot my magic sword."

I don't bother to tell him that, if my intel is correct, he's better off without one.

So we take the long way, and nobody tries to ambush us. We do not encounter anyone at all: no serial killers, no monsters, no talking birds or fish or forest critters. It's unnervingly quiet.

There's nothing to hunt or forage on the way, so we're living out of our dwindling supplies of canned food and dried goods. "This isn't the sort of post-apocalypse I was expecting," says Emmet.

"What were you expecting?"

"Oh, you know. Fire in the sky, and all that. Eight-thousand-foot monsters. All the fun stuff. I didn't think it would be the sort of post-apocalypse where you walk around an empty wilderness for days and then die of starvation."

"Weeks."

"What?"

"It takes weeks to die of starvation. Not days."

"Was that supposed to make me feel better?"

We spend the rest of the day walking along in irritable silence until we come to the highway.

Four lanes of crowned blacktop, with shoulders marked and concrete kerb-sides. Where necessary, the engineers who built it have blasted through hillsides in order to keep it straight and level.

"Well, fuck me," says Emmet.

"Does this lead to where we are going?"

"I have no doubt," says Emmet, squinting down the road in the hopes of seeing a destination. Whatever lies at the end of it is beyond the range of my topographical senses.

We make much better time walking on the road. My stomach is growling and I am optimistic that a good meal is near at hand, but Emmet is practically vibrating with fury. What kind of post-apocalypse in a magical kingdom builds roads fit for motor-vehicle traffic?

We stop and move to the side of the road when we hear a cart approaching. The driver draws the pair of horses to a stop and looks us over. He's the first person we've seen since the black thing visited us.

"Where are you two headed?"

"The Black River delta." I have to speak, because Emmet is still standing there with his jaw clenched.

"Indeed," says the driver. "That is the place to which this highway leads. What do you seek there?"

"We're looking for the merchant Ghesnuk Rethe?"

"Of course, you are."

Emmet uncoils a little, finds his professional demeanour. "Any chance of a ride?" he says. "I can't help but notice you have no cargo."

"What payment can you offer?" says the driver.

"We have nothing valuable," says Emmet. "All we can give you is our company, for the duration of the journey."

The driver considers us. "You are mortals, are you not?"

"We are indeed."

"In that case," says the driver, looking nervous, "I will take you to the headquarters of Mr Rethe, on two conditions."

"Name them."

The driver counts them off on his fingers. "First you ride in silence. Second, our commerce is done once I have delivered you."

"Can't say fairer than that," says Emmet.

We follow the river upstream through the Ore-Lands; a flat, arid territory pocked with mineshafts and gantries. In the distance, we spy the rusty towers of a city made entirely from metal. Black smoke purges from its smokestacks and wreathes the place in smog that remains oddly localized over the city. I am glad the highway bypasses it.

The black forest darkens the horizon to the east and the mountains curve around from the west. To the north, the river branches out as it rejoins the poison sea: we have come to the delta we have been seeking.

The driver turns the cart away from the delta and heads up into the foothills. We wind our way up a succession of switchbacks across the forested slopes. It's early afternoon by the time we jounce into a town that reminds me altogether too much of Sugdike's hotel district.

"Ruined. It's fucking ruined." Emmet has been grumbling under his breath the whole way. "Faerie Land isn't supposed to have *suburbs*."

I can see his point, but all this development gives me hope that there will be a hot shower my near future.

We pass through an industrial area and then through a tangle of silos and warehouses. The driver lets us off at a large factory with a sign front that says GR INDUSTRIES INC.

Emmet sighs.

We climb down out of the cart, and I thank the driver. He grunts and flicks the reins to get the horses moving again, keen to put some distance between himself and whatever trouble Emmet and I have brought from the mortal world.

Emmet follows me into the reception area at the front of the warehouse. I notice Conventional Earth magazines on a low table: *GQ*, *Better Homes and Gardens*, *Guitar Techniques*, *Guns and Ammo*, *Cosmopolitan*, *Forbes*. They are at least two years out of date and well-thumbed.

I go right up to the receptionist—a faerie in a low-cut blouse and cat's-eye glasses. She smiles falsely and says, "May I help you?" I'm pretty sure the lenses in her spectacles are blanks.

"Hello," I say. "My name is Zai. I'm here to see Mr Ghesnuk Rethe."

"Please have a seat, Mr Zai." The receptionist reaches for the phone and punches some numbers.

Emmet and I sit down. I start to rifle through the magazines, hoping for a National Geographic. I have not even finished going through the first pile when a pot-bellied elf in a Hugo Boss suit comes charging down the stairs from the office. His blonde hair is slicked down and his pointed ears are studded with jewels.

"Gentlemen! Mortals! Humans!" says the elf. "I am Ghesnuk Rethe, and I bid you welcome!"

I shake his hand, which seems too delicate to belong to a fat man. A Rolex flops about on his wrist—the band is too big. It shows the time as 12 midnight, so I'm certain it's not actually functional.

I introduce Emmet. Rethe claps him on the back like an old friend. "Humans! Today! This is a wonderful omen."

"I don't believe in omens," I reply. "I am here to do business."

Rethe leads us through the warehouse-showroom, past racks of strange and gaudy clothes; past boxes of souvenir jewellery; past shelves lined with snow globes and key-rings. At the very back of the building there is a curtained-off area guarded by a pair of eight foot tall, tusk-faced monsters. Trolls or orcs or ogres—something like that. I don't think the faerie folk fall as easily into the categories we humans like to assign them. The guards stand aside as we pass between them.

"The good stuff!" says Rethe, sweeping aside the drapes to reveal a small and carefully laid-out arsenal.

Swords, daggers, maces, morning-stars, axe-heads, spear-tips, arrow-heads; hanging from racks or lying neatly arranged on display pillows. The items are all made from a lustreless black metal that seems to suck the light right out of my retinas.

"Shadowsteel," says Rethe. "It will not bend, it will not crack, it will not break, or shatter, or burn, or melt. It will cut, it will pierce, it will kill, and it will never wear down or blunt, no matter how often it is used."

Emmet reaches for a sword, but I catch his wrist before he can touch it. He looks at me and I shake my head.

"I'm not here for these."

Emmet gives me a quizzical look. I'm not sure if the corporate shtick is working.

Rethe smiles astutely. "I did not think you were," he says. "I'm beginning to tire of these penny-ante players. Hustlers and racketeers. You did not use one of my Doors to enter the Realms, did you, Mr Zai? You did not venture here in the company of my agents."

"No, I did not."

"Which indicates to me that you represent the Big Dogs." He speaks the American slang more naturally than I do.

"The Sony Corporation." Emmet's eyes go wide. I thought for a moment that he would laugh, but he seems to have bought into the story as well. I wonder if I should feel offended.

"Ah, of course," says Rethe pretending that he knows what I am talking about.

I just stand there, channelling my father, looking at the open boxes of weapons expressionlessly. Rethe starts to fidget and eventually he says "Well, what is that you are after, Mr Zai?"

"I am not here to buy weapons. I am here to acquire resources."

Rethe twitches. "Resources?"

"After many years of pacifism, my country is re-arming itself. We take pride in doing things properly. In being the best. And that is why we want your people. Your engineers, your magicians, your blacksmiths, your overseers. Your organization. Your operation."

Rethe gapes at me.

"I want…" I gesture around the room. "I want all of this. Exclusively. Complete control of the manufacture and sale of shadowsteel."

Rethe's brow furrows. "You want to put me out of business."

"No, Mr Rethe. We want to *buy* you out of business."

We ride up to Rethe's estate in a hansom cab. It's not my first time in a horse-drawn carriage, but the experience is somehow more exciting in Faerie Land. Perhaps the cab used to be a pumpkin. Perhaps the coachman used to be a rat. The upholstered leather seats are a lot more comfortable than the floor in the back of the open cart.

The cab takes us up through the steep wooded hills and across a plateau. Rethe's manor house stands across a picturesque lake from a resort complex comprised of a hotel and a dozen cabanas. An eighteen-hole golf course lies between the lake and the rising flank of a mountain. "It's a fuckin' Club Med," says Emmet, appalled.

I wonder if there's somewhere I can borrow some clubs.

There are a dozen guest bungalows behind the main house, as well as a swimming pool with a split-level tiki bar. I am sure there's a tennis court somewhere.

All the furniture in my bungalow is hand-made, but it looks as if the designs were copied out of a timeshare brochure. It lacks the expected television set, telephone and alarm clock, but it does have hot running water. Even Emmet is impressed.

I have a shower and brief nap and then I head up to the tiki bar to have a drink with Emmet. We have a few hours to kill before our dinner with Ghesnuk Rethe.

The bar is full of Conventional Earth types: Englishmen, French, Germans; a clutch of Silicon Valley types. The only faerie folk I see are the staff.

The barman—a huge creature with a shaven, tattooed head—attends to us immediately. "What are you two human gentlemen drinking this fine afternoon?"

There are shelves full of spirits with familiar brand names on them, but there are no beer taps. I ask the barman what he recommends.

"I received a shipment of Stolichnaya vodka today."

"Do you have anything…local?"

"Wines, aye," says the barman. "Red or white, or rose. We have ale, too."

I order two of the latter, which the barman draws from a wooden keg.
I raise my glass to Emmet. "*Sláinte.*"

"Kanpai," he replies.

The ale's not bad. Smooth and a bit floral. I wonder if the process of fermentation is the same in Faerie Land. "So," says Emmet. "The Sony Corporation?"

I fix him with my father's gimlet gaze and give him one of Dad's favourite lines: "In the end, your paycheque and mine are signed by a man in a suit." I drown my sigh in a swig of beer.

"I dunno, man, I really thought you were just here on a holiday."

"You think breaking into a barred, politically unstable reality to seek out an illegal arms dealer is a holiday?"

"Well," says Emmet, "Adventure tourism, you know? I thought you were a collector or a thrill junkie or something."

"Do I look like a collector?"

"You look like a 1980s caricature of a tourist."

Of course, I know that. It's much better camouflage than he realizes. I wonder how long it will take him to realize that my cover story makes no sense. "Just because I'm away on business, that doesn't mean I can't enjoy the sights."

Emmet snorts and takes a long drink from his glass.

One of the Americans joins us at the bar; a young guy with a blonde buzzcut and a carefully groomed beard. He orders a Red Bull and vodka, then turns to me and Emmet while the barman mixes it. "I know, I know," he says. "It's very 2002." I guess that qualifies as vintage for someone his age. I wonder what he'd think if he saw my ancient iPod.

"Is it now?" says Emmet, coolly.

The man with the buzzcut turns to me and bows far too deeply. "*Konbanwa.*" Judging by his accent, he learned to speak Japanese watching anime.

"Hello."

"So you're the new guys in town?"

"Yes." I don't introduce myself.

The barman hands him a drink. "What do you think of the place so far?"

"I am enjoying the hot water."

The man with the buzzcut gestures with his chin. "I heard he has electricity up at the manor house."

"Now that is something," says Emmet, deadpan.

"I know that things aren't what they used to be around here," says the man with the buzzcut, "but even in a depressed economy, that kind of magic doesn't come cheap."

"Perhaps he outsourced it," suggests Emmet.

"You tell me where I can outsource industrial-grade magical engineering, I'll give you a hundred thousand dollars."

"I only take Euros," says Emmet. He pounds the rest of his tankard, sets it down on the counter and stumps off in the direction of his bungalow.

"What's his problem?" asks the man with the buzzcut.

I look him in the eye and say, "If I told you, he would have had to kill both of us."

In the early evening, Rethe's butler-cum-bodyguard escorts me and Emmet up to the main house for dinner. The butler is a scarred, pointy-eared veteran wearing a full-dress tuxedo with a sabre wagging amongst the tails of the coat. Although his right leg ends with a steel peg, he walks without a limp and carries himself with perfect posture. He is going to be a problem.

With exaggerated courtesy, the butler shepherds us through the halls and into the dining room, where fancy, upholstered seats are arranged around a long formal table. Ornaments that might have been purchased in an Ikea stand in niches along the walls. I take special note of the chandelier that hangs from the ceiling.

Rethe rises and comes to shake our hands. I cannot help but smile when I see his outfit: a Hawaiian shirt, khakis, and hiking boots. He tugs at the shirt and pants every now and again: they're brand new and he's not used to the fit. When I compliment him on his attire, he does not attempt to conceal his delight.

All through the six-course dinner, Rethe prattles about the food: leg-of-lamb with mint sauce and dryad's tears; salamander goujons with sky nectar and cloves; firebird stew that is disappointingly mild. It's pleasant, but unexciting. The sauces are rich, but lack any subtlety or surprises. Everything is heavy and somehow *literal*. But it's certainly better than campfire cooking.

After the meal, we move into a parlour, where Rethe offers cognac and cigars. I accept a cognac. Emmet asks for a double.

"You've seen what I have to offer," says Rethe, leaning back in his overstuffed chair, puffing away on his Cuban. "The question remains: what can the Sony Corporation offer me?"

"Do you like gold?"

"Gold I can use," says Rethe, "In limited quantities. Other metals are useful for the business, but if the Sony is going to take that from me, why do I need it?"

"Well, Mr Rethe, why don't you tell me what you want?"

"I like mortal things," says Rethe. "Things one cannot purchase or steal here in the Realms."

"I see."

"Right now, for example, I am particularly interested in rooms."

"Rooms?"

"Come, Mr Zai!" Rethe jumps to his feet with rather more energy than one expects of a man who has just washed down an enormous meal with three glasses of cognac. "Let me show you my *rooms!*"

Rethe leads us through a succession of hallways and down a short, but grand flight of stairs. The butler follows like a stalking wraith. Even when he comes to the head of the group to open a door, he manages to do so without turning his back to us.

We arrive in the first destination. "The den!" exclaims Rethe.

The den looks like a set from an American sitcom. A couch, an easy chair, an entertainment centre, a pool table, a fridge. A neon Budweiser sign on the wall above the bar. The furniture and the décor are all perfectly matched. There is a well-thumbed Pottery Barn catalogue, circa 2003, on the bar counter and I am certain that it contains a room laid out just like this one.

The clock on the VCR is flashing 00:00:00. There are no tapes, and I doubt there is a signal for the TV to pick up even, if it were properly tuned. The place is wired for electricity, just like the Californian at the tiki bar said, but I doubt Rethe knows what electricity is for.

The butler opens a door that leads into a study filled with empty filing cabinets and dated computer equipment. None of it is connected, or even plugged in.

Next is an enormous modern kitchen. A pair of faeries in aprons and tall chef's hats are preparing tomorrow's breakfast. They seem to have mastered the refrigerator and the oven, although I notice a stack of firewood in a corner.

For some unaccountable reason, the kitchen has a door that opens into a glassed-in Jacuzzi room. The tub lights are on, and the air is thick with steam, so I cannot see out of the glass properly, but I believe the sliding doors open onto a patio by the pool.

"This one..." Rethe stops, inhales a lungful of steam, and sighs. "*This* room is my favourite."

The butler produces some fluffy white towels and Rethe starts to disrobe.

Emmet is clearly embarrassed, and I'm feeling a little unhappy about the situation myself. I'm not afraid of being naked, but I would prefer that everybody shower and scrub themselves clean before getting into the tub. The thought of steeping myself in dirty water makes my skin itch.

But I put that out of mind. I have a plan.

"Emmet, please go back to my cabana and fetch my iPod."

"Yes, boss," replies Emmet, displeased at being asked to behave like a valet, but relieved that he doesn't have to remove his clothes.

I take off my own clothes and gingerly climb into the Jacuzzi. Rethe adjusts the jets and the lights while I settle in. The reeking chlorine steam bothers me a little, but despite my concerns about cleanliness, I am suddenly feeling more comfortable than I have in weeks. I sit, lean my head back, and close my eyes. The butler stands in front of the glass doors, hands by his sides, his full attention focused on me. I tip my head back and close my eyes.

Once Rethe has the Jacuzzi frothing and bubbling to his content, he turns to me and says "so tell me, Mr Zai. What do you think of the Shaedowlands?"

"This is the most comfortable apocalypse I have ever experienced."

"Think of it as a reimagining," says Rethe. "The Faerie Realms are still a Land of stories and magic, but they are not as they once were. In the past, there were powers that kept order, but none of them wielded supreme influence. The Council of the Magi, the Warrior Nation, a handful of the larger Queendoms. They have fallen now, and the Shaedow Empire has arisen in their place."

"New administration, new opportunities." I am quoting my father again.

"The only one who opposes the Empire is the Prince of Blood and Darkness. He strikes from the forests, under cover of night. His raids are brutal, but he does not have the numbers to take and hold any towns or cities."

"A guerrilla insurrection. That, also, is good for business."

A knock at the door. The butler opens it and Emmet returns. "Your iPod, sir."

"Thank you, Emmet." I ignore his sarcastic tone. "Just put it there by the towels, please. I'll meet you back at the rooms."

Emmet backs out of the room and closes the door behind him.

"Now, Mr Rethe, let me show you some of the many things the Sony Corporation can offer you."

"Please do."

I get dressed and fetch the portable stereo I saw sitting on a bookshelf in the den. Rethe watches me curiously as I put it on top of the bar fridge, which stands in front of the only power outlet in the room. I have to return to the den to find an adapter for the extension cord—I hope the voltage will be correct for this appliance. The butler just stands by the doors, disapproving.

Setting up the stereo is not difficult work, but the room is hot and full of steam and I am sweating profusely. Rethe lounges in the tub watching me, bemused. I connect the iPod to the charger and to the stereo system. After about twenty seconds it has enough battery power to wake up. I turn the clickwheel to choose a song.

A Tchaikovski piano concerto slowly fills the room, echoing off the tiles and the wood panels. Rethe sits up in the tub. "What is this?"

"Music."

Rethe looks around, confused. "But there are no musicians."

"That is correct."

Rethe listens for a moment while longer. Then he laughs. "There are no musicians!"

"This device contains songs that were captured as the musicians performed them. There are many songs, and you can listen to them whenever you like."

Rethe stares at me. "Aren't the musicians angry that you have stolen their songs?"

"Oh, no," I reply. "The musicians were paid for the recording, and the composer is long dead."

"This…is the music of the dead?" There is reverence in Rethe's tone.

I can only say "Yes."

"Necromancy." Rethe lies back in the tub and closes his eyes. Death is exotic to creatures that can live forever.

After a few moments, Rethe opens his eyes again. "I am growing bored," he says. "Much as I would like to have stolen songs at my disposal, this is unlikely to keep me entertained for very long."

Tchaikovsky is not to my taste, either. "May I play you something else?"

"Please do."

I turn the dial on my iPod and select a different playlist.

The result is immediate. Rethe's starts to rock back and forth. It takes about half a minute before he is waving his arms around and banging his head, shaking his fists.

"The Ramones. My personal favourite."

Rethe continues to splash in the tub like a child. He tries to sing along, although he can't understand the words. I switch from the Ramones to the Boredoms.

"This is wonderful!"

The butler, growing suspicious, moves closer to me. He adjusts his stance, and the pommel of his sabre becomes visible. I do not acknowledge him, I just turn up the volume. Rethe is vibrating around with delight.

"Louder! *Louder!*"

Finally, I glance at the butler. He takes another step towards me, hand on the sabre now. I look at him, wide-eyed, and pick up the stereo. The butler hesitates for just a moment, and I hand it to him. He stands there holding it for a moment, confused, until I kick out his peg leg. The butler somehow manages to draw his sabre as he falls into the tub, but it's too late now.

I jump back as the electricity pops and sizzles. Rethe and the butler convulse violently, sparking and glowing as the AC current arcs through them. The water starts to boil and steam. Neither one of them cries out.

The power shorts out with a bang and the lights go out.

My eyes take a few moments to adjust. Moonlight, filtered through the condensation on the glass walls, is the only source of illumination. The room is eerily quiet after the blasting punk music and the thrashing bodies. Tiny lapping noises are magnified by the steam and the tiles.

Rethe is floating face-down in the water. The butler lies half in the tub, half out, his blackened peg leg pointing up at a strange angle. Greasy smoke curls away from their corpses. I smell cooked flesh and burnt insulation.

The job is done. Now I just need to work out how to get home.

Emmet is waiting outside my bungalow. He's already wearing his pack and he has mine ready at his feet. "I saw the lights go out," he says. "I assume there's trouble?"

I hoist my pack onto my shoulders and tighten the straps. "Let's get out of here."

We set off at a jog, heading out towards the perimeter of the estate. "What happened up there?"

"I threw the stereo into the bath."

"You killed him?"

"And the butler."

"Is that what the Sony Corporation wanted?"

"I don't work for the Sony Corporation."

"I know. Who do you really work for?"

"You know as much about them as I do."

"I doubt that very much."

"Emmet, we need to move." We cross the road that leads down to the town and then turn onto a walking track that runs perpendicular to it.

"Where are we going?" asks Emmet.

I ignore the question and break into a jog. Emmet gets the idea quickly enough.

The track becomes steep, and it takes an effort not to skid down the hillside.

There is still no sign of a commotion at the mansion. The building is still blacked out. I doubt that anyone on Rethe's staff knows how to use the fuse-box.

The track fades to nothing and we are now stumbling down a sparsely wooded slope. We've long since lost sight of the manor house, but I can still feel it on the other side of the hill behind us with my growing topographical senses. It's closer to the sense of touch than any of the other senses, but there is nothing fleshly about it.

A horse whinnies somewhere behind us. Weapons clatter against armour. Soldiers shout.

"We're done for," says Emmet.

"Quiet." I drop down to a crouch, and Emmet follows suit, and the riders pass without spotting us.

There's less tree cover as we descend towards the plateau. We stop again when we come to the road. My senses are not acute enough to pick up moving objects; just gross features of the terrain. I listen carefully but I cannot hear the guards. We need to get out of here now. Even if we do manage to get away under cover of darkness, it's not going to be difficult for the guards to track us when the sun comes up. But we have little choice in the matter. Perhaps we'll chance on a portal I can open along the way.

I rise from my crouch and motion for Emmet to follow me, but after a couple of paces I realize that he's not following. I freeze on the spot. From the corner of my eye, I can see something huge and black looming behind me. I turn around slowly.

It's the black thing that followed us from the forest, sitting on a black horse. Mounted, the diminutive figure looks huge; like a pillar of shadow girded with black leather and buckles and knives. Emmet starts to scramble away, weighed down by the backpack, but a second black rider noses into the clearing, blocking his way.

"Oh, fuck me," says Emmet.

"Get on," says the first black thing, pointing to the space behind its saddle. I hesitate. "Get on, or we will leave you to your fates."

Emmet scrambles up behind the other rider, but I am not good with horses. The black thing offers me a stirrup and a hand. Despite its unexpected strength it doesn't have the leverage to haul me up onto the animal's back. The black thing hisses with impatience and a knife sprouts from between its fingers. Before I can recoil it reaches out and slashes the straps on my pack. Free of the encumbrance, and all of my possessions, I scramble up behind it.

Emmet is already sitting behind the other rider, pack and all. He looks pale. The black things spur their horses, and we surge away.

The ride is even bumpier and more nauseating than I remember from my previous horse-riding experience (does a pony ride at a summer festival count as experience?). The animal's muscles bunch and stretch between my legs; its flanks heave; its hooves strike the ground. I can smell its foetid horse-breath. But it does not snort or whicker, and its feet make no sound on the ground. The only thing I can hear is the air rushing by me and my own blood ringing in my ears.

We burst out of the tree cover and race over the lessening slope, angling across the slushy soil of the delta. I cannot see a horizon: it's as if the land just gradually blends up into the night sky.

Behind us, a dozen armed guards wheel off the curving road and charge down from the hill towards us, shouting in a language that might be English or might be Japanese or might be something else altogether. Ahead, the dark band of the horizon resolves into the dead trees of the black forest.

Our pursuers are closing fast. Their horses are swifter than our own black steeds, double-mounted as they are. I don't think we can make the black forest before they catch us. I hope and pray that they can't fire their bows or throw their spears while coming on so quickly.

"Can these things go any faster?" shouts Emmet, panicked.

"No," replies the black thing, "but the forest can."

The forest draws closer as we gallop towards it. The trees are somehow advancing, although I cannot see them individually moving. The trees proceed only in my peripheral vision. It's more like a great black tide coming in than an advancing army.

The guards draw up sharply and start to unlimber their bows. We continue to race onwards. The tree-line comes towards us.

The black thing kicks a final sprint out of our horse. Arrows zip past my head and I duck down and lean in, pressing against black thing's back so hard that I can feel the straps of its harness cutting into the side of my face. I have lost sight of Emmet—my eyes are shut—but I can hear him cursing.

And then we are in the forest. Even with eyes closed I can feel that the terrain underfoot is different. Were still moving, but there's a deathly stillness here; a lethargic calm that blankets my senses.

I exhale sharply and open my mouth to speak when something smashes into my right shoulder. My arm goes numb, and I slump forward. I'm hit.

The black thing reaches back and grabs me before I slide off the saddle. It hauls back on the reins, one-handed, and the horse canters to a stop. I can feel the animal's great chest heaving beneath me. Its flanks are wet, and I can smell its lather. I turn my head and see the shaft of the arrow sticking out of my shoulder like the stub of a broken wing. The pain, when it comes, is powerful enough to white out my vision.

The black thing turns in the saddle to look at me. "If I let you down from the horse, can you stand?" It has a hold of me by my collar.

"Yes." It takes me a moment to find the breath to speak. I'm full of adrenaline now, but blood loss will weaken me quickly. I hope the arrowhead isn't one of the shadowsteel pieces I saw in Rethe's warehouse. I wonder how I will explain the ensuing bout of monsterism to Michiko.

"Don't touch the ground or the trees with your bare skin. If you're going to fall or you need to sit, shout." The black thing dismounts and then helps me down from the horse.

The second black thing, already on foot, leads its horse around to us. Emmet follows it warily. "You alright?"

"I don't know. I've never been shot with an arrow before." I'm leaning against the horse for support, now. Pain comes in waves that make it hard to concentrate.

"Won't the riders follow us into the black forest?"

"Not at night," says the black thing, suddenly standing close enough to make me uncomfortable. "Probably not in the daylight, either." It turns to its companion. "Firewood."

The second black thing nods, bows, and silently vanishes into the forest. There's no underbrush, no deadfall, not even leaves upon the ground.

The first black thing moves suddenly. There's a sharp snapping sound, and then a fresh arc of pain that makes me gasp. He holds up the broken-off arrow shaft and waggles it in the air so the fletching quivers.

About an inch of wood still protrudes from the wound in my shoulder.

"*Itai!*" my squeal comes embarrassingly late. The sight of the wound is worse than the pain.

"I have to treat this," says the black thing. "It won't become infected in the Realms, but you will soon be crossing back to your own world."

"You'll take us back to the Door?"

"I'll bring a Door here."

The second black thing returns. It drops an armload of black wood and crouches to build up a small cone of kindling. The first black thing looks at it hard and says "burn," and it bursts into flame.

The first black thing grins at my astonishment. "Magic," it says. With a flourish, it produces a dagger from a hidden sheath and drops into a squat. It holds the blade in the fire, turning it over and over until it glows red, then yellow, and eventually white.

"Take off your shirt."

Emmet watches the proceedings quietly. He looks at the glowing knife, at the arrowhead in my shoulder, at the grinning black thing. "Oh, you're going to enjoy this part, you are."

The black thing grips my shoulder with one hand and raises the blade with the other. I can feel the heat from inches away. "Try not to move," it says. "I'm no surgeon and I'll not be gentle."

My skin sizzles as the knife goes in. I can smell the flesh burning. The black thing fishes around with the point, working the arrowhead out. I grit my teeth and hyperventilate and sweat profusely. Tears sting my eyes and I'm not sure if I sob or scream.

The arrowhead comes out with wet *pop*. I look down to see it bounce on the forest floor. In the firelight I can see that it's just ordinary steel. I'm still in a lot of pain, but at least one component of my anxiety ebbs away.

The black thing is still holding my shoulder. "I'm not done yet." I flinch away, but the black thing drags me back with irresistible strength. "Be still."

The flat of the white-hot blade against my bare skin is worse than the point of it digging through my muscle. "*Itai-yo!*" It's more of a creak in my vocal chords than an exclamation. Tears gush down my grimy cheeks. My cauterized wound continues to sizzle after the black thing withdraws the knife. It's going to leave an ugly scar.

When I have my breathing under control again, I wipe my eyes dry on the back of my hand.

"You did well," says the black thing, grinning. "For a mortal." It licks my crusted blood off the glowing, white-hot blade, spins the dagger over its knuckles, and makes it disappear.

Suddenly, I'm cold. I struggle back into my shredded shirt.

"So you're the Prince of Blood and Darkness, are you?" says Emmet.

"I am," says the black thing. "Some call me the Darkling in the Woods. Others name me the Black and Crimson King."

The black thing looks at me as if it's about to say something else, but Emmet interrupts. "That's a lot of titles."

"Indeed. Some I have earned; some I have been given. Others I have taken by guile or by force."

"But you've no territories, except the black forest?" says Emmet.

"The forest is bigger than you know, and growing," replies the black thing. "But you are correct. I have no court, no castle, no crown, no throne. I cannot yet face the Shaedow Empire in open warfare…but I grow stronger every day, and stronger yet by night."

"Why do you oppose the Empire?" asks Emmet. I want to shush him…it's dangerous to talk politics with a revolutionary…but it's all I can do not to weep from the pain of my wound.

"I do not oppose the Empire. I oppose the Emperor and Empress."

"You want it for yourself, then?"

"The Empire is mine by right of blood."

I wipe my eyes and clear my throat. Emmet ignores me, but the black thing turns his head in my direction. (I decide that he's male, since he calls himself a King.)

"Why did you help us?

"You did me a service," said the black thing. "Ghesnuk Rethe was negotiating an agreement to supply the Empire with shadowsteel weapons. Now that he is dead, I myself may enter negotiations."

Politics and commerce: the dirtiest partnership in any world.

"Thank you for your trouble. You saved our lives."

"Twice," says the black thing, evenly. "I believe that you are now in my debt."

"If there is any way I can repay you, I will." I feel obliged to say it, even though I know it's a bad idea.

"A man of your talents is always useful," says the black thing. "A killer of men and an Opener of Doors. I am certain that further opportunities will arise for us to do business."

"I do not plan to return here any time soon."

"The Faerie Realms are connected to many, many worlds," says the black thing. "And you are a Traveller. You'll be back."

The black thing puts a foot in a stirrup and swings back up onto his horse. His companion has already remounted its steed. "Enjoy the rest of your evening, gentlemen. I will see you again."

The black horses wheel about and vanish into the darkness, silent as shadows.

"Well, that was fucking charming," says Emmet.

The Door is nearby, as the black thing promised. Emmet adjusts his pack, and we strike out towards it. He is morose and the silence becomes awkward, so against my better judgment, I try to strike up a conversation.

"Are you pleased you got to see this place again?"

"Let's just say I'm keen to get back to my theme park."

I stop a few meters from the Door. It's closed, so I doubt that Emmet can perceive it. He fidgets uncomfortably; keen to be on his way. I grit my teeth and set my jaw.

"What is it now?" says Emmet.

I hold my stomach and put on a queasy expression. "I don't think the firebird stew agreed with me."

"Or maybe it was the outdoor surgery, conducted by a monster," Emmet suggests. "Can you hold it in for another minute, until we're safe in the real world?"

"I don't think so." I look around at the deadly trees, the lethal dirt. "And it's more private here."

Emmet grins. "Rather not shit yourself in a churchyard, eh?" He unclips the entrenching tool from where it hangs from his pack and offers it to me. "Go on. There's not many people can claim to have taken a bog in the black forest."

I start unbuckling my belt. "Do you have any toilet paper left? There aren't any leaves."

"No," he says, turning his back. "You'll just have to live with skidmarks until we get back to the B&B."

I smash the folded shovel into the back of Emmet's neck. He cries out, raises his arms, stumbles. I kick out his feet from under him and he falls. When he hits the dirt, his skin begins to darken.

Blackness seeps up into his hands and face, liquefying his flesh; eating through his clothes and dissolving his bones. It takes no more than ten seconds for him to collapse into a puddle of shadow. Another ten seconds and there is nothing left at all.

My gauntlet is still in the pack I lost in my flight from Ghesnuk Rethe's citadel, but the Door is much easier to open from this side. Or perhaps I'm getting better at this. The whorl in the fabric of the world parts beneath my fingers and I pull until there's a gap big enough for me to step through into the churchyard outside of Tramore.

There's no way I could have allowed Emmet to return with me, knowing as much about me as he does. I suppose he was a friend, and that I should feel bad, but all I really feel like is a shower. My watch says it's 9pm. My shirt is stuck to my shoulder, which is still wet and oozing.

I tramp the miles to the hill where I buried my luggage. I dig it up with the entrenching tool—not easy with only one functional arm. I'm relieved that the roller suitcase is still dry once I have stripped off the plastic wrapping.

I wipe myself down as best I can with a packet of wet wipes; spray on a generous amount of deodorant. The chemicals sting my burned shoulder. I still look like I slept in a hedge, but at least I don't smell like I slept in an abattoir. I put on a clean shirt (it has clover leaves and pineapples on it) and pack the old one away in a plastic bag, until I can find a rubbish bin for it. I've just murdered a friend, but I cannot bear the thought of littering.

Dragging my suitcase behind me, I walk down the road with my thumb in the air.

I take a room in a chain motel near the airport. I stand under the shower for about forty-five minutes before I go to bed. The pain from my shoulder makes it difficult to sleep, even after I wash down a fistful of painkillers with half a bottle of convenience store whisky.

Early the next morning I get a taxi to Waterford Airport for a puddle-jump to Luton. I transfer from Luton to Heathrow, where I have a five-hour layover before my flight home to Tokyo. The wound in my shoulder itches and oozes, although I have treated it with burn cream and bandaged it. I'm still not sure how I will explain it to my doctor, much less to Michiko.

In one of the terminal bookstores, I see a familiar book: *Doors and Ways*, edited by Raethe Marghison. The same paperback edition I have…or had. It was in the backpack with my gauntlet. I buy a copy.

I was reluctant to read the book before, but now that I have bought myself a second copy, I feel obliged. I felt embarrassed when Emmet questioned me about my abilities and this book is the only lead I have, unless I return to Sugdike. So I find a quiet place in the gate lounge and steel myself to read all of that English.

It's still difficult work, and I find myself flipping backwards and forward through the text, chasing threads, rereading sections that I previously skipped over. I circle the passages that seem to make more sense. I underline particular phrases, dog-ear some pages. The book is still in my hand when I board the plane.

I plan to continue studying on the flight, but once I'm in my seat with the book in my lap, I find that I'm far too tired. I cover it with my hands and close my eyes. Perhaps I will dream of Faerie Land; perhaps I will dream nothing at all. One thing's for certain: when I wake up, I will be home in Tokyo, where my fiancée is waiting for me. This story does have a fairytale ending, after all.

#6: The Wild Hunt

stranger holding a placard with my name on it is waiting for me when I come out of passport control at Mesra City International.

Unfolded Enterprises has never before been so imprudent as to send someone to meet me in public, here in their home city. If they were to send somebody, I would have expected it to be Rambo-san. Perhaps he is angry with me because I ditched him in Menlat Nir. Perhaps he's away on a different mission. Perhaps he slipped in the shower and hit his head.

Perhaps, possibly, maybe. This is unusual, and my suspicions are aroused.

The man with the placard looks at me uncertainly. He has the dark skin and pale eyes of a local, but he is dressed in a Brooks Brothers suit that was tailored for him in the Conventional Earth. He is wearing a chauffeur's cap and white gloves. I bet his name is James. I give him a small bow and wave away his stuttering offer to take my baggage.

James leads me to a VTOL limousine cab. I have never been in one of these before. Outside of Japan, all taxi drivers are suicidal lunatics, and the thought of a riding this city's looping, multi-strata expressways with some Unfolded Earth kamikaze at the wheel makes me nauseous.

I get inside and close my eyes.

ames pilots the limousine to our destination smoothly and without offering conversation. I will be pleased if he is Rambo-san's permanent replacement. He sets the vehicle down outside a shabby-looking restaurant in a part of Mesra City I have never visited before. Dingy plastic buildings; discoloured roof tiles; exposed plumbing; bizarre-looking antennae. It's not a slum, but it's definitely the low end of town.

"Mister is inside waiting for you," says James. "You can leave your luggage with me."

I have no questions as to the identity of Mister. There's only one person here who would have sent a cosplay English chauffeur to collect me at the airport. After he lets me out of the car, James gets behind the wheel and settles in to wait; double-parked out front of the restaurant with his hazard lights on. It looks like this is going to be a short meeting. I would fear for my life, if Mister hadn't made all this conspicuous fuss with the driver and the limousine.

The maître d' is wearing shorts and a tank top. He approaches and says something to me in Karachidaean. In English I reply, "Mister?"

"English," says the maître d', and guides me to a table at the back of the room where my boss, the Englishman, is waiting.

Jonathon is wearing the smug look of a Londoner on holiday in some warmer clime where the currency favours the pound sterling. He is alone tonight; no sign of Vashya or his usual bodyguards.

"Have a seat, Mr Zai." He does not get up or shake my hand. I bow and take the offered seat.

"I'm afraid I'll have to keep this brief. The clock is ticking on this one. Tick, tick, tick." Jonathon pauses and looks over my shoulder. "Ah, here we are."

A waiter is approaching with a small steel bowl containing a dessert that appears to be made of dry ice and mushrooms. Or maybe it's a soup. The waiter looks at me, but Jonathon waves him off. "This gentleman won't be staying."

That is fine with me. I just want to get to the hotel and shower off my plane trip.

Jonathon tucks into his dessert soup with a spoon. "So tell me, Mr Zai, do you feel up to killing a god?" Vapour oozes from his mouth when he speaks.

I try not to show it, but I am not keen on the idea. High profile targets draw too much attention. I am much happier murdering everyday people and staying out of prison.

Jonathon flips me a photograph of a line drawing. A one-eyed man wearing a wide-brimmed hat and a long beard. "You recognize this character?"

"No."

"His name is Odin...or Wotan, or Woden. Like that. He used to be the All-Father of Norse myth, but he fucked that right up, and...well, that's why you're here, isn't it?"

I nod politely, although I'm completely uninterested in this appraisal of my contact's character.

"The other gods in his pantheon—the Aesir—demoted him to a sort of folk hero. This led to a few episodes of self-mutilation, and, eventually, a suicide attempt. I guess he just wanted some attention." I wish Jonathon would hurry up and get to the point. He takes a moment to grin at me around his mouthful, enjoying my impatience as much as his food. "It worked, unfortunately. Odin's not the man he was, but he has made a bit of a comeback."

"He is still a god?"

"Yes, not to mention a world class arsehole. And he has a growing contingent of equally arseholish worshippers, and that's why our client wants him removed."

"Where can I find him?"

Jonathon flips a plastic envelope stuffed with tickets across the table to me. "These tickets will get you right up close," says Jonathon. "He's leading a Wild Hunt, and there are only limited places available."

"A Wild Hunt?"

"Odin really is down on his luck," says Jonathon. "He needs gold and glory like a diabetic needs insulin, so he's going to lead a band of wealthy tourists on a pillage-and-plunder raid through the skies of scenic Northern Europe, followed by drinks and dinner against a backdrop of the aurora borealis."

The job is starting to sound a bit more plausible. A hit scheduled to take place in a remote part of the world. All of the witnesses will be violent thrill-seekers. The contact is himself a mythical being, so there's unlikely to be an investigation into his death from conventional agencies. Still…he is a god. Somebody is bound to notice when he is dead. But I cannot refuse this mission. This is the problem with working for somebody else.

I take the envelope and inspect the contents. A fistful of airline tickets, an itinerary, and a small stone with a rune scratched onto it.

"The hunt departs from the *Dimmuborgir* in Iceland," said Jonathon. "Pickup is at 9pm on the fifteenth, local time."

I blink a couple of times. "Three days."

Jonathon grins. "On your bike, then, sunshine. James will take you back to the airport."

The return itinerary to the conventional world is not as bad as the one that brought me here, but going straight back to transit without even a proper meal makes it twice as miserable. By the time I hit Austin

I'm starving. Worse, I've got severe diarrhoea from eating nothing but airline food for fifty-six hours.

I spend the first half of my three-hour layover in the toilet. Then I stagger into the first restaurant I see and order big. I already have diarrhoea, so what does it matter?

The food is processed Tex-Mex chain restaurant fare, but it's so delicious after all that airline slop that I buy a souvenir t-shirt and a bottle of hot sauce on the way out.

By the time I land in Reykjavik, I am delirious from sleep deprivation, dehydration and minor food poisoning. I'm also starting to worry about my job.

Jonathon briefing me in a public place is ridiculously risky. Something is going on at Unfolded Enterprises—but it's far above my level. All I can do is put my head down and do the job and hope that whatever it is blows over.

Still, here I am in Iceland. It's not as exotic as Menlat Nir or post-apocalyptic Faerie Land, but it is a new country. Perhaps I will find a way to enjoy myself yet.

But first, I need to sleep.

Jonathon has arranged a rental car for me at Reykjavik airport. I'm supposed to drive it to the other side of the island to my accommodation at a bed-and-breakfast, which itself is an hour's drive from the rendezvous point.

I throw away the car voucher and check into the airport hotel. In my room, I pop five Lomotil and three Ibuprofen tablets, take a long, hot shower, and collapse in bed for fifteen hours.

The following morning, I still cannot face breakfast. I have a coffee and three glasses of water at the hotel buffet, and then I take the shuttle back to the airport.

First stop is the gift shop, where I pick out a bulky anorak with fur on the cuffs and the hood. It's like something Han Solo would wear, but with cute walruses printed all over it. I add a ski cap, a neck warmer, a pair of gloves, some thermal underwear, and a prepaid mobile phone.

Then I go looking for the information desk so find out about chartering a helicopter.

Waiting for the chopper in a glassed-in shack near the helipad, I notice that I am feeling something unusual. It takes me a few moments to work out what it is.

I'm angry.

I am not an emotional person. Sometimes I get annoyed or grumpy, but it is very rare for me to experience anything as intense as anger. That is what makes me good at my job. I do not enjoy seeing others suffer, although I admit that suffering does not particularly offend me, either. I do not believe in justice or karma; good or evil. I have never felt the need to revenge slights or indignities. But this? Flying all the way to Mesra City and then sending me straight back to the airport?

I do not kill personal acquaintances, for a number of very good reasons, but, if the need were to arise, I would happily make an exception for Jonathon.

Anger is not enough to keep boredom at bay. The wifi is good here, so I take out my burner phone and Google my contact. May as well do some research; this guy might be dangerous. He is a god, after all.

I skim the first paragraphs of the Wikipedia entry for Odin, but it's not very interesting. The Father of Victory. Never lost a battle. If Odin has any weaknesses, besides being blind in one eye, I cannot guess what they might be. Fortunately, I have no intention of engaging him in single combat. I have no idea how I am going to pull this off, but I'm certain I will figure something out.

Iceland is a more interesting topic. The geography, the sights, the people, the cuisine. Next time I am in a bookshop I will buy a Lonely Planet guide.

The chopper flight isn't going to be long, and the weather is good, so the pilot offers to show me some highlights on the way to the rendezvous. There is a lot to see: glaciers and fjords; volcanoes; waterfalls; barren arctic deserts. Green and grey and black; a lot less snow than I had expected. The days here are short in winter, but it takes a long time for what light there is to vanish altogether. I take nearly a gigabyte of photos through the cabin windows.

Eventually the chopper sets down at the rendezvous site, the *Dimmuborgir*, which the pilot tells me means 'Dark Fort': a massive and jagged formation of volcanic rock. It is beautiful and threatening despite the fact that, tonight, it's lit up by with garish coloured spotlights. According to the pilot, trolls and monsters are reputed to live in the caves below the ground. I wrinkle my nose against the stink. Apparently, the chimneys issue clouds of sulphur.

I take a dozen more photos before I climb down out of the cabin.

There are eleven tourists waiting on the scree, huddled under a temporary shelter where a noisy diesel generator provides electricity for the lights and heaters. Germans, Scandinavians, a clutch of Britons and Americans, a Polish skinhead in a Nazi greatcoat. All of them are men.

My arrival by helicopter does not impress anybody. None of the others greet me when I sidle up to the shelter and try stamping the cold out of my legs.

A cheerful man wearing a name badge emerges from behind the shelter and waddles over. Jonas. When I show him my ticket, Jonas claps his hands and says, "Oh good, we're all here!" He turns to the crowd and says, "Welcome to the *Dimmuborgir*!" He repeats this in German, and I think, in Danish.

A smattering of glove-muffled applause.

"The Wanderer will be here soon with your mounts and weapons, and then the hunt will commence," Jonas continues. "Tonight, you are his *Oskorei*!"

The applause is louder this time.

"Once you are underway, the Wanderer will lead you around the south coast, across the Norwegian and Northern Seas, and then over Deutschland, Danmark, and Polska. You will pass over the Baltic Sea, along the west coast of Finland, across the northern latitudes of Sverige and on to Norge.

"There will be periodic stops where you are encouraged to wreak whatever mayhem you desire with your special weapons.

"During your flight, you will experience time dilation effects similar to those which Father Christmas is said to undergo. This will be a fabulous and exhilarating experience that I am sure you will be telling your friends and family about for many years to come—if they only will believe you!" Jonas slaps his belly and laughs. There are a few chuckles, but nobody is here to enjoy the comedy routine.

"The Hunt will end in Norge with a meal by the Northern Lights, and an opportunity to socialize with the Father of Victory in an informal setting. We will be serving a traditional reindeer stew, and if you managed to secure any game our chefs will help you to cook that as well. There is also a vegetarian option."

"The All-Father will then depart and a *hubschrauber* will transport you and your trophies safely back to Reykjavik."

The group have a lot of questions for the guide. I keep to myself: I am still tired, and I am not remotely interested in the animals or the weapons or the '*hubschrauber*,' whatever that is.

Suddenly, the group falls silent. A spotlight swivels and I turn around to see what everyone else is looking at: a lone figure walking up the road, leaning on a spear. A tall man wearing a long coat and a broad-brimmed hat. The figure comes towards us, slow but sure-footed on the incline.

Despite the staged entrance, Odin cuts an impressive figure. Seven feet tall, with long, grey-blonde hair; grim-faced and self-assured. His face is a livid red mess around his missing eye, but the remaining orb gleams brightly, and seems unusually mobile in its socket. I am surprised at the stubbly chin: all of the illustrations I've seen show Odin wearing a beard. He reeks of blood and leather.

Odin does not greet us. He turns his head towards the *Dimmuborgir*, raises his spear and slams the butt on the ground.

Sulphurous steam billows from the rocks and I cover my nose and mouth with my collar. Thunder rumbles beneath a high-pitched shrieking. Twelve beasts gallop down out of the sky: mostly horses, but there are a couple of boars and a particularly ugly goat. Their iron-shod hooves strike sparks from the rocky ground. The animals snort and snuffle into a semicircle behind Odin; their breath steaming; tongues of flame, and coils of lightning playing over their hides.

Odin indicates that we should form up. When we have shuffled into something resembling a single rank, the Wanderer opens his coat and produces a short, heavy sword made of soft iron. He gives this to the first person in the queue, who bows timidly and accepts it.

Odin makes his way down the line, handing out swords and spears and axes, which he draws from inside his unnaturally capacious coat. One hunter gets a bow and a quiver of arrows. The Polish skinhead accepts a heavy mace, but he takes the time to show Odin that he has brought along his own weapon: an AK-47 carved with Norse runes and swastikas. Odin acknowledges it with an approving nod.

I am at the very end of the line. When it's my turn, I smile up at the All-Father as if I don't quite understand what's going on.

Odin gives me a look of derision and produces a long knife, which he offers to me. I shake my head and open my anorak.

"*Kamera.*" I point to the instrument hanging around my neck and nod vigorously. "I will take photo!"

Odin curls his lip puts the knife away. He would rather have disembowelled me with it.

Now that we are all appropriately armed, Odin directs each person in the line to a particular mount. Jonas and his helpers fuss about, helping those of us who are not trained cavalrymen get ready for the hunt.

My mount is the smallest and tamest of the beasts. When Jonas comes to assist me, I ask him what kind of goat it is.

Jonas shakes his head. "This is not a goat," he says. "It's a special Icelandic sheep." I cannot tell if he is joking or not.

It takes some effort to get situated on my hunting sheep. The animal is quite compliant, but I am not much of a rider, even after my recent experience in the Shaedow realms. Once my feet are in the stirrups Jonas helps to secure me with additional nylon straps, buckles, karabiners and Velcro tabs.

I am the last one to be ready. The animals paw at the ground while Odin discards his hat and shrugs off his tattered coat. He stands there bare-chested in the firelight, posing for the crowd. His hide is lean and hairless and covered in scar tissue.

"*Sleipnir!*" he commands. His voice is high pitched and musical, with an undertone of menace.

An eight-legged steed appears behind him, rising from a crevasse in the earth that was not there before he spoke. The beast is bigger than a Clydesdale; but sleeker even than the Black and Crimson King's horses. But this is not a horse. The longer I look, the more it seems to resemble an octopus. Or a spider. Shadows leak from its unblinking yellow eyes. Its mouth-beak is filled with triangular teeth.

Odin gives me a disapproving, one-eyed stare when I start snapping photos, but he does nothing to prevent me. He climbs onto Sleipnir's back and waves his spear overhead. "*Oskorei*, we fly! Let the Wild Hunt begin!"

I have to stow the camera and grab onto the reins with both hands as my battle sheep canters into the sky. We are the last to leave the ground.

The Wild Hunt is a lot more sedate than expected. There is no wind, despite the ridiculous speeds at which we are moving; nor is there a shortage of oxygen, despite the altitude. It's not even particularly cold—in fact I'm feeling a bit overheated in my anorak. The hunters chatter amongst themselves in their cliques as our mounts canter across the firmament.

As we skirt along the coast of Iceland and head out over the sea, I am able to observe the ground with perfect clarity. We pass over some fishing trawlers that do not appear to be moving, despite the thick plumes of wake behind them. We must be in some kind of a time dilation bubble. I can feel the weft of reality rippling around us, but it is unlike flying on the Way to Karachidor. I think that Odin—or perhaps his mount, Sleipnir—is carving a Way as we fly. I did not think this was possible, but I suppose that Odin is a god, after all.

My own senses are a lot more acute than before my trip into Faerie Land. Perhaps being immersed in such a magic-rich environment has helped to calibrate them better. Perhaps it's just the benefit of practice.

Our first stop is an oil rig. Odin leads us towards it in a curving descent; shrieking a high-pitched song in some old Norse tongue. Gouts of fire crackle around Sleipnir as we drop down out of the magical bubble that has kept us alive and healthy at altitude. Re-entry is uncomfortably warm, but it seems that the god and his steed have absorbed most of the heat for us. Once we have decelerated through it there is wind and cold and motion again. My animal's hooves clatter audibly against the sky as if it was cobbled like a road.

The hunters scream and laugh and hack and stab at the pylons and cables of the structure as we roar past it. We wheel about and come back for another pass. My mount follows the party without my guidance. All I have do is hang on.

A couple of beardy riggers stumble out onto the deck area, confused and sleepy. The Polishman tries to bring his AK-47 around, but he gets the butt tangled in the reins and it tumbles out of his grip. The weapon vanishes into the sea with barely a splash. At least I do not have to worry about friendly fire any more. It's also one less option for executing my mission.

One of the Swedes hacks at a rigger with an axe, taking off most of the man's arm. When we come around for a second pass Odin skewers the uninjured rigger with his spear. He slings the corpse across Sleipnir's saddle and frees the spear with one hand, keeping the other on the reins. I cannot get any good photographs—the Germans keep getting in my way.

The Wild Hunt rides on into the night, screaming with joy and fury. I wonder how much longer this is going to last.

We storm a small Bavarian village. We destroy a large section of the Øresundsbroen bridge-tunnel, which connects southern Sweden to northern Denmark by road and rail. We demolish a hamlet in Poland. We raze a ski resort in Finland. We obliterate a Sami village in the Lappish part of Sweden and then, finally, we cross over the border into Norway.

Most of the other hunters have managed to make some kind of kill, and many of them have trophies, but Odin is the only one who has managed to haul a complete carcass back with him.

The battery on my camera is completely depleted.

The terminus of the Wild Hunt is a remote fjord on the Norwegian coast, facing out onto the Barents Sea. The bonfire is already going. There are picnic tables, benches, a latrine block, and a temporary kitchen. The chef is wearing a white toque and earmuffs.

Jonas is waiting for us in front of the bonfire. The 'hubschrauber' — a well-appointed Sikorsky Skyhook — is standing off to one side and the pilots are leaning against it, smoking cigarettes. The aurora borealis shimmers in the distance; like disco lights behind a wet shower curtain.

Sleipnir hits the ground first. Odin is on his own two feet well before the rest of us alight. I am the last one to dismount. Jonas helps unclip me from my saddle and I climb down off my hunting sheep.

The hunters are still giddy with excitement. They rush around laughing and shouting, high-fiving and chest-bumping each other, waving their weapons and recalling the highlights of the hunt. The Swedes glance at me a few times, sniggering, but nobody else pays me any attention. When Jonas announces that the bar is open and the mead is hot, there is a stampede.

I stand and look at the Northern Lights, but not for very long. I have seen them before, and the view was better in Canada.

Odin is also hanging back from the others. I give him a thumbs-up and fumble out my camera. The battery is dead, but I'm more interested to see what he does than I am in taking another photo of him. Odin turns his back on me and stalks off to retrieve the corpse of the oil rigger slung across Sleipnir's back. Sleipnir growls something discourteous at him and he growls back. In this light, he looks more like a spider-horse than an octopus-horse.

I join the line of drunken hunters for the buffet. The Polish skinhead, I notice, is the only one who opts for the vegetarian meal. I'm starving; I haven't eaten anything substantial in days. My stomach feels ok for the first time in days. "More, please," I ask the chef when he spoons a pile of chunky reindeer stew and roast potatoes onto my plate. I wave away the slice of bread he offers with it: I can tell from looking that it's far too crusty for my taste.

Odin is making the rounds, asking everybody how they enjoyed the hunt and thanking them for their comradeship. The words are scripted and he speaks them bitterly. We are not true *Oskorei*, we're a bunch of tourists and he resents having to ride with us. I wonder idly why he agreed to this in the first place. Will none of the real monsters hunt with him anymore? Does he just need the money?

Odin's camaraderie grows more and more threadbare as he moves amongst the crowd, meeting his obligations to the tourist company under Jonas' watchful gaze. The Wanderer's single eye glitters with anger.

I still have to find a way to kill him.

But first, I need to eat. I am suddenly ravenous. I find an isolated spot by the fire to sit and dig in. I have shovelled down three mouthfuls and almost swallowed my spork before I notice how bland the food tastes.

I eat a couple more mouthfuls while looking around to see if anybody has a salt cellar or a pepper pot, but then I remember that I have something better.

I open the little bottle of hot sauce that I bought in Austin and stir some of its contents into the stew carefully, because it's marked Extra Hot. I taste it, add some more, and stir it again. I am just about to put another sporkful in my mouth when I realize that I have company.

Odin is standing over me, arms folded, seething with rage. "What are you doing?" he demands in a musical English that is all the more comical for his anger.

"Making flavour?" I give him the big smile that goes with the pidgin.

"There is not enough *flavour* for you?"

I look away in contemplation, then look back at the seven-foot-tall Norse god. "Eh…so-so."

"This food has nourished generations of hunters," Odin snarls. "Warriors and rapists and killers and *gods*. But it does not have enough flavour for *you*?"

"Not enough flavour," I agree, nodding and then shaking my head.

Odin thrusts his face into mine and jabs at me with one long, bony finger. "You insult my hospitality? In my own lodge? After I have shared a hunt with you?" Flecks of his spittle scald my face.

I blink at him. "This sauce is most delicious." I hold up the little bottle. It has a picture of a cowboy on the label. "Do you wanna try some?"

Odin's mouth works, but he can't find anything to say. His shoulders bunch. He's trying to decide if this slight is enough to warrant him slapping my head off my shoulders, which will no doubt cost him reparations to the tour company. I reach up and throw some hot sauce into his single staring eye.

Odin lurches away, screaming. He thrashes and stomps around, clawing helplessly at his face. Drunken tourists scatter. I drop my plate in my haste to get away from him.

The former All-Father backs into the bonfire, but he doesn't seem to notice—his skin does not burn in ordinary flames. Chilli oil, however, seems to be quite effective.

Odin staggers around in a circle, wracked with agony. He bellows for water in half a dozen different Germanic languages, but nobody has the courage to approach him. I am still trying to work out what to do next when the spear hits him in the face.

The spearhead smashes clear through the back of his head. Odin goes over backwards, and lands propped up by the shaft of the spear, which is now embedded half a meter deep in the dirt.

Sleipnir is standing up on two legs, with six tentacle-arms extended to give him maximum surface area. He no longer looks like a spider, an octopus, *or* a horse. He is something far older and more terrible than a patchwork of animal parts.

Sleipnir grabs the butt of the spear, puts one foot on Odin's chest, and hauls the weapon free of the god's ruined face.

"For fifteen centuries you rode me like I was some *beast*." Sleipnir addresses the corpse in English. He spits. "*Gungnir* is mine, now, and so, too, is your life."

I suppose that solves my problem.

Sleipnir turns to me. "Little human, I owe you a turn. Call me and I will come, for I do not forget my debts."

I don't know if I should take 'little human' as an ethnic slur or not, but I bow and thank him anyway. "How shall I call you?"

The horse god flips a small stone to me. I catch it and turn it over in my palm.

"My rune is Ehwaz."

I bow again. When I straighten up, Sleipnir has risen off the ground. His grey skin darkens to black...or perhaps it becomes translucent to the night sky. He vanishes into darkness; restored in some measure to his godhood and his power.

I bend to pick up the bottle of hot sauce where I dropped it. By some miracle it is still intact.

The hunting party is quite subdued while Jonas and his crew clear up the mess and collect the weapons. I ask the chef for another plate of stew and a new spork. It's pretty tasty, with the addition of the hot sauce.

Eventually, the rotors of the Sikhorsky spin up and Jonas directs us to climb aboard. I am the first one into the chopper and nobody wants to sit near me, so I have room to stretch out my legs—a blessing. I am saddle sore from having ridden a sheep all across the northern skies.

There are two hard-eyed Karachidaeans waiting for me when I get back to Keflavik International Airport.

I do not recognize them, so far out of the context, and it gives me a moment of vertigo when I realize they are Vashya's bodyguards. Aside from Rambo-san, I have never seen Karachidaeans travel anywhere outside of Karachidor.

This is bad.

One of the bodyguards takes my suitcase and the other leads me to a waiting Humvee. Neither of them says a word to me but somehow that seems preferable to a halting conversation in my beginner's Karachidaean. I am certain that neither of them speaks English.

We sit quietly in the Hum Vee for about forty minutes as it winds up into the mountains. The sky is a brilliant blue and the terrain is a brilliant white.

Eventually we pull up outside a modern, angular building: four stories of pale wood and mirrored glass. A spa hotel. The two guards escort me inside. My baggage remains in the car.

The lobby is tiled with polished slate. The artificial lighting is bright and cold. There is nobody manning the reception desk, nobody waiting to check in or out, nobody browsing the rack of tourist flyers, but the place does not feel deserted. It feels like it is holding its breath.

In the elevator one of the Karachidaeans enters a code on a keypad embedded below in a brass plate. I close my eyes and the elevator begins to rise. I do not open them again until the door opens.

A freezing wind ruffles my hair and my clothes as we step out onto the roof. Beside the penthouse, there is an enclosure containing an Olympic-sized swimming pool. Condensation makes the glass walls opaque. The guards march me inside.

We pass another guard and skirt our way around the pool. Vashya is waiting for me, sitting on the wooden slat bench near the change rooms. Two more guards bracket her.

Something is odd about the water vapour. When I wave my hand through it the sensation is cold and tingly.

"Zai, it is a spy filter, Zai." Vashya makes a vibrating gesture with her hand. "Nanites."

"Ah."

"Sit." Vashya indicates a space beside her on the bench. I do as I am told.

There's a silence. Then, "Zai, why here are you, Zai?"

I am not ready for such an existential question. "It's the closest airport to my mission?"

"Zai, you have a mission, Zai?"

"I just killed the god Odin."

Vashya looks at me gravely. "Jonathon sent you."

I nod once and make an affirmative "n" sound.

"Zai, he has left our organization, Zai."

"Has he retired?"

"Zai, I do not think so, Zai."

I think about that for a moment longer. "This mission. The Wild Hunt. That was not for Unfolded Enterprises."

"For Jonathon only." Her face darkens. "My resources, his mission."

When I get back to Japan, I will need to change my information drop. How much else about my life—my real life—can Jonathon access? At a minimum, he knows what I look like. He knows I live in Tokyo. He knows Federico.

What are his intentions now? Was this mission a final Fuck You to Unfolded Enterprises from a disgruntled ex-employee? I wonder how Unfolded Enterprises will react. They have been compromised just as badly as I have. I suppose a re-organization is order.

"Zai, go home, Zai," says Vashya. "This is not your problem. I will call you on when need you, I."

I stand up and give her a crisp bow. "Hai." I bow again from the doorway and then back out.

I killed a god today over some office politics. Regardless of what Vashya says, this is already my problem.

#7: Shin Edo

Ikari had been to many bad places, but this new version of Edo was by far the worst.

Its glass and concrete towers sprawled across the Kanto plain, choking the rivers; purging filth into the sea; sullying the skies and tainting the righteous sun. Sharp-angled buildings constructed from coarse, unnatural materials; strung about with rubberized wires and daubed with obscene swathes of neon. Sometimes he caught a glimpse of the city's true character showing through—here was a garden, there a shrine—but these were sad places, desecrated and unhallowed. This place, with its traffic and its stinking, teeming streets…this new Edo was an affront to the soul.

Worse yet were its people.

The respectable classes dressed like foreign merchants. The peasantry paraded around in boots and furs and synthetic fabrics, plastered with slogans written in barbarian script. Their skins were painted. Their hair was dyed and teased-up and ridiculous. The men looked like women and the women looked like whores. The people were children; jabbering to each other in an abbreviated version of Ikari's own magisterial tongue; punctuating it with jarringly singsong phrases and words stolen from uncouth foreign languages.

Not one of them wore a sword. Ikari's own sword was secured in the black canvas bag that his client had given him, because it was illegal to carry weapons openly in this terrible place. Ikari was no samurai, but he respected the warrior class for their traditions; their dedication; their skills. He respected their blades. There was no one in *this* Edo worthy of his respect.

Niklas was leaning against a wall, examining a map he had unfolded from a tourist brochure. "I think we should take the subway," said the big Finn, speaking in English, gesturing towards the subway entrance across the road. "It's only two stops, but these streets are a maze."

Ikari was displeased by Niklas' presence. One target, two assassins. It was wasteful and foolish. Ikari would speak to his master when he returned to the true country. It was demeaning to work with such barbarians. It was demeaning to take their coin.

Niklas was already halfway down the stairs. Ikari looked past him, into the mouth of the fetid tunnels where the city's degenerate inhabitants crowded into grimy carriages for transport. The Finn looked back over his shoulder, but Ikari shook his head.

"You take the subway. I will walk."

It's a lovely spring day in Tokyo.

The summer has cooled off, but the chill of winter has not yet arrived. I have my umbrella, of course, but I don't expect I will need it today.

All the characters are out, resplendent in their costumes: *sararimen* and students, delinquents and doormen, mutants and mothers-in-law. This is my home, my city; the place to which I will always return, no matter how far I travel. This is the best place in the world.

Today I am on a particularly challenging mission. While my Michiko rushes around organizing celebrants and cakes and reception halls and time at the photo studio, my job is to arrange the honeymoon. I am thrilled that, for once, I will get to book my own travel.

But first, I have a meeting.

Federico and I are in a cafe on the first basement level of the Omotesando Hills shopping mall, drinking coffee and eating cake. This place was new the first time he came to Tokyo, and he insists on coming here every time he's in town. I never miss the opportunity to see him— he is one of a very small number of people who knows who I really am, and the only one among that number I can truly consider a friend.

"I'm going for another slice. Can I get you something?" I speak English to Federico, because the Portuguese lilt in his Japanese embarrasses me almost as much as his shirt blazoned with the Brazilian flag and board shorts. He has certainly put on weight since I last saw him

"I'm on a diet, Zai," he replies in Japanese. Federico refers to me by my alias, sans honorific, because he thinks it's hilarious. Federico has retired on the finder's fee from Unfolded Enterprises and now he does nothing but lounge around resort hotels, stuffing his face.

"You look hungry, Federico-san, and the *Monburan* is amazing."

"I am hungry. And fat. Please don't ask me again, in case I say yes."

"Suit yourself." I get up and head for the service counter. I am absolutely not going to leave without consuming another slice of *Monburan* chestnut cream cake.

I am at the front of the line to order when the big gaijin walks in. I know it's rude to say gaijin, or even to think it, but something about this one just screams it. A modern-day barbarian.

I have been all over this world. I have been to places that do not, cannot, and should not exist. I have gone amongst blue people and red people; aliens and faeries; gods and demons. I do not find foreigners to be particularly stare-worthy, even when I am home in Japan, where gaijin-watching is a national pass time. But there is something about this one that draws my notice. Something about the razor-cut and the sunglasses and the sheer size of him. He looks like he has come tripping out of a 1980s action movie.

The gaijin looks around purposefully. I see his eyes alight on Federico. The fat Japanese-Brazilian, with his deep sun tan and loud shirt, is a natural centre for attention. Federico looks up at the gaijin and smiles uneasily.

The girl behind the counter bobs her head patiently while I pretend to vacillate over the cakes in the glass case and hope that Federico doesn't tip the gaijin to my presence. Out of the corner of my eye I see the gaijin approaching our table. Time to go, before he works out that I am still here.

I bite my lip regretfully and bow to the girl at the counter. "I'm sorry. It looks delicious, but I'm too full."

I bow again, and she bows to me, and I make for the exit. If the gaijin is part of a professional crew, he probably has a partner, but I cannot see any other suspicious-looking foreigners loitering nearby.

Federico shouts "Hey!" and I know the gaijin is onto me. I dive through the automatic doors barely a second before the gunfire starts.

Niklas was a heavy hitter who liked to shoot people, but this was not the sort of job he enjoyed.

Point him at a building and ask him to kill every living thing inside it? That was playing to Niklas' strengths. Give him a sniper rifle and a spotter to light up the target? That would also work. Give him a machete and lock him in a cage with a couple of other thugs? He wasn't a hand-to-hand fighter like little Ikari, but Niklas was big and tough and vicious, and he would get the job done. Send him to Tokyo to find a man described as 'average height, Japanese'? This was not the kind of work with which Niklas was comfortable.

Then, there was his partner.

Ikari should have been the one going in first. He knew the language and he could pass for a local. But he wouldn't ride the subway. On the other hand, Niklas was actually a bit relieved to be rid of him. He just didn't trust the little guy. Ikari didn't say much, but he was clearly furious 100% of the time. The last thing Niklas wanted was to see Ikari running up the walls and slicing open everyone that pissed him off. As best Niklas could tell, that was everyone the guy had ever laid eyes upon.

The only good intel they had was on one of the target's associates. The Brazilian was easy to spot, but he was alone when Niklas had barged into the coffee shop.

Niklas paused halfway across the floor, looked around. He was too late. Everyone in the cafe was looking at him now. An old man, a family, a young couple, a handful of singletons. When they saw him looking back, they all looked away and went back to drinking their coffee or eating their sweets. A customer got up and put her tray of dirty crockery onto the shelf near the counter. None of the empty tables had dirty abandoned plates on them. He liked that about the Japanese. They always cleaned up after themselves.

Niklas looked again at the Brazilian's table. A second plate and cup sat on a tray across from him. The Brazilian looked at him again, then glanced at the counter.

Niklas would never have looked at the guy twice, otherwise: an ordinary citizen dressed in slacks, a casual jacket, and loafers, apologizing about something to the cashier. Was that the target?

Niklas pulled his Glock, then hesitated. What kind of world-class assassin walks around in *loafers*, even on his day off? But then the Brazilian shrieked and the target darted through the opening doors, and he knew he was right after all. Niklas shot the Brazilian twice in the head, then turned and fired through the doors after the target.

A stray bullet struck a man standing near the door with an empty stroller. The young father went down and the weight of him set the stroller rolling forward into the coffee shop. Niklas discarded the empty Glock as he stepped around the stroller, but it cost him seconds that the target used to open some distance. Niklas drew a pair of mini-Uzis out of his coat and followed him out into the mall.

Perhaps he would just kill everyone, after all.

man behind me falls as I scramble to my feet. The gaijin is close. I still cannot see a partner, but I am certain that he has one. Shooting up one of the busiest shopping malls in Tokyo? Somebody really wants me dead.

Omotesando Hills is a wedge-shaped building in which the stores are situated on a spiral ramp, which starts at the third basement and winds its way up six levels around an open central space. I head for the grand staircase, which gives direct access to the three basement levels, ducking through the milling crowd. The gaijin rakes the ceiling with automatic fire and the general confusion becomes a panic.

I round a corner, stumble on something underfoot. A collapsible umbrella. I grab it and scurry on. It isn't much of a weapon, but perhaps I can throw it at my pursuer. I know the gaijin is behind me, but I am unsure how close. He squeezes off a burst and I push on with renewed vigour.

I kick and elbow my way up the ramp, fighting hard to keep the stampede from dragging me back towards the gaijin. The mall is built into the side of a hill, so there are street level exits on the top and the bottom floors, but crowds draining from a building behave like water leaving a vessel: the pressure forces them downwards.

The gaijin is on the stairs, intending to cut me off, but he's having a hard time fighting the stampede. He starts to fire into the crowd; intending to mow everyone down until he has a clear shot at me. I duck my head and press on.

The bodies sprawling down the stairs slow the gaijin's pursuit. I've been lucky so far, but he's gaining ground. Another burst and he'll have that clear shot.

The gaijin stops to reload, and I rabbit up the corner escalators. Out of the corner of my eye, I see him raising the weapon again. I dive off the top step to the right, taking cover behind a chest-high glass balustrade.

The gaijin seems surprised that the balustrade starts and shivers, but does not shatter. Suicide-by-jumping is a chronic problem in Japan, and the balustrade is made of tempered glass.

I'm back on my feet. The gaijin is still coming, taking the now-empty grand staircase two steps at a time. There are no exits on this level; no cover once he gets onto the ramp. My only hope is to play the angles.

I grab the top of the balustrade and get a foot up on the handrail.

The structure is sturdy even though the glass is cracked. The gaijin is one step to the top of the staircase, which, owing to the wedge-shaped floor plan of this mall, makes a very acute angle to the third level mezzanine. He turns to me in surprise as I jump, thrusting the umbrella at him and clicking the button on the handle.

As he brings up his weapon, the umbrella shoots forward on its telescoping metal stalk and opens, occluding the gaijin from my view. A burst of automatic fire rips holes in the fabric and I don't even know if I am hit.

The gaijin goes down under my weight. He cushions my fall, but I still hit the stairs hard, taking most of the impact on my left arm. I roll awkwardly off him, still clutching the umbrella. All that remains of it is a twist flapping black nylon and broken metal arms.

Panic and adrenaline somehow get me back on my feet. My arm is numb and likely broken. My shoulder, my head; the entire left side of my body hurts. I whirl unsteadily towards the gaijin, expecting that he will be coming after me again, but it takes me a moment to locate him. He is lying crumpled on the first-floor landing with his neck broken so badly that I can see his vertebrae.

I discard the umbrella and stagger down the stairs. I don't think I have been hit, after all. A miracle. More people are trickling out of the doors. I can hear sirens out in the street. There are casualties—have they been shot or trampled? Can anyone identify me? There must be some security footage. What will it show? Federico is probably dead, and I am sure he will easily be connected to his nefarious past. Will they be able to connect him to me?

But I have more important concerns now. Where is the gaijin's partner? A killer who carries this much firepower is a killer who brings backup.

I let the crowd bear me out of the main doors onto Omotesando Street. Police, fire brigade, and ambulances. The riot squad will be here soon.

I duck into a laneway, wend my way up and along. It's almost as crowded out here as it was in the mall. Weekend shoppers looking for fresh haircuts and trendy clothes in the smaller, artier boutiques; oblivious to the carnage that has taken place around the corner.

I catch a glimpse of a slight figure; dressed all in black amidst the funky Tokyo fashions. He's gone before I can get another look. But I have seen enough to know that this one is a very different kind of professional to the gaijin. This one, I have a feeling, is Japanese.

Keeping my head down, I cut left; salmon my way up crowded Take-shita Street. Boutiques with cringe-worthy Engrish names interspersed with chain restaurants: Women's Panic, Wooden Doll, Nudy Boy, Closet Child. Wolfgang Puck, McDonald's, Yoshinoya. I am suddenly hungry.

I pass between the curving, twenty-meter pillars that support the sign at the top of Takeshita Street. Harajuku Station stands directly ahead, between me and the green of Yoyogi Park. I wonder if my pursuer and his gaijin friend stopped to see the sights before they came looking for me in the mall. Did they make an offering at the Meiji shrine? Did they make time to check out the loli-goth girls, the rockabilly dancers, the row of garage bands?

I imagine not. These two killers are not like me.

Ikari was already outside the building when the shooting started. He was glad that Niklas had decided to go ahead without him. If he managed to eliminate the target by himself, the venture wasn't worth Ikari's time. If Niklas did not, then Ikari would have a stronger argument against pairing with undisciplined foreigners to report back to his master.

From the top level of the mezzanine Ikari watched the target defeat his Niklas with an umbrella and a show of unlikely courage.

Niklas was skilled at what he did, but he was not the right man for this job. The target was cunning and lucky. He used the terrain to his advantage, and he knew when to be reckless. If nothing else, the target had good timing. Niklas had rushed in and failed and now the target knew that he was under threat.

Ikari was pleased. He enjoyed a good hunt.

But it was too crowded outside the mall. Ikari didn't like crowds. He wanted an elegant kill and a quiet getaway. He had trained at this all his life and now that the Finn was dead, he was free to engage the matter with his own discipline.

Ikari shadowed the target through streets lined with gaudy shops selling decadent services; scandalous clothing. Shallow people in outlandish costumes browsed amongst them. They weren't impolite, but there was a wanton quality about them that repulsed him. All of this focus and energy being spent on the acquisition of tawdry goods. All this leisure time at their disposal.

Ikari showed himself to the target. Just a glimpse. Just enough to provoke a reaction; to inspire some fear. A fearful enemy was an enemy who would make mistakes.

The target crossed the road ahead of him and vanished into the train station.

At least it wasn't the subway. Ikari evaded the turnstiles and stepped onto the platform, where a train was already waiting. He had lost sight of his target, but there was only one place he could have gone. Ikari ghosted in through the doors just before they closed.

The carriage wasn't full, but there were no free seats. It was congested with commuters hanging from the wrist straps and the rails. The walls were plastered with advertising for all manner of worthless consumer goods. Flags hung from the ceiling of the carriage with more advertising, and LCD screens broadcast yet more exhortations to buy.

A female voice announced the train's destinations in a gratingly alien Nihongo, and then another in the English tongue that set his fingers twitching. An Englishman had had sent him to this horrible reflection of the true Nippon.

The target was not in the carriage. Ikari chose a direction and slid through into the next car. His shadow method would not work well in these carriages with their tight crowds and bright lighting. He would have to follow the target off the train if he was going to make this clean.

The train drew into Yoyogi Station. The stops were more frequent than Ikari had expected. He went to the door and watched to see who left the train. Too many to observe every one of them, but Ikari had techniques to narrow the search and he was confident that his target was not among them. He moved back into the train and continued his advance through the carriages.

Ikari had reached the front of the train by the next station, but there was still no sign of his quarry. Ikari got off the train. This station was the kind that he hated: underground, enclosed. Ikari did not like having the city on top of him. He didn't like the congested tunnels, the milling passengers, the lingering stink.

Ikari drew up his discipline and moved down the platform, seeking the man he was going to kill.

A sign overhead identified this place as Shinjuku.

I haven't seen my pursuer since Takeshita Street, but I have an intuition that he is close by. That level of tradecraft disturbs me. What is he? If he's been sent by Jonathon, he could be anyone. A super-killer, raised up in the mountains by some berserk *shinobi* clan. That would appeal to Jonathon's sense of humour, I think. Perhaps he's from my world, perhaps from some meta-Nippon, conjured out of jingoistic fantasies and political lies.

Whatever the case, Shinobi-san is appallingly good. The only advantage

I have is my knowledge of the streets. It has been more than a decade since I pulled the trigger for the Ishida syndicate, but this is still my home turf. I cannot think of a better place to lose a tail—even one as talented as Shinobi-san—than the tunnels and hallways of Shinjuku station.

I cut across into one of the retail tunnels, slip through a magazine store and into a side corridor. Toilets, an elevator, and a door marked NO ENTRY. I go through it, knowing from long experience that it will be unlocked.

Cleaning supplies. Storage space for the nearby businesses. I turn left, bound up a flight of stairs, turn right at an electrical switchboard. Pipes and plumbing. I move through another door and come out in an alley off Shinjuku Dori. I head out to the street, duck through a pedestrian underpass to Yasukuni Street. And there he is when I emerge into the square. Somehow Shinobi-san is already ahead of me.

He is dressed all in black. His garments are made from modern fabrics, but there is something severe and old-fashioned about the way they're cut. He has a long canvas bag slung across his back.

The pedestrian light is blue. I put my head down and walk, watching him out of the corner of my eye. I cross the street diagonally and hurry on. The light goes red behind me.

Shinobi-san steps into the traffic. He still isn't looking at me. Cars roar past him in both directions but he doesn't seem to notice them, or they him. Somehow, he traverses the busy street in a straight line, without provoking a single blaring horn or squeal of tires.

I turn and run, down past the Don Quijote discount emporium; past the crushed-together high-rises crammed with cheap restaurants and karaoke joints; left under the arch that leads down into the Kabukicho. Strip clubs, pachinko parlours, video game arcades, tourist trap theatre restaurants and pornography shops. I'm breathing hard. The fear and adrenaline are starting to wash out of my system. My injured left arm hangs numb at my side. I cannot keep this up much longer.

As I stumble along, I catch occasional glimpses of Shinobi-san, but he's gaming my sightlines. He does not seem to be working nearly as hard as I am, but he is slowly gaining ground on me, no matter how I duck and weave. He is close, now—level with me on the other side of the street.

I cut into an amusement arcade. Video screens strobe lights at me; speakers boom and chatter and squeal. Machine gun fire; slashing guitar chords; singsong voices; laser blasts. I spent half of my teenage years in places like this, but during my long absence, I had forgotten just how loud they get. Reflected on the convex glass of an ancient old

CRT screen, I catch a momentary reflection of Shinobi-san hesitating; disoriented by the sensory assault. What would my father say, if he knew that the video games he thought would ruin my vision and my mind had just saved my life?

For a minute or two, anyway.

I duck through a passageway that's concealed by a row of slot machines and follow it through the rear exit. I have won back a small amount of distance, and now I have a plan. A half-formed, desperate plan, but it's better than blind flight.

I cross the road to a soapland bath club and shoulder past the tout who is standing at the entrance. He calls after me indignantly as I barge through the doors; past the reception desk, where an alarmed hostess squawks at me to stop. Worse than my rudeness is the fact that I am still wearing my shoes. The staff call out behind me, angry but still polite. This bath club was run by the Otomo family, last time I was here. I don't know who is running it now, but Otomo is long gone from the local criminal landscape.

A couple of guys in suits with coiffed hair bounce out of an office at the end of the hall. Security. They look a little confused. These local yakuza don't know what to do if they don't have time to intimidate you first.

I glance over my shoulder to see Shinobi-san coming in the main doors. While the yakuza figure out what to do I rabbit up a flight of wooden stairs. I emerge into a hallway with half dozen closed doors on each side, leading to the bath suites.

Two more yakuza come around a bend in the corridor ahead of me. They have pistols drawn. Soft. Otomo would have had four gunmen up here.

I can hear a commotion downstairs. It stops before anybody has time to scream.

I force open a door on my right and slam it on gunfire. I wish the door latch was a proper lock.

This bath suite has fake wood panel walls and floors. In one corner there's a showerhead, a seat, a bucket. A cabinet full of soaps and oils and shampoos; washcloths and brushes and loofahs. A big mirror. Piles of clothes folded neatly in the baskets and three pairs of sandals on the mat just inside the door. A young *sarariman* is sitting in a Jacuzzi bath with a couple of girls, who are in the process of soaping him up. The three of them squint at me through the clouds of scented steam.

The gunfire outside stops abruptly. In the silence I put a finger to my lips. "If any of you call for help, I am going to kill you all." It has been more than a decade since I used the sneering yakuza cadence, but it comes out effortlessly. The sarariman and his two bathing beauties nod silently.

It will not take Shinobi-san very long to find me now that he has dealt with the two goons outside. I fill the shower bucket with hot water and take up a position near the door. I'm barely in position when it smashes open, the latch crunching out of the door frame. Three matte black shuriken zip through the doorway before the door has fully opened.

The thrown projectiles hit the faux-wood panelling on the far side of the room hard enough to crack the plastic. I am lucky that Shinobi-san is too old fashioned to use flash grenades.

He appears in the doorway with a short, square-bladed sword in one hand and a fistful of shuriken in the other, and I throw the contents of the bucket. Shinobi-san doesn't exactly stagger, but he sways as the scalding water strikes his face. I hope I've blinded him. I hit Shinobi-san with a low tackle and tumble past him into the corridor. Even blinded and disoriented, I am not prepared to grapple with him.

I scramble to my feet and pick my way over the two sprawled yakuza, who are dead on the ground with their necks sliced open. The blood spray on the wall suggests that Shinobi-san took them both down with a single cut. Their guns are lying where they dropped them. I scrabble for one, but my left arm still isn't working properly, and it skitters away from my fumbling. In my peripheral vision, I see a shadow cast. Shinobi-san is still coming. I forget the gun and stumble down the hall; throw myself into the turn at the end of the corridor.

The door to what used to be Otomo's office is open, so I dive into it. Three shuriken slice the air above me. If I have blinded Shinobi-san it does not seem to have affected his aim.

The office contains a single chair, a pot plant, and a desk covered with papers and vodka bottles. There is a drawer hanging open with a loaded .44 in it. I grab the pistol with my good hand and lunge for the door to the fire escape.

I tuck the gun into my belt and swing, one-handed, down from the ladder into to the alley below, nearly dislocating my shoulder in the process. The impact jars my legs and I stumble a few paces to regain my balance.

I turn and point the gun at the fire escape door. When it opens, I squeeze off a couple of hopeful shots. The recoil from the big pistol makes me stagger.

Shinobi-san leaps through the doorway horizontally, at full spread.

He does a handspring off the balcony rail, jack-knifes into a turn, kicks off the opposite wall, and hits the ground rolling. He comes up spraying shuriken and he would certainly have hit me if I wasn't already off balance and in the process of falling. The missiles thrum over my head and I land painfully on my ass.

Still sitting on the ground, I fire two more rounds. Shinobi-san doesn't exactly sidestep them, but he contrives to not be where the bullets are. It's not fancy footwork or even superhuman reflexes—he just knows what I'm going to do before I do.

I scrabble backwards and somehow get to my feet again by the time I have reached the T-junction at the end of the lane. I go right into the perpendicular street. There are vehicles parked all along one side of this laneway, allowing just enough room for a single small vehicle car to pass beside them. There are no people here; just the trade entrances to the businesses on either side. I burn what little energy I have left in a final sprint. If I can open a bit more distance between me and Shinobi-san I might be able to turn and plug him. I know this is a vain hope. I am sure he has more shuriken than I have bullets.

I stop, panting, beside a small shrine, nestled in a gap between two buildings. A tiny grassy area hosting a pair of trees a bench, an altar, guarded by a pair of stone foxes. This isn't unusual, even here in the Kabukicho. There are little pieces of old Edo all over the city, pressing through its flesh like scar tissue. I can't run any further, but this seems like a good place to die.

I turn and bring up the gun, which is now impossibly heavy. I fire four more times before the slide locks back. Empty. Shinobi-san evades every bullet and comes on slowly.

This guy could have killed me dozens of times over already, but, I realize, that was not his aim. He wanted to run me down, He wanted to get close enough to look me in the eye. Super-ninja or not, that is a poor strategy for an assassin.

He makes the shuriken in his left hand disappear and takes a double-grip on the sword. There is no expression on his face, which is red and blistered from the scalding water. How many people has he killed with that blade? Many. Many, many people.

More shocking to me is his youth. Shinobi-san is eighteen; nineteen at the most. He has spent his whole short life doing this.

I discard the spent pistol and extend my hands in front of me in something resembling a ready posture. I learned this in the army, but I have never been much of a fighter. Even if I was, I have got nothing left. This battle is already over.

Acceptance calms me, and my senses open out of the tunnel of fight-or-flight. There is a Door here. I don't know where it goes, but I feel it spring open as I flex my fingers.

Instinct takes over. I throw my arms wide, as if to welcome this strange assassin and his blade. Kill me, I am open. It is only fitting that I should die in the Kabukicho.

Shinobi-san advances, holding the blade in both hands at shoulder height. I draw my arms across and around as he comes, folding the portal over onto him as the blade sweeps in. I turn to the side and make a twisting motion, flipping the portal back onto itself. I close my fists and draw it tight; tie it off.

And Shinobi-san is gone.

I think he is trapped inside the folded-closed Door; executing one final perfect cut through a space-time loop; one moment of perfect swordplay repeated to infinity. I think, but I do not know. I am certainly not going to open the Door again and see what happens.

I kick away the empty pistol and stagger on. I'm bleeding, I'm bruised, and I think I have a broken arm. I am not aware of falling but suddenly I find myself lying in the street, facing the shrine. I see something scurry away from the corner of my eye. Something small.

The last thing I notice before I black out is that one of the stone foxes is missing.

#8: Exit Island

The full length of the Zurich International runway is visible through the plate glass window in the conference room. Jetliners prowl amongst the control towers, tail fins rampant; plumes of exhaust bluing the air behind them. In the distance I can see the Alps. Snow. Gingerbread houses. This view from the airport is all I am going to see of Switzerland today, but that's okay. I have been here before.

My employer has come all the way from Mesra City, and she looks tired, although her two bodyguards do not. Despite tens of hours in transit, they exhibit their usual easy alertness.

"Zai, it is very bad, Zai." Usually, I find Vashya's accent and circular phrasing to be mildly endearing, but today it is wearing on my nerves. Federico is dead, and I am lucky not to have shared his fate. Somebody knows who I am and where I live, and they sent two extremely dangerous killers to find me. It is very bad indeed.

But it could have been worse. None of the investigating police officers have connected me with either the shootings in Omotesando Hills, or the massacre in Shinjuku. Nobody has identified me from the mall. Nobody picked me out of the reams of security camera footage from Omotesando or the train station. No crime lab has found a set of my prints, which could easily be matched to my juvenile offender record or my military service file.

Footage of my umbrella stunt has been leaked onto YouTube, but a corporate karate champion has claimed credit for it. The man in the video looks more like him than me. I believe that Unfolded Enterprises has tampered with the data on my behalf, but Vashya doesn't say, and I do not ask. I am less interested in who cleaned up after me than I am in who tried to have me killed. "It was the Englishman. Jonathon."

"Russell Kilmer-Jones, is his name is true."

I knew that Jonathon was not his real name, but it takes me a moment to start thinking of him as a Russell. Russell is more difficult for me to pronounce, but it suits him better. "Where is he? England?"

"Zai, I do not know, Zai."

"You want me to go and look for him?"

She shakes her head. "Conventional Earth is not our territory."

I am beginning to understand. The Wild Hunt mission, which took place in the conventional world, was beyond the remit of Unfolded Enterprises. That should have been enough to tell me that the Englishman had gone rogue. "Alright. What do we know about the two assassins?"

"Yes. The one is Finnish man, is one."

"Finland is Conventional Earth"—Vashya nods, so I continue—"but the ninja...he's not from my Japan, is he?"

She nods. "Folded version Japan. Ōyashima, it is called, Ōyashima."

"I see."

I cannot help but smile. I am sure this is going to be dangerous, but it will be nice, for once, to travel to a place where they speak my language.

I take a short flight to Schipol airport, where Rambo-san is waiting for me. Rather than giving me documents for ongoing travel, he takes me to a suite at the airport hotel. I carry my own luggage up to the room, because Rambo-san has brought quite a lot of his own.

Once we have our bags stowed, Rambo-san collapses into the chair by the desk. I sit on the bed. "Have you been to Ōyashima before, Rambo-san?"

"No," Rambo-san admits. "It's difficult for foreigners peoples. But I have an briefing."

"Allow me to guess. Ōyashima maintains *sakoku*. Closed borders."

"Yes, Zai, closed borders. Except for Nagasaki."

Now I understand. "That's why we're in Holland. Only the Dutch are allowed to trade with them."

"And the Chinese," says Rambo-san.

The true Japan's *sakoku* policies ended when American warships rolled into Tokyo Bay in the middle of the nineteenth century. If Ōyashima has kept them, I expect they have kept the feudal mindset that goes with it. "What's it like?"

"I have heard that it's mega-gorgeous," says Rambo-san. "Like your Japan, man, but there are no earthquake or tsunami. No nuclear power for accidentisms. No bombings."

"Do they trade with Japan? My Japan?"

"Yes, of course, Zai-buddy. Very muchly. Ōyashima has not the factories of the real Japan."

"Then there must be some kind of a Way I can use to get there from home. Why are we flying in from Holland?"

"The documentations," says Rambo-san. He does not realize that I am asking what I need him for. "Bureaucracy systems too difficult."

That does make sense. The real Japan is like this, too. Even for an organization like Unfolded Enterprises, sometimes local is only for locals.

"These is you."

Rambo-san passes me a scroll in a leather case. It contains document with a watermarked digital photograph of me printed on it. It takes me a while to read the hand-drawn calligraphy around it, because I have to guess at the meaning of some of the more obscure kanji.

"Do you know what this says?"

"Homeboy, it identifies you as a merchanter?" he asks.

"A member of a *tekiya* organization. Yakuza. A gangster."

"So what, my duder?"

"This document identifies me as a criminal."

"Are you not one criminal?" says Rambo-san. "A yangster, in fact of the point?"

"That was a long time ago. Now I work for myself."

"Now you work for Unfolded Enterprises, same like me."

I concede the point. In my Japan, the yakuza do not even try to keep themselves a secret. The biggest syndicate publishes its own lifestyle magazine.

"There." Rambo-san indicates one of the luggage pieces that he brought with us. "Clothing for the local of Ōyashima."

The bag contains several pairs of trousers and some loose cotton shirts which fasten with traditional ties. Underwear and long-sleeved undershirts made of something like Dri Fit. *Tabi* that have the soles of running shoes. A kimono and a *haori* jacket, cut from an unfamiliar weatherproof fabric. It's good quality, practical clothing but I am going to feel like a cosplayer if I wear it.

I find a *wakizashi* inside a smaller duffel bag. Rambo-san tells me the identity scroll includes a license to carry the short sword openly.

I examine the scabbard, but I do not draw the blade. "I'm not taking this."

Disappointment blooms on Rambo-san's face.

I put the sword back in the duffel. If I go about with a sword, sooner or later, somebody who knows what they are doing will want to duel with me. I have no desire to be on the losing end of a fight with live blades. Or the winning end, for that matter—covered in blood and mostly likely cut.

"Let's hit the road," I say, in as American an accent as I can muster. Rambo-san brightens a little at the cliché.

We fly business class to Lisbon, Cape Verde, Cape Town, Mauritius, Jakarta and then Singapore. This Way approximates the sea voyage Dutch traders would have taken to Nagasaki four hundred years ago.

There is a fuelled-up Learjet waiting for us at Changi airport. After a brief but heated discussion, the charter company representative agrees to waive regulations and allow Rambo-san to fly the plane without a co-pilot. Some technicality about the weight of the unladen aircraft that sounds like a Monty Python sketch. Monty Python does not translate well into my language, and I have never liked it. It does not help that I am very sick of hearing Rambo's voice.

I had hopes that I could sleep in the passenger area of the plane, once we take off, but Rambo-san insists that I sit in the cockpit with him for purposes of load-balancing. Is this another Monty Python joke, or just the cruelty of fate?

About two hours out from our destination a patch of weather blows in out of nowhere. Rambo-san turns off the autopilot. He turns the yoke and pilots us right into the storm front.

"Rambo-san, what are you doing?"

"Zai, old buddy," he replies. "This is how we get to Ōyashima."

"Can't we fly…above…this weather?"

He turns to me and grins. "Zai, my friendly neighbourhood, Ōyashima is a place not like Karachidor. Is…protected, can I say?"

"It's protected by an electrical storm?"

"Yes. Inside is a Door." I'm no longer sure if Rambo-san is wearing a grin or a grimace.

I tune up my topographic senses. The storm is providing some kind of interference but there is indeed some kind of a node deep inside it. Rambo-san pushes the throttle.

Lightning coruscates over the towering masses of water vapour, forking down at us from all sides. Peals of thunder roll the plane to the left, then to the right. Rain pounds the canopy so hard that I fear the glass will break. The wind howls hard Japanese syllables at us, although I cannot make out the words.

Rambo-san grips the yoke with both hands. His head is craned forward as far as it can go, and I can see the tendons of his neck. Flop sweat drenches his hair.

On either side I see a coil of swirling vapour keeping pace with us. There are figures inside: one of them beating a drum; the other casting winds from a tubular sack. Raijin and Fujin, the gods of the storm and the wind. Their presence does not surprise me, although eighteen months ago I would not have credited their existence as literal beings.

The spirits peel away as the cloud masses darken. The rain and lightning subside, and Rambo-san turns the yoke so that the little aircraft banks right, into the still place at the eye of the storm.

Two pillars of cloud twist up and up and up, and then a pair of lintels condense perpendicular above them. Rambo-san opens the throttle and the Learjet yaws through the *torii* gateway and into the land of Ōyashima.

The storm quickly boils away to nothing. We have clear skies for the next thirty minutes before a landmass appears on the horizon. The island of Kyushu is immediately familiar, and soon Nagasaki becomes visible.

The port city spills down from the mountains into the harbour; striped with vivid green vegetation beneath a hot blue sky. This Nagasaki has none of the crowding skyscrapers that characterize modern Japanese cities. Aside from the cell towers there are few buildings over five stories tall.

An artificial island stands on pylons in the middle of the harbour. In my Japan, the island has since been reintegrated into the city, but I recognize this version from a high school history lesson. It is called Dejima. Exit Island.

Dejima is separated from the mainland by a canal and joined by a single bridge. A hulking grey American supercarrier is moored on the far side of it, threatening and crass. I believe this is the only landing strip Dejima is permitted.

We circle a few times while Rambo-san holds a conversation with the squawking radio, but there is no other air traffic that I can see. Finally, he sets down the microphone. Permission to land.

Rambo-san frowns with concentration, lowers the throttle and sets us down neatly on the flight deck. Once we have come to a stop, he looks at me. He is drenched with sweat and pride gleams in his eyes. It is quite a feat, to land a passenger plane—even one as small as this Learjet—on such a short runway.

"Good job," I say, as convincingly as I can manage.

We climb down a steep, steel flight of stairs from the deck of the carrier onto a floating pontoon, and then cross a folding gangway that leads up to Dejima's seaward gate. A pair of guards armed with MP7 machine pistols are waiting there to escort us into the customs hall. They are wearing future-fabric kimonos; olive drab and blazoned with military insignia. Each guard wears a pair of swords in a high-tech harness. The blades hang curve-up, samurai-style. I am very glad I left Rambo-san's wakizashi back in Schipol.

In the customs house, the immigration clerk, sitting at a dais, summons Rambo-san first. He is dressed in a fancy kimono that, judging by the sheen on his face, must be excruciatingly hot in this un-air-conditioned sweatbox of an office. He wears his hair in a *chonmage* queue.

Rambo-san proffers a Dutch passport. I wonder if the name in it is actually John Rambo.

"*Ben je echt nederlands?*" he says.

"Of course, from Netherlands," replies Rambo-san in English. "Require do you additional documentation?"

The clerk nods slightly and makes an affirmative grunt.

Rambo-san places a stack of American dollars as tall as my thumb on the dais.

The clerk says, in English. "Your documents are acceptable. *Dejima e youkoso.*" He writes something in his register and then looks at me.

I put on my best yakuza sneer and hand him the scroll Rambo-san gave me. The clerk twists it open and unrolls it. He reads it impassively, then twists it closed. The clerk gives me a small bow instead of writing in the register. I take the scroll and strut away. This is a role I am accustomed to playing.

According to the scroll, I am a local. Locals are not allowed to leave Ōyashima, on pain of execution…but the scroll shows me to be yakuza, and this place, the only open port in a world that has deliberately isolated itself from reality, is nothing if not corrupt.

Under the noonday sun it's even hotter outside of the customs house than inside, but at least there is the hope of a sea breeze here.

A single avenue runs the length of Dejima. Rambo-san and I follow it past the watch tower, some warehouses, a small grocery market, and a medical centre. It takes about three minutes to walk to the hotel, at the far end of the island.

The hotel is an old Dutch building, but the staff are Japanese, so I handle the check-in ceremonies. Rambo-san is annoyed. This is supposed to be his job.

I take the opportunity to quiz the concierge. If nothing else, this is an opportunity to get used to the local dialect, which is old-fashioned and a little stilted to my ear. "Excuse me. I wonder if you have had an Englishman staying here recently?"

He shakes his head. "Only Dutch barbarians are allowed on Dejima." Liar. It is obvious to anyone with functioning eyes or ears that Rambo-san is no more Dutch than I am.

"It may be only his name that is from England," I reply. Using this passive language in my native language feels good. Something about the practise of such etiquette is soothing, even though I am inquiring after a dangerous man. "He is a gaijin, after all. Perhaps you remember a Russell Kilmer-Jones?"

The concierge wags his head from side to side. He doesn't want to answer me, but I can tell he knows the name. "It is difficult to recall." This kind of prevarication means that he is not waiting for a bribe—he just doesn't want to tell me.

"It is important that I locate this man. I am from Edo, and my superiors wish to speak with him."

"Ah, perhaps I am starting to remember," says the concierge. Whomever I report to in Edo is not somebody a hotel clerk wants to cross. "Such a man may have stayed here, perhaps two months ago."

"And do you recall what he did? With whom he spoke?"

"It may be that a palanquin arrived for him. Perhaps it bore him into Nagasaki, and then to the magistrate's house."

Now I see the true source of the concierge's reluctance. It is forbidden for foreigners to cross the bridge into Nagasaki. If Kilmer-Jones went to see the magistrate, he must have government connections. My documentation as a yakuza might be useful with customs goons, but it's certainly not going to get me in front of anybody with genuine power. I bow my thanks to the clerk and sweep the room keys off the counter.

"What was that all?" says Rambo-san, who is waiting impatiently for me by the stairs.

"I asked him if there was hot water," I reply. "He says this is a first world country."

"That took a very lot of words."

"This is Japan. We are very polite." I shrug. "Also, there is no air conditioning."

In my room I have a hot shower and then collapse naked under the ceiling fan. It's like lying in an armpit, but at least I don't have to share the armpit with Rambo-san.

I awaken to the sound of fireworks. I can smell the powder through the open window. A summer festival.

My new clothes fit me pretty well. The *tabi* shoes are more comfortable than they look, and the moisture wicking undershirt is a blessing in this weather. I leave the _haori_ jacket in my room. It's still hot. The humidity is close to 100%.

Rambo-san is sitting in the bar downstairs, hanging out with a down-at-heel group of pilots. When he sees me, he calls to me across the room. "Hey what's up, my holmes-boy James?" He gets up and staggers in my direction. His pop culture pidgin is even more excruciating under the influence of alcohol.

"I think I'll go into town."

"At night?" Rambo-san looks sceptical.

"Of course."

He thinks about it visibly. "I'll get my coat."

I lean away from him. "*Gaikokujin* are not allowed onto the mainland." I use the polite word for foreigners, even though he doesn't know what it means.

Rambo-san blinks three times. "You took that Irish guide with you to The Fairy's Lands."

"Yes, and look what happened to him."

"What did happen to him?" says Rambo-san.

"He died."

"This Ōyashima is not like the Fairy's Lands," says Rambo-san.

"That's right. Here, you won't get ten feet before somebody notices you're a foreigner."

"I'll hide my face. It's night time."

"I don't think that is going to work, Rambo-san."

"But…"

"Stay here. I will report back in the morning, unless I am dead."

I turn on my heel and leave the hotel. I can hear him spluttering after me all the way out on the street.

The guards at the land gate let me through without difficulty and I cross the short bridge into Nagasaki proper.

The summer festival is bigger than I expected. There are *peiron* dragonboats on the water as well as a lot of other smaller vessels, all of them strung about with lanterns. Single fireworks erupt intermittently from a stationary barge, even though it seems the main *hanabi* display is over.

This Nagasaki is a strange place. The prevailing architecture is traditional, but the buildings are constructed from cheap modern materials. Concrete and fibreglass. There are a few very old European buildings, which look Dutch or, occasionally, Spanish. There are lots of cars and small trucks on the narrow streets: current model vehicles, probably imported from conventional Japan. The familiar JR sign near a train station makes me look for a McDonald's or a Lotteria, but there are no chain restaurants here, not even the Japanese ones.

On balance, it is prettier than a conventional Japanese city. No unsightly power lines; no high-rise buildings; no dumpsters or vending machines or neon.

The streets are thronged with revellers. Snatches of conversation are conducted in an ugly Nagasaki-ben dialect, inflected with Dutch and Chinese but with none of the borrowed English words that have colonized modern Japanese. Mobile phones are ubiquitous, but only pre-smartphone *garakei* models—the kind that were popular in the days when Japan had the most advanced cell network in the world.

The only people I see in Western-style clothes are speaking Chinese. I feel like a yokel in my kimono and hurry on. Say what you will about crass western fashion—the zipper fly is an invention worthy of a Nobel Prize.

I stop to let a palanquin pass. It is born by four scrawny men, shoeless and shirtless and wearing matching headbands. Security is provided by a phalanx of special operations samurai, armed with swords and Steyr assault rifles and armoured in Kevlar moulded to resemble lamellar ō-yoroi_plates. The procession is impressive as a show of status, but a limousine would be safer.

I turn right into a street lined with market stalls selling fried octopus and shaved ice and *yakitori* and crepes, as well as gewgaws imported from the real Japan. I wonder how expensive they are in this local market.

I pay particular attention to the stalls that offer games of skill; a traditional scam for low level yakuza. Before long I spot some obvious gang business: a runner who goes from stall to stall; interrupting the stallholders to relay some sort of a message. I shadow the messenger back to a small marquee set up in a far corner, behind the first aid and administration tents. I count to fifteen and then follow him through the door-flap.

Inside the tent there are half a dozen people: a couple of guards, slouching on some wooden crates near the entrance; a man and a woman counting and sorting money; an older man bent over a ledger; and a human peacock who is immediately recognizable as the *shateigashira*—the local boss. But for the outfits, this could be a familiar scene from my own youth.

The glamorous life of a gangster. Sitting around counting coins your men have bilked out of teenagers or extorted from working stiffs who have set foot in the wrong restaurant. If you kiss the right asses you might ascend to a rank from which you can manage the syndicate's trade in sex or drugs. If you are smart and ruthless enough, you might even have the opportunity to be involved in Far-Right politics. All the boredom of a salary job, with the added prospect of being mutilated or murdered.

But I keep the contempt off my face. Just because these people are assholes doesn't mean they're not dangerous. The two guards leap off their crates and train automatic pistols on me.

I raise my hands. "Good evening." I smile and incline my head without lowering my hands.

"Who are you?" says the peacock.

"My name is Zai. I represent the Ishida syndicate in Tokyo."

The guards keep their guns on me, but they are as surprised as the others in the room.

The peacock looks at the two money counters and the old man. "Go."

They scurry out of the tent through a concealed side exit.

"What do you want?" says the peacock.

"I'm looking for information, and I'm willing to pay for it."

"What kind of information?"

"Information about a man. A gaijin. He was here about six weeks ago."

The peacock gives me a look of withering scorn. "Gaijin are not allowed into Nagasaki."

"This one had a meeting in the magistrate's chambers. I want to know what they discussed. I want to know where else he went. I want to know who else he spoke with."

"What is the name of this gaijin?"

"He is called Russell Kilmer-Jones. An Englishman."

"What was his business here?" says the peacock.

I smile crookedly. "Among other things, I believe he wanted to hire a ninja."

The peacock guffaws. I cannot tell if that is because he doesn't believe ninja are real, or that he doesn't believe that a gaijin could hire one. I chuckle along, although I have scars to prove that both scenarios are quite plausible.

The peacock assesses me through hooded eyes. "The Ishida sent just one man for this job?"

"They sent as many men as they thought necessary." I purse my lips. "And as many dollars. I will pay you thirty thousand United States dollars, in cash, for this information."

The peacock pretends to consider my offer. "Sixty thousand."

"Forty," I reply. "Half up front, half on delivery."

"Fifty."

We agree to forty-five, and set a rendezvous location for the following evening. The peacock turns his back by way of dismissal, the two guards usher me out of the tent with menacing glares.

I head back out into the fair. Suddenly hungry, I stop and buy a taiyaki_pancake from a market stall, and a flask of ice-cold water from a nearby cart. With something in my belly, I am feeling better about everything. The streets have become less crowded as the evening wears on and many of the stalls are starting to close up. I think I will head back to Dejima to rest up and figure out my next move.

After the first crossroads, I become aware of a man with his hair greased up into a rockabilly coiffure watching me from across the road. He has a short sword in his belt, and I am sure he has a gun concealed in his kimono. He is very careful not to look in my direction, but I do catch him glancing back over his shoulder — he has at least one partner.

No policeman would wear such a ridiculous hairstyle. It looks like the peacock isn't taking any chances with me. I did not expect him to show this much initiative.

I cut right down a narrow lane behind a row of shops. This is my pursuers' home turf — I am unlikely to elude them in these streets. The only thing in my favour is the fact that they want me to get back to my lodgings so they can get the money. If they just corral me into a dead end and murder me, they will get nothing. Of course, if I lead them on too long a chase, they might torture me just for fun.

No sign of the man with the coiffure, but I catch sight of another pair of obvious yakuza goons, on either side of the road: a balding man and a sallow guy wearing a pair of mirrored Ray-Bans. Three to one. Even one-on-one would be bad news. I take a left turn onto another narrow street; this one brighter, crowded with residences.

"Over here!" A hissing voice, coming from a small garden in the front of a listing family home. The street lamp in front of the house is broken. I veer towards it for a closer look.

"Quickly!"

There is a small shrine in the garden, three-quarters hidden by an unkempt azalea plant. A statue of a fox sits on the ground beside it. "Idiot! Don't you understand Japanese?"

"I speak Japanese."

"This isn't the time for a chat. Come with me." The fox—no longer made of stone—turns tail and starts to trot away, down the narrow space between the side of the house and the fence that separates this property from the neighbour's. It is hard to tell in this light, but I think its pelt is yellow.

I hurry after the animal. "Hey. Where are we going?" I am feeling a little bit foolish.

The yellow fox does not look back. "You, of all people, should be able to figure that out."

The garden behind the house is both larger and wilder than I had expected. The back fence is rotten and some of its slats have fallen out. The fox slips nimbly through a gap and I follow.

We are in a small courtyard behind an apartment building. There is a single car parked in the space underneath it. We duck past and emerge at the front of the building into Chinatown. Here, the smells of incense, plum sauce and black powder mingle in the air. The fox trots on and I jog after.

"What are you?"

"What are *you*?" the fox counters.

"I'm a...traveller. Are you a Guide?" It's very dark now. The festival lights behind us are long gone.

"You're an opener of Doors," says the yellow fox. "I am a finder of Ways."

"Where are you taking me?"

"I am taking you out of danger."

We cross the Urakami River on a small footbridge and move into a narrow laneway. The man with the coiffure appears at the far end, up ahead of us. His two companions are hurrying to catch up to him.

The fox growls and ducks into another laneway. I rush after, having no better plan.

We wind our way through streets wide and small; past shops and houses, a police station, a library, some government buildings. I don't see the gangsters again, but I have an intuition that they are only a couple of steps from view.

As we head uphill the houses grow sparser and more dilapidated. Soon we emerge onto a lightly forested slope.

"Quickly," says the fox.

As we gain some higher ground, I can still see the glimmer of the city lights, the harbour. I doubt we've travelled two kilometres, but my hotel on Dejima seems very far away now. We are on a Way, but rather than passing from one reality to the next, the two worlds coexist here; superimposed as we pass along it. This journey has the quality of a dream about it, and it is not a pleasant one.

The fox trots up the slope into some scrubby trees, zigging and zagging for no obvious reason. We pass broken statues, rotting wooden homesteads, collapsed stone walls. The feeling of unease grows stronger. When I look back downhill, I can no longer see the city.

"Where are we?"

"Near to Nagasaki." The fox bounds over a fallen tree and I have to rush to catch it up. The sharp smell of pine needles prickles my nose. There's a new moon above, and the night has grown a little brighter. I am not sure what the moon over Nagasaki looked like, because the last time I looked up there were fireworks and powder-smoke obscuring it, but I am certain it wasn't the hammered silver disk I see hanging in this sky. Despite the added illumination, the trees up ahead of me seem very dark—almost burned. I draw up short.

"We're in the Faerie Realms." I speak in English.

"The *Youkai*_World," corrects the yellow fox. "The Goblin Countries are closer to Ōyashima than any place that remains in the Conventional Earth."

Up ahead, hulking shapes shamble through the dark spaces between the trees; snuffling and snorting and dragging their feet. The fox forges on blithely. I fear the yakuza, but that is a familiar kind of fear. The fox is leading me to a place where fear has a hairier texture. The terror of childhood nightmares, long since outgrown; of superstitions, long since abandoned; of urban legends, discredited or dismissed.

I glance backwards and spot the three yakuza picking their way up the hill, and in doing so lose sight of the fox. Panic wells up inside me. Monsters ahead and gangsters behind me. I start to jog across the flank of the mountain, seeking a path between. Perhaps I can find somewhere to hide, or a Way out of this juxtaposed world. My footing is pretty good in these *tabi* shoes, but I would feel much more comfortable in a pair of proper boots as I blunder through the scrubby thickets, scramble over rocky outcroppings.

The yakuza have spotted me. I can hear them panting and cursing as they labour in pursuit.

An old Chinese-style temple comes into sight. Gnarled oak and maple trees lean over its walls. I mount the stairs and move in through the gate quickly. I am sure the yakuza will follow me in here, but they have guns, and this is the only cover to be had.

The temple is not quite a ruin, but it has definitely gone to seed. The wood is grey with age through the flaking paint. Roof tiles are missing, and the decorations have been worn down by the elements. The courtyard shows bare earth and dust where the lawns used to be. Weeds have sprouted through the cracks in the stone paving. The doors to the main hall have long since been destroyed. Inside I catch a glimpse of broken statuary.

I work my way around the building, trying to keep to cover. Perhaps the yakuza will overlook it. A soft grinding sound draws my attention to a retaining wall covered with *Onigawara* gargoyle tiles. One of the stone faces turns to me and says, "Good evening."

"Good evening." I bow. "What are you?"

"I am just an old piece of stone."

"Why are you talking to me?"

"I am lonely," the gargoyle replies. "Not many people come up here. I wanted to talk to you before the ogres kill you."

"Ogres?"

"There's one just over there."

I turn slowly to meet the regard of a three-meter tall <u>oni</u>.

"Thank you for the chat," says the gargoyle. "Goodbye."

The ogre is mostly torso. It has short, bandy legs; a pot belly; and long, knotty arms. Steam roils off its skin like it is wet and very, very hot. The ogre's only clothing is a pair of pants made of tiger skins, and for the moment I imagine that it has just stepped out of a glam rock video clip from hell.

The ogre is breathing hard, whether from fury or exertion I cannot say. It tilts its bug-eyed head and hefts a spiked iron truncheon that is as big as one of my legs.

I turn and bolt.

I hear its massive feet slapping after me. How did it sneak up on me without my hearing it? Has it just stepped out of one of the goblin places? I don't know how to properly interpret the topographical qualities of this juxtaposed territory and there is no time to figure it out now.

I feel its wet breath on the back of my neck. It smells like incense and bile. I put my head down and try to make my legs go faster.

Screams from the courtyard. Human screams. As I come around the side of the main hall I catch a glimpse of a second ogre, laying about him with a club; smashing down palm trees and striking chunks of masonry off the walls in some red fury. The gangster with the Ray-Bans lies smeared across the walls and floor.

A third ogre comes through the broken doors in front of the hall, dragging the yakuza with the coiffure behind him. He screams and thrashes until the ogre picks him up with one hand and drives him face-first into the courtyard pavers. An explosion of bone and brain matter extinguishes the screaming.

My own pursuer's truncheon smashes into the wall near my head, showering me with a spray of broken tiles. I zig to the right and collide with the last gangster—the balding one. His eyes are panicked, and he has lost his weapon. I shove past him and stumble on, putting him between me and the ogre.

Gunshots. Three of them.

I throw myself into a headlong dive, slam hard into the ground, roll clumsily. Disoriented, I try to raise my head.

The balding yakuza is laid out flat with a hole in the back of his head. Nearby, the ogre is reeling about, covering its eyes with its hands and making small wailing noises. When it lowers its hands, I see that its bulging eyes have been replaced with a wash of red.

"Hurry!" The familiar hiss comes not from the yellow fox, but from a woman in an elaborate kimono, who is still pointing a smoking revolver at the ogre. It looks like a cowboy's gun. I wonder if she took it from one of the yakuza or if she has been carrying it in her obi. "There are more of them on the way."

The fox-woman turns away in a swirl of skirts. I notice that she is barefoot. As I rush after her, I overhear one of the ogres asking after the health of its blinded companion in high pitched, sarcastic tones. It sounds just like a yakuza.

"Why did you stop following me?" demands the fox-woman, once we're back inside Nagasaki proper and free of pursuit.

"I didn't feel like running into a nest of oni."

"We could have eluded them in the woods," replies the fox-woman. "Anyway, you disappeared."

"You weren't paying attention," she replies. "If you will not do as I say I cannot prevent you from blundering to your death."

"Why do you care about my safety?"

"I don't," she replies. "My master does."

"Who is this master?"

The fox-lady turns to look at me. Beneath a streetlamp I can finally get a good look at her. There is something beguiling about her features, and also something feral. A cunning and vicious intelligence. Her eyes are so black that it is impossible to tell the iris from the pupils.

"You know who he is," she replies, just as I notice that only one of her eyes is black. The other is a very dark red.

"The Black and Crimson King." I speak in English.

"Kurenai-sama." The Japanese name fits him better than any of his English titles, although it sounds a little feminine.

"What does Kurenai-sama want from me?"

"I don't know what he wants. You are still a part of his story—or he is a part of yours."

"My name is Zai, by the way."

"I know that."

"What's your name?"

"You can call me Chieko."

Chieko leads me into the Nagasaki JR station. Kiosks, benches, drink vending machines, digital displays showing the departure times and platforms. This could be any train station in the conventional Japan, but for the lack of advertisements and English language signage.

Chieko buys me a ticket from the machine, using only coins, and then we use them to pass through the turnstiles to the long-distance platforms. Even the turnstiles are the same. If we were riding the local trains, I could probably have used my Suica card to gain access.

"Where are we going?"

"The place you need to be."

If Chieko would tell me the destination, I could ride there by myself, and she could go back to catching rabbits or bamboozling horny teenagers, or whatever it is that *kitsune* spirits do when they are not running covert missions for guerrilla fairy kings.

Once we have validated our tickets, we get in line for a security check. This is different. At the end of each line is a robot: a sensor panel, a speaker grille, a blinking red light, and a spindly articulated arm with a katana blade mounted on the end of it.

I produce my scroll, but Chieko stops me. "If you show that, the sentry is going to cut you."

"The codes are legitimate."

"The codes are legitimate," she replies, "but the handwriting is not."

I had assumed the calligraphy on my scroll was just some neo-feudal decoration. It never occurred to me that they would run handwriting recognition software on it. Apparently, it did not occur to Unfolded Enterprises, either, who have otherwise been meticulous about providing me with valid documents, no matter where they have sent me.

We edge closer to the security robot. "How can we pass without proper documentation?"

"Magic," she replies.

"But it's a robot."

"That makes it easier," says Chieko. "It has no will with which to resist my charms. When the blade rises, you must precede me through the gate. I will follow to make sure the injunction holds."

We're at the front of the line. Chieko approaches the speaker grille and says, "I am Inari Chieko, and my companion is Urashima Tarō. We may pass."

I cringe at the alias, but the robot raises the sword and Chieko gestures with her chin for me to go through. I give a small bow to the speaker grill and proceed. Chieko follows one stride behind me.

I find that I am shaking as we proceed towards our platform. Would the robot really have cut me down in public if my papers were not in order? That is the moment where I cease to think of Ōyashima as a weird, fuddy-duddy part of Japan. This is not my home.

Chieko gives me a sidelong smile. I catch a glimpse of bright white teeth behind her lips.

The 11:40 to Hakata rolls into the station exactly on time and passengers debark. This part of the country is not serviced by shinkansen bullet trains, but the train we board is a handsome *Kamome* model capable of hitting 130 kilometers an hour. Chieko and I find our designated seats and sit down on the comfortable black upholstery.

I look at my ticket when the train pulls out. We are bound for Kageyamamura, an ominous-sounding place that I have never heard of. It does not appear on the route map above the doors. I lean back into my seat and watch the scenery pass, dark behind the glass. Chieko's reflection, overlaid on the landscape, looks wilder than her real face.

The carriage is about three quarters full, and I notice that some of the other passengers are not quite human. A woman sitting across the aisle from me, intently reading a phonebook-sized volume of *Shonen Jump*, has neither eyes nor a nose above a wide black mouth filled with shark's teeth. A man sitting three rows ahead has a neck that must be fifty centimeters long. I am almost certain that the passenger sitting by the door at the far end of the carriage is actually a ceramic urn wearing a kimono, but I don't want to stare.

The majority of passengers are ordinary citizens. None of them pay the *youkai* travelers any particular attention.

"Once, the whole world was like this," Chieko tells me. "The goblin folk could move freely amongst the humans, and humans would often venture into the fairy realms. Ōyashima is one of the very few places where this remains true."

"Why is that?" I ask.

"Ōyashima is halfway to being a dream," says Chieko. "The boundaries between worlds have not thickened as they have in the mundane Earth."

Deep inside, a part of me is screaming. I am accustomed seeing the strange, the supernatural and the weird, but only in exotic locales. Here, in a place that so resembles my home, it hits me right in the culture.

I look around the carriage again and then back at Chieko: "It's very Studio Ghibli, isn't it?"

"If you had said Harry Potter," she replies, "I would have bitten you."

The train makes two unscheduled stops before we get to Kageyamamura. The lady with the shark's teeth gets off at the first of these. None of the citizens appear to register that the train has even stopped.

Kageyamamura is exactly as its name describes: a small town built in the shadow of a mountain. Its station completely unmanned—not even an executioner robot on duty. Chieko and I put our tickets into the turnstiles and pass through without obstruction. Movement behind me draws my attention as we emerge from the main doors, and I catch a glimpse of something huge and dark gliding over the tiles behind me. I cannot bring myself to turn around for a closer look.

Seeing the look on my face, Chieko pats me on the arm. "Don't worry. It's one of ours. Probably."

That does not reassure me.

Instead of heading into town, we clamber down a cutting and cross the tracks. On the far side, Chieko leads us to a concealed pathway that winds up the mountainside. The sloped ground is thick with fir and cedar trees. It's colder here than it was in Nagasaki, and I wish I had worn the ugly *haori* jacket.

Ahead of me, Chieko's kimono slips down off her shoulders. There's a tattoo of a fox, rendered in a traditional style, all down the length of her spine. The kimono continues to slide, and somehow the rest of Chieko slides off with it, until the fox is all that remains. The kimono is gone, just the same as her human form. Chieko looks back at me with a grin on her triangular face. "Come."

We turn off the road onto a narrow trail through the trees. The vegetation and the lighting change subtly with every turn or bend. Wherever we are going, I hope there are no ogres this time.

After about fifteen minutes, Chieko calls a halt. "Over that ridge you will find the place you are seeking. I can go no further—it is warded against the likes of me."

"What is this place?"

"The thing that you are looking for."

"My enemy?"

Chieko gives me a scornful look and shakes her head. Of course, it wouldn't be that easy. "Go. When you return…if you return…I will find you in these woods."

"Can't you wait for me here?"

"There are patrols."

I do as I am told. I do not trust Chieko, but she did save my life a couple of times, and she has no reason to abandon me now. My own abilities might be adequate to find the Way back to the station, but I am not confident that I can safely ride the train unaccompanied. I am not confident that the train will even stop for me. I am certain that I cannot pass the executioner robots when I get back to Nagasaki.

Over the ridge, I find a handful of wooden buildings inside a rickety stockade. There are no lights. The place is not exactly camouflaged, but unless you approach it from just the right angle, it is very easy to overlook. My topographical senses give me nothing.

As my curiosity gives way to concern, I realise that I am not alone. I am uncertain how long the sentry has been standing in front of me. He slowly resolves in my vision, as if from a focus pull in a movie.

The sentry is dressed in high tech dark grey fatigues, complete with hood and bandana. His hands are wrapped, and he has *tabi* shoes on his feet. The sentry stands in a natural posture, holding a naked short sword with a black, Teflon-coated blade. I have no doubt that he could kill me faster than I can blink.

All I can do is I smile brightly. "Good evening. I am here to speak with the boss ninja?"

The ninja herds me into the hamlet at sword-point. The stockade, on close inspection, is a lot less rickety than I first thought. I wonder at the spell-wards that keep the *youkai* out and mute my senses. The *shinobi* clans are said to have had their own magical abilities, of course, but even after my encounter in Tokyo, I had always believed this to be nonsense. Most of what passes for knowledge about these people, up to and including the word 'ninja', was invented by novelists.

We cross a bare dirt yard and enter one of the huts. A single room, with rude wooden walls, exposed rafters, rotting tatami. I am surprised to see electrical fittings, although they have long since burned out. There is no furniture. No glass in the windows.

My escort lifts the corner of a tatami mat with a toe. "Get on the floor."

I get down onto my hands and knees.

"Open the trapdoor."

I grope around on the floorboards until I find a notch in the wood. I hook a finger through it and pull, and a section of flooring about one meter square comes away in my hands. A steel ladder leads down into, I presume, a secret ninja compound.

"Climb down," says the ninja.

I do as he says.

We are in a cave system. My escort leads me through a network of dim tunnels and caverns in a circuitous route that I think is intended to disorient me, and probably would if I was somebody else. We are moving downhill, deeper into the mountain. Sometimes the walls are bare rock; sometimes they are shored up with wood. Low wattage light bulbs enclosed in steel mesh cages provide just enough light to see by. I stumble along with exaggerated clumsiness, but my topographical senses have returned. I suppose the wards Chieko mentioned only protect the hamlet and its immediate area.

We descend further, passing through many chambers. Sometimes they are sealed by doors or portcullises. Sometimes there are mats on the floor. We pass an armoury, a kitchen, a laundry filled with racks of grey ninja pyjamas. Occasionally we see other men and women in their dark fatigues. They turn to watch silently as we go past. Nobody bows to anyone: the *shinobi* clans have no truck with samurai etiquette.

Finally, we come to a small chamber papered with maps, diagrams, and grainy surveillance photographs. A grizzled, shaven-headed man in his mid-fifties is waiting there, sitting slouched behind a low table. The table is also covered with maps, as well as a conventional-Japan smartphone and a loose pile of shuriken.

"Sit."

I kneel in *seiza* and force myself not to bow.

"Who are you?"

"I am called Zai."

He smiles crookedly. "You chose that yourself, eh?"

"I did."

"I am Minoru."

"You chose that yourself, too?"

"For tonight, yes. Tomorrow I will choose another name."

I think to myself, in English, the words *fucking ninjas*.

"Why are you here?" says Minoru.

"I am seeking information about a foreigner named Russell Kilmer-Jones. He hired one of your operatives for a mission in conventional Japan."

"I cannot divulge such information to a third party."

"I am not a third party. I was the target."

Minoru raises an eyebrow. "And what happened?"

"Your operative will not be returning to this mountain stronghold."

"Ah. Ikari-san. I will strike his name from the ledger."

"Ikari." Meaning 'anger' or 'anchor', depending on the spelling. A good name for a ninja.

"He was very young," says Minoru, as if to explain away the flamboyant name. He shows no sympathy for the young man's plight. "Talented, too."

"Now he will never grow old."

"Zai-san, what was your relationship with this Russell Kilmer-Jones?"

"I used to work for him."

"In what capacity?"

"I am a killer."

A slow blink is the only indication that he considers this to be unlikely. "Why did your employment end?"

"It did not. Mister Kilmer-Jones left the organization. I do not know where he went."

"And yet he sent an assassin to kill you."

"Two assassins. Ikari-san had a partner."

"Ah," says Minoru, as if that explains everything. He is right, too. If

Ikari had been alone, I would probably have died without even knowing he was there.

Probably.

I sit silently with my hands on my thighs. Minoru has admitted that the operative I killed was one of his own men. He is going to give me something now, I am sure of it. I just hope it's not a shuriken in each eye.

"As a professional courtesy, I will tell you that your Russell Kilmer-Jones' new appointment is a government position. He is now the head of Tactical Operations for the Secret Intelligence Service in the meta-nation known as Albion."

"I have never been to this place."

"Albion is an island nation, in many ways like Ōyashima," says Minoru. "*Sakoku*, just as we are. While we do not have an alliance, there are...political relationships...when it comes to...difficult situations... in the conventional world."

"You trade information. And sometimes, human resources."

Minoru nods. "Just so."

I start to get up. "Minoru-san, you have been most helpful, and I thank you for your courtesy." I say 'courtesy', not 'hospitality', because he has not offered me any refreshments. I would not have consumed them even if he had.

"Stop."

I freeze. I am in a half-kneel, bent slightly forward.

"Move half a pace to your right and then stand up."

I do so. No traps fire.

Minoru rises slowly but gracefully from his slouch. As he does so I see a lever that was concealed beneath one of his knees, a spring-loaded switch that was resting under his foot, a pressure plate at the small of his back.

"Best if I show you the way out." He smiles a little smile. "The path you took to this room cannot be safely traversed in the opposite direction."

Minoru opens a concealed panel and then leads me out into another corridor. We make three more turns, heading back towards the mountain face on a slight uphill grade. We come to a steel door.

"Behind this door there are no traps," he says. "If you can find your way out, you will emerge near to the place my man found you, and you may leave unhindered." He hands me a short sword and says "Take this. You will need it if you see me again. But I do not think you will see me."

The sword is like the one Ikari used: a bit longer than a *wakizashi*, with a straight, square blade. Not as sharp or elegant as a proper samurai blade.

I take the blade in two hands and bow. Dojo etiquette; a calculated insult. "Thank you again for your courtesy."

"I am not doing this out of courtesy," says Minoru. "I am doing this because I want to see what you can do."

He opens the steel door and I step through.

I am standing in a long, silvered hallway. My own reflection regards me from every direction. I would laugh out loud, if that was a behaviour of which I was capable. I am here in a genuine ninja stronghold, and they have set me in a mirror maze.

The blade feels good in my hand, although I am uncomfortable with the prospect of having to stand and fight somebody. My job is to kill people while they are unaware. To endure this inversion a second time—in my enemy's territory—feels like some kind of karmic adjustment.

Of course, I have some advantages, too. I am sensible about how mirrors work, and my topographic senses show me the layout of the terrain in advance. I still don't know how I am going to survive a confrontation with Minoru, but he will not be able to surprise me as easily as he thinks.

The most disconcerting thing about the maze is the way it shows me images of myself from angles I am unused to. Do my ears really protrude so much when viewed from behind? Do I really have those lines on the back of my neck? I have never believed myself handsome, but my small vanities have certainly been damaged by this experience.

Sometimes my reflection seems far away, and the hall seems very, very long. When I am close to my image it means that I am close to a mirror. I try not to focus on the reflections and extend my topographic senses. I am looking for creases or folds, for anything that might allow me to use my abilities to set some kind of trap for Minoru, but the only thing I learn is that the walls are very wide and probably hollow. There is enough space in between the mirror-panes for a man to walk and I am certain that's what Minoru is now doing. He told me I wouldn't see him coming, and with all these mirrors around, the only way that is possible is if he cheats.

My topographical sense does not give me any indication of motion, so I can't tell where Minoru is, but if I find the right position, I can predict where he will be. This is like an inside-out version of Tetris.

When I reach a favourable T-junction, I stop, pretending to be disoriented. In a motion that I hope looks like some sort of a calming tai-chi exercise, I spread my arms, describing a circle with my hands. Opening a Door.

I have been practicing, of course. Although I still have not succeeded in making a Door that leads to another place, I am getting quite good at controlling the time-gap on the opening side of the portal. I fold the back edges of the Door back, so that it will take longer to seal itself. My hands are slick on the grip of the sword.

I stand there, scratching my chin and feigning indecision for half a minute before the glass shatters and Minoru bursts through it. Even with the barrier he is lethally quick; more than quick enough to have skewered me before I could begin to turn...if I hadn't set that Door there.

I have set a ten second time differential, which gives me time to turn and bring my own weapon to bear. When Minoru's blade appears, after that ten second delay, I bring my short sword down as hard as I can. My blade cuts about halfway into his topmost arm, about an inch above the wrist. One of the bones breaks and he drops his weapon—a beautiful hand-forged katana. If he had given me that blade instead of the little home-made *ninjato*, he would have lost both hands.

I wrench the blade free, turn it sideways, and hack. The blade pierces Minoru through the neck on the other side of the Door ten seconds before the shock of it jars up my arms. There is no pain on his face, just confusion.

I let go of the blade and he collapses. "That is what I can do," I tell his dead body.

I am certain James Bond would have come up with something better.

At the end of the maze there is a door that opens out onto a rocky shelf on the side of the mountain. It closes smoothly behind me, offering no way back inside. I dust the broken glass off as best I can and wonder at how little blood has splattered across my kimono. Luckily, the fabric is dark. Hopefully, it can pass for spilled soy sauce.

I slip into the woods and start to head back in the direction of the stockade. Chieko finds me before I get there. "Did you get what you came for?"

"I did."

"Then, come! Come!" She uses the word as one might use it to command a dog or a small child.

Our route back to Kageyamamura is different, but just as meandering. I don't know whether this is because the Way there can only be traversed in one direction, or whether Chieko is trying to avoid an ambush. I do not bother to ask because I know she will not tell me.

The sun is coming up when we reach the station. There are three other passengers waiting there: a middle-aged woman; a disembodied foot the size of a briefcase; and a bushy-haired man seated on a pair of distended fleshy cushions that I take to be his testicles. The gliding shadow is gone—perhaps home to a hot meal, or maybe to some stranger's home to steal their children. Who can say?

The train pulls up and we all climb aboard.

Forty minutes later and we are back in Nagasaki, and Chieko and I are standing in line to show our papers. She seems to have relaxed now that the mission is over. I am suddenly starving—I skipped dinner and it has been a long, eventful night. When Chieko hears my stomach rumbling, she tells me that she knows a place where I can get a proper modern Tokyo breakfast: toast and coffee and cigarettes. I don't mention that I do not smoke.

Chieko approaches the speaker grille at the check point and says, "I am Inari Chieko, and my companion is Urashima Tarō. We may pass."

The robot raises its sword and I pass under it. Chieko follows. Is she swinging her hips a little? Her kimono is loose around her shoulders. I suppose I should expect that she would be a little foxy, now that she is able to be herself. Unfortunately, this has also made her careless.

A klaxon sounds and the sword comes down, executing a perfect diagonal cut as Chieko leaps through the checkpoint. The blade slices off a bushy fox-tail in a spray of black-and-red blood.

Chieko dives right into her fox shape, which is now lacking a tail.

"Go!" she barks at me and disappears into a sea of legs.

I need no encouragement to flee. There is nothing I can do to help her. Chieko's bleeding badly, but she is a wily fox: I think she will be okay. I let the motion of the panicking crowd bear me out clear of the guards. Like a dozen other people, I clamber over the turnstiles and scramble out into the street.

I do not think anybody has made me, but I am sure the security cameras have footage of the two of us coming and going. Time to get out of here before the authorities and/ or the yakuza can orchestrate a manhunt.

Rambo-san is still asleep when I get back to the hotel. I pound on his door until I hear him stir. He stumbles around cursing in Karachidaean for another minute before he opens the door; shirtless and wearing his fatigue pants back-to-front. His eyes are red, and he looks extremely hung over.

"Shower, get sober, get the plane ready," I tell him. "We're leaving."

"What?"

"Time to go, Rambo-san." I try to keep the urgency out of my voice. It is probably going to take the authorities a while to connect me, an undocumented foreigner, to 'Urashima Taro', but I am worried that they will close off Dejima in the meantime.

Slowly, Rambo-san's expression cycles from confusion to shock. He turns and shambles away without even bothering to close the door.

"Drink some water," I tell his retreating back.

I go to my own room and have a very quick shower. I cannot believe how much glass is in my hair. I change into a fresh set of clothes—jeans and a fresh aloha shirt, showing parrots and toucans against a jungle green. Downstairs, I scarf down a slice of toast and a hardboiled egg at the breakfast buffet.

Before long, Rambo-san shambles into the room, looking cleaner but not any less hung over. I hand him a cup of coffee and he drains it gratefully.

"You look rough," I say. "Are you able to fly?" There are plenty of other pilots here if he is not. I will pay whatever I need to…but I don't know if I can trust any of them.

"I'm able," he says, but his eyes are wide, and his body-language is edgy. I wonder at the strength of the hangover that has destroyed his usual unrelenting braggadocio.

In the customs hall, the immigration clerk stamps Rambo-san's fake Dutch passport, and then my own mostly-real Japanese one. It is illegal for natives to leave Ōyashima, but the authorities here are more than happy for foreigners to leave whenever they like. Even a foreigner like me, from the real Japan.

As we cross the gangway to the aircraft carrier where our Learjet is waiting, Rambo-san seems to come to a decision. He stops and turns to face me slowly. He has his hand inside his coat.

"Home-buddy." His voice cracks like a teenager's. "There's something you should know." Rambo-sane pulls a .44 magnum from inside his coat.

I raise an eyebrow.

"While you were in Nagasaki, some guy did come to me."

I raise both hands, to match my eyebrow. "Some guy?"

"Local guy," he says. "He heard you were looking for the English Man."

"And what did he tell you?"

"He told me, if I kill you, English Man will reward to me." Rambo-san's eyes are red and wet.

"And if you do not?" I take a timid, shuffling step towards him.

"Then in case of that, he will send a one to find me," replies Rambo-san. "Then us both? We die."

"And you believed some guy?" Another shuffling step.

"He was convincing," says Rambo-san.

"He paid you cash?"

Rambo-san's face reddens, but he does not deny it. "Cash a lot."

I lower my eyes and take another small step. "I thought you were my friend."

His pale eyes bulge with anger. "Your friend?" he says. "I wanted so your friend, but always you… 'No, Rambo, son.' 'Maybe next time, Rambo, son.' You tell I am you 'son', but next time is *never*." He takes a breath. "And now, Dad, next time is now."

"Rambo-san." I feel strangely touched, that he thought I was calling him my son. And I am shocked, that he thinks I am old enough to be his father. "Do you really think I will die so easily?"

"You, Zai, my buddy, I used to think were hard in the core," he says. "I thinked you were bad like the ass. But you are just a lucky one. You're not even dangerous. You are just an asshole."

I blink hard and glance over Rambo-san's shoulder, letting my mouth fall open. Before he can think twice, he glances behind him looking for whatever threat has startled me. I scream as I rush him, pushing the gun aside with one hand and slamming my shoulder into his chest. He squeezes the trigger. The gun blast is deafening, but the weapon is not pointed at me and the bullet ricochets loudly off the side of the aircraft carrier.

Rambo-san falls against the safety rail, still flailing with the gun. I grab one of his legs and tip him over the side. He screams as he falls, although I cannot hear what he says for the ringing in my ears.

I see him hit the water and go under. He's not far from the support pontoon but he does not appear to be a very good swimmer. Rambo-san surfaces, thrashing and gibbering. He goes under again and stays under.

I turn back towards the customs post and sigh. Now I need to find a trustworthy new pilot.

#9: Next Door to Alice

In a deserted gate lounge in an unused corner of Frankfurt Airport's miserable grey sprawl, Vashya and her bodyguards are waiting for me.

There is a manned security checkpoint to access the lounge, even though there is no flight scheduled here. I do not know if this is due to bureaucratic error or Vashya's influence, or both. Even so, the airport security team run my carry-on through the X-Ray machine and check my boarding pass before they allow me through. Vashya and her guards sit watching the proceedings impassively.

Since they do not appear to think this is funny, I open the conversation with an attempted apology about Rambo-san.

Vashya waves my explanation away. "He is gone, is he. Where is the Russell Kilmer-Jones?"

Vashya failing to repeat the Englishman's name takes me by surprise. Is it a discourtesy? To me or to him, or both? I don't know, but she clearly wants a direct answer.

"Russell Kilmer-Jones is in Albion."

Vashya shakes her head. "Albion."

Her body language is not encouraging but I feel obliged to press on. "How can I get there?"

"Heathrow."

"England?" I cannot conceal my surprise. The word escapes with a strained Japanese emphasis.

"Britain. Zai, the true Britain is Albion, as true Japan is Ōyashima, Zai."

"But…Heathrow is Heathrow, right?"

"Yes."

Great. Of all the airports in the world, I think I hate Heathrow the most. I put my irritation aside and take a moment to chew over what Vashya has told me. Albion is a meta-Britain; separated from the rest of reality out of spite and racism. This raises a new concern.

"Will I be able to operate over there? I am not...English."

Vashya takes long seconds to reply. "Zai, you must say you are Chinese, Zai."

If Russell Kilmer-Jones was here, he would be smirking as hard as he could. For the first time in my life, I think I would rather stay home.

Heathrow. Despite the fact that I am wearing a bowtie, a bowler hat, and a ludicrous fake moustache, the immigration guard allows me through with less fuss than usual. "Off you go, Mr Chan. Have a lovely stay."

I thank him and hurry on. I should be fine, as long as I don't run into any Chinese nationals. There are 1.3 billion of them, but I am certain they can't all fit into Heathrow airport.

Pushing my old-fashioned leather luggage on a hand cart I take the rail shuttle from Terminal 4 to Terminal 1. Then I change for Terminal 5. If Michiko saw me dressed like this, she would cancel the wedding without hesitation.

I take the exit for Ground Transportation and head for the inter-terminal buses. Within a few minutes an unmarked black minivan pulls up. The driver is wearing black livery with lots of brass buttons, a peaked cap, and patent leather shoes. He sits in the van with his arms folded and stares at me as I approach him.

"Terminal 7?"

The driver's attitude changes immediately. "Right you are, guv'nor. Let me help you with that." As he reaches for my ridiculous luggage, I wonder—not for the first time—if my life is actually a cartoon.

The minivan is a make that I have never seen before; fuddy-duddy in a way that's bereft of irony; like the Russian Lada, or the Hungarian Rába. The vehicle is modern, but it looks as if it was designed on some philosophy that was abandoned decades ago by the rest of the auto industry. I want to take a photo, but London is heavily surveilled, and I do not want to be caught taking snapshots of the mystery bus to the secret terminal. Certainly not in this outfit.

On the way to Terminal 7, the driver pilots the minivan behind the hangars and the maintenance sheds; around the far jet-ways; past ground crew pits and control towers and loading bays. Heathrow is only supposed to have five terminals—I wonder briefly what happened to Terminal 6. A mystery for another time.

We pass through several Doors along the way. The transitions are subtle, but I feel them in the bones of my hands. Each transition leads to a Heathrow that is subtly different than the one preceding it. By the time the minivan stops at Terminal 7, the drab concrete structures of the real Heathrow have been replaced by a multi-storeyed edifice that looks modern despite the fussy Edwardian design. Mirrored windows and automatic doorways recessed into tall, concrete archways. The shuttle driver lets me out and wrestles my enormous luggage from the back of the van.

Inside the terminal, I can see the familiar signs for the Underground, but I am not going to use the subway while so heavily encumbered. I join the queue at the taxi rank.

The residents of True London are every bit as rude as their conventional earth counterparts. They jostle me around, blow cigarette smoke in my face and talk self-importantly on ornate but state-of-the-art mobile telephones. Unlike real Londoners, these are all pasty Caucasians in hats. I feel less self-conscious about my suit and more self-conscious about my face.

When I get to the front of the queue a black cab pulls up and I get inside.

"Limehouse, please." I suppress a sigh. "The Oriental Palace."

The driver, who is wearing a chauffeur's double-breasted coat and cap gives me a look of sneering distaste. "Shadwell, you mean."

"Of course. Shadwell." The address Vashya provided says Limehouse, but I see no reason to provoke an argument.

The major landmarks in True London are the same as they are in the London I know, but the rest of the city is not. There are many more heritage buildings and many fewer skyscrapers. It is a technologically advanced city—satellite dishes on the roofs, power cables strung across the streets—but it seems much older than my real one. I do not believe that this London was bombed during the Blitz. Although it looks nothing like Ōyashima's Nagasaki, I am struck by the similarities.

The cab stays on the north bank of the Thames. This river, at least, is the same as the real one: congested and filthy. So is the traffic.

Soon we are in Shadwell. Chinese restaurants, opium dens, cathouses, laundries, tailors. Every Yellow Peril stereotype distilled here into this ghetto neighbourhood.

Outside the hotel, a bellboy in a standing-collared jacket and a flat-topped cap rushes over. He bows and addresses me in Mandarin. I gesture at my luggage and sweep inside, leaving the poor man to wrestle the enormous case out of the boot of the car. Better to be rude than to reveal myself.

The hotel was once a grand place, but that was a long ago. Now the

171

walls are grimy, and the carpets are stained. The furniture is chipped, and the fittings are cracked. It smells of sweat and antiseptic. At the front desk, an old man wearing a double-breasted jacket made of green silk greets me.

"We are in Albion," I reply, as haughtily as I can. "Speak English, please."

I show him my new Hong Kong passport and check in under its uncomfortable new alias, James Chan.

After I take a shower, I turn on the TV and try to relax. Australian soap operas with incessant commercial breaks. Lots of propaganda from the government, which calls itself the Crown. If there are any other political parties, they are very quiet. The news channels refer to the monarchy constantly and with much devotion, but do not present any actual information about the doings of the royal family. I can only tolerate about twenty minutes of it before I turn it off in disgust.

There is no point moping around in here in my underwear, so I change into a fresh suit of clothes. There are plenty to choose from in my voluminous luggage. There are five laundry businesses on this block—there is absolutely no reason for me to have brought so much clothing. I spend a full ten minutes grumbling to myself about the suitcase and the costumes it contains before I realize that I am scared.

Usually when I am working, I travel as a caricature of who I really am. But here I am in a police state and with a cover story that is thinner than single-single-ply toilet paper. My contact, Russell Kilmer-Jones, is in charge of the special operations police and is sure to be heavily guarded. And this is one mission where I cannot fail. My contact is my enemy. He knows who I am, and he already wants me dead.

What if he finds out about Michiko?

I'm scared, but for once I am neither tired nor hungry. The flight from Zurich was easy, and I ate well before I left.

I throw the fake moustache into the garbage bin, smooth down my hair, and head out into True London to see what I may find.

The tube in True London is cleaner than the real one, but the trains and the fixtures are otherwise identical. The stations look the same. There are occasions when we pass through Doors as we ride about the network, and I believe that some parts of the rail system are shared with the mundane London. I suppose it would be more efficient to share infrastructure, since both cities are geographically similar. I debark at Tower Hill.

Albion's Tower of London is not a tourist attraction. Here in Albion, it serves as a headquarters for law enforcement and domestic security services, including Kilmer-Jones' organization.

The inner and outer wards have been covered with a polycarbonate roof, and the windows are mirrored with one-way glass. There are no jolly Beefeaters to show tourists around. Instead of the Coldstream guards in their comical busby hats, there are soldiers with assault rifles and flak jackets. Snipers are posted on every nearby rooftop.

A black limousine with tinted windows draws up to the massive steel gates between the Cradle Tower and the Well Tower. After a good thirty seconds the gates open and the car coasts forward into a sealed steel vestibule. Before the gate closes again, I see soldiers with machine guns and sniffer dogs move up to inspect the vehicle. There is no way I can trick my way past that level of security.

I cannot see any other way in or out of the complex. If this was a movie there would be underground passages or a ventilation system with conveniently human-sized ducts, but I am certain that even if such passages and ducts exist, they will be just as heavily guarded.

This isn't a job for an assassin. It's a job for an army.

I cross Tower Bridge on foot and head west, towards the Southbank. The late afternoon air is crisp and I am finally getting hungry. I would love a curry, but I do not think there is any to be had in this part of True London. After a moment's consideration I decide that bland, expensive English food is preferable to whatever is available in Shadwell, so I head for the closest pub. A sign by the door names it the Loom and Spikenard.

I receive a few hostile looks when I walk into the establishment, but I ignore them as I belly up to the bar and find a menu. The barman glowers when I wave to him for attention. "Yes?"

"Can I have a roast beef sandwich and a pint of Newcastle, please?"

There's a long silence. Conversation throughout the pub stops.

"You think this is funny?" says the barman.

"A sandwich and a pint of Newcastle?" I enunciate each word carefully, in case he has misheard some insult in my accent.

"You think it's *funny*?"

I have no idea how to respond.

"You think you can just march your yellow arse into my fine establishment and demand *service*? From *me*?"

The silence hangs long enough that I attempt an answer. "Yes?"

"You might be King of all the Chinese in this and every world, but here? In my pub?" The barman spits the words at me. "I'll have no dogs or foreigners in *my* pub."

"The Crown should kick out the lot of you," says a voice from behind me.

Before I can look around, a couple of men grab my arms and drag me stumbling to the doors. One of them cuffs me across the face. The other plants a boot squarely on my backside and sends me crashing out into the street. I don't even hear the door slam.

Slowly, getting my wind back, I roll over and get to all fours. My suit pants are torn, and I have skinned my hands and knees badly. I touch my face and find my mouth swollen and bleeding. I am shaking. It takes me a moment to understand this unfamiliar sensation.

I am angry.

"Excuse me, sir, are you quite alright?" A man in a bowler hat and a suit. Goatee and a moustache. He holds out a hand. I take it gratefully and he hauls me to my feet.

"I'm fine, thank you."

I am still clasping the man's hand when his face changes. Flattens. He has monolid eyes now, and his brown goatee has darkened to black. He's East Asian, like me.

The man lets go of my hand and becomes once more an English businessman. The transition is faster, this time. Magic.

The magician smiles at my expression. "You must be new here."

I don't know what to say, so I tell him, "My name is James Chan."

He looks at me a moment too long. Then he smiles. "David Lo." His smile kinks, like he just told some kind of a joke. I nod as if I get it, but I do not smile back.

"Pleased to meet you, David."

"Call me Dave," he says. "I am a physician," says Dave. "My surgery is just around the corner. Come with me and I will treat your injuries."

"I'll be alright."

"I think you might be suffering from a mild concussion," he says, leaning uncomfortably close and peering into my eyes.

I know that I cannot trust a man who can change his face at will, but I am angry, I'm hurting, and I'm embarrassed, standing here on the street. And if he betrays me, well...

I have never killed a magician before.

had expected Dave's rooms would be filled with charts of the meridians and cabinets full of herbs, but it turns out to be a regular doctor's surgery. He leads me through an empty waiting area into an ordinary consulting room.

"Sit."

I sit down on the examination bed and Dave, again wearing his Asian face, proceeds to shine a light in my eyes, to listen to my heart. He tests my reflexes with a rubber hammer. He straps a cuff onto my arm to measure my blood pressure. While we wait for the cuff to inflate, he says "*Ni hui shuo yue ma?*"

"I'm sorry, my Mandarin isn't very good. Can we speak English?"

"Certainly," he says, smiling. Dave Lo smiles a lot. His voice has a strange hiss behind the upper-class British elocution. "You have a strange accent."

The blood pressure cuff is fully inflated now, tight around my bicep. "I came here after an extended time in Germany." It was a pretty long layover in Frankfurt, after all. I hope it's a plausible excuse for the accent of a Japanese man who sounds a little bit American but is trying to sound British, while pretending to be Chinese.

The cuff deflates and David takes a reading from the machine. He looks up and smiles. I haven't lied to him, but he knows I am not being honest.

He cleans my wounds with peroxide and tapes up the gash in my knee. There is something paternal about his attitude that is beginning to feel creepy.

"I'm pleased to say that you've sustained no lasting damage, James."

"No concussion?"

"I don't believe so. Keep the dressing clean and dry and you'll be just fine."

I slide off the bed and test my knees. I am still a bit tender but he's right—my wounds are only minor lacerations.

I feel like he is still examining me on some level, but he says nothing more. He just keeps smiling.

"Well, thank you very much, Doctor Lo. I feel much better now. How much do I owe you?"

"No charge. The NHS works very well here. And please, call me David."

"Thank you very much, David. I appreciate you going out of your way to look after a stranger."

Dave's smile develops a momentary kink. "Stranger than you think, James. What are you doing here, anyway?"

"I was trying to buy a sandwich."

"If you are still hungry," he replies, "I know a good place for curry."

I shake my head. "Right now, I just want to go back to my hotel and rest. But thank you for the invitation."

"Perhaps another time, then."

I give a small bow and back out of the room. Even when the door is closed, I can still feel that smile upon me.

By the time I emerge from Shadwell station it's full dark. Using the tube means there is a lot of CCTV footage of me, but I don't trust the cab drivers either. I must just accept that there is no escape from surveillance here. Even had I chosen to walk back to the hotel, there are cameras on every street corner which would have captured me.

In my room at the Oriental Palace, I have a shower and inspect the damage in the bathroom mirror. I have a fat lip and my jaw is bruised and tender. I have been beaten just badly enough that people will remember me. That's not good. Perhaps I should start wearing the fake moustache again?

The door explodes as I emerge from the bathroom. A sharp fizzing precedes the detonation of a flash grenade and I try to turn away, but it's too late. White noise buzzes in my ears. Colours too bright to distinguish dazzle me through my screwed-shut eyelids.

Someone takes out my legs with an extendable baton. Cops. More blows land upon my shoulders, my neck, my head and back, my ribs—some from batons, some from fists or boots. I am blind and deaf, and I don't know exactly how I have come to be lying prone on the floor.

The cheap carpet chafes my bare skin as rough hands roll me onto my belly. Someone slaps a pair of handcuffs onto my wrists, and manacles over my feet. My vision is just beginning to return when the black bag goes over my head.

I am unsure how long I have been in the cell.

I have only retained flashes of how I got here. Dragged through the hotel. Stuffed into a car. Carried bodily by men I cannot see, who bark orders in voices muffled by the fabric of the blind the ringing in my ears. A heavy door slamming shut. I am still finding it difficult to form a coherent thought.

I look around slowly, although I have been sitting here for some time now. Minutes? Hours? I do not know.

There isn't much to look at. A mattress, a steel toilet bowl without a seat, and a steel washbasin with a single tap. The ceiling, which is the same bare concrete as the walls and floor, is only a few inches above my head if I stand up. The door is a slab of scarred steel without any indication of a lock. I expect there is a tiny fibre optic camera embedded in the walls somewhere.

I am covered in welts and bruises, but I don't think any of my bones are broken. One of my eyes has swollen shut. Crusted blood in my hair. Also, I am cold. All I have on is the tank top and pyjama pants I put on after my shower.

More time passes. An hour? Three? Eventually, the door opens, and Russell Kilmer-Jones enters, accompanied by two black-clad Crown policemen.

"Help him up."

The two cops grab me under my arms and lift me into a sitting position. I blink hard and try not to moan.

"Konnichiwa, Mr Zai," says the Englishman.

"Good evening." It hurts to talk. Somebody must have hit me in the throat.

"Give him some water."

One of the cops hands me a bottle of water and I take a sip. Swallowing hurts more than talking.

"So here we are," says Russell. "I suppose you found me."

"Of course, I did."

Russell smiles thinly. "I had hoped never to see you again, Mr Zai."

"I am sorry"—I pause to swallow, but that does not alleviate the pain in my throat—"to disappoint you."

"Oh, you never disappointed me, Mr Zai," says Russell. "Not even once. You always did what I asked you to do—even when I asked the impossible."

"Killing a god."

"Indeed." He grins. "That, of course, was the operation that won me my new position. Odin was farting around out here, violating our territorial boundaries making a general nuisance of himself. With your assistance I put a stop to that and voila—if you will pardon my French—new opportunities became available to me."

"And then you decided to kill me."

"Well, of course," says Russell. "Odin had…well, perhaps he didn't have friends, per se, but he certainly had kin who might want to avenge him. Gods are right into that kind of stuff. It wouldn't do to have them coming back to me through you."

"I thought…" I suck down some more water. "I just thought you didn't like me."

"That may also have been a factor," he replies. "Can't say it isn't mutual, can we?"

I say nothing.

"Rest assured, Mr Zai, if there wasn't a viable business case for it, I wouldn't have gone to the expense. Whatever my personal feelings, your murder was a contingency, not a whim."

"I am pleased to know it." I don't even know where these words are coming from.

"In any case, it was starting to gall me that you were still alive, so I'm pleased you've turned up here in Albion and saved me the trouble of finding you again. Unfortunately, I have a meeting first thing tomorrow, so I won't be able to attend your execution, but if you would like to spend your final hours cursing my name I will understand completely."

All I can do is bow.

"Sayonara, Mr Zai."

One of the cops opens the door for Russell and precedes him out into the hall. The other follows and seals the door behind him.

I collapse back onto the mattress and try to sleep. Perhaps when I awaken, I will be dead. Being executed feels like more drama than I can handle right now.

More time passes. An hour? Three? Eventually, the door opens, and Russell Kilmer-Jones enters, accompanied by two black-clad Crown policemen.

The two cops grab me under my arms and lift me into a sitting position. I blink hard and try not to moan.

Haven't I been through this before? Perhaps I am in some kind of a time loop. Have I opened a time Door by mistake? Have I been condemned to relive this final conversation forever by some malicious demon?

Russell leans in close, peers into my face, squinting. Then he stands away.

"Bag him."

One of the cops drops a black bag over my head. The other claps a pair of handcuffs onto my wrists and they haul me to my feet.

"Let's go."

I suppose that Russell has decided to bring forward my execution. Perhaps he has changed his mind about watching me die. I don't care. This is still preferable to a time loop.

One of the cops gets an arm under my own and starts guiding me towards the door. He drags me a couple of steps before I start to stumble along. I can walk, with some help, but I am not strong enough to fight off a toddler, much less a pair of armoured cops.

We move down the corridor; make a left; then a right. My topographic senses indicate that we are in a fairly small room, but the impression is fuzzed-out. Perhaps this is some lingering effect of the flashbang, or a head injury.

We stop at a desk and Russell tells someone "I'm taking the prisoner for special interrogation at the Ministry." Something is different about his voice. The timbre is the same, but there's something sibilant about his accent.

A gate opens and we pass through some more corridors, down a short flight of stairs and then through a door into a wide, low-ceilinged space. Carbon monoxide and gasoline and rising damp: we're in a parking garage.

The cop guides me into a car seat and fastens my seatbelt. He shuts the door. I hear the other three doors open and close and then the car starts to move. We go up a ramp, wait for what I imagine is a boom gate to rise, and then drive smoothly out onto the street.

I clear my throat. "Is that you, Doctor?"

"Why, yes," says David Lo. "It appears that you are once again in need of a physician. And, perhaps, a new hotel."

The car pulls up outside a place called the Golden Pagoda Hotel. It looks very much like the Oriental Palace. "I've had your things brought here from your hotel in Shadwell," says David. "I hope you don't mind."

"I thought it was Limehouse."

"*This* is Limehouse." There is something proprietorial about the way he says it.

David hands me a key and tells me that my room is booked in the name of James Chen.

In James Chen's room, David tends to my wounds for the second time. My ribs hurt badly enough to make breathing painful, but he assures me the injury is just from compression. David nicks my swollen right eyelid to let out the blood. It hurts but it is a relief.

"How do you feel?" he says.

"I'm okay. Hungry."

"Clean yourself up and get dressed," he says. "It's time we had that curry."

Madhu's is a small place just off Druid Street in Bermondsey. David tells me that there is one like it in the real London as well, but on a different corner. I believe him as soon as I see the inside: poorly-lit and over-decorated with frescos and cloth prints. The waiters are all from the subcontinent. To a man, they speak better English than I do.

When the poppadums' arrive, I put it to David that our meeting yesterday was not accidental.

David smiles. "No," he says. "But you are lucky that I was the first person to notice your arrival...James."

"Otherwise, I would still be in jail."

David looks at his watch. "No," he says. "By now you would be dead."

"Maybe I will die tomorrow."

"They will have a more difficult time finding you now that I am looking after you," says David.

"Why would you do that?"

David takes a moment to answer. "You are not Chinese, are you, James?"

"No, I'm not." I feel no embarrassment at having been caught in a lie.

"And your name isn't James, either."

"I am usually called Zai."

"And what are you doing here, Mister Zai? Are you still looking for a sandwich?"

"Right now, I'm more interested in the Rogan Josh."

"And when you have eaten? What, then, will be your interest?"

It takes me a moment to parse out the English. "I am here to kill somebody."

"Russell Kilmer-Jones," says David.

"If you know everything about me, why are you asking me these questions?"

"I don't know everything about you," says David. "But I had my suspicions. When Mister Kilmer-Jones came to visit you in your cell, let us just say that my suspicions were confirmed."

"You suspected that I am an assassin?"

"Mr Zai, I think you are a great deal more than that. Let me tell you a story."

A waiter arrives with our meals, to my relief. If the story is boring at least the food will entertain me. I admit I am surprised that the curries are served with rice, rather than gigantic wedges of naan bread they serve in the Japonified Indian restaurants I am used to.

"London was once a great centre of sorcery," says David, "but that time is past."

I chew a mouthful of curry and nod. It is delicious.

"Although the Crown denies it, in the decades since they walled Albion away from the other worlds, talent has been draining from this place."

"Worlds, plural?"

David tilts his head. "I would have expected a man with your abilities to know *exactly* which other worlds."

"The Unfolded Earth."

"Albion is more isolated than Karachidor, or even Ōyashima," says David. "But it is a small place, and it is not self-sufficient. As much as the Crown hates to admit it, they maintain some trade with other nations—but since the separation they have had to forgo their vaunted fleets, and so shipping must be handled by the sea vessels belonging to other nations."

"China. Why did Albion close its borders?"

David steeples his hands above his curry dish. "The faction that became known as the Crown did not take the loss of the New World or the end of the colonial era very well and they deliberately splintered off a sliver of geography that they could rule as they saw fit. With an iron fist and a mouthful of spells."

"So, it's a..." I think back to my conversations with Emmet. "A deep clone of the real England?"

"No. It is a copy overlaid upon the conventional Britain, synchronized-with but walled-off-from it and all of the adjacent dream realms and hells."

"Tell me about these...walls."

"The dimensional barriers are strong enough to keep all but the most powerful out," says David. "I can sneak by them, with effort. A few of the old gods and demons who have transportation attributes can pass. But few others have the talent or power to make the passage, except for at the special Doors."

"Where are these Doors?"

"Oh, you can surely guess," says David, snorting over his smile. "Stonehenge has been heavily secured, and the other stone circles have been decommissioned, so now everyone who lacks clearance has to come through Heathrow."

"Like me."

Dave shakes his head. "You, my friend, are an unknown quantity."

"What do *you* want from me?"

David pinches his lower lip, shows me his teeth. "I think perhaps you can save this world."

That takes me aback. "I am not that sort of a person." This I know for certain.

"This place is dying. Albion is an old concept, and it's isolated itself from all of the other conceptual metaverses that might shore up its narrative power. Another fifty years and it will be an empty shell."

"Then why are you here?"

"I live here," he says. "This has been my home for nearly a century. This is the place where I belong." The face I saw when I shook David's hand was about my own age, but there is no reason for me to believe that face was any truer than Russell Kilmer-Jones' lardy English features. Who is this man, whose can change his face, and whose preferred home is a police state where he is hated and feared?

David leans across the table. "This is prime real estate, if the Walls come down. Albion would again have access to some of the rarest and most tightly sealed worlds. If we can wind back the rituals, the Ways can be reopened, and we can build a new fleet. This place could be a trade hub for the Unfolded Earth to rival Karachidor."

"How?

"It will take blood, and a man with a talent for opening."

"How much blood?"

"Not a lot, if you have the right kind."

"My own blood?"

"Ordinary blood won't work. This world is a reflection of the true Britain, a metaphor. Do you understand me?"

"I need metaphorical blood?"

"Yes. Royal blood would be the best."

"So...once I have bled the Royal Family, would I need to do some kind of a...a ritual?"

"You do not have to enact the rites. You will just have to spill the blood at each site. This will reveal a fault which somebody with your skills should have no difficulty in prising apart."

"How many sites are there?"

"Five."

"Where are they?"

"Whitechapel, and surrounds."

Of course, they are. I rub my eyes.

"The ritual upon which the Walls were built caused ripples that were felt in the real Britain," says David. His smile diminishes but does not vanish. "But the Ripper's crimes were a pale reflection of the horrors that took place in this London."

I mop up the gravy from my plate with a piece of naan. "This sounds dangerous. I don't see how this will help me with my own purpose here."

"Tell me, Mr Zai," says David, dabbing his mouth with a white linen napkin. "How are you planning to do away with Russell Kilmer-Jones? Before he finds you again?"

"I'll work something out."

"I have several dozen well-trained men at my disposal," says Dave. "And I have some abilities and talents myself, as you know. If you bring down the walls for me, I am certain I can find a way to assist you with your mission."

I put my knife and fork together on my plate and drain the last of my pint of Kingfisher.

"Surely somebody will notice if I start unravelling this old magic?"

David's covers his left fist with his right hand. "I can mask it, if you are quick about your work. And, of course, I can provide security."

"So, all I need is some royal blood and the luck of the Irish?"

"The Irish are banned from Albion," says David, grinning. "Best to rely on your own."

I rest in my room at the Golden Pagoda Hotel until evening, but I do not go to sleep.

I do not trust David Lo. Once I have brought down the walls for him, why should he keep his promise to help me? Even if he does honour his word, I am not keen to undertake some foolish caper in order to see my enemy dead. That is not how I work.

I now believe that Dave is the one who tipped off the Crown about me. If I had accepted his original offer of a meal, would he not have made his proposal to me then, and saved me a beating? I cannot know, but it doesn't matter now. I have my own plan, which will make his manoeuvring irrelevant.

I get dressed again. The costume failed to preserve my cover, so I am going back to civilian dress: jeans, boots, a cable sweater and a leather jacket. Gloves, a scarf, a pair of sunglasses, and a black Yomiuri Giants baseball cap. If I die on this mission, at least I will go out with some measure of dignity. I pour the contents of my aftershave down the sink and pocket the empty bottle. On my out the door I grab a camera. I am already feeling better about myself.

I ascend three flights of stairs up to the top storey of the hotel. I walk down a musty hallway and make a turn into a narrow corridor that leads to a service door. I force the door and take another flight of steps up onto the roof.

Up here the wind is strong, but I can still smell the stink of True London. The Thames cuts a dark swathe through the scattered lights of the Albionese capital. I shiver inside my jacket and fumble the runestone out of my pocket with gloved fingers.

"Ehwaz." I keep my voice low. I do not think that shouting is going to improve my chances of this working. "Ehwaz."

The night air thickens; bulges out into a three-dimensional shape, which then pours liquidly into the shaggy, hunched, eight-limbed octopus-horse-spider god of nightmares and mixed metaphors.

"Sleipnir, you promised me a favour."

Sleipnir holds the magical spear *Gungnir* crooked under the elbow of the upper-middle limb on his right side. "Slayer," he says. "Opener. I remember my promise, and I have come at your summons." He does not sound pleased about it.

I explain to him what I need.

Sleipnir sounds even less happy about my request than he did about the summons. "You saw what I did to the last arsehole who rode me around like a horse."

"You couldn't have done that if I hadn't blinded him first." I know it's insolent, but he does owe me a favour.

Sleipnir stares at me with eyes that are made of night sky. "Alright," he says. "This once, I will take you where you desire to be, and then return you here. But next time, there will be a price."

I am pleased that he has agreed to transport me. I am *particularly* pleased that he didn't strike my head off with his magical spear.

I heft my camera. "Do you think I could take a photo?"

Sleipnir stares at me with those terrible, empty eyes again and I wonder if I have pushed my luck too far. He spreads his four lowest limbs for support and spins the spear through some strange kata with his four remaining arms, coming to rest in a crouching posture with the spear levelled at my face. "Is this good?"

"That is perfect."

My hands are shaking as I snap some photos, with and without the flash, but I am grinning like a skull. Sleipnir tries some different poses for me, each one cooler and more intimidating than the last.

When I put the camera away, Sleipnir makes the spear disappear and drops down onto all eights. "Get on." He is definitely in a better mood now.

I mount up. There's no saddle, but my knees fold right in behind a shoulder joint and I jam my feet against a ridge in his carapace. Up close, Sleipnir is even more alien than I had thought. Can he truly be a god? What kind of humans imagined something like *him* into being? Or has he just accreted attributes as our conception of him has changed?

Sleipnir bunches his legs and leaps straight up. He finds purchase in the air and his limbs begin to oscillate. I cannot tell if he is running or swimming.

It's neither warm nor cold as we canter through the sky, and our passage does not generate any wind. I recall this sensation from the Wild Hunt, although that time I rode upon a sheep, not an Iron Age god.

London dwindles below us. Sleipnir accelerates so hard that, for one vertiginous moment, I think I am going to come loose of him. The moon fills my view, but it is not the moon that I know. This one is the flat and sharp-edged disk of metal that I last saw in the Faerie Realms.

Sleipnir decelerates as he comes about. Although I have never seen it from this angle before, but, mutable as it is, I recognize the planar geography of the Faerie Realms below. We descend towards a mountain range, skimming over the peaks and then wheeling over a dry, pockmarked landscape. In the distance, I can see a city made all of steel, glowing red from forges and foundries and blackened with the soot. Sleipnir angles away from it and veers towards the black river. We cross the running water and then come in low over a flat meadowland towards the skeletal trees of the black forest.

Sleipnir lets me off just outside of the tree-line. "I will await you here," he says. "The trees are too close to permit me flight, and I mislike the look of the soil."

I nod and bow to the demon god. "Thank you, Sleipnir. You are a true friend."

He nods and gestures with the spear. "Hurry up," he says. "I want to get the fuck out of here."

No sooner have I set foot in the forest than I am surrounded by chittering black things. Short, humanoid creatures with black skin, black hair; dressed in black leather garments that are all straps and buckles. They do not scare me anymore, but I still find the gaze of their cockroach eyes uncomfortable.

"Hello. I am looking for the Black and Crimson King."

The chittering subsides. I do not see any of the black things reaching for their weapons, but I am suddenly aware that they have their knives out.

"Why should he treat with you, mortal man?" I can't tell which of them is asking. "What can you offer him, besides the meat from your bones and the leather of your skin?"

"I owe him a favour, and I am here to make good on that."

The chittering rises again, and now I detect something deeper within it. A beat.

Hoofbeats; at some subsonic register that I can feel rather than hear.

Kurenai, the Black and Crimson King, boils into my presence on a horse that's as black as he himself. "Ho there, mortal," he says. "How the fuck are you?"

I bow from the waist. "I'm well, Kurenai-sama. No small thanks to your agent, Chieko-san. I hope that you are the same."

"I am well indeed." Kurenai's Japanese accent is just as perfect as his English accent.

"And Chieko-san? Has she recovered from her injuries?"

"She has."

"I'm glad to hear that. How goes your war with the Empire?"

The Black and Crimson King dismounts, his shadow rising to meet his boots as his feet come down onto the black soil.

"The war goes on."

"Are you winning?"

"The conflict has reached an equilibrium, and will remain there until some power changes or somebody intercedes."

I am beginning to understand how this place works. "Perhaps I can help."

"You have a debt to pay."

"If you help me again, I will open up a new territory for you to conquer and possess."

"I am listening."

When I have finished speaking, Kurenai says "My blood is precious to me." He stares at me, unblinking, while he says this. "Even more precious than it was to those I took it from."

It occurs to me that he took some of mine, the last time we met. I have not missed it. "You can always get more."

The Black and Crimson King laughs. "In copious amounts, if what you have promised me is true."

"I only need a little of yours."

"Hold your vessel ready," says Kurenai.

I remove the cap from my aftershave bottle. The Black and Crimson King unwinds a leather strap from his left forearm and rolls back the cotton sleeve beneath it. With a wicked black dagger, he opens a vein and bleeds into the bottle until it is full. He hands the bottle back to me.

Flames bloom from the fingers of the Kurenai's right hand and he uses it to cauterize his wound. He grins at me the whole time; firelight gleaming in his black eyes, on his black teeth. He knows he's cool.

I screw the cap back onto my bottle. The fluid inside it is black as shadow. "I expected that your blood would be…red." I think about it. "Or maybe blue."

Kurenai shakes his head. "No. My blood is black, for I am the Shadow: darkness is mine by right. That is my Princedom. Red blood is that which I take from others: power, lineage, life. That is my Kingship."

I don't know what that even means. I shrug. "I don't think it matters what colour it is, as long as it's real."

"The reality of a thing is difficult to judge, when it pertains to such as me," says the Black and Crimson King. "But I am sure you will find it to be *royal* enough for your purposes."

Sleipnir returns me to the Golden Pagoda Hotel in the small hours. I am tired and frightened and want to go to bed, but I am supposed to be executed this morning and I do not know how long Dave will be able to protect me from the Crown, especially once they find out that I am no longer in my cell. I have work to do.

Once I have memorized Lo-Pan's hand-drawn map I take the stairs down to the hotel lobby. The night clerk nods to me and mutters something disinterested in Mandarin. I grunt and nod as I head out to the street.

It takes about fifteen minutes to walk to the first site. Buck's Row is deserted. A four-storey schoolhouse glowers down over the street. The sky is thick and dark above. I find a plaque set into the pavement just where David's map indicates it should be. The text is too corroded to read, because the plate is made of iron, not the expected brass. In the real London, this is where the Ripper murdered Mary Ann Nichols.

I pour a little of the Black and Crimson King's blood out of the aftershave bottle. It flares when it touches the plaque, leaving behind a small soot stain. I cap the bottle and put my fingers on the stain, feeling around until I find a topographic seal. It parts easily enough in my fingers.

Perhaps this won't be so difficult, after all.

I drag my fingers through the seam all the way to Hanbury Street. I thought this exercise would be like trying to knock down a wall, but really, it's just like slitting open a poorly tailored seam. Once I have made the first cut it unravels with very little effort.

Which is good, because that lets me pay a bit more attention to my surroundings. Turns out, I am being followed. My shadow is well-trained: better than the Dejima gangsters, but not as good as my late nemesis Ikari. I do not know when they picked me up, but I believe they have been with me since I left the hotel. It must be one of David's men. Nobody else is supposed to know I'm here.

The building at 29 Hanbury Street is a now yarn shop. The window display shows stacks of coloured wool, pattern books, hand-knitted garments and toys. Glad of my leather jacket, I put an elbow through the glass pane above the doorknob. It shatters with a single blow. I reach inside and open the door.

I move quietly across the shop floor. If there is an alarm, it's a silent one. I let myself out of a side door and into the tiny garden at the back. Nobody stirs in the house.

The yard is mostly dirt and rocks and discarded trash, enclosed by a six-foot wall. It would have been easier to climb the wall than to break into the building, and under better circumstances I would have known that ahead of time…but I have had no time for proper reconnaissance. I need to get this done before Russell's men find me again. I doubt Dave will be able to spring me a second time.

The plaque here is buried under a few inches of soil, but the seam leads me right to it. I scuff the ground away with the toe of one boot until I can see a hint of metal. In conventional London, Annie Chapman was murdered here.

I pour some of the Black and Crimson Prince's blood onto the plaque, but there is no sizzle this time—I have already opened the seam. I think that my own abilities will be sufficient to finish the job from here on out. All I need to unravel the rest of the spell is a steady hand.

I wonder if I could have found and unpicked the seam at the first site, and saved myself the bargain with Kurenai-sama. But I suppose it's for the best. The Black and Crimson King is my insurance policy against betrayal by David Lo.

A light goes on in the house behind me. Perhaps the owners have heard me pottering around out here. Perhaps they spotted the broken the glass by the door. Perhaps there was an alarm. Perhaps they have detected the magic coming undone. Perhaps they just need to use the toilet.

I abandon any pretence at stealth and scramble over the wall. I drop down clumsily into the laneway behind and set off at a jog. I take a left turn, then a right. Another right. Lo's escort is still with me, but I see no signs of enemy pursuit.

In my haste to get away I have lost the seam. Luckily, I have more of Kurenai's blood in the little bottle. I hope I will not have to backtrack once I have opened all five points.

The cavernous, triangular buildings of Spitalfields Market loom ahead of me. I orient myself on the map and start to jog again. There's nobody around—just me and my shadow. A fox scampers between two parked cars but don't think it's Chieko: its fur is red and its tail is intact. Then again, she is a shapeshifter: if she can turn into a woman or a stone ornament, it is entirely feasible that she can change the colour of her fur. I imagine that she will have sharp words for me, next time we meet.

turn off Commercial Road into Dorset Street and on the first block I come to a small park. Three stunted trees, a bench, and a patch of ground that has been almost completely denuded of grass. Behind the bench, set into a concrete slab, is an iron plaque like the previous two. This is Miller's Court, where the Ripper butchered Mary Jane Kelly.

Now I hear sirens.

I dig out the aftershave bottle and spill some blood onto the plaque. It spits and sparks once again and I grope for the seam.

Red and blue flashing lights: the police are closing in. I still have two more sites to visit. The mission is hopeless now.

What am I doing here, fiddling around with vials of blood and mystical boundaries and attracting the police? I am a killer, not a magician. This is not how I do things.

I find the seam and tear it open.

A patrol car comes squealing around the corner and skids to a halt. Its doors fly open and three cops in flak jackets, armed with machine pistols and shotguns, spill out.

I put my hands in the air and turn around slowly.

A silenced pistol fires and one of the cops goes down. I turn with the other two policemen to see a man in a black suit duck behind one of the patrol cars. My escort. David Lo claims to be some kind of wizard, and I believe that he is…but mostly, he is an old-fashioned gangster.

The two surviving cops crouch behind their car, taking cover. I just stand over the plaque with my hands in the air, feeling stupid. One of the cops points his shotgun at me. "On the ground! Face down, hands behind your head!"

I put my hands on my head and drop to a half-kneel, but the triad in black has started shooting again and the cop ducks for cover. Now that he has lost the element of surprise the triad has discarded the suppressor, and the street is suddenly filled with the noise and smoke of gunfire. Three more triads appear: they have the cops surrounded. Still kneeling, I lower my hands and start to look for the seam again.

More cars pull in the street. Some are full of cops, other triads. A firefight develops faster than I would have credited. Muzzle flashes, automatic fire, shouting and grunting. This is like an action movie, except the hero is groping around in the dark for something nobody else can see instead of shooting baddies and looking cool.

Ah.

I feel a pressure on the seam from whatever lies on the other side of it. I yank on it, and it splits in both directions. This is unexpected. I have destroyed three of the five sites: apparently this has weakened the barriers enough to bring them down.

Sometimes you get lucky.

On my hands and knees, I start to crawl behind the bench, hoping that it will afford me some cover from all the shooting. While I am scrabbling around on the ground, I come across a pistol belonging to one of the dead policemen. I grab the weapon and shove it into the back of my pants. My philosophy about not carrying weapons, on the basis that it will encourage people to fight with me, does not hold in the middle of a pitched battle. Even so, it is my intention to hide behind the bench for as long as I possibly can rather than exchanging fire with Crown police.

The gun battle begins to wane. The police have numbers and firepower over the triads. The cop who yelled at me earlier is once more looking at me. I raise my hands again quickly.

"Didn't I tell you: get down on the…" He looks up at something behind me and he forgets what he was saying. The clamour of the gunfight ceases. Something looms in my peripheral vision, and I turn my head.

The stunted trees in the tiny garden have grown tall and twisted and black.

More of the black trees have sprouted at random intervals all along the street; breaking up through the asphalt and concrete. Buildings burst apart as black limbs push through their walls and windows. Some collapse inwards as tree roots pulverize their foundations.

A chittering sound rises, and Kurenai's black things fall upon the police like locusts swarming over a ripening crop. I have barely registered what's going on before the police are flopping around on the ground with black things crouched over them, grinning and licking their knives. Lo's triads have vanished.

The night comes alive with sirens. Black figures scamper across the broken buildings, over the crumbling rooftops. Obscene shapes flit through the air; dangling limbs and tentacles and antennae; flapping great dark wings or bobbing in the air like aerostatic jellyfish. And everywhere there are trees: growing out of the road way; clawing out of windows; pushing down walls. Dead black trees.

The sky bulges and a massive, eight-legged form congeals out of night air. Streamers of black mist curl from its shoulders as its outline firms up. "Mr Zai," says Sleipnir, whirling his spear over his head and slamming the butt into the ground at his feet.

"Sleipnir-sama." I'm not sure why he is still hanging around. "Have you come to watch the fireworks?" Or has he come to collect on my debt already?

Sleipnir's laughter sounds as if some small creature is being crushed inside his chest. Once he has recovered himself, he slouches down into steed form. "Climb on. We have somewhere to be."

I clamber onto his back for the second time tonight and the nightmare god takes to the skies. We circle central London a couple of times. There are black things everywhere. The trees have ruined many ancient buildings and plenty of new ones, too. The streets are filled with rubble and corpses. The dawn is thick with smoke and klaxons.

"London's burning," says Sleipnir.

"Do you know the song?"

Sleipnir surprises me by singing the first verse. I join in the chorus. We sing the song two or three times as we go swooping through the skies and then we switch to *Rock the Casbah*. I take a thousand photos.

Once we tire of the Clash's greatest hits, we move to the Sex Pistols. "Anarchy in the UK." By the time we descend towards the Tower of London, we're on the Ramones. "Blitzkrieg Bop." It's a bit like I am a *chinpira* punk again, eighteen and invincible, jacking motorbikes and strutting tough for the yakuza. But this is better. I am flying through the air on the back of a mythological creature while a city burns beneath me, and I don't remember the last time I felt this good.

The lattice roof over the Tower of London's courtyard has been ripped open by a couple of massive black trees and the gleeful application of many hands. Now all that remains is a tangle of broken girders and crumpled fibreglass.

Sleipnir drops in through the wreckage and alights in the courtyard. I climb down from his back, and he comes upright with a kind of grace that again reminds me more of an undersea mollusc than a land animal.

A black-skinned faerie creature mounted on a black horse comes trotting out of the smashed-in doorway to the White Tower. He grins and gives an insouciant wave. "Ho there, Opener! Hi there, godling!"

I bow to the Black and Crimson King. Sleipnir raises his spear in salute.

"You have made good on your promise, mortal man, and I thank you. Here is a token of my appreciation." Kurenai makes a gesture, and a double row of smirking black things march out of the White Tower. They form up in front of me, leaving between their ranks a corridor between me and the door of the tower.

Two more black things emerge, dragging a stumbling human between them. Kurenai motions for them to stop and they force the prisoner to his knees.

The Black and Crimson King grabs the kneeling man by his hair and pulls his head back so that I can see his face. "Is this the one you are seeking?"

The face is almost unrecognizable. Broken teeth, ruptured nose, a fractured cheekbone, swollen eyes. Dried blood all over half his face from a gash in his scalp. A diamond earring in one ear. He spits a mouthful of blood and somehow finds one last condescending smile for me. "Well, Mr

Zai, it appears that the tables have turned," says Russell Kilmer-Jones. He delivers the line well, but his voice cracks on the last syllable.

I draw the gun from the back of my waistband and put a bullet in his throat.

Blood froths from the Englishman's mouth. His tongue flops out from between his lips, but the only sound he can make through the remains of his windpipe is a sucking, whistling noise.

"He's the one."

"Shall I mount his head on a pike?" says Kurenai.

"Just leave him here."

"I'm glad you said that. I don't actually have a pike."

Kurenai lets go of Russell Kilmer-Jones' hair and the Englishman collapses face first. I stand watching until the sucking noises stop. It doesn't take long.

I turn to the Black and Crimson King. "I don't know about you, but I could really use a beer right now."

David Lo-Pan is waiting for us when Sleipnir and Kurenai and I alight at the Loom and Spikenard. He is smiling as if he meant for all this to happen, and I am certain he will claim credit for the invasion as soon as I am gone. But I imagine that he's angry. The world he wanted for his own is now occupied by a hostile army.

I also imagine that if I had just opened the seals, as expected, Russell Kilmer-Jones would be safe in his fortress, and I would now be dead at the hands of David's triads.

Regardless, he puts on a convincing display of high spirits and the four of us spend the rest of the day and most of the evening carousing. The locals who rousted me last time are gone. Today, the pub is suddenly staffed by triads and a handful of chittering Black and Crimson troopers.

When the kegs run dry David sends some men away. They return quickly with a crate of ice-cold Tsingtao. David, I think, is keen to make friends with the new ruler of the place.

The sun is just rising when Sleipnir and I stagger out of the pub. The Black and Crimson King, who is apparently immune to the effects of alcohol, has long since taken his leave. "Pillaging still to supervise and defences to erect," he said. "The Empire of Shaedows will test our strength before much longer."

Truthfully, I think he just got bored, as the sober do among drunks. Our bargain is complete; there is no further need for him to hang around.

I am not sure exactly when David Lo left, but it wasn't long after that. I recall seeing him staggering around in search of the Men's toilet. A short time later, a perfectly sober Englishman left the pub. I do not recall seeing David after that, but I admit my memory of that part of the evening is hazy.

Out on the street, I am surprised at the extent of the devastation. Wrecked buildings, guttering fires, dead bodies. I guess I had somehow forgotten that I started a war here. I don't feel bad about it, just surprised. And perhaps a little proud. This is a career first for me.

Sleipnir and I contemplate the scene. "I don't imagine there are any cabs about tonight."

"You want a ride back to your hotel?" asks Sleipnir.

"How about the airport?" Sleipnir looks pained. "I'm tired, Zai."

"You made the offer."

"I'm tired and drunk."

If I was sober, I would apologize, but alcohol makes me bold. "Are you okay? Did you drink some water? Maybe we should just walk around a bit until you feel well enough to fly again."

Sleipnir bangs the butt of his magic spear on the ground. "I am a *god!*" he bellows. "I'm perfectly okay to fly!"

"Well, okay, then."

Sleipnir succumbs to a fit of hiccups, which I politely ignore.

The Golden Pagoda is deserted. I grab my passport and my gigantic trunk and haul it up the roof, where Sleipnir is waiting. He rolls his eyes when he sees my luggage. "You have got to be joking."

I give it a moment's consideration, then drag the trunk to the side of the building and kick it off. It explodes in the street below in a shower of antique wood and terrible suits.

"He," says Sleipnir. I admit it's nice to have an appreciative audience. Sleipnir drops a shoulder so that I can climb onto his back.

We take to the air and Sleipnir orients himself towards Heathrow. The air is full of smoke and ash. I have no idea how he is able to navigate through it, but he is a god, after all. I hope he is willing to drop me at one of the regular Heathrow terminals, because I doubt the shuttle service to and from terminal 7 is running.

Sleipnir starts to sing *Next Door to Alice*. I don't know any of the verses, but I do know the chorus.

#10: The Grand Tour

They put me in my usual seat for the last leg of my final journey to Mesra City. I sit there in 34C, calm and alert, preparing myself for what I must do. The aircraft bears me on my Way, cruising through the ripples and folds in the dimensions of reality.

This is the last time I will ever fly to the Arisen City on the island of Karachidor, the secret colony of the lost continent, the transportation hub of the Unfolded Earth. I do not know how to feel about that, but I do know that I am ready for whatever's coming next.

"I'm thinking of retiring." I try to sound uncertain, as manners dictate, but of course I would not have broached the subject if I hadn't already made up my mind.

Vashya and I are in the Revectored Studio at the Epsidor Hotel, sitting on chairs that project from the walls at unnatural angles. Our personal gravities have been carefully oriented to make sure that we correctly adhere to the non-horizontal surfaces. I do not understand why such a highly instrumented environment is one of the few places in the hotel guaranteed to be unmonitored and unhackable, but Vashya says that it is so, and I am quite willing to take her at her word.

"Zai, your great enemy is destroyed, Zai." Vashya has no bodyguards with her today, which I believe indicates a new level of trust between us.

"That is correct. My enemy has been destroyed, and I would like to leave the business before I make a new one."

Truthfully, I am getting weary of it all. I like the travel, but I am now wealthy enough that I can go anywhere I want, as often as I want. But I am growing bored, doing the same thing over and over. The element of job satisfaction has waned as the tedium of it has waxed. What I did to Albion feels like a career best. I feel like I have achieved as much as I can, when it comes to murdering people for money—now it is time for something else.

Soon I will be married. I promised Michiko that I have matured, and I am ready to settle down.

"Zai, okay, Zai," she replies. If she is disappointed she does not show it. "But today, Zai, you still work for me, Zai?"

I bow to her. "Hai. Of course. One last time."

Vashya passes me an old-fashioned manila folder. It contains travel documents, photographs of my contact, and a copy of his itinerary. Already I am feeling nostalgic.

"George Diehl." I look closely at the itinerary. "One week Grand Tour of the Unfolded Earth."

The first three days of Diehl's tour are scheduled for Mesra City and Surrounds, but today is already day two. The schedule is going to be tight.

"Zai, you know what to do, Zai."

"Hai."

George Diehl is the kind of man who goes on guided tour holidays, and that will be the death of him.

I will be the death of him.

I take a taxi to the venue of George Diehl's main excursion for the day, because I am already behind schedule, and I would prefer not to have to follow him through a succession of impossible tourist destinations. And it is lucky I didn't try to find my own way there, because the Garden Path is not where I thought it was.

I always believed the Garden Path was just a fancy name for trail through the park where I used to meet with Vashya and Jonathon—Russell—under the gazebo, but it turns out that it is an entirely different place.

The taxi takes me through an unfamiliar part of the CBD, and I am just starting to feel uneasy when the strange towers and trunks of Mesra City suddenly yield to an expanse of parkland.

My first thought is that we have passed through a Door, but I know we haven't. It's just the geometry of the city and the geography of the garden that give the transition its abruptness.

I cannot see the full extent of the parkland from this vantage. The vegetation is dense and wild, more a forest reserve than a garden. It is very different to the parks we have in Japan.

There are half a dozen tour buses in the parking lot outside the main gate. I slap on a red JTB sticker with the name TANAKA hand-written on it go to the ticket window. "Excuse me, I have lost my group."

The ticket clerk waves away the itinerary papers that I offer her and gives me an English-language brochure-map. She ushers me through the gates, muttering to herself in Karachidaean. I bow and thank her, then hurry through the turnstiles.

The front courtyard houses a cafe, a gift shop, and a display panel that explains, in English and Karachidaea, that the Garden Path will lead me on a scintillating journey through the plant life of many strange and beautiful worlds. Traversing the path will give me a glimpse of the wisdom of the Green Sphere, bestow upon me a sense of the connectedness of all things, and enhance my appreciation of my place in the most wondrous of cycles. There are sanitary facilities and vending machines along the way, as indicated. Do not attempt to leave the path. Kindly do not litter.

I show my ticket to the woman by the door and step through into the green.

Gravel crunches underfoot as I step onto the Garden Path. Trees rise above me, and the ground off the track is thick with ferny growth. Blue sky is visible through the spreading boughs overhead. It takes a moment for me to realize that I cannot smell the leaves or the humus. I cannot hear any birdsong. I cannot feel the breeze that is waving the foliage.

I hurry past a sign on the handrail describes the flora on display without stopping to read it. According to the map in the lobby, the path is a big loop, with no forks or detours, so I should be able to catch up with Diehl's group if I hurry.

Once I round the first bend, everything changes.

The trees here are armoured. Fluids ooze from the joints where their limbs meet. The moss that grows upon them looks like chain mail. The sky is green, not blue.

I stop and look behind me. The armoured trees seem to extend back the way I've come. I must have passed through a Door, but my topographic senses give me no indication that there is anything unusual about the fabric of space here.

I walk slowly back around the bend, trying to find a spot where the forests change—where we pass from one world into the next—but the bend in the path makes it very difficult. There is no point at which I can see from one forest into the other. I am puzzled and a little bit worried. Have my abilities deserted me?

I proceed briskly along the path, passing through a jungle where the trees look as if they have been spun from spider-webs; a swamp where the plant-life has bubbled up out of the mud; an orchard where children's toys grow from padded nylon trees. The sky above is sometimes blue; sometimes veined with red; sometimes pregnant with storm clouds; sometimes blasted with meteor showers. Sometimes it is as empty as hard vacuum. Although I cannot locate the Doors, the Garden Path clearly passes through a succession of different worlds.

The path is not crowded, but there are always other people in sight. Couples, families with young children, a smattering of solitary tourists. Even if I catch up with Diehl, it's going to be difficult to find an opportunity to do this discretely.

Eventually I come to an amenities block. A dozen Karachidaean children are hanging around, assaulting the drink vending machine and climbing the fixtures. Their adult supervisors look harried and weary.

I duck into the men's toilet, on the off chance that Diehl is in there, but all I find is an empty, smelly concrete chamber. I wonder how the utilities are plumbed. Have the curators of this garden built some kind of an inter-dimensional sewage system? The signboards in the reception area did not provide a lot of detail about sanitation.

Behind the toilet block, water pipes connect to valves that protrude from a concrete slab. Each valve contains a very small Door. Perhaps not an amazing revelation, but I am relieved to find that my topographical senses have not completely deserted me.

Inter-dimensional sewage. It is definitely time I found a new line of work.

I continue down the path, into landscape where trees of black plastic grow out of a lake of bubbling green waste. The foliage glints and glitters — the individual leaves are razorblades. The sky is an arterial crimson hue. The path is elevated twenty meters above the surface of the lake. I wish it was higher.

I can hear the tour group before I can see them; the guide's voice declaiming facts and a hushed muttering below it. "...the Razorwoods are part of a myth-world that was spawned by a postmodern blood cult, which has enclaves throughout the English-speaking world..."

When the guide finishes expositing, the group spreads out a bit, posing for photos, scrutinizing guidebooks, flirting, complaining. A couple of eager customers pump the guide for more information. I spot Diehl standing by himself, leaning against the railing.

I pick up a tiny piece of gravel and flip it over the railing. It travels about fifteen meters before it bounces off an invisible barrier. Sufficient height. I look more closely at the hand rail, and spot a tag clamped onto one of the support legs, similar to the ones I saw on the pipes outside of the toilets. I think I have figured out what is going on. I extend my topographical senses and, now that I know what I am looking for, my suspicions are confirmed.

The Doors along the Garden Path have been turned inside out and stretched into tubes, which are joined end-to-end. The pathway remains a part of Mesra City's own reality that leads in a circuit through all of these deformed and conjoined Doors. I cannot decide if this is the cleverest thing I have ever seen, or the stupidest.

I follow the pathway as it winds out into a void in a downward spiral. There are no stars; the only illumination is from the crystalline tree-shapes that drift slowly and weightlessly, upside-down. I am uncertain what is holding the gravel in place beneath our feet—or holding us onto the gravel. Are we still subject to Mesra City's gravity? The crowd is silent and stays as close to the middle of the path as they can. The guide keeps on babbling.

Around the next bend we step down out of the void onto thin air, which is somehow even more disconcerting. Here the trees are once again upright, and each one has a bulb of turf hanging underneath it, held together with a mesh of root fibres. Bands of cloud scythe above and below us. Diehl is leaning over the handrail, perhaps trying to see if there is any land below. All I can see is more empty sky.

I bend down to tie my shoelace beside one of the railing supports. While I am kneeling there, I find the dimensional seal and slit it open with my little finger. I can feel the fabric of the Door sag in response. Perhaps I have miscalculated. I hope the Door will not tear open and kill us all. I stand up and move away from the support.

I am fiddling with my camera when Diehl yells out. The handrail gives way beneath him and folds out into the empty sky. Diehl loses his balance and lets go of the rail and—

—a young woman standing nearby catches him by the shoulder. She grabs his arm with her other hand and hauls him bodily back from the ledge.

Then there is panic and confusion. People gather around Diehl and he lowers himself, wobbling, into a sitting position. The guide jabbers into a walkie talkie.

I slip away, around the bend into the next garden. The ground here is a faecal brown colour, and the foliage that blows off the skeletal trees looks like hot ashes.

This is the first time in my long career that my contact has been rescued from death by an innocent bystander.

Back at the Epsidor, I sit in my room and brood about the day's events. I do not think I have attracted any undue attention to myself. I would be surprised if anybody is able to work out that I destroyed the seal. But next time some freak disaster befalls Mr Diehl, will some in his group remember me? Can I risk being seen with them again?

I know where Diehl is staying, but a hotel is a terrible place to pull an improvised murder. Even if I can locate his room without arousing suspicion, hotels are full of CCTV cameras precisely because they don't want criminals sneaking into guests' bedrooms.

I am going to have to follow Diehl to his next destination and wait for the right opportunity there.

I find Diehl and his tour group at the Port Authority, waiting at the gate lounge. Diehl is standing alone near one of the big bay windows. The ships at this end of the harbour are mostly cruise-liners and I suppose these vessels stop in plenty of Conventional Earth ports.

Diehl seems twitchy. I know how he feels: I was very nervous the first time I went on a submarine.

A stewardess in a pants suit and neck scarf informs us that the ship is ready to board, first in Karachidaean then in English. Diehl hangs back, and so do I. I have to make sure he gets onto the ship. Eventually he gets up, sighs, and trudges down the boarding tunnel, dragging his carry-on behind him.

A minute or two passes before the woman in the pants suit picks up the microphone again. "Passenger Zai, passenger Zai, please report to gate lounge 12."

"I am Zai." I slap down my passport and my boarding pass and bow repeatedly. "I'm late. So sorry. So sorry." I speak in Japanese and then repeat myself in English.

The attendant in the scarf smiles at me like I am an idiot and makes a shooing gesture down the tunnel.

"Thank you, thank you!" I rush through.

The tunnel leads to an escalator, and then to an airlock, where another attendant checks my boarding pass. He directs me through into the cabin, which is laid out like a particularly cramped passenger aeroplane—but there are no windows in the enamelled steel walls, and exposed pipes run along the ceiling.

I find my seat, stow my baggage, and settle in. I have no idea where Diehl is sitting. I can't see him, and I hope that he cannot see me.

The crew seal the hatches and the submarine begins to drift away from the dock. A submarine is much quieter than an aeroplane, and the motion is much gentler.

There are no windows, so I fold down the entertainment screen and choose a channel that shows camera views of the outside of the vessel. I drift off to the sound of the First Mate commentating on the marine life through the uncomfortable complimentary headphones.

An excited murmuring wakens me. All through the cabin I can see the other sleepers rousing. I look at my screen to see what the fuss is about.

We are coming up to an underwater city.

Some of the buildings are manufactured structures that have been crusted over with marine life. Others look as if they were actually grown whole from the floor of the ocean. Chapfallen castles made of stone and sand and coral; crumbling skyscrapers made of glass and ceramics and seaweed. Terraced reefs of low-density housing, thick with anemone gardens, divided by trenches and caverns. Artificial lights shine in some parts of the city; others are in themselves luminous. Some sectors are unlit.

Looping tubes sprouts from a particularly bright central building, spreading all through the city like tentacles. This hub is squat and black and round and ornate and new. The submarine turns and the new angle reveals a sign blazoned across the building's facade. It's the Marriot.

"We are now approaching the lost city of Mu," says a voice over the intercom. "If you tune in to channel one, there is a short infomercial describing the features and facilities of this wonderful entertainment destination."

I do as instructed. The view on my screen is displaced by a perky blonde woman with a smile that shows all of her teeth and most of her gums. Through a succession of costume changes and location shifts, she explains to me the history of the place I am visiting, in between advertisements for shopping malls and tourist attractions.

Many different cultures have myths and legends about sunken cities. The Karachidaeans believe that their homeland—Atlantis—was not the first civilization to be submerged. Unlike Atlantis, which was deliberately destroyed by some nebulous coalition of enemies, the Kingdom of Mu sank due to a series of natural cataclysms.

In the same breathless tones she uses to describe the boutique clothing district, the toothy woman informs me that Mu is still inhabited by some of its original citizens. The merfolk who live here were bioengineered to survive beneath the sea, but they no longer possess any kind of technology or culture. They do not make, they do not cultivate, they do not trade—they simply hunt and forage in the oceans like other marine life.

The toothy woman encourages me to spend extravagantly and offers a flirtatious goodbye that comes moments before the submarine coasts to a stop by the hotel. I switch back to the channel showing the exterior view in time to see tether lines draw up into alignment with the building. A trio of submersible drones connect an aquabridge to the airlock.

"Cabin crew disarm doors," says the skipper. Everybody tries to get out of their seat at once.

Despite the relentless corporate branding, the Marriot's lobby reminds me of Karl Stromberg's undersea lair from *The Spy Who Loved Me*. Bulging armoured windows show spot-lit views out into the ocean depths. The furnishings are seventies-futuristic, but with less velour and more fibreglass and fake marble. I check in while the tour group organizes itself. I haven't seen Diehl since he boarded the sub, but I do not think he can have gone very far.

The front desk gives me an unusual key dongle instead of the expected access card. It's a ceramic disk with a metal inlay showing the room number in ordinary Hindu-Arabic numerals, ringed by some unreadable Karachidaean script. When I swipe it over the lock plate beside the door to my room, I can feel a tiny Door open to release the lock.

I guess this is supposed to be an unpickable access control system, but with my abilities, it takes me about fifteen seconds to pop it.

order a scotch whisky and then a coffee in the hotel bar while I peruse my contact's itinerary. Diehl has no activities booked until tomorrow morning, which gives me the rest of the afternoon to have a look around. I might even bump into him somewhere. As big as this city is, there are only a dozen locations where an air-breathing human can venture on the transport network.

The tube station, which is accessible from the hotel's lobby reminds me quite a lot of the Maglev Transit network on Bravo Tango. I wonder if they used the same engineering firm to build it—or at least the same interior designers. A station attendant shows me into a four-seat carriage and instructs me on how to strap myself in. The ride is smooth and fast and makes a slurping noise as differential pressure draws our little train to its destination. I watch the lit-up city pass by through the glass-walled tubes on my way to the Inverted Aquarium.

The Aquarium is a three-storey facility with an observation dome on top. On the third floor, a U-shaped glass corridor extends out into the water. The second floor is a food court, and the ground floor hosts the transport hub, as well maintenance and deep-sea access.

I buy a ticket and go inside, ignoring the various information displays and the gift shop. Too much English. I want to look at the animals, not read about them. A crowd has gathered around a scientist who is explaining the facility and the sea creatures in English and Karachidaean.

The Inverted Aquarium engages a variety of methods to attract the marine life near to the glass for the viewing pleasure of its guests: flashing lights, subsonic bleats, electrical impulses, and chumming. As a result, there is a constant parade of wonders and horrors to observe: luminous viperfish with fangs too big for their jaws; distended gulper eels; armoured isopods. Vampire squid; chimaeras; krakens; deep sea jellyfish; acorn worms. The scientist becomes excited when he observes far in the distance, a Lesser Spotted Leviathan, but the beast is too far away for us to get a good look at it, and nobody is particularly impressed.

The crowd falls silent as a school of human shapes appears. They spiral up and around the aquarium walls in formation before they stream back into the darkness from which they have come. The merfolk have translucent skin threaded with luminous veins; mottled at the extremities and around the gills. They have two arms and two legs, as we do, but their joints are differently hinged. Their faces distorted by thrust-forward jaws lined with rows of triangular teeth. Their eyes are on the sides of their heads: dark and predatory and stupid. The merfolk do not seem to be particularly aware of the aquarium as they swim by it. They do not look in at us the aquarium and wonder what we are.

Like all humans, the scientist says, the merfolk are omnivorous. They are highly intelligent—smarter than dolphins—and, with enough time and patience, they can be trained to execute all kinds of tricks. They are also a lot more aggressive than dolphins.

There scientist explains that it is unclear whether these folk once had a kind of civilization, here in the ruins of Mu, but mounting archaeological evidence seems to indicate that they were bred as pets.

My ticket to the Inverted Aquarium gives me free access to the Archaeological Museum. As with most such museums, it is filled pieces of rubble, which are kept behind glass. Friezes and shards of pottery; weapon fragments; pieces of strange technology and stranger-yet artworks. An archaeologist is leading a tour through the maze, and I trail along behind them, close to enough to hear most of her talk but not close enough to be a part of the group. I want to be able to walk away without embarrassment if I get bored.

The archaeologist is speaking in English, and I am too tired to listen carefully, but the story itself is confusingly circular. The Kingdom of Mu was never a real city—it was a mock-up, built by yet another lost civilization, which the archaeologist refers to as Lemuria. Various signs and wall hangings that scientists have recovered indicate that Lemuria itself had legends of a precursor civilization which *they* called Mu, which had vanished beneath the waves. The Lemurians invented a lot of popular entertainments based around this idea, and these, in turn, led them to build what can only be considered a theme park.

I feel dizzy. Perhaps it's time I had some rest.

Back at the hotel, my sleep is troubled. I dream that I am speeding through the pneumatic tunnels of the city, sharing a car with an isopod and a pair of acorn worms. The platform at the station is guarded by a pair of mermen with Armalite assault rifles. I am hungrily perusing a leather-bound menu, but the only food on offer is seafood. All I want is a nice juicy steak.

The following morning, I catch the tube to the Extreme Undersea Adventure pavilion, a ring-shaped arena with a floor area about the size of a baseball diamond. I wander from floor to floor through a thin crowd of tourists, checking out the various submersible vessels on display, watching the animal handlers, and otherwise familiarising myself with layout.

Diehl enters with his group and spends about fifteen minutes dithering around, pretending to examine the displays, but I can see he is preoccupied with some other matter. Eventually he sidles up to the Adventurous Expeditions desk and, after a nervous exchange with the clerk, he signs a waiver and swipes his credit card. He has signed up for an Extreme Dive Experience.

Adventure sports were never my thing, but this could be a good opportunity, so I sign up too. The clerk ushers me through an archway and into a waiting area, where I join Diehl and ten other brave souls. My contact gives no sign of having recognised me.

Before long, a surly man with a crew cut emerges from the staff-only area. He examines us with a critical eye. He gives a grunt of disapproval and shakes his head. "I'm Henders, your dive master." He does not sound like a man who is happy with his lot in life.

Henders reads our surnames off a tablet computer, checking each of us off as we reply. Once he has established that we are all present he grunts and leads us to the briefing room.

Suddenly the holiday is over. Henders will brook no disobedience as he explains to us our mission: a cage dive with the merfolk. We, the Adventurers, will don our atmosphere suits exactly as he instructs. We will enter the diving cage in our allocated order and stand in our designated positions. Technicians in the control room will then lock the cage and drop it into the moon pool. They will then cycle the airlock will seal up and eject us out into the centre of the arena. Animal handlers will release the merfolk, who will perform some tricks for us.

Adventurers are not to look the merfolk in the eye. We are not to reach out of the cage. Adventurers are not to make any sounds or fast movements. The merfolk are omnivorous and highly aggressive.

Once the performance is over, the technicians will winch our cage back inside. Staff will then assist the Adventurers in removing their atmosphere suits. Photographs and video footage taken from inside the cage and from inside our helmets will be available for sale once we exit through the gift shop.

Henders herds us through into a long room full of lockers and bench seats and instructs us to strip. The change room is unisex, and

Henders will permit no modesty, but the room is so thick with fear that I do not think anybody is concerned about who is looking at them.

I used to have tattoos, when I was a young punk in the yakuza. Not a lot of them, because I didn't have the status and because tattoos are painful. But a few were enough, and shower time in the army was never fun as a result. Once I quit the Jeitai, I spent the first pay cheque I earned as a professional getting the tattoos lasered off. Besides the engagement ring I bought for Michiko, it's the best money I have ever spent.

Once we have donned the under-suits—Henders is already wearing his—we move to the dive chamber, where a heavy steel cage stands, open, beside the moon pool.

An assistant helps me climb into an atmosphere suit. Feet into the boots, hands into the gauntlets. She fits the chest and back plates, then the arms and legs; checks the joints and the seals. Satisfied, she touches a button on a control panel set into the wall and a fishbowl helmet descends from the roof, dangling hoses and electrical cables.

She steps up onto a small crate and guides the helmet down onto my shoulders. "How do you feel?" she says.

"No."

"What?"

"No." I shake my head.

"You'll be fine. Just do what Henders tells you. He's a professional."

I exhale three times, sharply. "No. Let me out, please."

"I promise you, sir, there is nothing—"

"No! No!"

My assistant sighs and turns to the dive master. "We have our drop-out over here, sir."

Henders turns smoothly and comes striding over in his suit, which is bulkier and yet sleeker than the ones issued to the tourists. I am certain it's military hardware and I wonder if he is armed. "You're out?" he says.

"Out," I say, working up some desperation.

Henders grunts and gives me a small smile. "There's always one." He turns away and makes a dismissive gesture with a chunky armoured hand. "Crack him out of the suit and turn him loose. I'll get these others into the cage."

"Yes, sir," says the assistant, concealing a smirk of her own.

It takes ten minutes to get me out of the suit again. Eyes downcast, I retreat back towards the change rooms. My assistant goes to help get the cage of terrified non-dropout into the pool.

Instead of turning left towards the showers, I make a right into a corridor marked STAFF ONLY, padding along in bare feet. I am still wearing the under-suit, which I hope will be enough to let me move around with impunity.

There are four control rooms in the new corridor. A light above the door of number one shows me that it's occupied, so I go for number three.

The lock on the door is the same kind that the Marriot uses. Using the pinkie finger on my left hand I find the seam and split it. The door opens and I slip inside.

The control room houses a chair and an array of blank monitors. I touch one of the screens and the console lights up. Three displays give me views from all of the cameras looking into and out of the cage, which is now filled with armoured tourists. Another screen shows schematics of the cage, and the last screen shows telemetry for each diver.

A crane lowers the cage into the pool. The divers' faces show fear and amazement as the water rises over their heads. An airlock door slides shut above them, and they sit tensely in the semi-lit airlock. A door below them opens and jets push them down into the open water. The Adventurers sit quite still. Even in the armoured suits, the immense pressure of all that water makes fidgeting difficult.

Jets reorient the cage and propel it up into the cavity in the middle of the Extreme Adventure pavilion. Lights attached to the cage fire up and suddenly the water is filled with radiance. This draws the merfolk in a rush of fins and flukes; a swirl of unnatural limbs. They circle it in shifting formations, linking hands or legs as they demonstrate some sort of undersea gymnastics. Scientists here found real life mermaids here, and they trained them to do synchronized swimming.

I touch the schematics on the screen and spring the cage door open.

I do not wait around to see what happens next. I wipe my prints off the screen and quit control room three as quickly as I can.

In the change room, I strip off my undersuit and get back into my civilian clothes. Fully dressed, I slink out past the photo booth, trying to look sheepish. The two staff members manning the reception booth snicker to each other. One of them says "hoser" to my back.

There is a hush in the viewing deck when I re-join the other tourists there. The door of the cage is open and two of the merfolk are trying to haul an armoured Adventurer through the gap. No sounds from the struggle penetrate the massive glass windows, but light classical music from the synchronized swimming routine is still playing.

The Adventurer tumbles out of the cage in a swirl of pale limbs and fins. I cannot tell who it is; they all look the same in the bulky atmosphere suits. The merfolk set upon the tourist, slashing with their fingers, biting with those triangular teeth. They are monstrously strong, but their teeth and claws break on the hard alloys of the suit. Soon they will figure out that the only way to get at the human inside is to tear it limb from limb.

Henders comes rocketing out of the cage, propelled by jets fixed to the back of his suit. He kicks his way through the crowd of merfolk and then rips the most aggressive of them off the feebly thrashing tourist. The waters are cloudy with blood and the merfolk drag their wounded away. More of them continue to hover nearby, trying to assess whether another attack might yield better results.

Henders gets an arm looped under the tourist's armpits. He turns 180 degrees, and jets back towards the diving cage. Two more of the merfolk see his turned back and shoot after him.

The dive master rolls the tourist through the open door of the cage and slams it shut. Inside, the tourists rattle around like bowling pins. He turns to face the incoming merfolk, who seize him like monkeys— one wraps its arms around his head and chest and the other latches onto his legs.

Henders smashes one of them away with a palm-heel to the chin. He executes a strange judo-like manoeuvre that rolls it over his back and sends it spinning slowly away. The remaining creature reaches up, but Henders' arms are free now. The dive master backhands it in the face and shrugs free of its loosened grip. It floats away with blood and brains spilling out of its caved-in skull.

The water is so thick and red now that it is hard to see what's happening, but I think Henders is hanging on to the outside of the cage, holding the door closed with those armoured fists. The winch hauls them down vanish into the darkness and they vanish from sight.

I eat lunch in one of the hotel restaurants. I have a table by a window, and I spend a leisurely hour working on my meal while staring out at the city of Mu, sprawled and luminous across the ocean floor. How does it exist under so much pressure? What a feat of engineering.

I do not think the tour operators will suspect foul play of the cage diving accident, but even if they do, I will be long gone before they start looking for suspects. Security here is lax at best.

After lunch I head to the submarine terminal and settle in to wait in the departure lounge. Before long Diehl's group arrives. I have spent a lot of time around these people, and I hope that I am just familiar enough that they won't notice me continuing to loiter nearby.

Diehl looks subdued when he arrives in the gate lounge, and he is not the only one. There were a lot of people at the Extreme Adventure Pavilion this morning. Others in the group are as boisterous as usual.

Nobody died today, but there is always tomorrow.

The submarine journey from the Kingdom of Mu is a short one, and most of it seems to be ascent. Even so, the captain apologizes for the slowness. This sub has an organic aeration system, he says, and it needs to decompress slowly in order to prevent nitrogen bubbles from forming in the transport layer.

Once the vessel is at the surface the cabin crew directs us up a steep flight of stairs and on deck. From there a floating walkway leads us to a larger pontoon, where there is shelter and a refreshment stand. The sea is calm and flat.

A circling airship descends towards us. It settles with the water lapping at its gondola. Members of the blue-skinned Menlat Niri crew extend a floating walkway to the pontoon and we board it carefully.

The dirigible flight is longer than the submarine ride. I drowse through it. By the time we dock amidst the familiar aerostatic canyons, I am even more tired than when we set out.

I am one of the last off the plane, but Diehl's tour group are still fussing around with breathing masks in the main hall of the airport once I come through passport control. I purchase an identical mask set to the one I wore the first time I was here and head for the taxi rank.

In broken Karachidaean, I ask the cab driver to take me to the Palisades hotel. My booking is for the Marriot again, but I want to get some space from the tour group. I need to get some rest and work out my next move.

I dream that there are merfolk hovering in the clouds outside my window, which is now barred like a diving cage. Henders bounces amongst them like a particularly aggressive pinball. He cannot fly, but he slams into them with incredible velocity, somehow maintaining enough momentum from each bounce to keep himself from falling. He is unarmoured but that does not seem to diminish his capacity to survive in the depths of the ocean—or the upper atmosphere. Somehow, we are in both places at once.

Henders punches a merman so hard that its head explodes, which causes the merman to abruptly lose his buoyancy. I am not sure when I cease to be a spectator watching from behind the bars of my room cage, but now I am that merman, tumbling towards the sea with my brains spilling out of my skull.

I doesn't hurt, but I do feel dizzy.

I wake up in a sweat.

This is unlike me. I have never suffered conscience-dreams before, if that's what these are. I have never felt sorry about the people I have killed. I am annoyed that Diehl has survived my first two attempts on his life, and I pity him a little, but I do not feel bad for what I am going to do to him.

Dreams or no dreams, Diehl is going to die and then I am going to go home and live happily ever after.

After breakfast, I put on my breathing mask and take a taxi to the Aeroponic Display Farm. I am one of the first guests through the doors. After two failures I feel like my usual improvisational tactics are not working and I need to reconnoitre like the professional I was and am…at least until this job is done.

The nodes of the Aeroponics Display Farm have been strung between a dozen dirigible surfaces. The tourist throng explores the farm from a series of gangways and catwalks, the scaffolding of which also serves as an enormous trellis. Fruit-bearing plants climb the curving meshes, which are suspended from gantries that rotate with the sun. The air is misted with nutrient fluids; sprayed directly onto the exposed root fibres of the various plants, which spread outrageously into the open air.

By the time Diehl's tour group arrives I have groomed three promising scenarios. Now I just need one of them to align with opportunity and I can go home and marry my fiancée and be forever done with the boredom of work.

Even with his mask on, Diehl looks edgy. I can't blame him. He stays in the thick of his group and I keep my distance.

The Orchard is actually a pen filled with spongiform animals; huge and lumpy and limbless and hollow. They excrete lighter-than-air gases that keep them buoyant in the atmosphere. Farmers can influence the composition of this gas mixture by manipulating their diet. The Menlat Niri waste no part of the animal, from the gas to the outer shell. They use them for food, fuel, and a variety of industrial processes that are well beyond my comprehension. The tour group makes a complete circuit of the perimeter before the guide leads us on.

I keep Diehl in sight, but this is not the place.

The Rookery is a multi-level structure where birds come to feed and to roost. The lower floors are used to farm free range chickens. An enclosed stairway winds up into the higher levels, allowing visitors to peer in at the different bird species present on each stratum. Diehl's tour guide decides that the climb is too strenuous for his group and leads them away without taking them inside. This is not the place, either.

I shadow the tour group as the guide hustles them off towards the Reservoir for a picnic lunch.

The Reservoir covers an area the size of twenty-four soccer fields, terraced over three levels by a system of locks and canals. The aerostatic surfaces that keep it aloft are housed beneath the massive rocky basin, so the whole place looks as though it has torn loose from the earth and is just now lounging around in the sky with nothing to do.

Menlat Nir collects water vapour directly from the cloud cover. Every building has its own tanks, but the reservoir is here to supplement them — or to collect overflow. It also used for aquaculture, hydroelectric power, and sanitation. I have no idea how this is at all possible.

A smaller floating island hangs above the reservoir, tethered by ropes and chains. This is one of the few public parks in Menlat Nir offering grass and trees, and many locals come here to enjoy surface earth pass-times: throwing Frisbees, kicking footballs, sunbathing. A handful of enthusiasts have cast fishing lines over the guard rails. While I am watching one of them pulls a glistening fat rainbow trout out of the water.

The guide leads us over a swaying suspension bridge towards the floating island. I look down: the surface of the earth is thousands of meters below. I am not afraid of heights, but my heart is in my throat the whole way. I stay well away from Diehl. This is not the place.

On the island the grass is lush underfoot. Perspex screens suspended between some of the nearby blimps protect this particular spot, reducing the vicious crosswinds to a strong breeze. It's nice and sunny out here; a lovely, quiet day. The guide hands out vouchers and the tour group queues up to collect their meals at the kiosk. My stomach is rumbling, but I cannot bring myself to steal somebody's lunch. I am a murderer, but I am not a thief.

Diehl takes his lunch and wanders away from the group. He sits on a rock near the guard rail and eats his lunch, staring out at the reservoir. He looks up at the curving balloons of Menlat Nir; the sickle-slices of sky above; the blazing mirrored surfaces directing sunlight down to us. He looks down to the dark blue of the oceans far below. The view enough to give anybody pause.

I have my camera out and I snap some photos, but Diehl's contemplative mood is infectious. Will I still be able to travel to these places… to the Unfolded Earth…once I have retired? I don't see why not. I will ask Vashya to introduce me to her travel agent. I hope that one day I will be able to avoid air travel altogether, given my facility for opening Doors and finding Ways, but I will still need somebody to arrange accommodation for me in places that are beyond the reach of *hotels.com* and Rakuten.

Michiko can never know about my work, but I would love to show her these territories; these worlds. These places that do not, cannot, or should not exist. I know there are many more to discover. Places I have never imagined.

The guide rousts Diehl's group, and they start to troop back across the bridge. I stay where I am, because this is still not the place.

About halfway across the bridge, Diehl hesitates. He stands, gripping the railing, staring straight down at the water. His eyes bulge: his neck is corded with strain. He stands like that for a good fifteen seconds before the guide grabs him.

I am too far away to hear the exchange, but it's full of strong, serious emotions. There are tears in Diehl's eyes. The guide puts an arm over his shoulders and escorts him very carefully to safety on the far side of the bridge. A medical team is waiting for him when he steps off. They drape a Mylar blanket over his shoulders and whisk him away.

Another first. I think my contact just tried to kill himself.

I head back to the airport and jump on an early blimp back to Mesra City. They're going to have Diehl under observation for a while and I don't want to get caught up in that. This whole thing is getting far too risky. I can't keep following him around; I'm going skip ahead and wait for him at the final destination on his Grand Tour. If he manages to kill himself before I get to him, I will still be paid. If he cancels the rest of his tour, I will probably lose the contract and the people who want him dead will find some Conventional Earth hitman to take him down. That's fine with me; I don't need the money. But I have agreed to do this job and I will do my best to see it through.

I do not want to retire on a failure.

In Mesra City I catch a taxi to the Port Authority and take the hydrofoil out to the Space Whip platform.

Lulled by my recent experiences in submarines and air balloons, I am surprised by the violence of the journey up the Space Whip. When I debark onto Space Station Bravo Tango, I am glad I skipped dinner.

Thankfully I've been here before. I find my way to the hotel on the MT without conscious thought. I have no memory of the journey; just of the relief I feel when I find my suite and collapse onto the bed.

I dream that I am fishing in the Aeroponic Farm's reservoir. I have an ice box beside me containing a six pack of Sapporo beer and a bento full of delicious food, lovingly prepared by my darling Michiko. Of course, I know that the real Michiko has never been much of a one for cookery, but this does not shake me out of the fantasy.

The rod flexes and the line goes taut, so I start to reel it in. I am humming a Social Decay song as I turn the spindle. I have never been fishing in my life. Whoever knew it was this much fun?

Ah! I have caught a giant sky-sponge from the Orchard. My line goes slack as it comes floating towards me, drawn on by inertia, perhaps. Suddenly I am worried, because the sponge is far too big to fit in my bucket. I pick up a rusty fishing knife, which has been embedded in the splintering planks of the deck beside the ice chest. It's hard to get a grip because the handle is slippery with fish guts—or perhaps cold soba noodles.

The sponge looms huge overhead. It has a pair of weeping yellow eyes and a mouth full of perforated gums. Ichor drips from its maw and splatters, sizzling on the decking. The sponge's drool is strongly alkaline and will dissolve my bones once its gums have abraded the skin and meat off them.

I abandon the knife. There is only one thing left to do. I put one foot up onto the rail and launch myself into the air. The reservoir below is gone, and there is nothing but sky below me. I cannot see the earth. I don't know if I am falling up or down, but that doesn't really matter. This fall will be forever.

I awaken at 11am, having forgotten than the station doesn't keep a day/night cycle. Three dreams in a row. I would find that disturbing, if I was the kind of person who was easily disturbed.

I shower and get dressed, but I am feeling oddly dull and lethargic. This is my last chance to kill George Diehl. Today is my last day on the job, if you don't count time for traveling back home. Perhaps I have let this go on for so long because I am not ready for this part of my life to be over?

I break out a new shirt to raise my spirits: white cotton, with blue *tapa* patterns on the hem and a giant turtle on the back. I ordered this shirt from my new favourite website: *aloha-shatsu.com*. It looks good, and I feel better as soon as I put it on. This is it. No more Mr Nice Assassin.

George Diehl is as good as dead.

I am already waiting at the observation deck above the space dock when Diehl's tour group arrives. I pick out his face in my peripheral vision but stay well clear of him.

Outside the station, alien ships go about their business slowly, attaching to different nodules on the dock, disgorging shuttle craft, reconfiguring themselves. Last time I was here I thought that they resembled winged animals: swans and dragons and ducks; luminous and graceful and bejewelled. This time, I feel less inclined to poetry. They ships are hideous, like insects that live in dark, wet places; like microscopic parasites blown up large; like bacteria; like worms. I am certain that their civilizations are just as ugly and petty as our own. Why else would they tolerate us?

Diehl's group is enraptured with the view, but luckily, I have seen it all before, so it does not distract me from my contact, who today is wearing a cotton Aloha shirt. I think it's actually nicer than mine and I cannot help but feel a twinge of jealousy over it.

The guide ushers Diehl's group along to the far side of the room and I trail behind, taking photos that I will delete before I get home. But the guide takes the group out to the starboard area, and I find myself in a corner of the observation lounge that I somehow overlooked the first time I was here. Quite a large corner, as it turns out.

The guide gestures through the view glass to a scattering of some empty hoop structures, hanging fixed in the void of space. My topographic senses tell me what they are before the guide does: they're Doors. Interstellar Doors, that open into distant regions of the galaxy. Some of the aliens on board Bravo Tango have starships that can move at non-relativistic speeds, but the use of Faster Than Light drives is forbidden inside the solar system. Too dangerous to the satellite worlds, and too difficult to cloak the evidence from amateur astronomers.

These Doors are more modest option for alien species who do not have the energy to burn on long-haul FTL travel, and who are willing to trust the operators of the network.

We humans do not have the technology or political clout to travel out of our own territory, which, according to the tour guide, legally extends as far as the Oort Cloud. Our trading partners from abroad guard their secrets carefully.

We are just in time to see an Opening, the guide says. He will not speculate on what is coming through, or why. On cue, lightning crackles clockwise around the rim of one of the closer hoops. It arcs down from the uppermost edge of the hoop to the bottom; branches horizontally and then splits through the diagonals. The lightning bulges inwards like a net, coruscating through the visible light spectrum. The vertex of the bulge opens to blackness, and the bulk of something huge and alien pushes through it.

A star ship squeezes through like a turd that has been filigreed with gold lace and lit up like a Christmas tree. Its reticulated bulk coils down into a neat spiral as it eases out of the portal into terrestrial space. Once the turd-ship is through, the portal flickers off.

The guide says that only two of the twelve visible hoops are still in use. Most of the others have been decommissioned—not because they're broken, but because the natural expansion of the universe has drawn the matching Doors away from shipping routes. A middle-aged woman with a tea cosy on her head suggests that this is wasteful, but the guide assures her that materiel is plentiful when you have an entire galaxy's resources available to you. It is almost always cheaper to build a new Door generator than to move an old one.

After the Opening the tour group disperses through the observation lounge. Diehl, looking queasy, heads for the Men's toilet. I gave it thirty seconds and then I follow him inside. I round the corner from the wash room to the toilet area just in time to hear the lock on his cubicle drawer snick shut.

We are not alone in the toilet. A man is at the urinal, focused on his business. He is very careful not to look across at me when I step up. Toilets might be a dirty place to execute some already-dirty business, but they do have some advantages. I stare at the flush button and pee into my own urinal bowl. Diehl is having a loud and runny bowel movement from the sanctity of his cubicle. I feel embarrassed on his behalf.

The man on my right finishes up and flushes. I stay where I am while he very slowly washes his hands. Then he puts them under the drier. He is very thorough. It feels like he takes half an hour to dry his hands. When he finally turns and pulls open the door, another man enters.

"Excuse me," says the newcomer.

"No, excuse *me*."

Maybe I should kill them all.

Inside his cubicle, I can hear Diehl pulling on the toilet paper dispenser.

I elbow the button to flush the urinal and then, at the washbasin, I turn on the tap with the blade of my right hand. I do not want to leave any fingerprints. I have my hands under the drier when Diehl flushes his toilet. The newcomer is still busy at the urinal.

I leave the Men's room with my hands still damp.

A few minutes later Diehl emerges from the Men's. He looks around furtively and then rushes off, abandoning his tour group. I do not think he's made me, but he knows something is up. I set off after him briskly. Looks like I will have to make my own opportunity.

Away from the tourist precinct, the corridors have bare aluminium walls, unadorned by information displays or advertisements. We are in a derelict area near the shipyard offices. Diehl doesn't know this area, but I do.

I pick up the pace. I am sure my contact can now hear my footsteps banging on the metal flooring, but he blunders on without looking back. Diehl makes a left, then a right, but he has no destination in mind. He's spooked and he just needs to *get away*.

I could probably run him down, but I don't want to turn this into a footrace. I cannot keep chasing him. Sooner or later, we are going to be seen.

Despite my eagerness to get this done I stop, look around, think for a moment. And there it is, right in front of me. A little red button behind a glass panel. I wrap my hand in a handkerchief and use my folded Swiss Army Knife to smash it.

Klaxons sound and ceiling lights begin to flash. I continue after

Diehl as the corridors begin to fill with workers. They mill about, uncertain. I hear one of them complain loudly that they had a fire drill only a week earlier. This complaint leads to an argument about the location of the rally point, which most of them failed to attend the last time this happened.

Alarms are still screaming in the corridors. Illuminated strips appear in the walls, ceiling and floors. Over the intercom, a female voice with excellent diction advises us to calmly follow the flashing lights.

I have lost Diehl in the confusion. I turn right, left, right, but it's harder to make headway now that the halls are choked with dithering workers. I need to finish this. Find Diehl, drag him into an office, kill him. If there is anybody else in there, I will kill them, too. I do not think I'm going to get another chance.

There he is. I bang down the corridor after him and he immediately starts to sprint. At no point does he look behind him. Left, right, left, right. I am close enough to hear him panting. He comes to a T-junction. A large group of people are gathered in the left arm—it must be a rally point—so he goes right, and I follow. The milling crowd is too flustered to pay us any attention.

I follow Diehl through one more turn, which leads to a short dead-end corridor with three bubble-shaped doors set into each wall. He ducks through one of the doors and disappears surprisingly quickly. The door seals itself behind him and the lights on it cycle from yellow to red.

I slap at the door, the doorframe, the wall around it. It will not open for me, but I can feel it vibrating beneath my hands. The clank of machinery startles me, and I recoil. I hear something like an engine starting and then a heavy jolt.

I step away from the door and look at it again. The words EVAC POD 159 are stencilled above it in bold letters.

I move over and the door for pod 160 bubbles open for me. I step through carefully but once I am over the threshold some kind of webbing enfolds me and drags me inside, strapping me down into a heavily padded seat. Seals hiss and a succession of hatches open and close as the pod drops and slides forward through a channel in the hull.

The engine roars and, with a sudden kick, my escape pod accelerates free of Station Bravo Tango and spins out into the vacuum of space.

Once my pod is clear of the station the main engine goes off. The roar is replaced by a series of short hisses as the directional thrusters expel bursts of nitrogen, arresting my spin and allowing the pod to drift slowly away from the space station.

Diehl's pod is drifting loose about three hundred meters away: a bulb of white metal, blistered with gas tanks and thruster nodules. The pod trails a long array of antennae and sensors and has a large round window at the front, which makes it look very much like a disembodied human eyeball. The numerals 159 are blazoned on the side in black. It's about the size of a Toyota Vitz.

The pod's joystick controls remind me of many happy hours spend playing games on my family's old home computer. Analogue dials on a dashboard show fuel and oxygen levels, and an array of mirrors show me what's going on above, below and behind me. The controls are surprisingly low-tech—I suppose that's to conserve energy. These pods are not designed to last for an extended duration. Or perhaps they're made cheap because nobody expects them to survive a genuine catastrophe.

Pod 159 fires a thruster and moves into a slow yaw. Another thruster fires, and another, and it wobbles into a spin. Diehl is struggling to get it under control.

I touch the right-hand joystick and my pod starts to turn. I touch the left to trim it up. Soon I am bearing down on Diehl's Pod 159 at a leisurely clip. Its thrusters fire and it veers away, rotating out and up at a dizzying angle. Diehl has seen me coming and panicked.

I set off in pursuit, but I do not know what I am going to do when I catch up to him. There are no weapons systems and ramming into 159 will be as dangerous to me as to him. I need to manoeuvre him into something fatal before he runs out of propellant and before someone on Bravo Tango figures out that the emergency is a false alarm and sends a shuttle to haul the pair of us back in.

Diehl fumbles out of his spin and jets along in a reasonably straight line. I ghost after him. The only sounds in my ears are those of my own breathing and the occasional hiss of the thrusters when I make a correction to my bearing.

It's like a very slow-moving video game. I stay on Diehl's tail and I keep him between me and the space station. He is learning to better control his vehicle, but I have the advantage of topographic senses and a past life as a juvenile delinquent spent mostly playing arcade games and intimidating senior citizens. I have Diehl on the defensive.

I chase Diehl in a spiral that takes us all the way around station

Bravo Tango and most of the length of it. When the shipyards come into sight, I try to drive him down towards the dry docks, hoping to herd him into some of the heavy equipment there, but he lurches his pod away from the cranes and the gantries and into a crazy yaw. Fearful of getting caught in his tail, I hang back while he struggles to bring his pod back under control. If he crashes and dies that will be okay, too. But today I am not so lucky.

What feels like a pulse of frustration propels me as I scoot up behind him. Diehl pulls away again, but I stay close behind. My topographic senses flare as the hoops of the interstellar Doors come into view. Finally, I know what to do.

I push closer to Diehl, getting more aggressive, and it has the desired effect. Pod 159 jitters around, accelerating towards the hoops. I zoom up, recklessly close, and he jerks the ship towards one of the abandoned dimension hoops.

There is still a Door here, or at least a weak spot where there was in the past, and I am certain that I can open it. I turn my pod and send it careening towards Diehl's. He panics and falls into an uncontrolled spin as I rocket past him, through the hoop. I tear the Door open as I pass through, drag its fabric with me to hold it open…hold it open…

Long moments pass before Diehl drifts through behind me. I allow the portal snap closed.

Now it's just him and me.

We are somewhere dark. There's no star system here. In fact, there are barely any stars at all. I can see some distant galaxies, but they are faint and very far away. The low-wattage lamps on the two evacuation pods cut the darkness like lasers. The void of space is thin in this region of the universe. No wonder this Door has fallen out of use.

Diehl's pod drifts by above me. Or perhaps he is below me, and I am upside down. There is no frame of reference against which to make the judgment. I fire my thrusters to twin his position; coast up alongside him. Diehl makes no further attempt to flee. My vehicle bumps up against his, glass to glass, with a soft *clank*.

I am not even sure why I am doing this. Perhaps I just want to make sure it's Diehl. This is my last job and I want to be thorough. Perhaps.

Upside down, Diehl peers out of the glass at me. He looks drawn, but relaxed. He wipes his eyes and meets my gaze. Seeing myself in the glass—facing my contact through my reflected image—gives me a moment of vertigo.

"I like your shirt."

Diehl looks down, touches the fabric with his left hand. "This? Really?" His voice is faint. The glass-to-glass contact would permit better sound conduction if the windshields were thinner.

"*Alohashatsu.com*?"

"What?"

"Did you buy it online?"

He shakes his head. "Old Navy."

"Ah." I nod, disappointed.

"Who are you?"

"My business name is Zai." I don't know why I'm telling him this. "My real name is Retsuya."

"Pleased to meet you," he replies automatically. "I'm George."

"I know who you are."

"Oh. Of course, you do." He just looks at me.

"George, may I ask you something?"

"Is it about my shirt?"

"No."

"Oh. Well, sure, I guess."

"When did you work it was *me*?"

"You?"

"When did you work out that I was the one who has been trying to kill you?"

He shakes his head. "I've never laid eyes on you before."

"I stalked you across four different worlds."

"Didn't notice."

"But you did notice that someone was trying to kill you."

"I wasn't sure. I thought...maybe...um. Accidents happen, you know?"

"You tried to kill yourself."

"No. That was just...I guess I did know, deep down inside. I knew they'd come for me. I knew I wasn't allowed to be there."

"Where?"

"Well, you know. Karachidor. Mesra City. Mu. Menlat Nir. The Unfolded Earth. Normal people aren't allowed there."

"How did you get onto the tour?"

"It's a boring story."

"I am a forgiving audience."

"Well, it was...is...I have a business rival. Boring stuff, really. Air conditioning parts. Boring. But he was kicking my ass and I couldn't work out why, so I...acquired...some material from his office. It showed that a lot of his funding came from a place called Mesra City."

"A place that doesn't exist."

"Yeah. I know it sounds stupid, but...I went and confronted him. My rival."

"Why?" I ask myself the same question. Why am I prolonging this? This isn't thoroughness. Am I getting sentimental?

Diehl looks away. "Because he's my brother."

"He told me to go home and forget I'd ever heard of the place, or... bad things would happen. Sell up my business and leave him alone. So, I did."

"But then you changed your mind."

"It was eating me. I had to know. Where the heck is Mesra City?"

"How did you manage to get tickets?"

"I also acquired a copy of a travel itinerary when I stole all those documents from him. I called up his travel agent and I told her I was Troy's brother and...here I am. With you."

I am tempted to ask George Diehl if he would share the name of the travel agent, but perhaps that is pushing the discourtesy a bit too far after I asked him about the shirt, so I just incline my head. Perhaps it's a bow, perhaps just a nod.

"So, what happens now?" he says.

"Now? I'm going to leave you here."

I can see him looking around. At the veiled darkness; the thin scattering of stars. To my knowledge, this is as far from the earth as any human has ever ventured.

"That's it? You're not going to kill me?"

"You will die here, I'm certain. You'll run out of power, or air, or water. If not, in two or three weeks you'll die of starvation."

He nods, digesting all of that, considering his options. He could put up a fight. Try to trick me into reopening the gate, or to damage my pod. Try some stratagem to take me down with him. But he won't. George Diehl is done fighting.

I just stare at him. I have never had to face someone like this; someone who knows that I have just caused their death.

Diehl just sits there thinking about it. Then he opens his eyes again. "I don't suppose you'd reconsider?"

I shake my head.

"Had to ask."

"Goodbye, Mr George Diehl."

"Goodbye, um, Mr Zai." Diehl is the first person I have ever told my real name to while out in the field, and he hasn't even remembered it.

I touch the joystick and break contact with Diehl's pod. I turn mine about and squirt it back towards the portal. In my rear mirror I see Diehl give his own jets some power; accelerate away from the portal. I do not know if he's rushing towards his death, or he just wants to get away from me.

I make the transition back through the Door and pilot my pod back towards the docks on the far side of Bravo Tango. The vacuum-space there is a lot more crowded than before, with around twenty more escape pods milling around under supervision of a squad of blunt-nosed shuttle craft. Big flashing signs proclaim that the emergency was a FALSE ALARM and advise us to REMAIN CALM.

I wonder how long the rescue teams will search for Diehl's escape pod before they give up.

Back in Mesra City I check into the Epsidor for the last time. My flight home is first thing in the morning, so I have one final afternoon to kill in Mesra City.

I take the subway into downtown, and I just walk around. With a breeze from the harbor and grey skies overhead, I need a jacket today.

I have left my camera in the hotel room. I want to remember this place with my eyes, not with flash memory. Many shops are closed and there is a strange quality about the place today. It's not a ghost town or a zombie city, but it feels like it might be some kind of transit stop on the way to the underworld.

Out of the corner of my eye I spot a neon sign. I am certain it wasn't there a moment ago, but when I turn it's plainly visible. The foreign language bookstore. I'm certain it was on the far side of the CBD the last time I saw it.

I descend the steps into the store. This time I understand the skin tingling, pressure-drop sensation for what it is: passage through a Door.

The shop is even brighter than I remember it. The light seems *newer* this time. Even the smell of it is somehow fresher.

There is no cashier at the front desk, and I am starting to feel self-conscious. I'd feel terribly embarrassed if the cashier comes back and finds me walking around in here by myself. Will she suspect me of stealing?

But the longer I remain in the store the more comfortable I become. Nobody is going to disturb me in here. This time is mine.

The Japanese language section is not where I remember it. It's on the other side of the store, right in between Hindi and Korean. Something about this offends me, so I gather up all the books—there are only six of them—and move them to the place where I feel they do belong. Right next to Self Help.

After a moment's consideration I take my battered copy of Doors and Ways out of my bag and add it to the shelf, sandwiched between a Karachidaean-Japanese dictionary and a Mindfulness volume with Deepak Chopra's face on the cover.

Feeling strangely satisfied, I head for the exit.

One of Vashya's bodyguards is waiting for me when I check out of the Epsidor the next morning. He does not greet me, but he takes my bag and gestures for me to follow him. Out front of the hotel, he opens the door of a waiting limousine and ushers me inside.

I sit opposite Vashya, with my back to the driver. The bodyguard sits next to me and the door closes.

"Well, this is a surprise." A sentence I have never uttered before in English. I sound just like the late Russell Kilmer-Jones.

The car pulls away from the kerb and I settle back.

"Zai, I want to say goodbye, Zai."

I feel unexpectedly touched. I bow.

"Zai, you were excellent employee were you, Zai."

"Thank you. I have enjoyed working for you. I was able to see many things that I would never have believed possible."

We are on the expressway, jetting towards the airport. The limousine is a lot more comfortable than a taxi.

"Zai, gift for you give, Zai." Vashya produces a small wooden box. She opens it to reveal a gold wristwatch, nestled on a bed of velvet. There is no brand marking on it, but it looks like fine Karachidaean craftsmanship. I bow again. "Dōmo arigatō gozaimasu. You shouldn't have."

I feel bad that I don't have a gift for her, and her bodyguards, but I honestly never expected to see them again. In Japan, I would be mortally embarrassed.

I remove the cheap Casio watch that I wear for work and try on the new watch. It has a nice weight to it; like wearing a slab of wealth on my wrist. The band is soft leather and fits perfectly.

"It's beautiful. Thank you for everything."

"Zai, it was my pleasure, Zai. Hard work for thank you, Zai."

We ride the rest of the way to the airport in silence. When we arrive, she does not get out of the car, but she does lean out of the door and say "Zai, goodbye and farewell, Zai."

I bow. "*Sayonara. Okarada o taisetsu ni.*" This is the last time I will ever see this woman. I do not know her real name, but she has changed my life.

The bodyguard hands me my suitcase and gets back into the limousine.

I buy myself a nice Karachidaean meal in an airport restaurant with a glass of *shnkwer* to wash it down. I am feeling good. I manage to navigate passport control and immigration without incident. The guards even smile at me.

At the gate lounge I settle in to wait, feeling unusually rested and free of stress. I listen to the Damned on my iPod until it's time to board. *So, Who's Paranoid?* Not their best album, but still one of my favourites.

My flight is mostly empty and I have an entire row to myself. I cannot expect such luck on all of my connections, but with fifty hours of transit time ahead of me I am ready to make the most of every luxury. I am, of course, in my usual seat: 34C.

When the doors are sealed, I slide across to the window seat so that I can watch the take-off. Right on time, we begin our taxi up the runway. The engines rev up, the control surfaces on the wings open, and the plane becomes airborne. The skies are blue and bright and clear. Our ascent is smooth and unfaltering.

I lean back into my seat. I am done with it all. The risks, the adrenaline, the thrills, the criminal antics. It's over. I am going home to live happily ever after.

I am not at all surprised when the bomb goes off

The first explosion rips through the back end of the plane, shearing off the tail and smashing the aircraft into a sickening yaw.

Is this the work of some enemy I never knew about? Was it revenge for what I did to Albion? Or Odin? Was it Vashya, or some other department from the Unfolded Enterprises group? Who knows?

I lean back into my seat as I feel the plane start to slip down onto its nose. There is no point assuming the brace position; nobody on this plane is going to survive a landing. The white noise of the cabin depressurizing is louder than the explosion. I am still relaxed. What can I do but sit here and die? If I was at the back of the plane, I would be dead already.

I will never go back home to Tokyo. I will never get married to Michiko. I will never be a normal person with an ordinary life. But I have no regrets. I wouldn't trade any of the things I have experienced. Not even the theme parks.

A second explosion starts at the cockpit and rolls backwards towards me. I see the fireball coming and I know this is the ending I have earned. This is the death that I deserve, and I accept it willingly.

I am not a religious man. If there is an afterlife, I do not know to which Hells I am going—but I hope I will get to see them all.

#11: Palace of the Dragon God

That's one version of what happened to me, but there is another. Which is not to say that it didn't happen, because it absolutely did. I died in that bombing. I have memories of it. I remember sitting in that seat with the plane coming apart. I remember the firestorm engulfing me; my flesh igniting; the burning gases blasting me to cinders. Such pain and violence is hard to forget, even if it only lasted a few moments. That happened to me, but it is not what happened to me.

I think it's some sort of a quantum thing.

I have known that I could make time Doors since my trip to Faerie Land, but I did not know what would happen if I myself stepped all the way through into another time. Now I do.

Now there are two of me—one who died in the explosion, and one who escaped back into the past. I have the memories of both of me, although one set is very brief, truncated as it was by my violent death.

I am the cat who died in the box, but I am also the cat who lived.

One other thing I was right about, though. Time travel gives me a headache.

I am sitting in my accustomed seat—34C—in the cabin of an empty aeroplane. We are on the ground at Mesra City International Airport. My seatbelt is unfastened. I rise tentatively, but the plane is still around me; still intact.

I check the overhead locker but there are no bags up there, because my earlier self has already taken them.

It is five days prior to my death.

It is ten minutes since I disembarked from this very plane to attend the briefing for my final mission: follow George Diehl on his Grand Tour and kill him.

All I have are the clothes on my back and the travel wallet I brought with me from the very near future.

Hustling down the aisle towards the exit, I surprise a flight attendant who is in the process of collecting his personal belongings from a locker in the front galley.

"Who…how did you…?"

"I'm sorry." I put one hand on my stomach and touch my forehead with the other. "I was feeling ill."

I am feeling generally woozy and nauseous, but the flight attendant looks sceptical, so I retrieve the crumpled old boarding pass out of the travel wallet and show it to him. The attendant examines it and then returns it. "I'm sorry, Mr Zai. I hope it wasn't the food."

"I had the chicken."

The attendant makes a face that suggests I should have known better. He gives me directions to the airport pharmacist, and I thank him profusely.

I rush through the arrivals hall without catching sight of my other self. I suppose he is still waiting to collect his baggage. I take the escalator upstairs and head for the ticket counter to book myself on the earliest available flight back to Tokyo.

I have five days' head start on whoever is going to kill me.

Michiko is waiting for me at Narita, unmistakable in her army boots and studded leather jacket. She is wearing a charcoal tartan skirt that I have never seen before, and black hose. In the days since I left Tokyo, she has shaved off the pink Mohawk and dyed her eyebrows green. Michiko looks more like an assassin from a weird comic book than I ever have or will.

She squeals my name when she sees me and runs up to embrace me. A few people stare at us, but most are polite enough to hide their disapproval.

Michiko takes me by the hand and leads me up through the parking garage. "What happened to you?" she asks. I know I'm looking a bit frayed right now. The quantum headache comes and goes but never recedes altogether. She touches the singed cuff of one of my sleeves and says, "Barbeque accident?"

"Terrorist bombing."

"And you couldn't find a shower?"

"I would kill for a shower."

She does not ask where my luggage is. This is not the first time I have returned without any.

Michiko leads me to the big black Mercedes Benz. "Get in," she says. "You stink. We're stopping at the nearest *onsen*."

Technically the Benz is still mine, because she dumped me before I could sign it over to her, but now that we are back together, she has taken ownership of it, in principle if not on paper. Sooner or later, this is going to be a problem.

I look at my beautiful gold watch. We have still two full days before I am going to die, and I really could use that bath.

I leave the watch in a trash can, and we get on the road.

Michiko takes the Higashi Kanto expressway west to Chiba and then turn south at the interchange onto Keiyo Doro Avenue. These are toll roads, and I am unhappy about the cameras, but I want to get away from the airport as fast as possible, and also to avoid Tokyo proper. A couple of hours later we are in Chikura, on the coast near the bottom of the prefecture. We check in to a private room at the Chikurakan *onsen*. Michiko pays for it with cash.

I scrub myself clean in the shower room; wash my hair twice. Then I open the screen door and settle myself into the tub; immersing my tired body in spring water that is so hot it's barely tolerable. I lie back and close my eyes. I am not sure whether the bombing, the time travel or the airline food was more stressful, but after what I have just been through, I needed this badly. I can barely feel that strange headache anymore.

About ten minutes later Michiko joins me in the tub. She is so clean her skin seems to sparkle in steam. Her eyebrows are very, very green.

I tell her everything. None of it surprises her.

Not even the quantum stuff.

We get back on the road at dawn, heading back up through Minamiboso to the Kanaya ferry terminal. Michiko and I wait there for about twenty minutes for the ferry. We drive the car right onto it and then, forty minutes later, we drive off at Yokosuka.

We are in Kamakura less than an hour later.

Michiko parks the Benz in Genjiyama Park in the hills near the Daibutsu hiking trail. I see the occasional jogger go past, but it is still too early in the day for school groups to be. We have the place to ourselves.

Michiko follows me around with her arms folded, pretending to be sceptical about my claims to supernatural powers. I haven't been here since I was a child, but some half-remembered instinct tells me that there is a Door, or at least a Way, in this vicinity. If I had known how to use my topographic abilities when I was little, how changed would my life be?

Not very, I decide. I would probably still be dead.

But there is nothing here. We tramp up and down the hillside for more than an hour before Michiko loses her patience. "It must be at the shrine," she says.

I shake my head. That's too obvious. But eventually I give in, and we head towards Zeniarai Benten.

The Zeniarai Benten Ugafuku shrine has been located inside this cave for 900 years. A rare place that is holy to both Shinto and Buddhist beliefs, people still come here to wash their money in the spring water. Superstition claims this will cause that money to double, come the springtime, but this idea has been losing popularity since paper money was introduced. Even with Japan's epic deflation spiral, you cannot buy much with a handful of coins.

There's nobody in the cave washing money—or anything else—on the green bamboo rollers. There's no Door, either.

I give Michiko a shrug that is partly an admission of failure and partly an I-told-you-so and we head back outside. I am out of ideas. Should we try our luck back in Tokyo? Will my enemies really send a clean-up crew after me, now that I am...now that I will shortly be... conclusively dead? I do not think they know about my abilities, but they are thorough, and if they check the airline's records it will be clear that something is amiss.

The headache is pulsing behind my eyes now, so I pinch them shut and lay an open palm against my left temple. "I'm going to try something."

"What?"

"I'm going to make a Door."

I spread my hands and tear open a portal. I try to think of a motel that I know in the Florida Keys, but the harder I try, the more difficult I find it to visualize the place. Meanwhile, the feeling of familiarity is growing strong all the time. I just wish I could properly remember what it was that I experienced when I was here as a—

A child stumbles out of nowhere. A fat little boy, seven or eight years old. He's wearing a school uniform. His shirt is untucked and there are tears on his face. Sweat stains under his arms.

The pain behind my eyes spikes and it's all I can do to stay upright.

Michiko approaches him cautiously. "Are you alright, little brother?"

The child looks up at her and starts to blubber. "We were at the temple, and I was hungry so I went looking for candy and then it was hot so I went into the trees and I don't know where I am and it's late and there are bears—"

"There are no bears here," says Michiko, firmly. "Where is the rest of your class?"

"I don't know!" The boy continues to sniffle. "I've never been lost before. I've never been alone."

I approach the boy, trying to place each foot on the ground in between the pulses of my headache. I try to look him in the eyes but I'm not sure I can locate them on his face through my blurred vision. "It's alright to wonder off by yourself," I tell him slowly. "But you must always remember which way you came."

"How can I remember?"

"Pay attention. Look at what's around you. Study the map before you go."

"I will." the boy wipes his nose. "I promise. I always will."

"Very good. Are you paying attention now?"

"Hai."

"Good. Now follow this trail down the hill until you come to the road. Turn left, then turn right. When you come to the traffic light, turn right again. At the next traffic light, turn left. This road will take you all the way to the giant Buddha statue. Your class will be waiting for you over there with the bus home."

"Thank you!" The boy bows and turns away.

"No, no. This way." I usher the boy through my portal, and he vanishes.

Michiko looks at me for a long time. Then she says, "Looking for candy, huh?"

I take a long, shuddering breath. The headache is receding now, but I feel like throwing up. "He was seven years old, Michiko."

"And you forgot all of that, did you?"

"I remember some creepy stranger scared me," I reply. "But he told me how to get back to safety."

I think it's some sort of a quantum thing.

Down the hill from the shrine is a path that leads through a tunnel of *torii* gates. As we approach the big red pillars, a yellow fox slinks out from behind one of the posts and walks right up to us.

"*Kawaii*." Michiko bends down to pet the animal. "It's tame!"

"Good day," says the fox.

Michiko straightens up. "Did this fox just speak Japanese?"

"Hai."

"You must be Michiko," says the fox. It bows its head. "Pleased to meet you. I am at your service."

Michiko bows in return. "I have never met a *kitsune* spirit before." She looks at me and says, "You two know each other?"

"We've met. I'm pleased to see that your tail has grown back, Chieko-san."

"Oh," says Chieko, dismissively, "I have plenty more of those, Zai-san." Michiko snorts. "Zai?"

"It's my work name."

"Zai, as in…*zainin*?"

"As in *rin, pyo, to, sha, kai, jin…*"

"*Retsu, zai, zen.*"

"Yes."

"Ninja magic? Really?"

I hang my head.

"Retsuya, you play too many video games."

"So do you!"

Michiko thinks about it for a moment. "It does sound cool, I guess. But the kanji's wrong."

"It's a pun."

"The lowest form of humour."

My cheeks go red. "It's the name on my fake passport."

Michiko gives me a look of scorn that would kill the hardiest of weeds.

"Are you going somewhere, Zai-san?" asks Chieko, the familiar a note of impatience in her voice.

"Yes."

"Where?"

"Far away. Wherever you are prepared to take us."

Chieko nods slowly. "Do you have a car?"

Chieko sits on my lap in the passenger seat and Michiko drives down through Kamakura proper and then along the waterfront to

Osaki Park. We leave the Benz in the day lot. On foot we follow the trail down past the playground and into the woods. The fox skips along primly ahead of us.

The trees are not very dense, but the ground is rocky and the slope down to the beach is quite steep. Michiko and I skid and slide after Chieko, down to the narrow strip of black mud beach.

From the tree line we look out over the choppy waters. The view is nice enough, but it is not a good place for a beachside frolic. If it were up to me, I would have gone all the way to Fukui.

Chieko stands up on her hind legs, puts her paws in her mouth, and whistles.

Before long, a bulky shape appears in the water. It starts paddling towards us.

"It's…a turtle," says Michiko.

It is indeed. The turtle beaches itself right in front of us. Chieko struts up to it, licks the turtle's face.

"Good morning, fox," says the turtle.

"Good morning, turtle," says Chieko. "How do you fancy taking us to the Palace of the Dragon God?"

"It's a lovely day for a trip."

Chieko jumps up onto the turtle's back. "Grab a flipper," she says, "and don't let go until we get there."

Michiko gives me a sour look. "If I had known we were going for a swim," she says, "I would have brought my new bikini."

We are standing in the grand hall of Ryūgū-jō, the Dragon God's palace, several hundred meters beneath the surface of the ocean. Yet another sunken kingdom, but this one the most beautiful of the three. Spires of red and white coral rise from ramparts cut from solid quartz. Though it is old and abandoned, this place shows no evidence of ruin. Not even the weight of the ocean has eroded its wonder.

Despite being so far under the water, the palace is as bright as heaven. Some of the radiance ripples refracted down from the surface, but the structure itself is also luminous. There are no shadows.

Michiko and I are neutrally buoyant in the water, but we are breathing air that tastes sweet, like plum blossoms in the spring. I do not find this at all disconcerting. This is a place out of myth, after all, and I am a man of magic. I hope Michiko is impressed. I am uncertain now if the strange feeling in my head is due to the pressure or my continuing headache.

The skeleton of *Ryūjin*, the long-deceased dragon god of the sea, lies coiled upon the sandy floor. Chieko leads Michiko and me through the spiral of his bones, scattering white stones in front of us.

Finally, we come to the centre of the room, where *Ryūjin*'s skull lies. Its gaping eye-socket is twice as tall as I am. The expression on his face is one of smug contentment. Michiko leans close and whispers "*Kawaii,*" in my ear. I can only agree. This is the cutest dead dragon I have ever seen.

Sleipnir is standing in front of the skull, upright on two legs, with his other six limbs are arranged in a ceremonial pose. The spear Gungnir is planted in the sand behind him with a banner waving in the currents. David Lo stands on Sleipnir's left, and Kurenai, the Black and Crimson King, on his right.

Half a dozen dark figures stand in the empty galleries. I can identify three of them: Federico, Emmet, and Rambo-san. Federico looks happy and well-fed, as always. Emmet looks a little sour. I do not blame him. Rambo-san is sulking like a child who has been denied his dessert. My dead friends are translucent in the strange light, though the substance of them is made of shadow.

I squint at the other shades, but I cannot be certain who they are. I think one of them might be George Diehl, although he's not even dead yet. I am certain that Russell Kilmer-Jones is not among them.

Sleipnir speaks some words in a language that I do not understand. When he stops speaking, David gives me a sparkling grin and opens a small box. It contains a silver ring with a dragon skull on it. The skull has rubies for eyes.

I take the ring and turn to Michiko, who is holding a ring that she received from the Black and Crimson King. Kurenai smiles at me encouragingly. His teeth are as black as David's are white.

I put the skull ring on Michiko's finger; she puts a plain platinum band on mine.

"You may kiss," says Sleipnir.

We do.